# Into This World We're Thrown

# Into This World We're Thrown

## Mark Kendrick

Writers Club Press
New York Lincoln Shanghai

Into This World We're Thrown

Writers Club Press
an imprint of iUniverse, Inc.

For information address:
iUniverse
2021 Pine Lake Road, Suite 100
Lincoln, NE 68512
www.iuniverse.com

Any resemblance to actual people and events is purely coincidental.
This is a work of fiction.

ISBN: 0-595-21468-1

Printed in the United States of America

# PREFACE

---

As in *Desert Sons*, this dramatic conclusion to that story contains a mixture of real and imaginary events and place names from the Mojave Desert's Morongo Basin in southern California. The purpose was to establish a real environment without making it sound like a dramatization. And, although this novel is a conclusion to *Desert Sons*, it can be read apart from it. Nonetheless, some of the references to past characters and events may be unclear without having read the *Desert Sons*.

Enjoy,

*Mark Kendrick*

# Acknowledgements

To Glenn, who puts up with my long hours at the computer.

To Larry, who provided invaluable input on the therapy sessions.

Special thanks goes to Ron Donaghe, author of *Common Sons,*
whose encouragement caused this sequel to be written.

Last, but not least, to all the fans of Scott and Ryan
who've been the best readers a novelist could hope to have.

"I, walk alone in the dark, without you
And deep, in the shadows I run, without you
And here, here I stand, the king of fools.
Now love's here, where are you?"

Journey, <u>Trial By Fire</u>, "Message of Love" © 1996

"Preoccupied without you,
I cannot live at all.
My whole world surrounds you,
I stumble and I fall…
I wonder what you're doing,
I wonder where you are,
There's oceans in between us,
But that's not very far."

Puddle of Mudd, <u>Come Clean</u>, "Blurry" © 2001

# CHAPTER 1

Scott Faraday was on his back holding his breath. Ryan St. Charles was probing Scott's mouth with his tongue as he rested his upper body on his elbows. He had both of his hands clasped around the back of Scott's head. Finally, Scott couldn't stand it any longer and pushed him away. The sheet slid down Ryan's back and stopped at his waist. Scott turned his head and exhaled loudly. "Ugh, something died in your mouth," he announced with exaggerated disgust.

"If you'd let me kiss you longer it wouldn't be so bad." Ryan slid completely off Scott's belly and ended up next to his side, his face in the pillow. He was smiling goofily, something that Scott couldn't see just now. He then raised his head up. "I hope they left already." He rose up even further now, trying to peer out through the mini-blinds, but they were tightly shut. He wanted to know whether Scott's parent's cars were still there or not.

Shakaiyo, Scott's three-year old black Labrador Retriever, who was lying in the floor near the foot of the bed, lifted her head and sighed noisily, then went back to her half-snoozing again.

Scott's bedroom, which was the detached guestroom in the Faraday's backyard, was perfectly isolated from the house. Nonetheless, Ryan, having been clandestinely driven in last night, was concerned. He still hadn't told Howard, his uncle who he lived with, about their relationship. Scott still hadn't told his father either. But today was that day. They had made a promise to each other.

Scott had completely changed Ryan's point of view in the last couple of weeks. He had stuck with Ryan even down to the last minute back in Crescent City. He hadn't rejected him over that stupid lie Ryan told him about his ex-girlfriend. He had even come looking for him under the bridge. Scott was one unique person, and worth more than anyone he had ever known.

Despite the crap he had dealt out to him all summer, Scott was still with him. It made him feel warm inside whenever he thought about them together.

Indeed, he thoroughly enjoyed the playfulness which Scott seemed to exude almost all the time. He used to think that someone with that kind of energy was the ultimate in queer. But he discovered that he loved Scott's unique style. And the part about it being queer? Well, he was gay, too, so what had his struggle been all about anyway? *Oh yeah, I've been trying to hide it from everyone, including myself, for a long time.*

After their return, it had taken him two days before he became completely comfortable saying 'I'm gay' to the mirror. At the end of the second day, and after having said it what seemed like a thousand times, it became just another phrase. But, telling Howard was next. And for Scott, his father.

It wasn't as if they were going to clobber them over the head with it. No, it was because they were in a relationship. They wanted it to be known only because of that. There was going to be no more hiding from those who were important in their lives. Ryan had thought about it enough to know Scott wasn't kidding about that. And there was going to be no more denial on Ryan's part. Scott had convinced him that it was the right thing to do and that it was going to be easy. He was sure it would be, but being bigger than his fear wasn't something he was completely used to doing just yet. He was still as moody as ever, but now Scott was his anchor. He had never experienced that before with anyone and was still marveling over it. He was also surprised that he had allowed all these realizations to surface in the first place. Scott had turned out to be a catalyst for all sorts of positive things.

Ryan got off the bed, stepped to the window, and lifted one slat of the blinds. He looked out over the driveway. Both cars were indeed gone.

Scott drank in the sight as he observed Ryan from behind.

Ryan's almost jet-black short hair was sticking out all which way. His trim waist had an even tan line across it. Dark hair graced his legs from his ankles to about three-quarters of the way up his buttocks and disappeared into the fold of his cheeks. From this angle, he saw Ryan's rounded shoulders and the pointy ends of his collarbones. With the slat raised, the light that streamed in framed his head, making him look angelic. Perhaps he *was* an angel sent specifically to Scott. Perhaps he was just an average slim eighteen year old. Regardless, he was Scott's and that made all the difference. He sighed and an easy smile crossed his face.

Ryan turned around and saw him staring. Now Scott could observe the gentle curve of his pecs, the dark nipples that dotted each one, and the sparse wisps of dark hair that spread across them. He looked at Ryan's navel and followed the thin trail of hair to his semi-erect penis. Ryan dove on top of him after he reached the bed. Scott emitted an 'oof' sound. Shakaiyo didn't like what appeared to be an aggressive move on his part and placed her front paws up on the edge of the bed. She emitted a low growl as she eyed him suspiciously.

Scott reached out and scratched behind her ears. "It's okay, girl." Ryan scratched as well and she decided it was so. She returned to her place on the carpet near the bathroom door.

Ryan looked down into Scott's green eyes then picked a piece of sleep sand from one corner. "Ready?"

Scott could feel exactly what he meant since Ryan was laying on top of him. *He's kidding.* Scott smirked, then extended his index finger as he started counting off. "Let's see, nine-thirty last night, three in the morning," he glanced at the clock, "and an hour and a half ago. Not even *you* could do it again."

Scott's senior year was going to begin in two days. They had no more than seventy-two hours left before they would see each other, what, maybe twice a week, if they were lucky? They had both gotten used to having intimate moments together whenever the urge hit them. That was going to drop to almost nothing compared to this summer once Scott started school again. His schedule would be even more crowded than before. Ryan was well aware of that and seemed to be getting in as much extra recreational time as he could recently, something that Scott didn't mind at all. Nonetheless, he knew he wasn't good for another round. He had had to ask anyway. He started flicking his tongue across one of Scott's nipples.

As much as Scott loved it and despite being hard again he had to get out of bed. He gently pushed Ryan aside and looked down at himself. "I can't go running like this."

He had decided that even though he wasn't going to be on the track team his senior year, he would still at least try to keep in shape. Ever since he'd met Ryan, he had stopped training. That was changing starting today. There was a trail behind the house that led to Inauguration Peak in the foothills some distance away. Scott used to run on it last school year. Out of the routine over the summer, he wanted to get back into it and stay in it. Ryan lay on his back watching the fan whirling above them. "And you have to go home after I come back," Scott told him.

Scott started picking up their clothes that had been tossed all over the room in their frantic effort to strip each other last night. He deposited them into two piles. Last weekend, Ryan stopped wearing his ever-present painter's cap. When Scott asked him where it was, he said that he didn't like how it matted down his hair anymore. Scott liked it since it gave Ryan a unique look, but he didn't like the constant hat hair either. He'd finally grown used to not seeing it anymore.

Laying on his desk across the room was the rolled up poster that Ryan had drawn as a promotional graphic for the band. Draped across it was his underwear. How it had managed to get flung up there he couldn't figure. He wadded it up and threw a drop shot into his dirty clothes hamper. The poster had survived their trip back two weekends ago completely intact. No dents on the edges, no smudges to its carefully drawn surface. He had been waiting for the right time to spring it on the band. He was sure they'd love it.

He let Ryan drift back to sleep while he donned running shorts and shoes and took off. Twenty minutes later he returned and came back to a still-sleeping Ryan. "Hey, get up," he said as he shed his shorts. Ryan obeyed and, still yawning, started shaking his clothes out. "I guess Howard's gonna know what you want to tell him this morning since you didn't come home last night," Scott added.

"I told him I was sleeping over."

"Are you sure you don't want me to be there with you?"

"I can do it myself."

Scott was still wondering if Ryan would go through with it. He asked only to make sure. Actually, he wasn't at all ready to tell his dad today, but figured if he didn't do it then Ryan would have one up on him. He couldn't allow that.

Ryan dressed while Scott took a quick shower. He then drove him back to his house.

Ryan's uncle, Howard, had been dating Krysta for several months now and she had been showing up at the oddest times these last few weeks. Her car wasn't there now. He had no excuse to back out.

Ryan gave him a quick squeeze on the thigh and jumped out. Scott took off for band practice. It was only Labor Day weekend and the band had plenty of time to get ready for the upcoming gigs they had booked for the end of September. Nonetheless, practice would be long and involved today.

Ryan strode up the driveway to the back entrance of the house and stopped at the railing of the raised deck. The far end of the backyard was bordered by a cement irrigation ditch that was perhaps twenty feet wide and more than one hundred feet in length. Its sloped sides delineated the backyard and the greater neighborhood from the huge circular fields that produced three yearly soybean crops. A lone hawk hovered way beyond the ditch, then dove down onto something he couldn't possibly hope to see this far away. He turned and drew in a deep breath as he came into the kitchen.

Howard St. Charles was dumping his coffee cup out in the sink. "You're back early."

"I didn't want to go with Scott this morning." The band didn't need any distractions with him being there today. And besides, he wouldn't get to interact with Scott due to their heavy schedule this weekend.

Howard knew that Ryan liked watching the band practice. "That's a switch."

"I need to talk to you anyway." His heart started going full blast now, but he knew he had adequately prepared himself. *It's okay. You're not telling him every fucking detail.*

"You need to talk? To me? This I gotta hear."

Howard had let Ryan live with him since the beginning of June. After Ryan's grandmother had kicked him out for his out of control behavior in June, Howard agreed to take him in until he started college. It was a decent arrangement. He didn't mind the company and had grown to know his nephew quite well over the last three months. Ryan had seemed to mellow out somewhat, too. Perhaps it was the change of environment that had precipitated his change of character. He wasn't exactly sure. But there was something else he was quite sure of. Was Ryan going to tell him?

Ryan realized he was hungry and probably should have eaten before starting like this, but he wanted to get it all out in the open, and fast, before he backed out. "You might want to sit down."

Howard was concerned now as he sat. "Okay." The gravity with which he started speaking struck him as odd. And Ryan wasn't sitting, so this was clearly an announcement of some sort.

Ryan tightly gripped the back of one of the kitchen chairs. "I'm gay."

"Hmm. I know I'm supposed to be surprised."

"You aren't?"

"I'll act that way if you want me to."

"You knew?"

"Of course I knew."

"How?"

"Ryan, I have a Master's Degree. Granted, it's not in social sciences. But what it means is that I'm not a dumbass, like you sometimes like to think. I figured it out, oh…a month ago?"

"Really?"

"Yeah. Those sketches? You and Scott 'playing' that one day in the living room. Spending the night with him all the time, like *last* night." He chuckled. "Could you be a little more obvious?"

"Fuck," he replied softly.

"You and Scott an item?"

"He's my boyfriend."

Howard tried to keep the grin from his face at seeing his expression. He wasn't succeeding. "Boyfriend. That's more serious than I thought." He knitted his brow now. "What made you want to tell me?"

"We made a promise."

"A promise?"

Ryan was white-knuckled now, and after realizing it, released his grip. He pulled the chair out and sat down at the table with Howard. "We promised to tell. Me to you, and him to his dad."

"What about his mother?"

"She already knows. He came out to her last year."

"Wow. He was out at fifteen?"

"Sixteen. You're…taking this rather well."

"I had an undergrad roommate who was gay. I partied with him and several of his buddies our entire junior year."

"Oh. I was sure you'd wig out."

"How long have you lived here?"

"You know. Since June."

"You should *kinda* know me by now. I could care less if you're gay. I wouldn't go around announcing it to just anyone though. This is a small community. Not nearly as small as Crescent City, but there are some small minds here."

"I never told anyone up there." That wasn't exactly the case, since Crawford certainly knew, but he had never announced it to anyone either.

"It must've been hard."

*Is he making some sort of sexual reference?* "What?"

"Having to 've kept something like that a secret in high school. How did you handle dating and socializing? And Crescent City has what, maybe four thousand people? I'm sure you knew practically everyone."

The sting of last year came to mind, though it was softened a little due to Scott's influence on him. "Yeah, four thousand and a couple of strays. I had a girlfriend senior year. It didn't work out, of course." There was no way he was even going to mention Crawford.

"Well, not to worry. Just don't let Krysta see any more sketches of Scott. She's got a religious streak in her that could take a turn for the worse if provoked. You know, the whole religion and homosexuality thing. For some people those two don't mix."

Ryan made a face. "Why are you going out with her if she believes crap like that?"

"I'm not dating her for *you*. I like her. She's nice, she's fun to be with, and she's all woman, let me tell you."

Ryan cracked a smile, feeling so much at ease now he couldn't believe it. His stomach rumbled loudly.

"Haven't eaten yet?"

"No."

"Neither have I. How about you and I go to *Nelson's* for an all-you-can-eat breakfast? On me."

"Sure. Let me take a shower first." He could still smell Scott's scent on him. He was sure Howard would too if he didn't wash up.

*              *              *

"Sound Dude!" the guys yelled when they saw Scott at the Royal Garage entrance.

The Royal Garage was the name they had dubbed Colleen's parent's garage. An attempt had been made to sound deaden the aluminum structure by using dozens of two-by-two foot squares of purple-colored, fiberboard egg cartons. Nailed all over the walls and ceiling of the structure, they served their purpose well. The name for their practice area had been practically screaming at them when they completed their handiwork.

Scott waved at them as he looked around for Colleen. She was nowhere to be seen. Darryl Osterhaus was behind his keyboard stack, accessing something from the LCD panel of the lowest one on his A-frame rack. Bryce Owens had just sat at his drum set, and was already twirling a drumstick in his left hand. Barry Rhodes, their lead guitarist, was wiping down his sleek, black, six-string guitar. Mitch Jenner was attaching the shoulder strap of his bass guitar. Sparks, their lighting guy, was stacking gels into a box.

Scott rested the poster on top of their Fostex 8-track reel-to-reel. The reel-to-reel was patched to the 4-tracker which was used to make the cassettes he mixed for the band.

"What's that, young Jedi?" Bryce asked as Scott set the poster and a couple of blank cassettes down.

"You have to wait until Colleen gets here."

She came in the side entrance and shut the door behind her. She was in her usual shorts, sandals, and t-shirt. She noticed right away that Ryan wasn't there.

"Good, you're all here. Take a look."

Colleen eyed the poster as he picked it back up. He carefully pulled off the rubber band, handed one edge of the posterboard to her, and started to unroll it.

"Ooh, I know what this is," she said.

"Hold it tight," he told her. Mitch and Barry placed their guitars on their stands while the other guys came forward. "Voilà. Whadda ya think?"

"Bitchin'," exclaimed Bryce. "Ryan drew this?"

"Dude, he did it in one freakin' day."

Colleen joined in now. "It's just the right size and it captures the essence of everyone: you're all a bunch of animals, just like I've been saying. I see he carefully left *me* out of the poster."

"Hey, I'm only half animal," Bryce added with a disappointed affect.

Scott grinned at the remark. "You're the centaur with the boobs," he told Colleen as he pointed.

Darryl and Scott both saw the look of concern on her face.

"Not to worry. We'll keep the Jarheads from groping them," Darryl offered. He was referring to the fact that the poster would be used in at the Twentynine Palms Marine base for their upcoming concert nights.

She studied the poster. Satisfied that nothing as graphic as boobs were nowhere to be seen—that Scott was kidding—she emitted a 'whew'. "Silly boy," she told him.

Barry was eyeing the poster thoughtfully. "Good color, right size, tells everything we need to say. He's hired. For cheap, that is."

Sparks nodded. "It needs a good spot right above it when it sits on the stand. I gotta find a way to keep it from rolling up. Hey, I'll put it in a frame." He made a silly face at his revelation.

Scott handed the poster to him and let him put it aside. Weeks before, he told Mitch he wouldn't embarrass him with the news. But he needed more practice before he told his dad. He cleared his throat.

"I have something to tell you all, too."

Bryce was returning to his drum stool but turned his head back. "You're pregnant?"

Scott raised his eyebrows at the thought. "We haven't busted any condoms yet, so no. I'm a homo."

Colleen and Mitch glanced at each other. They knew, of course. Unknown to Scott was that they had talked while he and Ryan were up north. Mitch couldn't contain himself any longer and had asked Colleen how long she had known about Scott. They had discussed that they wouldn't push the issue with him, but nonetheless talked with the rest of the guys about it. Why it was an issue with Scott was something they couldn't quite say, but Mitch had decided he had figured it out. Scott was a guy and he was young. There was the unwritten Boy Code of Conduct he was conforming to at school. Yucca Valley Regional High School, simply called Regional by most everyone, wasn't the most gay-friendly place he could think of, at least when he had attended. Plus, now that they knew Ryan was more than just his friend, it seemed clear that Scott's relationship was something he had to work out before he felt comfortable telling just anyone about it. It was a lot to sort through, even if they were his friends.

Barry tried to break the obvious tension. "Who's a homo?"

"I am." Scott sat down on his stool behind the soundboard, waiting for their reaction. It was dead silent in the garage.

Sparks spoke up. "So, that's here my bulbs have been going."

Scott eyed him. "Your what?"

Sparks feigned a look around. "Are you sitting on them?"

"Eat me."

Sparks jumped back a step, clomping his feet loudly. He tried to sound mortified. "Not *here*. The guys are watching." He had been carefully keeping his face expressionless, but now he started laughing.

Scott was filled with alarm. "Why are you laughing at me?" He was getting really uncomfortable now.

"I'm not laughing *at* you. We knew."

Scott scanned the group. "Am I that obvious?"

"In this town? Are you kidding?"

"Come on."

"Uh, Colleen, you better tell him," Darryl said.

"Scott, we don't care if you're animal, vegetable or mineral. Just keep doing the excellent job you've been doing on sound and with all the equipment, and you can come dressed in a feather boa for all I care."

Mitch looked at her, sounding dead serious. "No he can't. *I'm* the only one authorized to wear one."

They spent the next couple of minutes escalating the joking around, but then congratulated him on being their 'brave little boy'. He loved them for being supportive yet still felt somewhat awkwardly embarrassed at having revealed himself like that in front of all of them at once. It was like he had divulged his entire sex life to them out of the blue.

They were half an hour into practice before he suddenly felt so good he couldn't believe it. He grinned as he adjusted the main line-in levels to the reel-to-reel as the band practiced. Nothing had changed. Telling Ralph, his dad, would be easy.

\*　　　　　\*　　　　　\*

Scott knew his dad would be home earlier than normal today since he had specifically checked the schedule. When he arrived home, Ralph was on the couch flipping through TV channels.

Still reeling from not having been shunned by the band, he was feeling quite exuberant. He poured himself a glass of soda, and then walked into the living room. "Hey, Dad, how was work today?"

Ralph looked up at him. It was odd for his son to begin a conversation with that kind of question. "Same as the rest. Why?"

He took a sip, set the glass down, then cleared his throat. He sat across from his father in the leather chair. "I have to tell you something." It was more difficult than he thought actually. What he thought was a cool lack of unease didn't hide a look of concern, nor did his voice.

Ralph muted the sound, but didn't turn off the TV. He could tell something was up. "Did you have an accident?"

"No. This is way more important than that."

Ralph pressed the 'off' button and set the remote down. "You got someone pregnant."

"No, but that's the second time someone's said that today." *That's weird.* "I guess it's kinda related to that though. I'm gay."

"You're what?"

"I'm gay."

"Uh, right."

"Well, it's true. You had to know. And I'm sorry I have to tell you this, too, but I'm not going to High Desert College. No way." He had blurted it out in one long breath.

"We already talked about that, son!"

*Uh, oh. He's already yelling.* Scott hadn't even had a chance to explain himself. Maybe he should have had Ryan here for support after all. Which reminded him that he hadn't even found out how it went with Howard. "Dad, I'm gay. Please. Let me talk about that first."

"Have you told your mother?"

If Scott was reading him correctly, he seemed to be panicking. "I told her last summer."

"You told her you were homosexual a *year* ago?"

"Well, that's when I figured it out. And do you have to use that word?"

"She never told me?" He it said mostly to himself. He was silent for a moment as he mulled it over. His wife hadn't told him this very important piece of information about their son for a year. It was evident that something was wrong with his marriage, but he didn't want to think about that just now.

Scott answered. "She asked me not to tell you then. The restaurant. You know, the bills and the repairs. It was a bad time. I'm sorry I didn't say anything after that was all over, but I can't keep it a secret anymore because I'm-I'm going out with someone."

"With a boy?"

"Of course."

Ralph was becoming visibly agitated now. "I won't have anybody molesting my son!" With that, he stood up.

Scott was the one taken aback now. His father's reaction was quite disturbing. "He's not *molesting* me!"

"Who did this to you?"

"Who did w-what to me?"

"Turned you into a homosexual."

"What the *fuck*, Dad? Nobody! And will you stop using that word?"

Ralph pointed at his son. "Don't *you* use that word with *me!*"

Scott stood up. This was supposed to have been easy. He hadn't been prepared for his reaction, much less a fight, but it was rapidly turning into a full scale one. *Why is he yelling? And what the hell was that about being molested?*

"I've been gay ever since I can remember. You just didn't know it. I didn't really understand it until last year. And why are you so upset? Just because I'm going out with someone?"

Ralph didn't seem to be listening. He gestured, beckoning him. "Out with it. Who is he?"

Scott thought for a second. Should he tell him? Yes, he had to get past this point. He had to talk to his dad about that damn college. There was no way he was going to let this go. He had a promise to keep. "Ryan."

"Howard's nephew?"

"Him." Scott's voice cracked as he said it. His throat was terribly dry now and he felt hot all over. He glanced at the soda. He badly needed another sip.

"*Goddamn it!*"

Scott nearly stumbled over his words as he spit them out. His heart was in overdrive now. "Dad, please! Ryan and I like each other. We're gay. It's just a fact."

Ralph slowly sat back down. He leaned forward and put his head in his hands. Scott could see his forehead getting red between his fingers. It was only one of two emotions that Scott could figure.

"Are you crying?"

Ralph leaned back and dropped his hands. His face was really red. "I should have gone to more of your track team events," he began. "I should have been more involved with Scouting. I should have been there for you instead of trying to provide for my family." He wasn't crying.

Scott read the anger in his voice. "It's not like that! You didn't do anything. I did." Wrong choice of words. He shook his head. "I mean I'm gay. Nobody molested me. No one made me this way. Why are you saying all those things?"

Ralph still wasn't listening to him. "You're going to business school, by God. I planned this a long time ago."

Scott didn't care anymore whether he was communicating or not. His father hadn't even tried to listen, which quickly put Scott in no mood to explain it either. He stamped his foot. This confrontation was way too intense and way too peculiar. "You can't make me do something I don't want to do. I'm studying *music*." He felt unbelievably angry now and stormed into the kitchen so he wouldn't end up taking a swing at him. He had no idea it would turn into an all out row. He had his dad figured out completely wrong!

Just as he got to the kitchen, Elaine, his mother, pulled the sliding glass door open and stepped in. She took one look at her son and knew something was wrong.

Ralph was right behind him. "Don't walk away from me when I'm talking to you."

His tone told her everything. She immediately dropped her purse onto the kitchen counter. It fell over onto its side. A hairbrush tumbled out, skittered across the countertop, and fell to the floor. She ran to Ralph, grabbed him by the upper arms, and stopped him in his tracks. "What is going *on* in here?"

"Our son told you that he's-he's *gay* last summer, and you never told me?"

She looked over to Scott. He looked away from her as she made eye contact. She was sure Scott was on the verge of tears. This was awful. And her husband was tense with anger. She knew Ralph didn't handle stress well, but it had never come to having arguments with Scott. She gripped his arms more tightly. She was even bracing herself in case he lunged after him. "Honey, I'll tell you why later. Right now, you apologize. Look, you're scaring him."

Scott spoke up now. "Huh! I'm not scared." Anger was in his voice. "He thinks I shouldn't be with Ryan. That's not *his* decision. And it's not *his* decision where I go to school either." He yanked open the sliding glass door, pulled his keys from his pocket, and jumped into the Jeep.

Through the still-open door, she heard the vehicle start up, then pull away from the house.

"He's our *son*, Ralph," she said with an urgency she normally didn't use with anyone. She looked back and forth at both of his eyes as she slowly let go of him.

# CHAPTER 2

Incredibly, the day had turned into a complete disaster. It had started out with the boys being together in what could easily be described as a bliss-filled night of passion, as usual. Just this morning Scott had felt happier than he had in a very long time when the band perfectly accepted his announcement. Ten hours later, he was more pissed off than he had ever been in his entire life, after having the most bizarre argument with his dad for the first time in his life.

He ramped up to past eighty miles per hour once he got to the freeway. *Fuck the speed limit.* Where to go was the issue, though, as he weaved around cars on his way east. It wasn't until he was through most of Twentynine Palms before he felt more in control of himself. He finally turned around at a dry wash just past Cactus Jack Avenue. *Why did he react like that? Am I just naïve to think he'd be okay with it? And I didn't even get to argue my case about school.* He had to make sense of it, but talking to his father right now wasn't the answer. He pulled over to a gas station and parked by a pay phone. Howard answered.

"Ryan there?"

"Hey Scott. Yeah, he is. Just a minute."

With his free hand, Scott tapped out a beat on his thigh with his thumb and little finger.

Ryan was on a moment later. "Hey, boyfriend."

"Fuck."

"Fuck what?"

"My dad freaked out on me."

"I hear traffic. Where are you calling from?"

"A gas station."

"Why?"

"I took off."

"Oh."

"He's a fuckwad."

"You don't sound right."

Scott sighed. "I need a hug."

"What are you waiting for?"

This was a switch. Ryan remembered several weeks ago, when it was he who was freaking out, and he had asked Scott to come over to help console him.

Scott knocked on the door fifteen minutes later. Howard's car wasn't there. Ryan had convinced him to take off. At first, Howard had balked but then acquiesced when Ryan explained that all wasn't right at the Faraday household and he wanted to talk to Scott in private. Howard needed to buy some groceries for tonight's dinner anyway.

Ryan opened the door and Scott immediately draped his arms over his shoulders. They hugged as they stood in the hall. "You stood up to my stupidity and you can stand up to your dad, too," Ryan offered.

Scott pulled away. "I thought he'd just say, 'Okay, you're gay, wanna watch TV?' But *no*, he freaked out instead."

"Maybe he just needs some time to get used to it. Or-or maybe he had a bad day."

"He said today was like all the rest. So, I told him. Then he spazzed so fast that I didn't have a chance to explain anything."

"Was your mom there?"

"She got home when he was chasing me down."

Ryan's eyebrows went up. "Chasing you down?"

"I thought I was gonna punch him so I went into the kitchen to get away from him. Right as he came in after me my mom came home and stopped him from wigging even more."

Ryan let him calm down for a moment. The house was completely quiet except for a clock ticking in the den. He took Scott by the hand and led him to his bedroom. They sat side by side on the bed where he proceeded to give Scott a long kiss. Ryan's touch made him forget for a moment that he was feeling angry.

Ryan leaned back on his elbows. "Howie knew about me, and us, for a while."

"Just as I figured. And?"

"He's cool with it."

"I told you. And you were freaking out."

"And I told you that your dad *would* freak."

Scott looked down at the floor. "I guess that makes us even, huh?"

"What about the band? What'd *they* say?"

"*They* didn't care. And no one *should* care. I'm still in."

With that, Ryan's eyes lit up and he started kissing him again. This time, ever so slowly, he started to pull Scott's t-shirt up. It was like that with them. In a moment's notice, they would get naked with one another, even if one or the other felt out of sorts. After all, it was a great way to get cheered up. Once the shirt was off, Ryan squeezed Scott's little nipples one at a time. He knew exactly what he was doing. It was all Scott needed to feel horny beyond words. Noticeably aroused, Ryan crossed the room to lock his door. It took all of eight and a half minutes after which Scott dipped a finger into the splatters they both made on his chest. He made Ryan lick it off. Ryan did the same to him. Scott sucked his finger then tried to bite it. Both giggled like little boys.

Scott wiped his chest again, then stepped into his underwear. He stared at Ryan's naked body next to his bureau. He pulled on his shorts and zipped up. "I hate you," he said with an impish grin. He tossed the towel to Ryan, then slipped a foot into his tennis shoe.

Ryan caught it, wiped the tip of his penis off again, then wadded it up. "I hate you more," he replied with the same grin, as he stuffed it into the drawer.

*       *       *

"I didn't tell you because I know how much some things stress you out," Elaine said. She was doing some stressing of her own. She heard the tires angrily squeal on the pavement out front and hoped he wouldn't do something stupid. She stepped over and slid the door shut.

"You knew he was gay and never told me? How could you?"

"Ralph. Honey. That was his decision. *He* was supposed to tell to you. Which he did." She pointed to the driveway. "But you made him go away. How could *you*?"

"A whole year?"

"He was sixteen! You remember how difficult *everything* was at sixteen, don't you? Don't turn him away now. He loves you. And please don't do that again. Don't lay into him like that. It's not healthy."

He knew what she was talking about. He had gotten like that once with their elder son Steve many years ago. She had stopped him that time as well.

When they met, Ralph was sixteen and Elaine had just turned that. He hadn't even been on a single date yet. She was going steady with someone anyway. They were just friends at first. Ralph dated a couple of girls after meeting her, but nothing serious ever came of them. It wasn't until almost two years later that they started dating. Ralph had just graduated from high school and was still living at home. Elaine had been broken up with her boyfriend for a couple of months at that point.

The generation gap had been very wide on Ralph's side of the family. He and his father argued about a lot of things. Ralph was the baby of the family. None of his brothers and sisters were living at home anymore and his father was considerably older than him. Once Ralph had started dating Elaine, the arguments shifted to Ralph's marijuana use. The elder Faraday had been in AA for a number of years and was still singing the praises of sobriety. When he accidentally found a bag of pot in his son's bedroom, he was convinced that Ralph had inherited the family tendency to get high way too often. After all, one of Ralph's aunt's was in an alcohol rehab center at the time, his grandfather had died of cirrhosis of the liver, and it was well known about the other aunt who had been addicted to prescription painkillers for years. It appeared to Ralph's father that his son was taking another path to the same end. At his father's behest, and then Elaine's, he dumped the pot down the toilet. It was that or be kicked out of the house. It was several months later when he finally made the big decision, mostly for Elaine, but he did indeed give it up for good. His father was happy, Elaine was happy, and he was happy because she was. Eleven months later, he and Elaine were married.

Unfortunately, it was true. Ralph had inherited the Faraday's addiction gene. He simply used work as his escape. The more work the better was Ralph's unconscious inner mantra. So, despite never having smoked pot ever again Ralph had always dealt with stress in a less than optimum way. Perhaps one of the worst ways he could have chosen.

"You can't stop him from being gay. You know that."

Ralph looked at his wife. Despite the fact that he had known the occasional person who was or seemed to be gay since being in the restaurant business, it didn't make any sense to him. He simply ignored gay people. And he hadn't given himself an opportunity to process that his own son might be one of 'them'.

"It's more than that. He doesn't want to go to High Desert College. He has no idea what he's doing. He's making a huge mistake. I can't have that happen again."

"Again? What are you talking about? What kind of mistake?"

"The same mistake I made. Not planning for the future until it's almost too late. He has a chance to make a better life for himself than I did at that age and he's throwing it away with the notion that he can have a career in music. Besides, how many people do we know who've made it being in a rock band? Huh?"

"Ralph, our son is in a completely different generation. Our old friends were just playing around. Half of them were…drug addicts." There, she said it. "They didn't buy equipment or write music, or play in public like the band he's in. Theirs just might make it. You never know. He has something going, and he has to make his own mistakes. I think he should make them himself, don't you?"

"On my dime? I don't think so."

"So, this is about money? When did our son's life become about money? His life is his."

"It's not about money. It's about a sound future. That's what I've been telling you. You're—he's—not listening."

"We're his family. We're there for him when he needs us."

"You mean, to pick up the pieces when he's finally figured it out? Not when it's obvious what he needs to do."

Elaine knew when to stop arguing with him. This was that time. And she knew he was referring to his parents having been virtually penniless when they died.

Ralph would be angry for a while, maybe a long time. He'd line up all the points and argue his case. Eventually, though, he'd understand an opposing viewpoint. His hardheaded tendency to be right at all costs was something she had never liked. But he would come around like he always did. And in this case, if he didn't, she would make sure of it.

*            *            *

Scott arrived back home late. Late enough for there to be only the one light left on—the one that was on the timer in the living room—and for his parents to be asleep. He parked his Jeep at the curb since both their cars were in the driveway. He let Shakaiyo out of the backyard and they went for a slow lazy walk up the dark street and back. Twenty minutes later, he returned to his bedroom with her in tow. He turned on his desk lamp and looked at the magazine stack to the left of the terrarium, where Legs, his tarantula, sat on a hollow Cholla cactus branch. A single leg of the banded spider was moving up and down in what appeared to him to be a slow motion beckoning. The spines of nearly two dozen neatly stacked and assorted magazines were all facing toward him next to the terrarium. He read their titles: *Hi Fidelity, Sound Equipment Review, 90s Musicon, Spin, Rolling Stone,* and a couple of others. He moved them aside. Underneath were miscellaneous papers. One was a test from last April. He'd kept it since it was a trigonometry exam where he had made an 'A'. A rare 'A'. He hesitated, but then dropped it into the trash can. Trig was last school year. Old news. The envelope and the triplicate forms had been there underneath the exam this whole time. He picked up the application to High Desert College and looked at it. The only thing he had filled in months before was his name: Scott Andrew Faraday. He didn't give it a second thought. He held the forms with both hands and tore them down the middle. Putting the halves together, he turned them, then tore them down the middle again. He kept going like that until he could no longer rip through them. He let the pieces fall down into the trash can.

"Here girl," he said to Shakaiyo. She got up and came to him, tail wagging. He got down on the carpet, lay on his back, knees up, and let her lick his face. He felt even better now.

*                    *                    *

Scott woke up shortly after the sun crested the far mountain range in the east. Ryan had shown up just before he had fallen asleep last night. Shakaiyo had heard him first, as usual, and when he looked out the window, he saw Ryan waving at him from the driveway.

They had completely messed up his bed due to them having rolled around on it so much. One of the pillows, along with the blanket, was still on the floor. He had only his longer pillow along the length of his body and the completely untucked sheet partially draped over him. Scott had made Ryan shower with him before he left shortly after one-thirty. Ever since that first shower together in Parker, Scott couldn't get enough of seeing Ryan wet under a showerhead. And he couldn't get enough of licking water droplets off his shoulders and pecs. It was like drinking liquid dynamite, what with the feelings it gave him. The smile that was on his face from last night's antics disappeared as he remembered what happened yesterday after he talked to his father.

After visiting the bathroom, he flopped back into bed. He reached over, took the phone off the cradle, and speed dialed his aunt in Parker, Arizona. He was glad he had his own line. He was assured of complete privacy when he talked to her.

"Atcher House, Cinnamon Atcher speaking."

"Hi, Aunt Cin." He never found it difficult to be cheerful, even this early in the morning, when it came to talking to his favorite aunt.

"Good morning. How's my nephew?"

"He's fine." He adjusted the pillow so he could rest the phone on his ear without having to use his hands. "All except for one thing." His joyful demeanor disappeared again.

"That's what I'm here for. What's going on?"

"I told dad everything."

"Everything? As in you're gay?"

"That, about Ryan, about not wanting to go to that stupid junior college. That's all I was able to say, though, since he freaked out on me."

"Was this at work?"

"No way. I know better than that. I waited 'til he got home."

"And he still freaked out?"

"There was yelling and shouting and I wanted to hit him."

"Hit him?"

"It didn't happen. I retreated before it came to that."

"Ugly words were thrown around?"

"A few. Some from him, some from me. It coulda been worse though."

"I know your father pretty well, honey. I thought you would, too. He's not too terribly good at listening to big messages like that, especially all at once."

"But he had to listen." He exhaled loudly. "I might as well move away right now."

"Scott," she said with emphasis.

"I won't do anything he says. Especially if he's gonna be a dick."

"You have to talk to him."

"I did!"

"You need a different approach. You can't just up and tell off your father like that."

"Well, *he* started it."

"Then *you* end it."

"I'm sorry it happened. But really, what can I do about it?"

"Hmm. Make him aware that you understand his concerns, and talk to him again. But this time go over only one topic at a time."

"He's so busy all the time I may never even get to the second one if he won't handle the first one."

"Which one's going to be first?"

"The college deal. That's coming up fast. And I need to talk to a school counselor soon."

"Which one are you thinking about?"

"UCLA. That's where Ryan's going."

"Good luck honey. Keep your eyes open. Keep your heart still. And listen to yourself."

"I know, I know."

"Okay, you know. Now continue applying it."

"Thanks again, Aunt Cin."

"It'll turn out just the way you want it to. Just give it time. Do I always have to tell you to go slowly with everything?"

"Yes," he reluctantly replied.

*That Scott. He just gets into a tizzy sometimes.*

They talked about miscellaneous family matters for a while before saying their goodbyes.

Scott went to see Ryan early on Labor Day. They spent the first part of the morning goofing around with Howard. When it seemed that Howard wouldn't leave the house after Krysta arrived, Scott drove Ryan back to his place. He packed a backpack with a big container of water, sunscreen, a sci-fi paperback with the back torn off, cassettes, snacks, condoms, lube, and his Walkman. He drove them out to a rarely used dirt road he knew way beyond Pioneertown. There, they discarded their clothing except for their boxers, and lay out on a huge blanket he had brought.

They alternately lay in the sun and in the shade of a collection of nearby boulders. Ryan listened to Scott's tapes with the headphones. Scott had gotten hard the moment he shed his clothes, stayed that way, then deliberately distracted Ryan to get him aroused, too. Three times over the next two hours and forty-five minutes, Scott let Ryan use first his hand, then his mouth, and finally his penis, to help empty him out. Scott reciprocated the same way each time, of course. Neither could do it a fourth time. Not even blanks. Scott ended up reading only seven pages of his novel. Ryan didn't quite get through the second tape before the batteries died.

This was the last day of freedom for Scott. He was almost heartbroken that the summer had unofficially ended. Tomorrow would be the first day of his senior year. He'd have to adjust his entire life to accommodate school, band practice, and not seeing Ryan nearly as much.

Just before they put their clothes back on and returned, Scott lay on top of him and hugged him as hard as he could. They were both hot, covered with a layer of salt, sweat where their naked flesh touched, and crusts of dried semen. Who cared? God, it felt so good to be with him. He hoped it would last forever.

✳                    ✳                    ✳

*The blackboard stretched endlessly into the desert far beyond the classroom/Royal Garage. A fat piece of chalk was in his hand. It was heavy. Scott had on only underwear and socks. Chalk dust landed on his neck, his bare chest, at his feet, as he wrote, furiously wrote.*

*'Grand Plan' was across the top of the board. Row headers read '18, 19, 20', then continued for many years after that. Mr. Platt, his junior English teacher, was reading off something. He had six fingers on his right hand, his thumb on the wrong side. His voice was distant and difficult to hear because of loud Centauri original tunes filling the classroom. Ryan was there, too. He was sitting at one of*

*the desks. Naked. God, he was hot. He was looking out into the distance, not participating in the conversation.*

*What's that, Mr. Platt? Add as much information as I can? Fill the rows up? What am I going do next year, and the next, and the next? What are my plans for today, tomorrow, the endless future?*

The dream faded into oblivion and Scott found himself looking at the whirring fan above his head. Sitting up, he propped his pillow up and glanced at the clock. It was the middle of the night.

*All this grown up stuff to do before I graduate,* he thought. But trying to predict what was going to happen this coming year, much less the next, seemed like the stupidest thing. And it wasn't about what school to go to after all, was it? It was about what he wanted to do with his life. It was his life after all, not his father's. *What the hell does passion mean if it can't be my own? What the hell does anything mean if it's not mine to own?* Why was it so important for him to be 'obedient' to his father if it meant he would ultimately end up unhappy? None of it made any sense and this early in the morning, with only the air conditioner to override the silence, he could find no sense in any of it.

He lay back down again, messed around with his balls, then lazily stroked himself purely out of habit as he got hard. But he didn't continue and he let himself go flaccid again. Slowly but surely, he drifted back to asleep even while anticipating the first day of his senior year.

# CHAPTER 3

Preston Tyllas sat at his desk, third row from the door, three rows back from the board, in calculus class, that second day of the new school year. He slowly let the pages drop from the index to the table of contents as he inspected the well-used textbook. The odd-numbered answers were pre-printed in the back of their books. Quite a few of the answers to the even-numbered questions were written in along the margins in the last nine chapters, where the really difficult stuff was. Excellent, he thought as he smiled. He tried to figure out when they'd get to those chapters. He counted weeks off with his fingers. *Hmm, looks like about January of next year.* He'd made a lucky draw yesterday. *I hope these are right.* He scrutinized them a little more carefully. It didn't do any good. He had no idea what any of the questions meant in the first place.

Scott was directly to Preston's left. He was leaning back slightly as he talked to Doug Sandefur, his best friend and buddy from the track team. Doug was about an inch and a half taller than Ryan, was lithe and slim, and was one of Regional's star relay runners. He had light brown eyes, a distinct chin, and short brown hair. It was even shorter this school year. He normally spiked it on top with plenty of gel, like he did today.

Doug was a popular jock despite not being on the football team, mostly because he was a consistent champion, was good looking, and likable. Although he was talented athletically, Scott had assisted him in winning several competitions last year in the 4 x 800 Meter Relay, which they were both best at. Scott may have been short and stocky, with a solidly built body, but he was trained for speed. Last year, they, along with their teammates Evan and Aubrey, had assisted each other into their top positions on the team. Scott knew Doug was the fastest of them all, though. He had no illusions about that.

If he hadn't known Doug was completely straight, he could have easily gone for him. And until Doug started going out with Jill, his girlfriend, he always had his pick of the girls. He was totally popular with them. In addition, Scott knew that Doug had exactly what girls liked between his legs. He had seen it enough times in the showers.

Preston overheard their conversation, as was his intention.

"I said, I'm *not* coming back to the team," Scott repeated.

"You're a douche nozzle if you don't," Doug whispered back.

"I'm doing way too much stuff with the band. I don't have time to be in the band and on the team. I told the coach yesterday."

The girl in the fourth row, Kay Delavan, was directly across from Preston. She was doing some inspecting of her own. Preston dragged a hand across his thick brown hair in an attempt to push it back from his forehead. As always, it fell back down in a heap, when his head was tilted down, like now. Parted in the middle, his hair was just long enough in front to reach down to almost the tip of his nose. She watched as he unconsciously blew a wavy lock out of his eyes.

Preston was six-foot-two, slim, but not skinny. Thin lenses surrounded by shiny pewter-colored frames sat on the bridge of his short, sloped nose, and didn't hide what she thought were his adorable hazel eyes. She loved the tiny hoop earring he wore in his right earlobe. She liked his soft even tan and the dozen or so different-sized dark moles that dotted the right side of his face then ran down his neck before disappearing beneath his collar. They were so sexy. He always wore the nicest clothes, like today, and other than his unruly hair, was meticulously neat. *Why doesn't he ever ask me out?* She'd hinted several times last year, but he never made his move. She would, instead, have to ask him out this year. Nonetheless, she wondered what was wrong with herself for him to rarely even look at her, then dismissed it.

As Preston scanned the book from back to front again, she saw he was smiling. *Who could smile looking through a calculus book?* She looked down at hers, wondering where the humor was.

Preston wasn't concentrating on his textbook at all just now. He was intently listening to Scott and Doug as they talked. He had made it almost his duty to keep up with what Scott was up to last school year. He had gone to all the public Centauri shows, watched the last three track meets that Scott had run in to see him in his Regional tank top, and just happened to have seen him pull into the parking lot this morning in what could only be a new Jeep. He knew Scott had had a pretty crappy car last year. He also knew exactly where the Jeep was parked right now. The newest bit of information he just logged was that he wasn't coming back to the team. He'd miss seeing Scott on the field in that tank top.

Preston was smitten. The crush had started about midway through junior year and never waned. To him, Scott was the perfect blend of good looks and enthusiasm, even if he were a bit short for his own taste. Scott was totally into that band, was a great runner, and had the most bizarre sense of humor. But what he loved the most was the dark red hair. There were several other boys in the senior class that had red hair, but they mostly tended toward orange. He especially liked it dark red. Scott's was the darkest, and his skin tanned more easily than most redheads' skin. In addition, his deep green eyes were impossible to believe. It was an intense combination of features. He never understood why he didn't always have girls flocking around him.

Despite being completely unreligious, Preston had prayed one night a couple of months back, hoping Scott was gay like him. And seeing him again in the only class they had together this year only served to stoke the fire of his imagination all over again. Scott had been the object of more than half of his erotic fantasies in the last eight or nine months. This afternoon, directly after school, would be no different.

Doug continued. "Why didn't you say something before? And how the hell are we gonna beat the Wildcats this year?"

"Remember when we all went out back in July? I told you then."

"Fuck. All of us thought you were kidding. By the way, what the hell happened to you all summer? I hardly ever saw you." He remembered only four times they even saw each other.

Doug and Scott had been friends ever since Scott had joined the track team at the beginning of sophomore year. They just plain liked each other. They had gone on several pizza dates with girls, went to Wolves football games together, and had gone rappelling twice the previous spring with other members of the track team. In fact, Scott had been particularly proud to have introduced his favorite sport to him shortly after they became friends. They had always ended up with each other at parties, at dances, at every one of the public Centauri concerts, in the locker room, on the track, in classes they had together. Everywhere. Doug even liked the silly accents Scott did for comic relief, along with his odd brand of humor.

Scott had felt a bit guilty for not having let Doug into his life all that much since school let out last June, but everything had changed, of course. Doug wasn't someone he wanted to know why. He liked him way too much to end up losing him as a friend. Having a boyfriend had meant he had to be a little more selective with his time. Unfortunately, his friendship with Doug had been one of the things to suffer. He still felt bad about it but had had to prioritize. "I'm really sorry. I had a lot of stuff to do all summer. That's why I'm not coming back to the team."

"Douche nozzle," Doug whispered as he crossed his arms over his chest. But he was grinning.

Scott studied Doug's face. He knew when Doug was kidding. And he was now.

Doug knew Scott had a lot of things going on, and he loved Centauri himself. What was he going to do, tell him to give up on perhaps the best rock band Yucca Valley had? No way. Still, Scott had virtually vanished all summer. He hoped his absence like that wouldn't continue or happen again.

"Sorry, dude. Coach already tried to get me to stay. I told him no."

"I hate you," Doug said as Ms. Dunn, their calculus teacher, came into class. Scott grinned as he recalled having said that to Ryan just a couple of days ago after they had sex in his bedroom. He continued to grin as he opened his book to the first chapter.

✳   ✳   ✳

Joe Engle strolled into metal shop several seconds after the tardy bell rang. He had no interest in being on time for this class, although he knew if he kept it up, he'd eventually get nailed. How many times had he seen the counselor last year for being tardy? Nonetheless, he had to break in the instructor early in the year to show him who was boss. He rarely skipped classes, so why didn't they just let him in whenever he wanted?

He briefly studied his reflection in the window of the door before he entered. He didn't care that his left cheek was covered with zits. Last month it had been his chin and under his right ear. His mousy-brown hair was regulation military short. Although that style was growing in popularity with his crowd, his cut was an attempt to mimic the ever-present Marines that lived nearby. Joe's skin was darkly tanned down to the bottom of his neck and up his arms to about mid-bicep. The rest of his torso and his legs were pasty white under his Western clothing. He briefly surveyed his boots. They were scuffed along the sides, but he had shined the tips earlier in the week. All he could muster was a once a week shine job just to keep them from looking completely ragged.

Joe had failed and retaken sixth grade. Since he had been held back that year, he was a year older than most of his classmates. Regardless, his six-foot-three frame carried a boy who looked older than he really was at nineteen years old, mostly because of his weight and the fact that he simply didn't look much like a teenager anymore.

Joe could have been the poster boy for the cowboy culture at school. He had the hat, the belt buckle, the tooled belt with his name across the back, the requisite pickup truck, several pairs of well broken-in cowboy boots and plenty of Western shirts to complete his look. Despite being a bit pudgy around the middle, he fit well into the garb. He listened to country music exclusively, all on cassette, and blared it with plenty of distortion across the parking lot at school. He had been in FFA briefly but quickly realized he had no interest in agriculture or what the organization offered. Carl and Stu, his two buddies, were still FFA members and wore their blue logo jackets as often as possible. They both smoked like he did, but they all preferred to dip. Perfect rings had formed in all of the right back pockets of Joe's boot-cut straight leg jeans from a ubiquitous can of Skoal.

Metal shop was his last class, and when it ended, he went to the parking lot, headed for a gas station to fill up, then pulled up to the back of the machine shop in the nearby town of Yucca Mesa where he worked part-time. It was the only machine shop in the entire Morongo Basin that was open for two back-to-back shifts. The shop had several skilled full-time mechanics, drill press operators, lathe operators, and others. Joe was one of two unskilled minimum wage laborers. His and Roberto's job was to sweep up, dump ashtrays, clean the owner's office before going home, clean up scrap metal, move empty barrels when asked, and other assorted odd and end tasks. It was great since he didn't have to think about anything important and still get paid.

Despite his abrasive personality, he kept his position. Months previous he had strategically stopped an air compressor from exploding. He had noticed the pressure gauge was registering in the top end of the danger zone. He pulled the emergency relief valve and was later hailed as the shop savior. By default, Joe had saved several people from injury or even death and had kept the shop from being destroyed. It turned out that the compressor was on a manufacturer's recall list.

Most of the time, Joe kept a cup with him to spit in. Unfortunately, he had to set it down whenever it came time to do the sweeping. Styrofoam coffee cups were readily available in the shop so he simply got a new one when he couldn't find his old one. That meant he had to find them all before he left for the evening. The senior lathe operator had told him many times to keep his cups out of his workspace. Unfortunately, Joe found that it was at the exact spot he needed to set it down when he started his sweeping rounds. He would regularly deliberately 'forget' that particular one was there when Jack was away from his press. Luckily, Jack took several smoke breaks during his shift and was gone again. He snickered to himself when he set his one-quarter full cup down on top of the bin next to Jack's lathe, started sweeping, and promptly 'forgot' it was there again.

Shortly after nine-thirty, he left the shop and drove home. Lights were on all over their five-bedroom split-level ranch-style home. Joe lived with his mother, Liddy; his stepfather, Roger; Mary, his younger sister by a year; his older sister Susan, who was a year and a half older than he; his step-uncle Bob, and Bob's live-in girlfriend LuAnn. They all had their cars parked in the drive, out front, or near the house. Joe couldn't remember another home except this one.

Joe's father had mysteriously disappeared after a rather nasty divorce. He was never heard from again. His mother never spoke of him after that, nor revealed where he might be. Joe was sure he knew why and didn't want to know where he was either.

He remembered very little of Cade, his father. What he did remember, when he let the memories intrude, disturbed him. His father would occasionally come home in a rage after the bars would close, which would wake everyone up. That would make his mother yell at him. When Cade would get thrown out of his own bed, which was every time he had come home like that, he'd sometimes come stumbling into Joe's bedroom and pass out on the floor. Other times, Cade made the rounds to Joe's older and younger sister's bedrooms. He'd hear his sisters softly cry or whimper when his father visited them. On the occasions when Joe's bedroom was visited, and his father didn't just pass right out, his rage would be completely gone and he would paw at Joe while telling him to stay quiet. He would then make himself 'comfortable' in the bed with him.

He got slapped twice before he learned to shut his mouth when the touching started. That's when he realized what his sister's whimpering had been all about. After a while, Joe pretended he was asleep. His father's visits had started when Joe was eight. It continued like that, periodically, for a year and a half more before the divorce. But it was too late for Joe. His antenna had been permanently bent. The touching, showing Joe where to touch, and the deliberate arousal his father had introduced him to at too early an age had already hard-wired him.

When Joe started puberty at twelve and a half, he was already fighting the dreams. He was only somewhat successful in doing so. To this day, though, he had never thought of himself as anything but heterosexual, despite the wet dreams caused by images of a man's mouth on his erect penis or the memory of his father's semen discharged all over the front of his naked body.

Roger Pitley started dating Liddy shortly after the divorce and started living at the house about three months later. Since his brother was part of the package, Roger laid a cement slab at grade, and with his brother's help, constructed a new addition onto the back of the house. The new construction included a bedroom with full bath for his brother and his girlfriend, and a large game room that doubled as a den for the whole family. Shortly after it was finished,

Roger and Liddy married. His mother got a new last name. Joe and his sisters stayed Engles. All that had occurred just over eight years ago.

But nothing had changed. Sure, the house looked different, but inside it, Joe's family life never got any better. To him, his older sister had merely been upgraded to bitch, his younger sister got older but still had a six-year old's voice, and his step uncle Bob went from merely lazy to becoming an outright slob. In the last five years, the longest he'd kept a job was nine months. LuAnn used to stomp around and fume every once in a while, but was angry about nothing a lot more often nowadays and spoke her mind way too much. His mother went from working dayside to second shift, so he rarely saw her awake anymore. And his stepfather was getting more and more sullen due to his warehouse job which had had him working alternate second and third shifts for the last several years. Joe stayed pissed off at everyone nearly all the time and rotated whom he had arguments with. Indeed, the entire family rotated with their arguments as well. The cycle went on incessantly.

To escape the chaos or when he needed a good night's sleep he went to his girlfriend's house. Hardly anyone noticed when he was gone. But sleeping over always presented a problem. There was always the threat of another one of those damn dreams, which would have him in the bathroom wiping himself up or cleaning the sheets off. Always it was the same. Some shadowy male figure would be over him masturbating or having his way with him. Even having as much sex as he could with his girlfriend didn't stop the dreams.

There were eleven holes in the walls of the garage. All of them from his fist. Eleven of the fifteen or so times he had woken up from the dreams over the last year and a half, he had gone out to the garage and punched a hole through the drywall. Punching something would make him fully awake. The adrenaline rush of his anger would make the dream fade completely away. He could see where the studs were through the tape, since the drywall had never been primed. He had never hit a single one of the 2 x 4s. Since there were various things nailed up on the walls in the garage no one ever noticed when there became one, then two, then all eleven of them. No one cared about any hole that might develop anywhere in their detached garage anyway.

Two years ago, he had punched his step uncle the first time. The resultant smack on the head had landed him on the floor. He thought it had been Bob and not a dream that time. It wasn't. Nonetheless, it started a series of confrontations. The fights became more and more frequent until last May Joe landed in jail for twenty-four hours after having punched him again. Since Joe had just turned eighteen, the incident was on his permanent record. He had to remind himself to not punch Bob anytime soon or he'd go to jail again. Next time for a much longer time. The police had answered calls to the Pitley home due to a couple of domestic disputes in the last year and a half. His was the first jail sentence, though.

Joe had had a string of escapades with eight girls over the last five years, starting on the night of his thirteenth birthday. Wasn't it normal to have sex with as many girls as he possibly could? At least he hadn't gotten any of them pregnant. That was more than either of his sister's could say for themselves. Each had gotten pregnant at least once by the time they were fifteen, both of which had ended with an abortion.

One of the numerous things that Joe hated was the thought that anyone might be gay. He had fought his battle against the intruding thoughts, dreams, and images in his head for a good long time now and couldn't even imagine anyone thinking it was a good thing, much less giving in to it.

Only on one occasion had he joined in with one of his buddies, Stu, to taunt another kid in school. Stu had cooked up a plan to harass Alan, that kid Scott Faraday used to hang out with. Alan was little, quiet, and somewhat shy. But the fun wasn't there because Alan fought back almost immediately. That wasn't supposed to have happened. The desperate shame and guilt he felt about his own bizarre thoughts and dreams made him uncomfortable doing it. Alan might have been queer, but who knew? And he was way feistier than any queer should have been, or so he had thought. Luckily, Alan ended up moving away and he didn't have to deal with it anymore.

It was shortly after that that he started taking an almost morbid interest in Scott. He had kept his eye on him purely out of his own subconscious attraction to him. That led him to mess with Scott on occasion. He'd come by and smack Scott on the back of the head then make an excuse for having done so. He had done it only so he could touch Scott. He couldn't ever figure out why he wanted to do it, but couldn't help himself. He had done it several times and Scott never did anything about it either. He even made comments about how pretty certain guys were, just to see what his reaction would be. Then there was that time he tested Scott. He half wanted it to be true, but felt disgusted with himself for even thinking about it. He had invited Scott to come by the football stadium bleachers that one night a while back. Scott hadn't given him a firm no and that kept Joe on high alert.

Joe's head was a confused mess of repulsion about thinking about sex with boys and the lure of images that wouldn't disappear from his dreams, and occasionally flooded his idle thoughts. It was his personal hell, but he'd make it through it, even if he went crazy trying, he had told himself on several occasions.

*                    *                    *

"I'm, like, totally weirded out," Scott said to Colleen in the Royal Garage. He was there alone with her since no one else had arrived yet. In fact, he had arrived early, rousted her from the house, and made her sit and listen to him. "I had this big argument with my dad last weekend."

Colleen sat on a chair next to him. "That's news. I never heard about you guys arguing before. I'm sorry to hear about it."

In a way, her concern was refreshing, but Colleen really wasn't one to lend an ear in situations like this. It was his feelings he was talking about, not a gig, or what was wrong with a tune, or anything like that. He nonetheless told her everything.

"It wasn't just any ole argument either. I told him I'm gay. I told him about Ryan, and I told him I didn't want to go to junior college like he wants."

"You told him all that at once?"

"I promised myself, and Ryan, that I would."

"You know, I thought you were smart."

"Oh, stop it."

"I'm serious. You knew he was gonna freak, didn't you?"

"I figured he'd get mad. He wigs out pretty easily. But I didn't expect him to freak out on *me*."

"Why? Did he hit you?"

"No, but I thought I would hit *him*. It was more like what he said. Like, he wanted Ryan to quit molesting me. And he said I was going to High Desert College whether I liked it or not."

"Molesting is an odd choice of words."

"I'd say."

"I thought you had a good relationship with your parents."

"I have a decent one with my mom. You know I told her last year. But I never told him. And with Ryan in the picture now, and all, I had to."

"Hmm. So, is he speaking to you?"

"How'd you figure? He hasn't said a word since then. It's like I'm grounded without being grounded. He's more silent than usual."

"So, what's the deal about college?"

"I was going to ask you."

"I asked first."

"I had this revelation while we were coming back from Ryan's grandma's that I had never asked you how you paid for it."

"Student loans. How else does one do it?"

Scott looked pensive. "I could have kicked myself for never asking before. Dad told me he was gonna pay as long as I took the classes *he* wanted me to take. I just went along with it since that's what he did for my brother. I guess I won't get the same treatment now."

"He's really being that way? That's awful. You should talk with a school counselor. But you should still try to talk to him again."

"Yeah, I'm gonna talk to the counselor soon. And if *he'd* talk, I would. I'm not saying another word until he does. I don't want to talk about him anymore."

She shook her head. "Men." He looked at her questioningly. "You guys are all alike. I'm glad I don't have an ounce of testosterone in me." She was quiet for a moment as she thought about what Scott was going through.

Mitch, the bassist, and Barry, lead guitarist, came in through the side door of the Royal Garage. They were in a heated conversation about something. Colleen and Scott listened as they entered.

"He lives in San Diego," Barry said. He had seen Scott's Jeep in the driveway as well as Shakaiyo running around in the backyard, but suddenly seemed embarrassed that he was talking out loud when he saw them.

"San Diego? I hope he's coming up *here*," Mitch replied. He saw Colleen and Scott, too, and stopped talking as well. Their silence was overwhelming.

"What's all that about?" Colleen asked. They were obviously withholding something.

"Tell them or I will," Mitch said.

Barry tightened his lips, then sighed. "Damn it."

"Uh, what's going on here?" Colleen asked.

Scott surveyed them both. Something was clearly bothering Mitch, and Barry seemed reluctant to talk about it.

"Barry got an offer to join a band in San Diego."

Scott shot up off the stool, looking at Barry. "You what?"

"I didn't say yes."

"Oh boy," Colleen said. "I knew this was coming."

Scott looked at her now. "You did?"

"It was a surprise to me," Mitch stated. He looked at Barry. "We have a band here and we have gigs. What're we supposed to do for a lead guitar if you decide to take off?"

Barry went to his instrument and hoisted the strap over his shoulder. "Here's the deal. My friend Nick is in this jazz band in San Diego and he wants a jazz guitarist. You guys know I like jazz." They were all familiar with Barry's appreciation of jazz, a genre none of them particularly liked. "Well, we've been talking on the phone. Their band's thinking about changing their lead guitarist. I said I'd think about it."

Scott became even more alarmed. Whenever an offer to join another band was seriously entertained, the inevitable was next.

Scott had grown quite enamored with Barry's ability to keep the band together over the last year, and he had been one of the founding members. Granted, he was the oldest member of the band. At twenty-three he could do just about whatever he pleased. And as good as he was he could certainly join any band and get serious with them in a short period of time.

"Barry, man, you *can't* go," he said. They all heard it in his voice, desperation even. All heads turned to him.

Barry stopped what he was doing. "I didn't say yes."

But he didn't say no.

After everyone else arrived, band practice didn't start on time. In fact, they barely got any practice in. They spent the next hour talking about the issue.

Barry's friend had started the contemporary jazz-fusion band in San Diego called Pacific Moon about the same time that Centauri was formed. They were hoping to cut a CD by spring of next year. They had almost signed the deal when their lead guitarist started making trouble. Their producer ended negotiations. Now they were talking about restructuring the band, maybe even removing their guitarist, so they could eventually get a new recording deal. Barry was unhappy that Centauri had only gotten a three-gig deal at the Marine base in Twentynine Palms and nothing else on the horizon. Colleen was their default promoter since they didn't have the money to hire someone. But she worked a lot during the day and didn't have a great deal of time to spend shmoozing. The sheer lack of gigs seemed to be putting a damper on Barry's enthusiasm, especially in light of the fact that he had an offer to do his favorite type of music. So, the discussion boiled down to the fact that Barry wanted more exposure. A lot more.

During the discussion, which wasn't heated by any means, Scott became more and more agitated. Getting a good lead guitarist wasn't that easy. He knew exactly three guys in the area who played a decent lead. Barry was the best. The others were a combination of being either not as good, didn't want to be in a rock band, or their sound didn't fit in well enough.

*Wait a minute. Why are we always just looking to Colleen to book gigs?* Scott's mind went into overdrive. Maybe it would be up to him. Perhaps he'd have to show them he was more than just their soundman and occasional lyricist. Whatever it took, he'd do it. He'd go door to door to every bar in town that had a venue. *They can eat me if they think I can't talk to bar managers.* And there was Grubstake Days coming up next spring. Ever since 1951, Grubstake Days had been the Morongo Basin's tribute to the area's mining past. Nowadays, since it was such a much-loved event, there were contests, re-enactments, a parade, and bands that played. Perhaps even theirs this time. Granted, it was a long way off, Memorial Day of next year even, but maybe he could find the right person to talk to and beg them to have Centauri play, for cheap, if necessary. Wouldn't Barry have to stay if he booked that gig? Centauri hadn't played at Grubstake Days last year because they had that crappy soundboard.

Scott's eyes lit up. He was sure he could talk to someone at school to have them do a dance gig or two, too. The list of potential venues was far greater than he ever thought possible. Regional had a decent-sized auditorium. Why he didn't think about that before was beyond him. And how many people in school did he know who loved Centauri? Lots. The action plan was already in his head. He'd force Barry to stay if it was the last thing he did.

✻        ✻        ✻

Ralph pushed aside the time cards he had been fidgeting with while he sat at the desk. He had the phone to his ear. "Yes," he said. "Middle name, Andrew. Fall 1991 enrollment year."

"I'm sorry, sir. The computer just doesn't show anyone by the name of Scott Faraday for '90 or for '91. Is it under a different name or maybe a different enrollment period?"

"No it isn't. Thanks."

Ralph hung up the phone. He had been passed to three different people in the last five minutes. The admissions office had no record of Scott's name being on file at High Desert College. That could only mean one thing. His son had never filled out the application.

When he returned home later that afternoon he knocked on Scott's door. His Jeep wasn't there but he wanted to make sure he wasn't in his bedroom anyway. *When was the last time I was in his bedroom? Six…eight months ago? That's odd. I don't remember when it was.*

He pushed open the door, flipped on the light switch, and surveyed the room. Scott's stereo and sound recording equipment was displayed prominently in the rack on the far wall. The overhead fan was rotating slowly. The mostly opened bathroom door showed a drinking cup and toothbrush next to the sink. The closet door was wide open but everything was neatly hung up. The concert shirts Scott wore were on the near end of the rod. They were quite noticeable due to their wild color, spastic designs, and exotic materials. Scott's fully made up bed (that was a surprise) had his Mexican blanket folded up on it. The large wooden box that contained his rappelling gear was at the foot of the bed. His Frisbee hung on a peg above his headboard. His desk had a stack of magazines on it, his tarantula in a twenty-gallon terrarium, and the ebony

Buddha that his brother Steve had given him for his birthday were next to the stack. Other assorted odds and ends lay on the desk as well. The sum total of Scott's life. Ralph had decided that his son's future had depended on the next step.

His only intention was to find the form, complete it himself, and mail it. He stepped over and scanned the desktop. A small piece of paper begged his attention. It was torn on three sides and the only thing he could make out was 'ERT COLL'. He picked it up, and then looked down next to the desk. The forms were there, shredded, and covering the bottom of the waste can. Ralph dropped the single piece into it with the others. *Why is he doing this?*

Another thought came to him then. He pulled the chair out from the desk and sat. He picked up the top magazine from the stack and absentmindedly flipped through it. Maybe it wasn't his son who was being selfish. Maybe it was him. Elaine's admonishment was still making his ears ring. It had been gnawing at him most of the day anyway.

# CHAPTER 4

Ralph was in his office filing invoices. Elaine came in and pushed the door closed behind her. It stopped and opened back up about three-quarters of an inch. She sat down across from him. No one else was in the back of the restaurant just yet.

"Ralph, we need to talk." She used that tone. The one that meant stop and listen to me.

Ralph immediately stopped filing. The chair creaked as he sat down. "I'm listening."

Clark Hanson, the evening shift headwaiter, pulled his car up to the back entrance of Faraday's and parked it. He flipped down the visor and inspected his face in the little illuminated mirror. He dragged his fingernails across his left cheek. Despite the fact that he had shaved before he left his apartment, one could perfectly see where his beard grew. He usually shaved his dense whiskers twice a day due to the fact he was in the public eye nowadays. Satisfied with his inspection, he flipped the visor back up. He pulled his lean six-foot frame out of the car and surveyed the quiet parking lot behind the restaurant.

A little over eight months ago, he had moved here from Mission Viejo. At thirty-two years old, and being a single gay man, Clark should have been completely out of his element in this small town. Nonetheless, after he had moved here his life completely changed for the better.

When he came out with a vengeance, at twenty-four, he had been on a fast track of all night partying, drugs, and more sex than he could ever have imagined. That lasted almost six years before he realized that he was becoming burned out. He figured he could live that kind of life for decades until AIDS caught up with him. It never found him, but too many of his friends back in Orange County had low T-cell counts, became sick, or simply weren't safe and were quickly on their on their way to becoming viral-loaded.

When the only person he had ever fallen in love with died in his arms while in hospice care a year and a half before, he knew something had to change. It was he who had to do the changing. It took months to execute his plan. What it had involved was an acknowledgement of the fact that he had been taking way too many drugs, never got enough sleep, and that he needed to get away from the people he was hanging around with. There were a lot of loose ends he had no idea how to tighten at first. But he found out how. Shortly after his thirty-first birthday, he did it. He moved away to Yucca Valley and rented an apartment in the nicest complex he could find. It was far enough away from L.A. to keep him from partying, but not so far as to not be able to visit family when he wanted or needed to.

The Morongo Basin had very few of the things that L.A. offered, and had plenty of drawbacks. At least it was sunny virtually all of the time and never got any of that damned L.A. smog.

The Basin, with its scattered adjacent communities, was small in population, and had little in the way of the culture he had grown up with. Nonetheless, he generally liked the people he'd met, despite the fact that there were some vocal religious zealots around who stuck their noses into people's business on occasion.

There were things to do here, but they were quite benign. The list of amenities was actually longer than he had thought at first. And it was quiet here. He found the solitude inviting. He could think, which was something he did very little of for the first couple of decades of his life. He even went hiking on occasion. He had never hiked in his life until he came here. There was even this great restaurant he worked in and the tips were excellent. He hadn't expected that at all, given how small the community was. But Faraday's had a reputation he hadn't been aware of. It attracted people from all over. In the last ten months, he had waited on two Hollywood directors, a bestselling author and his wife, two famous actresses, and an actor from one of his favorite movies. Most all of them, except for the screen personalities, he recognized from the names on their credit cards. All at Faraday's.

Clark already showed how responsible he was with both Ralph and Elaine since he had a key to the back door. He inserted it and quietly came in. He was adjusting his tie in the mirror near the punch clock when he heard Ralph and Elaine talking in the office.

One of the first things he had noticed after starting work at Faraday's was that although Ralph and Elaine worked hard, they seemed to be in a frenzy most of the time. It was if they should never have been in the restaurant business. It was tiring work and not for those who didn't tolerate long hours. Ralph didn't tolerate chaos very well. He was always pushing himself and trying to stay in control at the same time. It rubbed off onto Elaine, who was generally a pleasant person to be around most of the time. It seemed that success was always just out of reach for Ralph, and rarely was anything good enough for him. Clark figured he noticed it because he had had to slow down and take an assessment of his own life. *Everyone has their own pace, though, and it may be a long time before Ralph realizes what he's doing to himself*, he thought. Clark noted that he was becoming a little more philosophical as he was getting older, which was odd. He never used to think like that before.

Clark couldn't help himself and listened. Elaine's voice was distinct behind the mostly closed door. "You have to talk to him. It's not fair that you've not spoken to him ever since he told you," she maintained.

"I'm mad at *you*. How could you keep the fact that our son's gay from me?"

Clark's ears perked up immediately. *Gay? Their son? Scott?* This was one hell of a conversation already. Now he was holding his breath so he could hear every word.

"I told you I'm sorry. And he told you, didn't he? He had to take his time. I'm sure he felt it was that time, now that he's going out with Ryan."

*Ryan? Who's Ryan*, Clark wondered. *I don't know anyone by that name. Wait a minute. Come to think of it, Ryan must be that dark-haired kid that's been here a few times. Howard St. Charles is his uncle or something. And this is amazing. In three seconds, I've just gone from knowing exactly five other people in town who're gay to another one, and hearing about his boyfriend. But, the Faraday kid? I can't believe I never knew it!*

Cute or not, Clark rarely took notice of boys under twenty. Youngsters just weren't his type, mostly because they were arrogant or just plain airheads. But this was different. The Faraday boy was right under his nose, was gay, and he didn't even bother to properly get to know him.

Ralph continued. "He's way too young to make the kind of decisions he's making on his own."

"And just how old were you when we first met?"

Ralph didn't say anything. Clark heard the chair creak. Finally, Ralph spoke up. "His age."

"My point exactly. Look, I know why you're really upset. Steve complained about High Desert College too, didn't want to stay here, and your parents never pushed you to get an education. Scott knows exactly what he wants and he should have that."

Clark wondered for a moment who Steve was, then recalled that he was the Faraday's elder son. He heard the chair creak again.

"Talk to him, honey. Tell him that *he's* right. Tell him that *you're* wrong. Leave it at that."

That was all Clark needed to hear. He figured he better act like he just came in before the office door opened and they saw him standing there. He tiptoed to the backdoor, made a noisy entrance by deliberately slamming the door shut, and went down the hallway toward the punch clock again. The office door opened. He put on a wide smile for them as Ralph and Elaine both said hello and passed him on their way to the kitchen. He could tell there was a strain between them even though they were nice enough with their greetings.

Later, when Scott came in on his shift, Clark was all set to talk to him. Unfortunately, it was a busy night. That was always good for tips though, so it didn't really matter that much after all. Nonetheless, he wanted to have a real conversation with Scott and here he was, too busy to even talk. He passed by the host station when Scott was by himself near the end of the evening. "Hey, Scott. When are you off?"

Scott looked at his watch. "The usual time. Why?"

"Wanna go get some ice cream? It's on me. I need to ask you something."

Scott had always figured Clark was gay although no one had ever confirmed it for him. It wasn't until this summer that he even had an inkling to ask him. Nonetheless, ever since Ryan had entered the picture he had completely shut out all ideas of even bothering. It just didn't matter. Besides, Clark was what, at least fifteen years older than him? That put him outside the ballpark of people he normally had casual conversations with, much less conversations about whether they were gay or not. Regardless, Clark was always friendly toward him and never participated in any of the gossip that the waitresses engaged in, which Scott liked about him. And the fact that Clark wasn't married at his age made him sure he had Clark pegged correctly. Scott wasn't sure what he was up to, but it was a friendly invitation, so why say no? "Sure. How about the Dairy Queen?" He was sure that would get at least a grin out of him. When it did, he was suddenly a little uncomfortable having said it.

They pulled up to the Dairy Queen shortly after nine-thirty. They each ordered a small dish of soft-serve, then found a table toward the back of the dining area.

"Okay, I'll be direct about this," Clark began. "I overheard your parents talking about you this afternoon."

"Arguing or talking?"

Clark gave him a face. "Just talking. Seems that you've let them in on a little secret. I, uh, wanted you to know that I'm gay, too."

Scott leaned forward and whispered. "Are you coming on to me?"

Clark half-expected that kind of response but wasn't sure Scott would just come out and say it. Now he laughed. Scott saw the ice cream that had coated his tongue as he did. "Not *even*. You're way too young for me." He wanted to add that he never even thought about making a pass at a kid, but decided to leave it at that. "Besides you're going out with someone, huh? I completely respect that. That's what I wanted to talk to you about actually."

Scott stopped digging into his ice cream. "They said all that?"

Clark held up a hand, palm out. "Like I said, I overheard them talking about you. Seems your dad is upset about the fact that your mother was told and she didn't tell him. Is that accurate?"

"Jeez, are there no secrets anymore?"

Clark leaned forward a little. Scott could see the tiny pupils of Clark's eyes in the bright dining area. He even noticed a little black spot in the lower part of the bluish-green colored iris of Clark's left eye. Suddenly, Scott thought Clark was handsome for someone who he thought was at least twice his age.

"Don't tell them I heard all that. I swear I wasn't listening on purpose."

"So, what else do you know?"

"Something about your brother and something else that I forgot. But imagine my surprise hearing about *you*. There are very few out gay people in this town as it is and when I found out that I worked with another 'kindred spirit' I just had to let you know."

So, at Scott's inquiry Clark told him everything. How he had come to live in Yucca Valley and about his friends back in Orange County. Scott told him about the issue Clark said he had forgotten. The one where his father was practically forcing him to go to a junior college against his will. Soon enough he was lit up like a sparkler. He had discovered that despite their age difference Clark was a very likeable guy. In fact, he could have clobbered himself for not having found out all these things earlier. What was even more odd though was that the more Clark talked the more handsome Scott thought he was. *Hanson, handsome? What a coincidence.*

"What I really would like to know though is about that boyfriend of yours. How the hell can you be out in school? I mean, I would have killed to be out at your age."

"At Regional? Huh, I'm not out at school."

"Oh. Well, how'd you meet him?"

So Scott told him about last June: about how they had met at the restaurant that one evening, and how he slowly but surely built up his nerve to come out to him. Clark listened so intently that the rest of his ice cream melted before he could scoop up another bite.

"Do you have any idea how brave you are? To do all that here in the Basin? To be out at seventeen? To have a *boyfriend* at your age?" Clark asked. He was incredulous. All this had occurred right under his nose.

"I told my aunt when I was fifteen, but I didn't come *out* out until I was *sixteen*."

"I wish I could be ten, no, fifteen years younger, and be you." He fell silent and shook his head as he tried to process the bubble of innocence Scott lived in. He looked at his watch. "It's getting late and I know you have school tomorrow. Look, I'm not perfect by any stretch of the word, but if you want someone to talk to, I kinda doubt there's much you've gone though that I haven't already. Not like I'm an expert on relationships or anything. But..."

Scott cut him off. "You don't know how glad I am that we talked. I had wanted to ask you if you were gay before I met Ryan. But that was before I had come out to anyone else except some of my relatives and our lead singer. Then when he came along everything went on hold. I-I just wanted to be with him every second. You know what I mean?"

"Are you kidding? Of course, I do," Clark said with a huge grin. "Friends?" He stretched out his hand. Scott smiled as he shook it.

They tossed their cups into the waste receptacles then stepped outside. Scott pulled out onto Highway 62 and took off toward home. Clark shook his head. *I swear he's the most courageous gay boy I've ever known. I wish I hadn't been so scared.*

He thought wistfully of the two aborted attempts he made to edge out of the closet, once when he was eighteen, and the second time when he was twenty. He had been too scared. White bread, suburban Mission Viejo just wasn't the place to find oneself that easily. He did, though. Late by today's standards, but he did. Clark watched Scott's taillights heading away. *Damn that boy.*

Back home Scott parked the Jeep at the curb on the cul-de-sac. He was feeling a mixture of elation and sadness now. Clark was this unexpected ally, which was an incredible find, yet his father's continued silence weighed heavily on him. Plus, what Barry had announced was still disturbing him. It was as if he was being tortured from two directions for no good reason.

Shakaiyo greeted him at the gate. She placed her front paws across the top of it and he let her lick his face. His watch showed that it was shortly after ten-thirty. The sliding glass door opened and Ralph came out. Scott was surprised to see him there in the dark. Ralph came toward him and Shakaiyo went up to him looking for an outstretched hand. He offered it to her while Scott continued to stand at the gate.

"Son, I, uh, mind if we talk?" Ralph asked while he scratched behind Shakaiyo's ears.

"About what?"

"I shouldn't have yelled at you last week. And I'm-I'm sorry I haven't been talking to you."

Scott's heart leapt. His father was speaking to him! Scott knew how difficult an apology was for him. He opened the gate and Shakaiyo came trotting out.

"Let's walk," Ralph said.

"I need to take her for one anyway."

This was one of those rare moments of solitude with his dad and Scott wasn't about to pass it up. Perhaps his father had figured it all out just like Ryan had said. They started down the driveway then up the street.

"Your mother and I've been talking. She's reminded me that you're no longer the little boy I've been watching grow up."

He gave his father a sideways glance. "Duh."

"Son, look, I got upset because I want you to have the future my parents didn't provide for me. They never even nudged me to go to school. When I was growing up, they didn't bother to give me a good example of how to be successful. And they died destitute because my father didn't think about the future. I don't want you to end up like him."

"Dad, I love music more than anything in the world. I love Centauri more than any band in the universe. I don't mind working at the restaurant. It's okay, but I can't make a living doing that. And that means that I can't go to a junior college. I have to go to a school *I* choose. And pursue subjects that mean something to *me*. Besides, I don't see how what your parents did has anything to do with me."

"Maybe it doesn't. Maybe I've just been hearing you say that you don't want the things I know are important. Maybe you have different priorities."

"Yeah. And do you have any idea how awesome the band is? You know we have the three gigs coming up at the base. We're gonna kick butt! That's what it's all about. That's what makes me wake up in the morning. That's what makes me feel alive. That, and Ryan."

Ralph looked at him. Their eyes locked momentarily. "I didn't mean what I said about him either."

Scott stopped dead in his tracks. "You mean that? You don't mind that I'm seeing him?"

"If I had a choice you wouldn't be gay. But I don't have that choice. You made that one."

"I don't recall saying, 'Hey, today I'm gonna be gay'. It doesn't work that way. And do you think I was happy about it? I mean, at first. I had to lie to everyone for a long time. That was the worst part, the *lying*. I kept it a secret from you for a freakin' year. I keep my mouth shut in school *every single day*. It's no fun, believe me. I can't be myself with any of my friends. Not that I think I'm screwed up because of it. It's just then I'd have to deal with the assholes that'll make my life hell. The kids at school wig out about gay people."

"You don't have to paint me a picture."

"But it's not something I chose."

"Okay, wrong words."

"Yeah, wrong words. But thank you for understanding that I'm going to keep seeing him."

"It's going to take me a while."

"To what?"

"To get used to it. It's, you know, embarrassing."

"Embarrassing? When have you ever even see us kissing?"

"Well, never."

"Then why is it embarrassing? It just…is," Scott didn't understand what his father meant at all.

"Just give me some time."

"You've had my whole life, all seventeen years, to get used to it."

"You know what I mean."

"Do you know what *I* mean?"

Scott wasn't fully satisfied. He wanted him to come around immediately, but then thought he might be going too fast once again and quieted down. He actually heard his Aunt Cin's voice admonishing him in his head.

"Maybe if I got a book or something to read about it."

Scott wondered how that would do any good. "Yeah, a book," he replied with noticeable sarcasm.

"Okay, forget it. Look, son, make the right decisions. I guess I can't tell you what they are, although I tried. But I want you to make them for me anyway. Don't be stupid like I was. Make sure you know what you're doing."

It seemed like he was rambling now as he continued with a long story about his mother's illness, their misuse of money for most of his life, his lack of direction when he was a kid. In fact, many of the details Scott had never heard before. None of what he said made any sense though. It was history. And none of it related to him at all. Scott just let him talk now without rebutting anything. His dad rarely had conversations like this with him. And for him to completely forgive Scott for both things he had said, much less talk this much was cause for celebration.

They finally returned and stopped at the gate. Scott let Shakaiyo into the backyard. Ralph took his son by the shoulders, then hugged him tightly. He loved his son regardless of who he was or what kinds of decisions he was making. He had to master forty-seven years of conditioning to get past the gay issue. He still hadn't completely figured out why he was letting Scott make his own choice about school. But he knew that at the core of his issue was something about identity and being seventeen. He was completely incompetent when he was Scott's age. As a teenager he had worked menial jobs, didn't know what he wanted to do with his life, and had little ambition. Elaine was his impetus to get his life in order. Before that, he was virtually adrift. He had been working hard for a very long time now, wasn't aimless at all, and had no idea that Scott had mastered his identity in ways he hadn't even begun to understand. He thought he'd get used to what his kids did. But there was always something he wasn't prepared for.

# CHAPTER 5

Warren Tyllas, Preston's father, had started in the car dealership business with a small used car lot outside of Flamingo Heights, one of the small communities just north of Yucca Valley. That progressed to a larger dealership within the city limits of Yucca Valley, and now to the huge new one down in Palm Springs.

Preston never rode the bus to school because he had a car which his father had given to him on his sixteenth birthday. In fact, he had chosen his cherry red Nissan Maxima right off the lot in Palm Springs. As Preston exited the school parking lot, he took his time getting home. After all, it was barely three miles to the Sky Harbor neighborhood where he lived. He pressed the remote to the garage door, pulled up the driveway, and parked his car in the third stall. No other cars were in the garage. His father was still at the dealership and wouldn't be home for another couple of hours, as usual, so his stall was empty. Preston's parking spot was the last one on the right. The middle stall had one of those new molded plastic picnic tables, still boxed up waiting for Fred, their handyman, to assemble. Ever since his parents had gotten divorced when he was thirteen, that stall had been vacant. His mother had gotten the other house in the divorce. During lengthy custody hearings Preston begged to live with his father, and he had done so ever since he was fifteen.

Rosa Morales, the Tyllas's El Salvadoran housekeeper, was in the kitchen when he entered the house through the garage entrance. A pleasant aroma greeted him.

"I'm cooking a special dinner tonight," she said with a broad smile as he passed by.

"Okay. I'm extra hungry today. Can't wait. But I'm gonna eat at work," he replied in a snide sing-song way. He always thought she was a little too cheery for his taste and just gave her that passing acknowledgement. She paused and briefly looked at his schedule posted on the refrigerator. He was supposed to be off today. If he were working tonight, it wasn't the first time he hadn't written it down. He passed by her and raised his voice so she could hear him. "I'm gonna study for a little while before I go to work, so don't bother me."

She was all too aware of his need to deliberately sound nasty for no apparent reason. She didn't know many other Anglo teenagers, but this one seemed particularly surly. None of her kids would be caught dead talking to her like that. She still thought that if she stayed nice to him he would eventually come around. But it had been nearly four months and he still hadn't warmed up much. Maybe it was because he didn't know how well off he really was? She didn't know for sure. What she did know, though, was that Mr. Tyllas paid her handsomely to keep house, and cook for him and his only son. She could endure a little teenage insolence for that kind of money.

Preston walked down the plush carpeted hallway, ignoring the framed photos that hung on both walls. They were mostly of his father in a suit and tie, shaking hands with politicians and other famous people at the dealership. Others were of early family outings with his mother, his father, and himself skiing and sailing. One was taken in a gondola in Italy when he was seven, another at Disneyland, and one was just of him taken in front of the Golden Nugget in Las Vegas. The largest photo was of the entire compliment of aunts and uncles on his father's side, with he as the only boy in a sea of seven other younger girls. He was five years older than the next in line. He was an only in several respects, and at the top of the heap.

He turned the corner and went up the stairs to his bedroom, closing the door while locking it at the same time. He had perfected the quick close-and-lock technique years before. He placed his backpack on the bed.

Months previous he had carefully explained to Rosa to not move any of his stuff when she dusted. He surveyed the room, making sure everything was in place. On his desk, the diskette holder next to his PC hadn't been moved even an inch. His small dot matrix printer sat next to the computer in its low cradle. The doors to his bathroom and walk-in closet were both closed. None of his books had been moved, and the blinds were shut. He twisted the rod to open them and briefly looked out over the backyard. A ten-foot stretch of various sized palms in large terracotta pots sat at the bend of the kidney-shaped pool that was surrounded by brick pavers. Two cottonwoods hugged one corner of the yard. The entire backyard was enclosed by a very tall redwood fence.

He unbuttoned his shirt, shook it off his shoulders, and draped it over his desk chair. He went into the bathroom and brushed the hair up off his forehead. He surveyed himself in the mirror on the back of the door. He had gotten his annoying once-every-other-month zit a week ago, and it had faded considerably. It was almost undetectable now as he inspected it near his hairline.

He kicked off his shoes and went to the large walk-in closet. Way in the back corner, under a pile of folded clothes, was his locked box. The box that contained the Polaroids and other assorted photos. Some were of himself, naked and aroused, of course. Most were pictures of other boys. He had a couple of photos of boys from the football team, one of Vic, the cute skater boy from down the street, who only let him take two (*damn him*), and quite a few of boys at the pool at work. Every picture featured a shirtless boy. He loved chests. Flat ones, built ones. It didn't matter. As long as he could see nipples. In fact, he called his little collection his 'chestposé'.

He unlocked the box, and pulled out the manila folder. The pictures of Scott Faraday, his special collection, were in it. He spread some of the choice ones out onto the nightstand, while the folder slowly slid down the edge of the bed and fell to the floor. He reached up to caress his pecs. He worked a hand down into his pants and grasped himself. He had been completely hard before he even got the pictures spread out. In another moment, his pants dropped to the floor and he kicked them aside. He dropped onto his back on the bedspread and conjured up another fantasy scenario of he and Scott together as he slid his boxers off. While checking out each photo in turn, it took a little more than three minutes before he was done. He hated stifling his moans, but didn't want Rosa to know he was beating off. He had wanted to drag it out as long as he could but rarely lasted much more than eight minutes, even if he slowed down or stopped completely at times.

He looked around himself to make sure he hadn't gotten anything on the bedspread since his first spurts occasionally went right over his head. Satisfied with his inspection, he went to the bathroom to wipe up. He really had to study before he went to work and, after stashing the photos and changing into some shorts and a t-shirt, managed to get in about half an hour before he finally hung up his school clothes and left.

Work was at Cottonwood Springs Resort and Country Club. The club was a bit unique in that they had no overt policy about member's relatives being employees. Yet, why his father didn't just join one of the nice clubs in Palm Springs was beyond him. Warren was insistent that it was the nicest resort in the high desert. He hadn't been kidding. The country club had horseback riding, a driving range and an 18-hole golf course with pro shop, tennis courts, a couple of sports clothing stores, dining facilities, corporate condos, a huge pool, and all the other amenities that could be found in Palm Springs on several hundred acres, but all at about half the cost. It was a cinch to secure a part-time job stringing rackets at the tennis shop. It was at the club where he met Casey. Casey was the latest in the limited number of males Preston had managed to seduce in the last two years.

Preston and his father had traveled to Nuevo Vallarta, next to Puerto Vallarta, Mexico, when he was fifteen. It was Warren's way of celebrating with Preston after he had been given custody. He had spent quite a few hours skimboarding that first day on a decent stretch of beach near their rental condo. The only other skimboarder he saw that day was a gorgeous boy named Dean. They skimboarded while Preston wished he could get into Dean's swim trunks.

Even while conjuring up his fantasy, he was incredibly nervous about the prospect since he'd never had any sexual contact with anyone before. Nonetheless, he had been working up the nerve to do something 'gay' for a couple of months at that point. He had figured it out when he realized that not a single one of his masturbatory scenarios or sexual dreams ever had a female in it. It was always guys. He had to have one in real life. He simply knew he was gay. And when Dean and he were the only two people on the beach that day, the fantasies wouldn't quit.

The next day, Dean and his family just happened to be on the same booze cruise with he and his father. They met again while in line at the dock before getting onboard their vessel. They sat together on the way out to the bird refuge island at the end of the bay, ate together at the isolated beach during the picnic lunch, and generally became inseparable. Since the adults weren't doing much more than getting blitzed on the ride back, he and Dean sat and talked even more. Dean was two years older than Preston, which made him a little more than seventeen at the time. The more they talked, the more they kept staring at each other. The more they stared, the hotter it seemed to be getting. And it wasn't from the sun. Preston was being obvious about trying to hide his erection under his beach towel. Dean noticed it, of course, and teased him about it. Preston didn't mind it. It was the perfect icebreaker. So, he came right out and asked Dean if he could give him a blowjob. At first, it was just joking around. When Dean kept pretending he hadn't heard the question right, he became persistent, then downright serious about it. None of the drunken adults noticed them both go into the little head at the same time. They did nothing more than feel each other up and kiss in there. Dean quickly realized what a great find he had made. So did Preston. They made plans for that evening.

He gave his first blowjob a little more than five hours later. It almost didn't happen though. He had trouble finding their condo since they weren't well marked, Dean's father had invited him inside for a late snack which took up valuable time, and then Dean's mother wanted to know all about Yucca Valley since they were from Nebraska. Yucca Valley? Who the hell wanted to know about that place?

Once they got away and he got Dean's rock hard penis in his mouth, he had arrived at a complete understanding of himself. Dean didn't reciprocate that time, but rather gave him a handjob to even the score. That was okay with him though. It was just the ability to rack up the point that he had been going for anyway.

Several days later on the plane trip home, he thought he had permanently hurt himself from the number of times he and Dean had done it. In fact, there was even a little blood in his urine in flight. He had gotten his blowjob, multiple times. He got more handjobs to go with it as well. He had never had that many orgasms in such a short period. He knew then that he was only checking off the months until he could move away from Yucca Valley. His sexual hiatus lasted only thirteen months. He didn't count on being able to find others to be intimate with back home.

Shortly thereafter, Warren joined the country club. At first, it was so Preston could have a place to swim. The pool that was in their backyard was still a drawing on the architectural plans. Preston went to the club as often as he could. He made an effort to become friends with all the lifeguards, which led to being friends with other employees, which then got him his part-time job when he turned sixteen. Much to his dismay, all of the male lifeguards had turned out to like girls. He had hoped that at least one of them wouldn't, but that wasn't the case.

Since Preston had been stringing rackets in the tennis shop, along with selling clothing and other tennis items there, he had met not only quite a few of the other members, but their guests as well. Patrick Casten was in his early twenties, was an average tennis player and son of a long-time club member. He had invited a college buddy from Vermont to stay with him for a month last fall. John Hammon turned out to not only be decent on the court, but he was very good looking, had just turned twenty-two, and took a liking to Preston right away. Patrick had no idea his buddy was gay.

Starved for sexual adventure, Preston had been on the lookout for any prospect he could get. The burning eye contact had been his first clue. The lingering touch of John's hand each time Preston had handed him the assortment of rackets to check out had told him even more. When John wanted a personal tour of the grounds, Preston knew right away why he was being asked. When asked how old he was, Preston lied. He wouldn't be seventeen for eleven months. He figured John wouldn't have cared anyway.

John had taught Preston things he never knew were possible. He learned how to overcome the gag reflex problem he had encountered with Dean. He used a condom for the first time. A lot of them. He learned the importance of lube, the more the better. He learned how many fingers could go inside him at one time. He also learned how exquisite a tongue could feel in every nook and cranny of his virtually hairless body. It was the most rewarding month of his life. Exhausting even. And somehow, Patrick never found out about their many clandestine rendezvous.

Before John left at the end of that month, Preston told him how old he really was. John was angry that he had lied. But Preston had done it for a good reason. His father had taught him a very valuable lesson: never get deeply emotionally involved with anyone. Pretend you're enjoying the other person's affections and simply feign interest back.

Warren hadn't formally taught him that. Selling cars was a completely impersonal act. Hiring and firing salesmen or managers was a completely impersonal act. Marrying his mother, and cheating on her twice before she found out had all been impersonal acts. His mother's failed second marriage, due to her being almost the same sort of person, reinforced the notion as well. So, Preston was good at it. He had learned, by sheer osmosis, exactly how to conduct himself when it came to interpersonal relations. He practiced as often as he could on Rosa. He also had been savvy enough to know that his and John's age difference could present a serious problem for John. And he knew that John had fallen for him by the end of the first week.

John got over being angry the week after his return to Vermont. He demonstrated it by writing Preston a long romantic letter expressing how much he missed him, asked when he would visit him in Vermont to go skiing (all on John), and told him he couldn't wait to 'put my tongue inside your sweet young ass again'. Preston thought it was cute, but promptly burned the letter. A second one never found its way into their mailbox at 17250 Quail Valley Trace.

*          *          *

Casey Sekalic turned seventeen at the end of the last school year. In fact, the last day of his junior year coincided with his seventeenth birthday in late May. At the end of this school year, he would be graduating on his eighteenth birthday. He looked forward to that double celebration.

Teller Academy, where he attended, wasn't part of the Morongo Basin school system since it was a private school in the nearby town of Joshua Tree. Most of the kids that attended there were from the wealthier families in the area. Teller only had one hundred thirty-four students, smaller than any school in the region. Casey was one of forty-two who were seniors this year.

Preston could have gone to Teller, but had rejected the idea before his freshman year. He liked the fact that Regional had a lot more boys than Teller. The 'scenery' was a lot better there, too. He didn't count on the twist of fate that had brought he and Casey together.

Casey's father, an internist in town, had enrolled him at Teller three years previous. Being from the former Yugoslavia—more specifically the Dalmatian Coast of Croatia—his father had been seeking ways to leave their Communist country behind. A well-paid bribe to a coastal patrol boat captain made sure that his cabin cruiser would get them unimpeded to Venice. He, his wife, his six-year old daughter, and then fourteen-year old Casey, made the exceedingly dangerous trek across the open Adriatic to start their new lives. Several short hops across Europe, then through North America, eventually landed him in Joshua Tree, well away from any fighting back home. There, he was able in due course to setup a lucrative practice.

Casey remembered a lot about Croatia before Communism began to crumble all over Europe, which eventually included his patchwork country of origin. One thing he remembered well was how homophobic Serbians were. When Casey was eleven, Uncle Lovro had been taken out to a hillside one evening by a group of militiamen. He had been summarily shot and the body was never recovered. All due to one important fact. It was well known in his family, and apparently to others, that Lovro was gay.

Casey felt he was very lucky. If he had been back in Croatia now, he would be the next one in his family shot on that hillside. Lovro was all of twenty-seven at the time, and resembled Casey in many ways, the same blonde hair, the same blue eyes, similar in build, and the same liking for males. Luckily, Casey was too young to know that last fact about himself at the time.

Casey's real first name was Vedran, a Croatian name that had been in his family for generations. Casey became his nickname the first day of school at Teller. He didn't know who first came up with it since he barely understood any English, but for some reason no one used his real name. Nonetheless, he liked it and Vedran became the name only his family used now. Although his last name ended with a 'ch' sound, he still didn't want to change it. Heck, he barely owned his first name anymore, his father continued to use the single 'c' in print, and he sure wasn't going to change it just for school.

In less than a year, he was speaking English almost perfectly. He had never spoken it before coming to the States. He still got tongue-tied on longer words. Although he had learned how to mask some of his Slavic accent no one seemed to mind it, even here in the somewhat isolated Morongo Basin. It may have had something to do with his curly blonde hair and blue eyes. It seemed to attract a lot of attention.

Despite the fact that others thought he was exceptionally good looking, Casey nonetheless maintained a full set of teenage doubts about his appearance.

His saving graces, he had decided, was that he was fat free like many of the other boys he knew, had finally stopped burning in the sun and had a nice even tan now, and he liked sports, which made him fit in well with the guys.

He was well aware he was gay due to the fact that he only fantasized about boys, especially the half-naked ones at the club pool, and had never developed any sexual interest in girls. Luckily, his avid interest in anything that resembled sports had kept his proclivity completely hidden from others. It also led him to work in the golf shop at the club. Still, though, he didn't dare join any of the sports teams at school for fear of what might happen in the locker room. His penis had always had a mind of its own and still wasn't listening to him.

René Geiger lived three doors down from him and didn't attend Teller but rather went to Regional. She was his best friend and knew he was gay. It was their little secret. They met the week he moved to the neighborhood. At school, he was a member of a small all-male clique. Although they were all totally into sports, he kept them just at arms length. Somehow, it was always easier to be better friends with girls than with guys. It was something he never quite understood.

He had never been sexually active until he met Preston at the club in early June, two weeks after his seventeenth birthday. Since that time, he'd had more sex than he thought he'd ever have. More than all his buddies combined.

Casey spun the dial of his combination in the employee locker room before going to the punch clock. He passed the mirror on his way out and checked his attire. He wore the requisite khaki shorts with black dress belt, tennis shoes with short white athletic socks, and the standard maroon polo shirt with the Cottonwood Springs Country Club logo on it. The maroon shirt alone singled him out as an employee to everyone. His tight curly blonde hair was always in place, so he didn't bother to do anything with it.

He ran a finger up the timecards and found his. He checked the time on the punch clock and waited for the machine to click to exactly five o'clock before he placed his card in the slot. Punched in now, he strode off to the driving range. His first task was usually to take the tractor out and pick up all the golf balls. That would take a while. When he was done with that, his next task was to handle the golf carts that were being brought in from the day's games. That usually took the rest of the evening. It was menial work at best, but he didn't mind it at all. It was just the right amount of physical activity, which he enjoyed, he got free golf tips from one of the golf pros, and he always had enough downtime to go over and talk with his boyfriend Preston.

Preston arrived at the shop at exactly six o'clock. He checked the order slips and placed the first one behind the plastic holder. He had four today, two catgut and two nylon orders. All the rackets had already been carefully tagged, as usual, with the member's name, the tension requested, and the color code they used for the strings. He had started on the second racket when Casey arrived.

Preston had been working at the club for almost five months when Casey came on as a new employee. He had come to find out that Casey's father had been a member for over a year but he never remembered either of them before that day. Boy, that day was killer.

It had started out like any other June day. Preston came into the locker room to change for work and saw the manager showing the new guy his locker. Casey only had on tennis shoes and the club's khaki shorts. A folded maroon shirt, still in its plastic wrapper, was in his hand and his street shirt lay in a heap on the bench in front of him. The manager had been looking at a form on his clipboard, completely uninterested in Casey's upper body. Preston, on the other hand ran right into the bench and bruised his shin while scouting this new handsome blonde boy. Clearly a new employee, he had the most beautifully tanned smooth pecs topped off with nickel-sized dark brown nipples. And that curly blonde hair was to die for. When Casey raised his arms up to don a t-shirt, he saw real blonde tufts in his armpits. So, the blonde was real. Preston was determined to find out who this new guy was before he left the locker room. So he did. He went right up and introduced himself. He knew almost instantly that Casey was his next prospect. He could tell from his voice alone.

It took five days, but Preston had sex with him. Casey had been asked to go look for Mr. Touhy's three iron that he thought fell off his cart on the fairway somewhere near the fifteenth hole. Preston was already off for the evening and happened to come by when the assignment was being given. He couldn't believe the luck. Under the guise of being a Good Samaritan, he offered to ride with Casey since it was getting toward dusk. Plus, he knew the way. He was merely being friendly, wasn't he?

He was more than friendly. After Casey stopped the cart on the fairway near the green, Preston took Casey's hand, placed it on his crotch, and asked him if he wanted it. The fact that Casey didn't say no or pull his hand away was all he needed to seal the deal.

Preston unzipped Casey's shorts, pulled them and his underwear down to his ankles, and proceeded to give Casey his first blowjob. Casey had been fully erect before his shorts made it to his feet. It was a first for them both. Casey had never had sex with anyone and Preston had never been with an uncircumcised boy. In fact, he had barely seen an uncircumcised penis before.

Infatuated as he was, Casey decided there and then that Preston was his boyfriend. Over the last four months, he had had sex with him at least once a week. Most of the time, it was twice a week. It was always on Preston's terms: incredibly hot, yet ultimately unrewarding; passionate, yet oddly unfulfilling; always clandestine, but sometimes out in the open at night in one of their cars in the parking lot, or on the fairway, or behind a boulder in the wide open desert. Casey knew if he only gave in a little more each time, he could win Preston completely over.

He still had no idea who he was dealing with.

Sara, one of the other girls who usually worked evenings, was up front folding shirts on a large Lucite cube when Casey came into the shop.

"Hi, Casey." She was particularly fond of him. She loved his accent and his curly blonde hair. But she really liked the fact that he was exotically nice. No other guy she knew was as nice as he. And even though he seemed to act a little less masculine than all the other guys she knew, she figured it was a cultural thing.

"Hi Sara. Busy night?"

"Are you kidding? I've sold exactly two things in the last hour, despite the invitational. Preston's doing all the work."

He looked back at the corner of the shop. The racket-stringing machine was attached to the floor on a slightly raised platform. He could see Preston running some string into one of the feeder holes. Despite being slightly raised up from the general floor area, it was far enough from the front of the shop and the rest of the clothing racks for the boys to hold private conversations. Casey always knew Preston's schedule and visited him when they overlapped. That amounted to two nights a week. In between times, Casey never went into the shop. He tried to avoid Sara and the other salesgirl, who wasn't on tonight, since they tended to ogle him a little more than he cared for.

"I see him back there. Talk to ya later."

She gave him the usual coy smile. "Sure, go see your boyfriend," she said sarcastically. She meant it as a joke. She'd said it like that several times in the last month. It was her disappointed way of saying, 'Damn you, go see him. Don't even bother with *me*.' She couldn't figure out why someone as nice as Casey was friends with someone with such attitude as Preston.

Casey walked to the back. He knew what Sara had meant by that, but it wasn't something he hoped she'd say to anyone else.

Casey leaned on the railing at the platform. "Hey, P." That was his nickname for Preston. Secretly, it meant 'penis', although he would never tell him that.

Preston sighed. "Hi, Casey."

It wasn't that Preston didn't like Casey. Casey was one very hot boy. It was just that Casey wanted way more than he could ever hope to offer in return. Leading him along had been fun at first and Casey was an easy way to get his rocks off. He certainly didn't figure Casey would stick around this long. But he couldn't find it in himself to tell him to go away. Besides, he would be stupid to do that. Someone else might get him. Who, he didn't know, but it might happen.

Due to Casey's childhood experiences, and despite the relative safety he felt living in the U.S., he harbored a mixture of complete trust in people and an unconscious fear of his equilibrium being disturbed by them. Teller was a mostly stable assortment of kids, the club was the same day after day, his father and mother were home about the same time every day, and the climate here in the high desert was virtually the same all the time. That was the good part and the baseline of Casey's life, about which he felt blessed. Preston, on the other hand, was a seriously complex person. He was the roll of the dice that caused Casey to wake up in the middle of the night; to chew his fingernails, which he just started doing; and to wonder what Preston really meant whenever he said virtually anything. Casey was confused a great deal whenever he interacted with him. Preston was the most puzzling person he knew.

Weeks previous they had talked about Preston enrolling at Teller so they could be closer together. Now he could no longer keep silent about his clear absence. "Why didn't you enroll like you said you would?" He had been avoiding the question for days.

Preston stopped what he was doing, looked up front to make sure Sara was still there, and leaned over the railing. "My dad said it would cost too much. Besides, I don't want to leave all my friends." All lies. He never intended to change schools.

That hurt. Preston had sworn he would go to Teller for his senior year. In fact, Casey had done a lot of footwork for him to help make the change. He hadn't figured his boyfriend might have been lying each step of the way.

Preston started with his smooth talk again. He knew when he had him in his spell: he simply watched his face. Whenever Casey was apprehensive, felt confused, or got worried, a wrinkle formed under his left eye. It seemed to happen a lot. When the wrinkle disappeared, he knew Casey was calmed down or quit trying to figure it out. It was so simple it was almost no fun anymore. He leaned down and whispered. "But don't worry. Just because I can't go to Teller doesn't mean I don't love you."

Casey didn't exactly like it when Preston talked using that tone, but it was typical of the communication they had. It was a little different when they were alone together, but only slightly. Always, Casey tried to get closer. Preston would verbally dance around, tell him he loved him, and give him that certain look that meant there would be incredibly hot sex later that evening. And it was always hot.

When Preston entered him the first time, Casey actually cried. It wasn't only because of the pain. He'd been dreaming of what it would be like in the days after he had gotten that first blowjob on the golf course. When it happened and Preston had been the one to take his cherry, he was ecstatic. He couldn't get enough. He didn't like taking on the active role. Luckily, Preston did. More recently, Preston had been teasing him, telling him he wasn't going to do it anymore. He had done that three times in the last month. That had led to Casey begging him. He told himself that the next time Preston pretended he wasn't going to do it he wouldn't beg again. He knew he would give in though. He always gave in. And he always hated himself afterward.

Despite being highly disappointed about what he'd just been told, after they got off work Casey walked with Preston to the playground below the hill from the dining room area of the club. All the windows were dark indicating that the wait staff was gone. The playground area was normally viewable during the day from the big windows at the left end of the dining area. Now, since everything was dark, it was their private make out place. They spent the next fifteen minutes kissing and feeling each other up on the merry-go-round before Preston led him to the backseat of his car in the parking lot. Ten minutes later Preston was swallowing every drop Casey issued. *God, he is so hot,* Preston thought as Casey went down on him.

# CHAPTER 6

Scott's guidance counselor's office was decorated with plants, her diplomas, knickknacks, and scribbled pencil drawings from her small children. She was searching in the top drawer of a four-drawer file cabinet and finally drew out a sheaf of stapled papers. Scott was sitting in front of her desk trying to place the odd smell. *Maybe it's lavender soap*, he thought. He wanted out of there as soon as he could since it was starting to nauseate him.

"This lists the names of all schools in the entire California higher education system." She studied the top sheet briefly, then flipped the page up. Taking a seat at her desk, she scanned the next page and marked some items in red pen. "These are some of the schools I think have good music programs. But you'll want to check into them more thoroughly. We don't have application forms for any of them so you'll have to send for them once you've decided. You still have time to decide, although doing all this last year would have been a lot more appropriate. It'll be difficult to get the classes you want. Don't worry about transcripts though. We'll have all that ready when they ask." She stuffed informational brochures about student loans, military service and other post-high school items of interest into a folder and gave it to him.

He unzipped his backpack and slid the folder in. "Thanks," he said. He made a quick exit and inhaled deeply after he left her office. *Whew, maybe it was flavored douche?* The thought was oddly amusing and disgusting at the same time.

Her off-handed admonishment worried him though. Sure, he should have done all this during his junior year. But last school year he thought he knew where he was going after he graduated. At least last year he had taken all the proper college entrance exams, had decent grades, and plenty of points needed to graduate. So far. He still had to keep his grades up all year to stay on track.

\*　　　　　　\*　　　　　　\*

Scott leaned back on his elbows on Ryan's bed and watched while he changed clothes. It was striptease, then a reverse striptease. He was actively resisting diving all over him. "So, Friday night he finally talked to me."

Ryan pulled the t-shirt over his head. "It's about time." He pulled his arms through. "What'd he say?"

"You know, all those stupid adult things parents always say to their kids: I love you, but I don't understand you. It's okay to see Ryan, but don't poke him on the driveway again since it took all day to spray the stain off with the hose. The usual stuff."

Ryan stopped dressing and looked at him. He had an odd look on his face. Scott couldn't help but grin, which made Ryan laugh. Again, Scott hadn't used any of his usual funny accents, so it took Ryan a moment to realize he was kidding. "What did he really say?"

"He apologized. He told me to make sure I knew what I was doing and stuff like that. He really thinks I should be a business major no matter what though. But he was okay about me being gay. It's just he's 'embarrassed.'" Scott made quote signs in the air.

"How can he be okay about it if he's 'embarrassed?'" Ryan mimicked the quotes.

"Maybe he thinks it'll rub off on him or something."

"I rub off on you sometimes."

"Make out with me," Scott whispered.

Ryan came forward and, with his shorts still unbuttoned, stood in front of Scott. They kissed quietly for a few minutes while Scott tried to keep his erection from breaking through his shorts. Neither had time to do anything beyond that, since they needed to get going. Besides, Howard was home.

Scott pulled the Jeep into the parking lot of the *Stage One* Bar. It was only six o'clock and not a single vehicle was there except for his and another one. He figured it might be either the bar manager or some one else who could help him.

Ryan watched him put it in park. "How many stops you gonna make?"

"Just two tonight."

They hopped out and went to the back door. Scott had to knock several times, each time pounding with more force, before anyone answered. Finally, a short mostly bald man, with a round face and a ragged mustache opened it. "Can I help you?"

"Hi. I'm Scott Faraday and this is my friend Ryan. I was wondering if I could talk to someone who's in charge of hiring bands. We're called Centauri and are a local rock band." He hadn't rehearsed much of what he would say and ad-libbed most of it.

The man seemed friendly enough. He had been looking back and forth at both of them with dusky eyes. "I ain't the business manager, but if you give me a card I'll give it to him when he gets in tomorrow."

*Damn.* "I don't have one, but I can write down my name and number. Can you see if he'll contact me?" This was his very first cold call and he had no idea what the rules were.

"Sure," the man said.

Scott went to the jeep. He scribbled his name and phone number on a band flyer and returned to hand it to the man. "I have an answering machine," he said with eagerness in his voice.

"Don't worry young fella, I'll have him call ya." With that he turned around and the door banged shut. The two boys stood there in the long shadows of the waning day. Ryan spoke the obvious. "That didn't amount to much."

"I was expecting to talk to someone who could help me. Fuck it. On to the next place."

They hopped back in the Jeep and went to the Chamber of Commerce office. Scott disappointedly discovered that it had been closed since four-thirty. He'd have to try them another day when it was open and he could get there after school. That was it for his list anyway. The rest of his prospects were listed on a piece of paper back in his bedroom.

"Sorry it didn't work out," Ryan offered.

"How the heck am I gonna help the band if I can't even get to the right people?"

"You only went to two places. Selling stuff is pure math. You'll only get so many to buy your product. In your case, it's the band."

"Well, it sucks." Scott was more concerned about getting more gigs booked as soon as possible. *Why doesn't Colleen see the urgency?* She was the one who could book a gig on charm alone. He knew she was able to do that because of her looks, her way with business owners (usually men), and the fact that she had bucketloads of charisma, which was the reason she was their front person in the first place. His list only had five places on it and he'd just been to two. Without anything even worth pursuing so far, he felt that he had just become a failure at the onset. He briefly thought about who he needed to contact at school again for the upcoming school dances.

"Why'd you pick me to go with you? You should have gone with the rest of the band to do this."

It was his secret agenda to help them out. "I don't want them to know I'm doing it."

"Well, it's stupid. You should have Colleen or Barry with you. Since they're over twenty-one they'd have more credibility going into bars. Besides, who's gonna believe that we're serious?"

"I'm wearing a button-down shirt. I even ironed it. I was nice to him. I have flyers. That's serious."

"Our age, dumbass."

Scott looked at him. "It's a secret." Then, "Tower Road Drive-In?"

"Yeah, food."

They parked at Tower Road Drive-In and went in to order. Scott took their number to an empty table and they waited for the food to be delivered. He had meant to tell Ryan at some point, but hadn't done so just yet. "I wanna go to UCLA with you."

Ryan's eyes lit up. "Really?"

"I don't know if they have a decent music school though, so I have to find out. I just want to be with you. I can't stand the thought of you going away and never seeing you again."

"It's not gonna be like that. I'll be coming back here during breaks and holidays."

"Still, I talked to a school counselor. She didn't have any apps for UCLA though. She just gave me a huge packet of stuff to sort through."

"D'you have it with you?"

"Yeah, in the Jeep."

"Go get it."

"They're about to bring our food."

"I wanna look through it."

He had an ulterior motive, which he hadn't told Scott about yet. Ryan had been thinking about it for a couple of weeks now. He had been mulling over what Scott's dad had been wanting and looking at what Scott's passion was. He had decided that if Scott combined business with music, it would make them both happy. He hadn't factored in that Scott's dad would capitulate so quickly or that Scott would want to just follow him to school. But what if Scott did both anyway, he had thought? There had to be someplace that offered a music major with a minor in business. He might be able to find it and help Scott get in good with his dad. Hell, Scott *had* a dad. It wasn't right that they didn't get along so well. It was worth the effort.

Scott pushed the plastic numbered marker toward him. He went to the Jeep and returned moments later with the folder. Their food was on the table. He handed the folder to Ryan. "I don't know what you're gonna find that I can't find in there myself."

"I have a UCLA catalog at home. Remember? Oh, wait. It's just for the Engineering school. I can send off for the music school one though. Not to worry. I'll do all the checking for you."

Scott slipped off his sandal, raised his foot up, and briefly placed it against Ryan's inner thigh. The unexpected touch made Ryan jump and he looked up at Scott. Scott was looking at him, smiling as he munched on a fry. Ryan was just awesome.

*       *       *

By the middle of September, the band was practicing three times a week which was a higher rate than normal. Not everyone had to be there for each practice. Due to Scott's schedule, and the fact that he was simply not so good at higher mathematics, he was already finding himself falling further and further behind in his calculus class. The first pop quiz he made a C. The second one he made a C minus. In a way, two pop quizzes in this short a time was good since it made him realize how bad he was at calculus. He knew he was going to have to find a different approach to studying than the one he was most comfortable with which was studying alone with the stereo blasting.

In fifth period calculus, Doug was wearing a faded Wolves t-shirt. It had shrunk enough to be a little too small for him. Because of that, it perfectly outlined his deltoids whenever he moved his arms. Scott loved that about Doug's body. He had an interesting build with his broad back and wide rounded shoulders, which resulted in a somewhat shallow chest. But even though he thought Doug had a nice body, he didn't particularly think his face was all that cute. He figured Jill, Doug's girlfriend, thought so though.

Scott had known Jill Stokvis since junior high. She had since become quite the perky brunette. She met Doug through him. Her interest in Doug started out with her going to the track meets. Then she started walking with him in the hall all the time. Scott was crushed when Doug started going out with her halfway through junior year. He was, at first, annoyed when he realized that Doug was nudging him aside in favor of being around her more often. But he knew Doug was one hundred percent straight. It became even more obvious on their rare double dates where they went parking.

When Doug started going out with Jill exclusively, it made it very difficult to keep their relationship the way it was before. Then Doug told him about his sexual exploits with her. Scott had hoped the purity of their being friends would return, without girls being all that involved in their lives. After he discovered he didn't like girls that way, he hoped there would be some time for just the two of them. But Jill kept that from happening. Her almost ubiquitous presence rapidly put distance between he and Doug.

It was at that point that Scott had decided he hated her. After all, Scott had come first, hadn't he? He stopped thinking that way the very moment he caught himself saying something nasty about her to him. Luckily, he had caught himself in time and never said it. From that moment on, he stopped thinking that way altogether. He felt somewhat left out though, and refused to tell Doug he was gay, despite the fact that he considered Doug his best friend.

"Jill asked me if you're gonna go this afternoon," Doug said. He was in today's relay.

"Of course I'm going. I may not be on the team anymore, but I still support the Wolves."

"Great. See you there."

Preston leaned over to get Scott's attention. He had overheard the exchange, as usual, and this was his opportunity to be with Scott in the bleachers for a change.

Scott had known Preston since they were freshman and had talked with him on and off over the years. A lot of people knew Preston due to his father's car dealership. Scott had always thought Preston was cute, too, but then there were a little over two dozen boys in the senior class that he thought were cute, all in their particular ways.

Actually, he had his own classification system. There were The Nine. They were the nine most handsome or cute boys, but not necessarily the most popular ones, although some of them were certainly in that group. Doug was one of The Nine, mostly because he was an outstanding athlete, was good looking and because they were friends.

The second group contained eleven guys. They all had their good points, but somehow didn't quite go into the first category because of some flaw he decided they had. Preston occupied that group. He was certainly one of the good looking ones, but he didn't quite pass muster to be lumped into The Nine. He was always sort of aloof. He didn't mingle with many of the other students like Scott did. Scott had once thought it might because of the fact that Preston was from a different economic class than most everyone else he knew. After all, he wore only expensive clothing, his glasses frames were always trendy (last year they changed mid-way through the school year), and Scott had overheard him talking one day about his father's wine collection to one of the teachers. Faraday's served wine, of course, but it was for drinking. Their collection was a stockroom, which constantly rotated. And, Preston just acted differently, even if he was way cute.

The third group, and the smallest by count, consisted of good looking or cute ones that had at least one trait that made them lose most of their points. They smoked, were stoners, were just plain losers, or had a combination of those traits. Still, they occupied a third group because of the fact that they were, well, hot.

Of those two dozen and some boys he knew or knew of, not a single one outshined Ryan in either looks or occupied that one special group: boyfriend. And even though Ryan admitted to the occasional toke, at least he didn't smoke cigarettes or use pot regularly, so he just couldn't put him in the third group. Hell, Ryan occupies his own unique spot in the universe, Scott had decided.

Doug turned to talk to someone else. Preston took that moment to speak up. "Hey, wanna sit together? I'm going, too."

Scott leaned his way. "Sure." He was surprised Preston had asked since he had never asked before. Maybe he was becoming a lot less aloof nowadays. The opportunity to talk with him at a meet was going to be great, he thought.

Later that afternoon, Scott met up with Jill at the pre-designated location at the track. They waited while Preston found his way to them as well. He had his backpack slung across his shoulder.

Jill didn't know Preston personally, but recognized him by sight. Scott introduced them and they started talking. Then Scott noticed how Preston seemed a little agitated as she talked to him. He actually stammered a couple of times, too. When had he ever heard Preston stammer? Never.

The only thing Scott disliked about Jill now was her obsessive need to have perfect hair. What a contrast: Jill with her perfect hair and Preston with his unruly long locks. Scott then noticed something he had never really thought about before. Had he ever seen Preston talking with *any* girls at school? Why was that? The only exception was the ones he drove to school every once in a while. As he wondered about it, Preston ran his eyes from Scott's face, to his chest, then to his crotch. He did it all in a sort of slow motion pan. *Whoa, what was that all about?* Scott's radar started to peg, but just as it did, Preston looked away and turned his attention back to Jill. That left him wondering if it was his imagination or not.

They found places in the bleachers near a group of other juniors and seniors. The Wolves were running against the Desert Hot Springs Demons today. Today's competition would consist of the 100 meter high hurdles, the 4 x 400 relay, and the one Doug would be running in, the 4 x 800 relay. The Demons weren't particularly good but Doug was going to meet his match if he wasn't in good form.

The coach usually put Doug at the last leg of the 4 x 8. He had amazing energy and usually crushed the competition. That was always assured if the baton was passed correctly. Today it would be. Aubrey was a master at passing it. It was a no-brainer that the Wolves would kick butt. Scott was sure of it.

Doug was loosening up down at the sideline. Preston unzipped his backpack and produced a 35mm camera. He deftly twisted off the 50mm lens and twisted on a zoom telephoto. Scott was impressed with the equipment and realized again why Preston was in Category Two. Everything about him was first class. Not that Scott thought that first class was bad or anything. It was just that Preston always seemed to be or look somewhat elitist or pretentious. That was part of his flaw.

Preston didn't start taking pictures right away but rather set the camera aside. He leaned over to Scott while the next runners took their places. "How about that Ms. Dunn, huh?"

Scott saw the look on Preston's face and knew what he was talking about. "Yeah, no kidding."

"We lucked out and got the easiest math teacher in the entire school," Preston replied sarcastically.

"Yeah, I knew she'd be tough."

"I didn't think she'd be this hard. I hate calculus anyway though."

Jill nudged Scott. "Look, Doug's ready now."

Preston took his camera, stood, then started down the bleachers.

"Where're you going," she asked. "Isn't that a telephoto lens?"

Preston pointed to the bleachers below. "The angle and the lighting's better over there." That wasn't entirely true. He planned to get some shots of not only Doug, but Scott as well. "Not to worry, I'll be right back."

Scott sidled up next to Jill. She clutched his bicep with both hands. She was obviously excited. *What a smile. No wonder he likes her. No, it's more than her smile, it's her boobs. He already told me that.* His eyes went from her mouth to her cleavage. It was jiggling considerably now that she was bouncing up and down.

On the front and back of Doug's tank top were the large green letters YV, with the name Wolves emblazoned in diagonal italics across them. His running shorts were satiny white with a green stripe running vertically along each side. Preston's eyes lingered on Doug's upper body. He snapped a couple of shots. *Even though Doug's cute as hell, he doesn't come close to being like Scott,* he thought. He snapped a couple more close-ups, including one of Doug's hard round butt, then turned to face Scott and Jill up on the bleachers.

Scott was leaning back on his elbows with his legs crossed in front of him. His feet were up on the bleacher in front of him. His shorts were bunched up at the crotch. The wind had caught his dark red hair, blowing it around wildly. It framed his rosy cheeks and that incredible smile. Preston raised the camera to his eye. It was a perfect shot.

Scott felt as if someone were watching him. He glanced to this left. *Someone is watching me.* Preston was a good forty feet away and had his camera aimed in their direction instead of at the track. Seeing that he was apparently going to be on film, he tilted his head ever so slightly, raised his hand up in a brief wave, and smiled even more broadly.

*Bonus! My god is smiling at me.* Preston took that instant to snap the picture, immortalizing him on film. He snapped a couple of extra shots of Scott now that he had stood up to see over the students who were in front of him. Finished with that, Preston came back up and stood with them.

Scott checked out the Demons runners. Mario Navarro was up against Doug in the last leg of the relay. Scott knew Doug outrun him. He figured it would be by at least a second. He knew Mario's running speed since he'd run against him several times in the past.

The baton pass was perfect. Jill yelled *Go! Go!* Scott yelled with her. Doug beat him as predicted. The Wolves won the heat. Preston snapped a couple more pictures. He couldn't wait to have the roll developed.

Later at the pizza parlor, with Doug, Evan, Aubrey and Spence—the relay team—in tow, and after they had all discussed the meet, Preston took a moment to talk with Scott. "You know, I wasn't kidding about not liking calculus. I think I'm gonna get some tutoring for the next chapter."

"Why? We haven't even started it yet."

"I looked ahead."

"Really?" *Who did things like that?* He never looked ahead in the textbooks of his hardest subjects. He didn't like to freak himself out about schoolwork.

"I couldn't help it. I wanted to see when it was going to get harder than it already is. It starts to get impossible in the next chapter."

*Actually tutoring's an excellent idea. A preemptive strike against declining grades would be mighty helpful,* Scott thought. "Maybe I should go with you."

Preston's eyes grew wide. "Really?"

"Yeah, I need some extra help, too."

*Hmm, I sure could find a way to help you,* Preston thought.

The next day, directly after class, both boys walked down the hall to the designated classroom to sign up for tutoring.

They signed the sheet at the teacher's desk, marking the subject they needed help on, and sat with the other waiting students. The teacher showed up a few minutes later, reviewed the sheet, and called out names.

"Classroom 303. Give her these slips," she said to Preston after the boys came up to the desk.

They took the slips and went down the other wing to room 303. Annette was a known calculus brain and only too eager to help them. As much of a geek as she was, Scott was relieved that she seemed to know exactly what she was talking about. It took another half hour, but both boys found themselves able to do at least the example questions in the next chapter.

On the way out of the session, Preston posed the question. "Hey, Scott. If you want, you could come over and study with me when you don't wanna go to this tutoring class. I have a pool and we could take a dip before we study."

Scott found that totally appealing, but knew that due to band practice that he wouldn't be able to come over any time soon. "How 'bout after we're done with the gigs on base?"

"Anytime. Just ask. When are they?"

"The first one's next Saturday. Then we have two more the following two weekends. Too bad they're on base. Nobody from school can go."

"That sucks." He said it that way not only because he wasn't going to be able to see the concerts, but also because Scott wouldn't be able to come over for weeks. That is, if he did at all.

Scott figured he would be seeing Annette again before that time. The homework was probably going to be way too difficult to do alone, and since his second to last period was free, it was the perfect opportunity to have Annette tell him everything he needed to know to keep up. No more goofing off in the library anymore.

# CHAPTER 7

Finally, the big day. The first gig of the season was tonight. It was almost eight and everyone was at Colleen's place loading up equipment. Scott was stoked. It had been months since the band had had a paid performance and he was glad today had finally arrived. He had even gotten permission to get Ryan on base. He was their official roadie and the band couldn't be happier since he was an extra set of hands.

Howard's car pulled up in Colleen's driveway. Ryan was behind the wheel. Scott approached the driver's side window. "You don't have a license," he stated.

"I do now. And a scooter license, too. Howie was happy about that since I'm no longer riding around illegally. The slate was wiped clean when I turned eighteen. I just didn't have time to get them until yesterday."

"And he let you use his car? That's telling a lot."

"Next weekend we're going to get me a new one. Well, actually a used one. But at least I'll have my own freakin' car for a change, huh?"

"Good. That means I don't have to haul your ass all over town anymore." He skipped backwards a few steps. His adrenaline was revved up and he was virtually dancing anyway.

Ryan parked, then helped them load up the last of the equipment cases into Barry's vintage VW van, assisted Scott in stuffing sound equipment into his Jeep, and did whatever else they needed for the endeavor.

Sparks had put the poster that Ryan had drawn for them in a frame the week before and had taken it to the venue on base. Weeks earlier Scott had mailed in a promotional tape to the audio dubbing company they used in San Bernardino. So they could avoid the shipping costs, Sparks had driven there the weekend before to pick up the fifty copies. He folded and stuffed the cassette inserts himself to further save money. If they sold only twenty tonight they would have made a profit on them. He had then gone to the printer to pick up the fifty copies of Centauri bumper stickers. The stack was in his car now. Announcements on base had been put up weeks before by the department handling the event.

All the pre-show hype paid off. Although at first only one hundred twenty people showed up, they soon had the place packed. After they reached maximum capacity, a shouting match had ensued outside when the MPs wouldn't let anyone else in. Inside, they got several requests and did three encore numbers before the auditorium lights were left on and the MPs got everyone to leave.

With Ryan's help, they were able to load up their equipment in record time despite people asking for band stickers, talking to the band members, and in some cases being just plain annoying. On the way back, Scott felt like he was on speed. They had sold almost all the stickers and twenty-one tapes, the soundboard performed perfectly, Colleen's voice was in prime form, and there was only a couple of mistakes, one by Mitch and the other by Darryl, which no one seemed to notice. He talked Ryan's ear off about every detail of the evening.

Finally, Scott calmed down enough for Ryan to get a few words in himself. Ryan told him what he had turned up in his school search. "Hey, I've been checking through the UCLA catalog and going over the rest of the papers your counselor gave you. I'm not so sure it's the right place for you to go."

"What? It's not a good school?"

"No, it's good. It's just not the best place for you go to with me."

"Are you trying to tell me something?"

"Nothing more than what I just said."

"Admit it, you're trying to kill my buzz."

"I'm just telling you what I checked out."

"Well don't tell me any more, okay?"

Ryan felt a little exasperated, but Scott was still zooming, so he quieted down. He still felt he needed to tell Scott what he had uncovered but figured he had plenty of time later.

He had been investigating other universities with his idea in mind. The more he had thought about it, the more he was convinced that Scott should combine music with business. His investigation had turned up exactly three schools that fit his criteria. Each had had to be relatively close by, had to be a California State University school, and had to have an equally good engineering and music college. He had requested applications by sending query letters to their admissions offices. But now, as he thought about it, he was beginning to wonder what would happen if Scott decided not to go to college at all. What if Centauri got all the gigs they could handle and Scott became a permanent member of the band? Then where would *he* be? He had been all excited by the prospect of Scott accompanying him and now this nasty thought intruded in on his neatly laid out, albeit sneaky, plan.

It was shortly after two by the time they had finished unloading the gear. Scott was as tired as he could be once he got home since all his adrenaline had finally been used up. But it didn't make any difference when it came to his dick. He wouldn't let Ryan leave. After they showered, Scott let Ryan make love to him for a lot longer than normal before he let him come. Each time he got close to climax, Scott made him pull out or stop thrusting. It was excruciating for him as well, but he wanted to tease him. Finally, he quit playing around and they came at the same time. He was sure their collective moaning would wake his parents. That didn't happen, but they laughed when Shakaiyo whined a couple of times.

Scott woke Ryan up just as it become light outside. Ryan didn't pull the same kind of stunt. He lay flat on his back, his feet resting on the side of Scott's pectorals, attempting to tickle Scott's armpits with his toes as Scott entered him. When he was done, Scott looked down at the single thin white steak that had started at Ryan's left pectoral and ended just above his navel. It had taken him a mere five minutes to come, Ryan only slightly longer. Scott hadn't pulled out yet, nor had he released his grip from Ryan's penis. The view from his angle was one he wanted to preserve for eternity. Ryan's face seemed to be one wide smile.

Scott was able to have that moment for only another twenty seconds though before Ryan gently, then forcibly made him let go and pull out. *God, I wish I could stay inside him forever,* Scott thought.

On Sunday, they were listening to tapes in Scott's bedroom. Ryan sat on the floor and had the bottom drawer of the large six-drawer tape case pulled out, inspecting the ones in the back. These didn't have Scott's handwriting on the labels. They were store bought instead. *Jeez,* he thought, *he must have four hundred* tapes. He also had several Sound Equipment Review magazines opened. He wasn't all that interested in the articles, just the full-page ads featuring the latest in digital recording equipment. He had gotten a little more savvy about the equipment the band was using, and the components that were on the shelves of the Wall of Sound, as Scott called it, here in the bedroom. This was the third magazine he'd looked through so far, and was going in chronological order on purpose. He noted that prices of digital mixing equipment from the major vendors were dropping considerably. "Hey, have you noticed that these DAT recorders are becoming affordable now?" He spun the magazine around.

Scott sat down next to him. "Yeah, if this one," he pointed to one of the pictures, "comes down another two hundred dollars we're going in on one. Our analog stuff is gonna be history soon. Studios use digital equipment exclusively now. We just can't afford it yet."

Ryan spun the magazine around again. "Hmm, I'd love to hear a DAT recording of Centauri."

He pushed the still-opened magazine aside and continued looking through tapes.

"Ozark Mountain Daredevils," Ryan said as he pulled the cassette out of the drawer. "Who the hell are they?"

"More 70s stuff. They're never played on the radio anymore."

Ryan inspected a few more titles and, not recognizing any of them, looked at the dates printed on the labels. "These are *all* old bands. What's up with that?"

"Everything in that drawer was my brother's. OMD and Jethro Tull were two of his favorites. Dude, they're the reason I play the flute."

Ryan pulled the OMD tape out of its case and looked at the song list. "What kind of music is this anyway?"

"Kinda mellow, easy listening, hillbilly even. It's hard to define, really, but it's got lots of flute intros and stuff. It still sounds pretty cool. It's not typical of that time at all."

"So it's not disco, huh?"

Scott made a face as he started for the bathroom. "Ugh, I'd rather be staked out in the desert at noon than even *own* a disco tape."

Ryan was waiting for that moment. As soon as he heard Scott unzip, he went to the desk. A stack of cards that one might normally find in a wallet was next to the stapler. Ryan was sure that he recognized the edge of Scott's social security card. He quickly lifted off the top card. Sure enough, it was right underneath. He quickly marked the numbers down on a piece of memo paper and thrust it into his pocket. He needed the number for what he had planned. He figured that if he filled out the college application forms for Scott, once he got them all, he could surprise him. He was sure Scott would think that would be the coolest thing. He put the card back and neatly stacked the pile before dropping back down to the floor. It had taken him all of six or seven seconds.

Scott came out of the bathroom just as the phone rang. Ryan only glanced up. *Good, he doesn't suspect a thing.* Scott plopped down on the bed as he reached over to pick it up. Ryan popped a tape back into its case and continued his perusal.

"Scott, warm up," Colleen said.

"Warm up what?"

"Your lips."

Scott glanced over at Ryan and grinned. "What makes you think I haven't already warmed them up?"

From the way he answered, she knew what he meant. "Is your boyfriend over there?"

"Yeah," he replied slowly.

Ryan had just pulled out Marshall Tucker Band's debut recording. His eyes grew wide. *Jeez, this one's almost as old as I am.*

"I'm not talking about using them on *him*. You're gonna use them at the next gig."

Scott's heart skipped a beat. "I'm the soundman in case you forgot."

"*Someone* has to do the live flute for *Fly By Night*." She was referring to the Jethro Tull tune by the London Symphony Orchestra that he liked.

"On base? Who decided that? We'll get booed off stage!"

"We're going to do it the way we practiced it way back. You know, your flute routed through the effects box, Barry's lead, and the rest of the bands jammin' sound. The tune will rock their world."

"Are you sure about this? I mean…"

"Look, you know Darryl has the symphonic tracks, except for your part, already programmed into the keyboards. If you don't want to do it, we could hire, oh, say the first chair flute from your school."

"Uh, no way!" he exclaimed as he stood up. Ryan looked over at him and wondered who was on the phone now.

"Then be at practice this week. What's your schedule like?"

He wasn't working much this week since his parents knew he was in a crunch due to the gigs and schoolwork. "I can be there Friday night." He was off Wednesday but needed to practice before showing up at the Garage.

"Then be there," she said cheerfully. The phone clicked.

He punched the off button. "Bitchin'!" he exclaimed. He slung the phone up with a good spin. It went almost to the ceiling. As it came back down, he deftly caught it behind his back then let it drop onto the bedspread behind him. He kneeled next to Ryan on the floor and put up both hands in the high five position.

Ryan smacked his palms. "What am I fivin' you about?"

Before Scott answered, he sorted through one of his CD stacks for *A Classic Case*, his prized 1985 London Symphony Orchestra instrumental release. They had practiced *Fly By Night* several times before, but it had all been for fun. Now they were going to do it live on stage? With him as lead? It was a pleasant surprise to be sure. "I'll tell you all about it," he said excitedly.

When Ryan came over on Wednesday night he heard that Jethro Tull tune about a dozen times. Scott was amazing. He didn't even have the sheet music. He practiced it all by ear. He would listen to a few chords, pause the CD, write down a few things on a scratch pad, play what he heard, then un-pause the CD again. This went on until he equalized out the flute and played the whole thing through. It would be a matter of practicing the tune with the rest of the band again to get it just right. Ryan had come over for a little smooching, but Scott was so concentrated on the tune that they barely even kissed.

On Friday, it took hours but Scott was able to mesh his practiced sound with the band's previous recording. It was pure rock, more so than the arrangement on the CD. Ryan showed up for the last hour of practice. He could tell Scott had it down perfectly. It was so endearing, he could have screamed. His very own boyfriend was uniquely talented as well as cute.

The poster had somehow managed to survive the entire week intact. No one had damaged it, or otherwise even touched the frame it was in. Scott was relieved since they had forgotten to pick it up last weekend.

The gig started after a fifteen-minute delay. The same issue had arisen as last week. Lots of people wanted to see them since word had spread even more. Luckily, the MPs loosened up a little and let far more people into the auditorium than was normally allowable. Colleen had negotiated a bonus based on ticket sales, which no one else had found out about. The extra cash came as quite a surprise when she told them the next day. Before the end of the evening, though, they had done so many requests that they never even got to the tune Scott and the rest of the band had practiced so diligently. Nonetheless, so many people were hooting and hollering at them by the time they were done with the second encore, that it didn't seem to matter much.

Afterward, Sparks couldn't sell tapes fast enough. He also had over one hundred more band stickers which sold rapidly as well. Two guys who were really into recording equipment bent Scott's ear until he finally had to shake them off. Then they bought the remainder of the tapes and told Sparks they were going to sell them at their own marked up price. That was okay, the sale to those guys already gave them their profit.

Several groups of people decided they had to talk to every one of the band members. One had told Colleen she sounded like the lead singer of another popular band. Another wanted to know if she dated Marines. No, she had said. She told him she was too 'old' for him. The auditorium was finally quiet once the last Marine left. Scott loaded the soundboard into his Jeep. Colleen handed him an errant cable. "Sorry we didn't get to the Tull tune," she told him.

Scott was still feeling completely upbeat despite that. "We still have the last gig. Maybe we should do it first thing, just to get it out of the way. Besides, I gotta do sound the rest of the evening anyway."

"That's a good idea. I'll tell Barry on the way back."

Ryan was a little disappointed as well. He had wanted to hear it done live and had waited up to the end to see it get played. But, hey, who could ignore their fans? In a way, Ryan had found it extremely exciting. Where else could he scan an audience of testosterone-filled males and not get noticed he was checking them out?

They barely slept that night. Ryan kept him up in more ways than one. It wasn't that Scott's naked body next to his wasn't enough for him. It was more that his mind had been filled with hours of watching all those sweaty guys in the audience. Somehow, the images weren't emptying from his mind as rapidly as his penis was. Finally, though, he relented and they fell asleep. Neither of them woke up until almost ten-thirty the next morning.

"Wanna go with me today?" Ryan asked as he dried off from the shower.

Scott pulled on a tank top. "Where to?"

Ryan stepped into his shorts. "Howie and I are going to the dealership to buy the car."

"Oh yeah. Why didn't you say anything about that last night?"

Scott still had only his tank top on. Ryan glanced down at Scott's crotch. "I guess my mind was on other things. Besides, I told you last weekend."

They went into the house where Scott poured each of them some cereal, then he drove him back to Ryan's house. Scott realized he hadn't seen Howard for several weeks. Krysta came over a few minutes later. She had a full day of activities planned with Howard once they got Ryan's car in Palm Springs. Scott noticed that Howard hadn't said a word about Ryan and he being together. Maybe it was because Krysta was there with them now. Hadn't he said anything to her?

They all rode in Howard's sports car. It was cramped in the backseat, but he didn't mind. If he had Ryan pegged correctly in a few hours they would be freewheeling all over Palm Springs and he would be in a front seat instead. About halfway there, Ryan stuck his head in between the front headrests. "When I get the car, Scott's riding back with me. Both of you are on your own."

Krysta looked back at him quizzically. "Really Ryan, what makes you think we need to have you around any longer than necessary?"

"Well, you know. You have to be supervised so much." He shook his head. "Sometimes I think I need to get a chaperone for you both."

Howard was delighted that Ryan was being so lighthearted and enjoyed the comical banter which continued for a few more minutes. It had been a while since he'd seen him so animated.

Scott was equally surprised. But clearly, Ryan was in a rare upbeat mood. *Must be 'cause of the car*, he thought.

Long streamers of pennants were strung tent-style from high atop a central light pole to eight other poles at the edges of the car lot. The wind was flapping them all noisily. Once Howard parked and they all got out. Scott looked up at the huge sign by the road. He didn't know they would be going to Tyllas Nissan. In fact, he hadn't asked which dealership they would be going to. "I'm in school with the son of the guy who owns this place," he said to no one in particular.

Ryan was busy thinking about sitting in the used dark green '89 Mustang again and didn't acknowledge the statement. *Whew, it's still there*, he thought, as his gaze went down the third row of cars. Howard came out of the show-room with the salesman from last weekend and they all went back inside to start the paperwork. Howard and Krysta were going to spend the rest of the day doing some sightseeing and shopping. So, a little less than an hour later, the boys were tooling down Rodeo Drive.

Scott glanced at the odometer. The Mustang was barely two years old but seemed to run well for having a little over 30,000 miles on it. He fiddled with the air-conditioning, turned it to maximum, and felt the cool air streaming out before he turned it back down to low. He scanned through the instruction booklet that was in the glove box. He programmed in radio stations for Ryan, then settled on KROQ. Ryan seemed to be in bliss as he drove all over town. Finally, though, they stopped to eat before heading back home.

"Hey, do me a favor," Scott said after they had started up the huge hill at Morongo Valley on Highway 62.

"What's that?"

"Once all the gigs are done and we get paid, I'm gonna have that roll bar speaker set that I was telling you about installed in my Jeep. Can you take me to school that day?" Earlier he had told Ryan how he wanted to get better speak-ers in the Jeep. The roll bar unit was the perfect match for what he wanted.

"Why can't you install it? You put in those other speakers."

"It's too time consuming to do it now that schools in and all, so I'm gonna have the stereo place do it for me. They said I could drop the Jeep off and come by that evening to pick it up."

"Sure."

It would be hours before Howard returned home. So, they spent some qual-ity time in Ryan's bedroom. They were both on their knees on the carpet. Their clothes had been tossed about everywhere, as usual. Ryan entered Scott from behind and worked on him from the front at the same time. Scott's moans reverberated against his chest as he got close. He had to brace Scott's torso with his left arm so Scott didn't double over and accidentally make him pull out. It was the most awesome feeling when they both came at almost the same time.

He didn't care that Scott left a wet trail next to his bed. He'd done that himself a number of times, only he was alone each time.

*    *    *

On the night of the final concert on base, and before the band got started, the Marines were as rowdy as ever. Scott even recognized some of the faces from the previous concerts. Since this was their third date in as many weeks, they really had to mix things up to make it work. Scott wore his shiny shirt with the red and gold Mylar threads in it. That way when the spotlights hit him, he would reflect the light back at the audience in a true blazing light show. True to their set list, Scott played for the opening number. It was exhilarating getting up on stage, act crazy as hell, do all sorts of funny faces, play his heart out, and get paid for it at the same time. They got so many 'oo-rahs' from the tune that Scott was disappointed they hadn't come up with a second one to follow it with. But his appearance on stage was just for fun. The evening wasn't about him, and he knew it. Colleen, with her wild hair, her skintight leather pants, and the armbands was the focus. His job was sound.

Once back at the soundboard Ryan joined him, slapped him on the back a couple of times, then briefly hugged him. He couldn't believe what a showman Scott was. It was a new dimension to Scott about which he had only the slightest of clues. It took another fifteen minutes before Scott came down from the intense high of being on stage.

After the gig ended, they packed up all their gear, and finally made it back to Scott's bedroom. Ryan slowly pulled off Scott's clothes while Scott stood there, hard as a rock. Ryan gently held him down on the bed while kissing him all over, never once letting Scott touch him. Scott was squirming like a worm. Finally, he rolled a condom down Scott's rigid dick and lubed it up for him, pumping him slowly in a tease that brought him right to the edge twice.

Finally, he stopped teasing; slowly sat down on it and only minutes later was wiping up Scott's chest, neck, and chin. Again, they came at just about the same time. Scott didn't want to pull off the condom after Ryan unstraddled him. Ryan loved it when he did that. It was such a turn-on to see how long he would be able to stay at attention. It was always quite a while. Finally, though, Scott removed it and cleaned himself off. They snuggled close together on top of the sheets. Ryan reached around and felt Scott's penis. He was still mostly hard. *How does he do it,* he wondered, just before he fell asleep.

First thing Monday morning, Scott went to the administrative office and looked at the school calendar of events that was posted on a corkboard. He placed his finger on the paper and ran it down the page as he read. It included the year's football schedule, along with the Homecoming date, later than normal this year, since it was going to be the last week of October. There was a Halloween Haunted House event at the end of the month, sponsored by the sophomore class. The Thanksgiving Dance was in November and the days off for Thanksgiving were highlighted as well. Winterfest, the annual school party which was always held the week before Christmas was there, too, along with the Christmas holiday schedule. The rest of the school year's events hadn't been scheduled yet. In fact, nothing for 1991 was listed anywhere. He needed to ask the coordinator about scheduling Centauri to play at the Thanksgiving Dance and at Winterfest. He really should have done it three weeks ago, but had been too busy to think about it.

Held annually at school since the early eighties, Winterfest was a symbolic gesture to thumb their noses at the dark days of winter. About a dozen classrooms were open for crafts and displays, events were scheduled such as comedy and variety shows put on by some of the students, and on Friday night, a band played in the auditorium. The best part about it was that the seniors could choose the band—not the teachers, or the staff. The school district was even generous and paid for whoever performed. Scott didn't want to let any event escape his notice. He was sure paid gigs would keep Barry interested.

As he traced his finger down the rest of the page, he found the name of the scheduling coordinator. It was Mr. Turner from freshman Physical Science. That was going to be his next stop. He knew where Mr. Turner's class was and, just to check, he went down the freshman wing to his classroom. He was at his desk reading the newspaper.

"Hi, Mr. Turner?"

Mr. Turner knew right away it wasn't a freshman. He looked up, smiled, then folded the section he was reading. He knew Scott from three years previous and had seen him here and there in the halls more recently. "Hi, Scott."

"I noticed you're the school scheduling coordinator this year."

"It's my turn again. Every five years. What are you trying to schedule?"

"My band Centauri. I saw that the Thanksgiving Dance band hadn't been picked yet."

Mr. Turner furrowed his brow. "Thanksgiving Dance, huh? I think you're a day late."

"A day late? How's that possible?" *Yesterday was Sunday. And the paper posted in the admin office indicated that no band had been scheduled,* Scott thought.

Mr. Turner pulled out a 1990-1991 scheduling calendar from his briefcase and opened it on his desk. Scott stepped up as he flipped pages.

"Here it is," he said as he pointed. "Late last Friday, Joe Engle, one of your fellow seniors, recommended The Jesse Copper Band."

Scott was greatly alarmed. *Joe Engle?* "You said yes?"

"I couldn't just tell him no. It's a popular country quintet, with two pretty vocalists, I might add. If you insist on a different one we'll have to put it to a vote. You know that."

Scott knew all about The Jesse Copper Band. He and Mitch even talked with Jesse at the Fairgrounds last May. Plus, he knew all the bands in the area. "Then, we'll have to. Please put Centauri down, too." Scott was fuming. This event was worth nine hundred dollars!

The bell rang in the hallway. Freshmen had been milling around in the corridor just after he had arrived and a couple of them came in the room now. Mr. Turner closed the calendar book.

"Wait," Scott said. "What about Winterfest? Who's playing then?"

"No one's asked me yet. I guess you're going to recommend Centauri?"

"Of course."

Mr. Turner opened it again and turned to December. He wrote down Centauri.

"You know what the payment is?"

It didn't matter. He needed a gig date badly. "No."

"Six hundred. Payable the first school day after the event. That would be next year. Will that be okay?"

"Absolutely! So, we're set?"

"Last year's band was awful. I know Centauri is a lot more professional than some of the others we've had play for that event. So, this one's a go. If anyone suggests another one, I'm going to tell them no. You were at the last Winterfest, weren't you?"

Scott hadn't liked that band either. "No, I wasn't."

Mr. Turner closed his schedule book and chuckled. "I guess you'll be there this time." He pointed to his students taking their seats while looking at Scott. "Class."

Scott looked out at the freshmen. He was glad this was his last year of high school.

Now there was Joe to deal with. Joe was already a thorn in his side. Now this. It was almost as if Joe had been reading his mind. He'd have to track him down and confront him. Maybe Joe would withdraw his suggestion if he asked him just right. It wasn't going to be fun having to even talk with him. He didn't even like being near the guy, but he had to do it. He rarely saw Joe in the halls, though, and looking for him would be weird. Perhaps he'd spot him in the cafeteria. He usually ate lunch with his cowboy friends at the table near the 'Employees Only' door.

✻ ✻ ✻

On Tuesday, Scott saw Preston and caught up to him before third period started. "I'm taking you up on that invite."

Preston's heart skipped a beat. "Really?" He said it with way too much enthusiasm, he realized. But how could he help himself? "I'm off tonight. How about you?"

"Good. I am, too. You don't mind?"

"Are you kidding? With your help, I'm sure we can drive right through the problems. How's six tonight?"

"Six it is. Since we only have to answer the odd-numbered ones, all we have to do is look in the back of the book and figure out how to get there, huh?"

They only had to do four questions for the homework. That was enough. Scott figured that with both of them working together they might be able to get them all done in less than an hour. He was really anticipating that pool though, which was one of the main reasons he wanted to come over so soon, and hoped Preston wouldn't mind them swimming before they worked on the problems.

Scott pulled up to the driveway at Preston's house a few minutes before six, braked, then thought better of it. He didn't know who's car was in front of him. He let the Jeep roll backward then pulled to a stop at the curb. This was the first time he'd been here. *Nice house*, he thought as he pulled the key out.

He grabbed his backpack and went to the front door. The front yard had an annual flower garden plot at the foundation of the two-story house. The rest of the landscaping was native vegetation. He had no idea how much it cost, but was sure it was several thousand dollars worth. He rang the bell and Rosa answered. She smiled nicely and asked him to wait in the entryway. She gathered her purse from a nearby table as Preston came around the corner.

"I'm going now," she told him. The nice smile she had when she greeted Scott disappeared when she stated that. Scott noticed that and the fact that Preston barely acknowledged her. She then went through the kitchen to a side entrance.

"Sorry about that. She's the housekeeper," Preston stated.

Scott heard her car start. "So?"

He whispered but it was purely for effect. "I told her to leave early."

Scott thought he might be completely out of his element here. Preston could tell an employee when they could and couldn't work? He didn't have that kind of power even at the restaurant.

Preston was barefoot. He had actually not been able to decide what to wear. He wanted his first impression at home to be special, so he had chosen a silk button-down shirt and some nice shorts with a belt. He wondered if Scott would notice that he had chosen his favorite shirt. Not quite completely obsessed with Scott, he still nonetheless had thought about him often, even when he wasn't fantasizing about him in his bedroom. "We're studying back here."

He led Scott through a spacious den. Tall picture windows were on both sides of the sliding glass patio door. Scott could see an awning that covered the full length of the tiled back patio. There were several pieces of carefully arranged, expensive-looking furniture on the patio that had a similar design to the furniture in the den. Outside to the left was a retaining wall. In front of it was a wet bar. Its entire counter surface was covered with bright-colored Mexican tiles. To the right was what appeared to be a closet. The door was open and as they stepped out on the back porch, he saw that it wasn't exactly a closet, but rather a large utility room. It held a washer and dryer, a built in bench, the pool filtration system, several open shelving units which held towels, pool toys, and other miscellaneous items. The pool, with its large potted plants clustered on the far side of it, looked quite inviting.

Preston stepped around behind the wet bar and opened a squat refrigerator. He pointed in. "Cola?"

Scott was busy scanning the backyard. He could get used to this rather quickly and realized that Preston was quite lucky to have all this.

Scott didn't answer. Preston thought that was a negative. "Juice instead?"

That got Scott's attention. "No. I mean, yeah. A cola."

Scott dropped his backpack on one of the cushioned chairs under the shade of the awning. While Preston put ice in two glasses and poured the colas, Scott slipped off his sandals, went to the water, and skimmed his toes in it. It was just right. And the deep end—all of ten feet—would be perfect if it were cooler than the water he just tested.

Preston set the colas down on the glass tabletop in the shade, retrieved his books from the chair next to him, and sat down. Scott returned to the shaded patio and took a sip.

Preston was feeling nervous as hell. Here he was alone with Scott and he was choking. Maybe it was because he admired Scott so much. Scott was ideal in a number of ways, not just because he was so good looking. He seemed to have the perfect life. He seemed happy all the time, unlike himself. Whereas Scott's parents owned the best restaurant in town, he had to eat Rosa's cooking most of the time. He knew about Scott's detached bedroom from conversations he'd overheard with Doug. His bedroom was across from his father's. *It would be like having his own condo,* he thought, as he visualized what it must be like. He knew about Scott's dog, had wondered what it would be like to have one, too, but wasn't about to be responsible for one. And, of course, he knew all about Centauri. That really cool band seemed to be one of the highlights of Scott's ideal life.

"So, you wanna get in the pool before we start?"

"Always swim before studying," Preston replied as if it were an adage.

Scott grinned, then unzipped one of the compartments of his bag. Out came bright red trunks with a white strip that ran horizontally across the front and back about three inches down from the waistline. Right there, Preston wanted to own them. He wanted to slip them on and rub himself through the fabric. Just as quickly as the fantasy popped into his head, he quelled it. He was sure he'd embarrass himself in another second.

"You can change in there," Preston said. He pointed to the built-in padded bench in the utility room. "I'll be right back. I, uh, left my trunks in my room." He would have offered Scott to change in his bedroom, but didn't want to be obvious. And he was afraid he'd get hard if he did. He dashed to his bedroom and, standing next to his bed, nearly fell over trying to get his shorts off. He slowed down, pulled his swim trunks up, and snapped the front together. He felt like he was divided in two. Scott was actually in his backyard, so close he could reach out and touch him, yet he didn't dare. *Fuck, I'm totally nervous as hell.*

Scott absentmindedly surveyed the spacious utility room as he changed. Although Preston seemed completely harmless, Scott couldn't quite place the odd looks he kept giving him, the certain way he talked, the nervous way he did everything. It was as if invisible bolts of electricity were shooting between them. He wasn't sure if it was just himself wondering about it too much, but was sure something was going on. He couldn't shake the feeling. He was sure his radar was picking up something again. He looked over his memories of the recent track meet. There were the glances of each other's crotch, the too-long stares, the hesitations when they spoke to each other. *This is just too weird,* he thought, as he tied the string on the front of his shorts. *I gotta know for sure, but I bet…I just bet!*

Preston leisurely sauntered back to the patio. *Calm. Calm,* he said to himself. Scott had his calculus book open. He was wearing nothing but those bright red swim trunks. Preston could have died just then as he scanned Scott's tanned upper body, lingered on the bumps of his little nipples, then glanced ever so briefly at Scott's crotch. *So what if Scott's half-naked in your backyard. Yeah, right. He's half-naked and you tell yourself 'so what'.*

"Hey, this way," Preston said. He set his glasses down on the patio table, then went over to the pool and immediately dove in.

Scott followed him in. They both came up in the deep end. They whipped their hair around simultaneously and Scott wiped his eyes. They did a couple of laps, then rested at the shallow end as they caught their breath.

Preston leaned back with his arms outstretched against the lip of the pool. He grasped it as he kicked upward, keeping his lower body afloat. "So, how was the last concert?"

Scott floated on his back, trying to keep his ears from going under. It wasn't working, so he stood up. "It was bitchin'! I even got to play a tune we've been practicing."

"I thought you just did sound."

Scott told him why. Then, "It's an old one by Jethro Tull. I tried to sound just like Ian Anderson, but I'm sure it didn't even come close."

*I bet you're perfect on anything resembling a flute.*

Scott had to tell him who Jethro Tull and Ian Anderson were, then continued. "We sold dozens of stickers and all our tapes, got 'ooh-rahed' until I couldn't stand it anymore, and Colleen shook her booty all over the stage. We made some good cash. I'm trying to drum up some more business for the band though. We're turning up dry for a while."

"If we weren't in the Basin, I bet you guys could probably take your pick of places. You know, like down in Riverside or Banning, or further west."

"Yeah, but the closer you get to L.A. the more bands there are. The competition's fierce."

"Maybe you need to do more marketing."

"Yeah, that's what I'm doing. But I really suck at it." Scott deliberately used that word. He wanted to see Preston's reaction. He was on high alert now after having his radar go off again. He was glad that he had had practice with Ryan, feeling him out and trying to determine if he were gay. He had been completely right about that one. But Preston was his classmate and he had never had this suspicion before now. And what if he were wrong? If he was, and he gave himself away, and Preston wasn't gay, his life could easily be in the danger zone once the news made it back to school. It was definitely best to wait to see if Preston gave him some obvious clues. *Hmm, what if he's just not out yet?*

Preston wanted to say he sucked really well, but refrained from even attempting to vocalize that. Scott talked some more, but Preston hardly heard him now. He was mesmerized by Scott's upper body reflecting sunlight off virtually every bead of water on him. The rest of him was too distorted beneath the water to see anything worth looking at. Besides, his nearsightedness was hindering that view anyway.

They did a few more laps and soon were shaking the water off themselves at the side of the pool. Preston produced two thick beach towels from the utility room and they dried off.

They downed their sodas and dug into their books. Twenty minutes later, Preston announced that they needed to raid the refrigerator. They padded into the kitchen and Preston took out several containers of lunchmeat. They fixed two huge sandwiches each, poured a large bowl of corn chips, and brought everything back to the patio table. Preston poured them more sodas. It was dusk before they were done with the problems. It took a lot longer than Scott had anticipated. That was bad. It would mean he'd have to study extra hard until he was a little more confident about the class. Nonetheless, they managed to figure out each one of the problems well enough to understand how they got to the correct answers.

Despite wanting to peel off Scott's swim trunks the entire time, Preston contained himself and kept his attention focused, but barely. Despite being distracted, it was a good thing Scott was there. He knew that without Scott's help he would have no idea where to begin. That's when it dawned on him that unless he kept seeing Annette—if Scott weren't available—that he'd really be in dire straits.

Satisfied that they had all the problems worked out correctly, Scott announced he was leaving. He hefted his backpack, Preston walked him to the front door, and Scott took off.

Not more than five minutes later Warren returned from work. But the timing was fine. Preston had already unloaded the pressure that had built up and was cleaning the sticky mess off the faucet, the far edge of the sink, and the bottom of the medicine cabinet mirror when he heard his father come in downstairs through the garage entrance.

As promised, Ryan came by at six forty-five that Thursday morning. He wanted to get Scott to school as early as he could so he could get to work on time.

Scott actually took Ryan's hands out of his pants pockets this time. Ryan loved doing that. He would often come up behind Scott, slip his hands into Scott's front pockets, or simply down the front of his pants and start kissing his neck. While fumbling around, or unzipping him, it would invariably get Scott hard and there would have to be some relief before they could leave the bedroom. This time, though, they only had a few minutes. Scott leaned against the door and thought about innocuous things while he grew soft again. Finally, he adjusted himself. "I wish you wouldn't do that unless you were planning on finishing me off."

Ryan shrugged his shoulders. "I would have but you stopped me."

Ryan followed him to the stereo installation shop. Scott quickly confirmed the speaker model he wanted and gave the clerk his keys. He hopped into Ryan's car.

Just as they pulled up in the school parking lot Scott unzipped one of his backpack compartments and pulled out a Centauri sticker. He held it up. "Can I?"

"Ooh, yeah!" Ryan pointed to the back of the car with his thumb. "Put it on the bumper," he said as he came to a stop. Scott started to get out of the car.

"Wait!"

"What?"

"You have a pen?"

Scott pointed to his backpack. "In here. You need one?"

"No. You do. Sign it."

"You want the band to sign it, not me."

"Duh. You're *in* the band."

Scott grinned as he dug out a pen, adding big flourishes to his signature as he wrote.

The students that didn't live on the bus routes drove or walked to school. Some of the kids carpooled if they lived near each other. Preston sometimes drove Jamie and her little sister Marion from across the street when they missed the bus. Today was one of those days. After he parked, they went in the side entrance. He sat with his window rolled down while sorting through some papers from his chemistry folder.

Joe sat in his truck with his girlfriend Brenda Hedding. He spit into a little Styrofoam cup he had in one hand. His still-opened can of Skoal was sitting on the dashboard. He had Garth Brooks' new August release playing in his tape deck, and at a reasonable volume, since she was there with him. He was scanning the label. He liked the 'No Fences' title. It reminded him of his backyard. In addition, he really liked this particular band and wondered how popular they might become.

Brenda only liked guys that had a flair for chaos. The boys she had been dating up until the time she met Joe were way too nice. Due to the fact that they didn't fit the bill of enough drama for her taste, she had dropped each of them in turn. That made for two boys last year when she was a sophomore.

In Brenda's mind, Joe was her perfect blend of exasperating personality, argumentative attitude, good looks, and boyish charm. He wasn't nearly as nice to her as the other boys she'd dated and that made him okay in her book.

She loved his truck and the way he drove it like a bat out of hell. She also did-n't mind that he had sizeable love handles. None of the other guys she had dated had had them. She had decided they were too skinny for her taste.

She noticed that Joe didn't let much get by him, which she thought was particularly applicable at home. She believed every word he said about his family. It was *they* who had all the problems. *He* was just fine.

When the dark green Mustang rolled to a stop two rows from Preston's car, its movement got his attention. He didn't recognize it. He couldn't see who the occupants were either because of the other cars between it and him, so he continued looking. One of them eventually had to get out.

Joe watched the dark green Mustang pull to a stop four rows in front of and just to the left of his truck. Since he had the back end of his truck to the wall next to the dumpsters, he could look out over the entire parking lot. Brenda was talking about something stupid again, so he was just smiling and nodding at every other sentence so he could feign paying attention. He was more interested in this evening when he would be able to pull her panties down to her knees again, like last Tuesday. He was more interested in softly caressing her creamy inner thighs again, like last Tuesday. He was much more interested in pulling his dick out and letting her suck it again, like last Tuesday. He absent-mindedly watched the car while being lost in his little fantasy.

Scott got out and rested his backpack on the trunk of the Mustang. Preston was suddenly very interested when he saw who it was. Scott wiped a spot on the bumper, peeled the backing off the sticker, and deftly applied it. Preston could tell it was a Centauri sticker even from this distance. He'd recognize their logo anywhere.

Joe saw Scott get out of the car, go around back, and kneel down. He watched with mild interest now as he tried to figure out what he was doing. Seemed he was sticking something to the bumper. When Scott stepped back, Joe couldn't make out the lettering, but recognized the design right away. It was another one of those God-damned Centauri stickers. He hated that band. It represented the very worst that Yucca Valley offered. Rock music was like stale beer. It stank. What was worse was that Scott was in the band. He rolled his eyes as he watched him rub the side of his fist over the sticker. The next thing he saw nearly made him cause a small disaster on his lap.

A broad smile had crossed Preston's face as he watched Scott kneel down to apply the sticker. He had a perfect view of Scott's waist since his short t-shirt rode up the small of his back and his shorts came down a little. If he had been close enough he might have even been able to read the brand of his underwear. Then he saw the Tyllas Nissan sticker on the trunk and the temporary license affixed to the inside rear window. Fresh from his dad's very own used car lot, he noticed. *Good choice*, he said to himself as he nodded.

The next thing he saw Scott do almost made him stop breathing. Scott took his bag, slung it over his shoulder, and went to the driver's side window. He looked to his left, then to his right, clearly checking to see if anyone was watching. Somehow, though, Scott didn't look in his direction. Then, it happened so fast Preston almost thought it hadn't really occurred.

But it had.

Scott stuck his head in the window and ever so briefly kissed the driver full on the lips. It wasn't a girl he kissed. He could see the back of the side of driver's head now. It was a guy!

Preston's mouth dropped open.

The window started going up and the car started moving slowly down the lane. Scott watched the car leave. He had a silly smirk on his face. No, it was a smile.

*Did that really happen?* Preston had squirmed around so much now that all of his sorted chemistry papers slid off his lap to his feet, getting all out of order again.

The driver was pulling around and would have to go behind him to get out of the parking lot. Preston quickly turned his head to see if he could recognize the driver. When it went by, still at a slow speed, he got a good look at the boy. He figured he had to have known who it was. No, he didn't recognize the face from anywhere, but he certainly was good looking. Quickly, he turned back around, completely in a quandary, and looked for Scott. He was headed into the school. *Oh, my fucking god*, Preston thought. *Could it be true?*

The cup of Skoal spit in Joe's hand dropped two inches to his lap, but he caught it before it turned over on his crotch. He was speechless at first, but somehow managed to find his voice. When he did, he yelled at Brenda. "D-did you just see that!"

She had been rummaging in her purse and hadn't been looking. Now she looked at him, then to the parking lot where he was pointing. "See what?"

He pointed to Ryan's car going past one row away. "That Mustang." He then pointed at Scott who was now on the sidewalk. "You see who's over there?"

"That's Scott Faraday," she said matter-of-factly. *Joe knows who he is. Nearly everyone in school knows Scott, at least by sight, since he was on the track team. And he's in that band that Joe can't stand.* She also knew that Joe wasn't particularly fond of Scott for reasons he kept to himself.

Ryan was now driving down the out lane. While Brenda watched Scott head toward the side entrance of the school, Joe attempted to scrutinize the driver of the car. He didn't recognize the car or the driver. But he certainly could tell that the driver was male. He wasn't exactly sure he saw a kiss since the rear window frame had partially obscured his view of it. Nonetheless, the look Scott gave the driver, and the general circumstances that surrounded the quick act, told him everything.

Now he knew exactly why he didn't like Scott *Fairy*day.

# CHAPTER 8

After the bell rang at the end of fourth period, Preston wasn't sure how to react. He had run the scene over in his mind dozens of times by then. The object of the majority of his erotic fantasies had kissed another boy in the school parking lot? Had his prayer been answered? Was this too good to be true? More importantly though was the fact that Scott was clearly gay. How else could he explain it? With his head swimming with questions about this incredible turn of events, he went to his locker, pulled his calculus book out along with his math notebook, and walked down the corridor to class.

Preston dragged his fingers across his head. The hair he had pushed back promptly fell back down in front of his eyes. He eased himself into his seat. He dared to look at Scott only from the corner of his eye. Scott was sitting in the back talking with Doug and Lynn. Ms. Dunn, who had been outside the class-room talking with another teacher, come in and shut the door. Everyone started to take their seats.

Preston found himself getting hard. It had been almost three years since he had gotten a spontaneous hard-on in class. So far, he hadn't ever been called on to work out any of the problems at the board. He hoped today wouldn't be an exception because, as his plan formulated, the harder he got.

Scott took the bus back home that evening. It had been quite a while since he had ridden in one. Ryan wouldn't be back until after five. Scott knew this particular route had a stop about two blocks from the stereo speaker installation shop. He walked leisurely to the shop, paid the man, and picked up the Jeep. He pulled out their now-published Centauri tape and slid it into the cassette player. He turned the volume down at first, afraid they might have messed things up, but then when he was sure he heard sound out of each of the speakers, he adjusted the fader and cranked the volume. It was as good as he was going to get from a set of car speakers, even if this unit cost a lot. Nonetheless, it was way better than before.

\*              \*              \*

Finally, a Friday. Scott stood by his locker wondering why he'd been targeted. He couldn't remember the last time one had been vandalized. The combination locks had keyholes in the center. His had clearly been gouged with a sharp instrument and there was gum jammed in the keyhole. The combination wouldn't budge. The only way he'd be able to get it open now is if he took a hammer to it. He knew it would take at least a week to get it fixed if he did that. He glanced at his watch. It was a few minutes before lunchtime and he figured he might be able to at least get someone from the janitor's office to help him get it open. He got someone only a few minutes later.

He was mortified when Mr. Morton the maintenance man, opened it. Scrawled in large black permanent ink letters on the inside was one word: 'FAG'.

Mr. Morton only glanced at them. He could care less what was on the inside of lockers until summertime when they had to be de-stickered, cleaned, and sometimes repainted. Nonetheless, he noticed the look on Scott's face. "You look like someone just punched you," he said, as he unscrewed the lock from the inside.

Scott was busy inspecting the scrawled letters, wondering who could have done it and why Mr. Morton didn't seem to care they were there. This changed everything. Whoever had written it knew he was gay and appeared to be harassing him. His first thought was Preston. He was the only other student he had recently had contact with who might have had a suspicion. But then he wasn't sure. His mind raced as he thought through all the possibilities. Maybe Jake, the asshole from third period? No, he had never harassed Scott for any reason. Maybe it was Al and his jackwad burnout buddy from the across the hall. He glanced over to Al's locker. No, it couldn't have been him either. He only hassled narcs. There were only a few other kids at the end of the hall quite a way down. It could have been anyone, he realized. And now he had to be on the lookout.

Mr. Morton removed the lock, installed a new one, then gave Scott the paper with the combination on it. He kept the key for himself and dropped it into his pants pocket. He poked the gum in the old lock with his screwdriver. "Looks fresh." He sniffed it. gum."

Joe had been leaning against the wall far down the corridor. Scott hadn't seen him. Joe went out the side entrance to the parking lot to get the can of Skoal he'd left in his truck. When he got to it, he opened the glove box, tossed the permanent marker into the box, and then retrieved the Skoal can. *That's just the first taste, Fairyday.*

Mr. Morton left just as Preston saw Scott. He went toward his locker. Scott slammed it shut so Preston wouldn't see the inside. That startled him and he stopped short.

"What are you pissed off about?" Preston asked.

"What?"

"You just slammed your locker door. I thought you were pissed off about something."

"It's nothing." Suddenly Scott wondered again if he had anything to do with it after all and furrowed his brow while he looked at him. He knew that criminals were known to return to the scene of the crime. Maybe this was that situation?

Preston wondered what the odd look was all about, but then dismissed it. He felt nervous as hell. "I, uh, came by to see if you wanted to, uh, come over this week to study." He could have just told Scott that he saw him kissing a boy in the parking lot yesterday morning, but he wanted to start executing his plan instead. He had thought about it a lot in the last twenty-four hours. He really didn't care who the boy was. All that was important was that he would be the next boy to have him. The fastest way to do that was to get Scott alone with him as soon as possible. Whoever it was that Scott kissed would fast be history once Scott understood what was what.

Scott's initial agitation lifted considerably, which Preston noticed. "How about next Sunday afternoon?"

"Next Sunday?"

"That's the earliest I have time."

*Damn, that wasn't part of my plan.* He'd have to wait over a week now? "Yeah, next Sunday's fine, I guess. Hey, I have some enlargements of the track meet. I wanna give you one." *That should do it for sure.*

"Serious?"

"Yeah, you'll have to come over to get them though."

"As long as your pool's available."

Preston raised his eyebrows as his enticement took effect. "Of course."

He left and Scott went to look for a large permanent marker in one of the art classrooms. If he scribbled enough, he'd be able to completely cover over the letters. After that, he planned to plaster the inside of the locker with Centauri stickers just to make sure it would never be noticeable again.

Toward the end of the school day, Scott saw Joe walking down the hall and figured he was going toward the shop wing. It was about time he'd seen Joe. In a way, though, he was happy he hadn't seen him recently until now.

Joe seriously creeped him out. Last school year he would break off on occasion from his little group of cowboy buddies, come up to Scott, talk to him about the most bizarre things, or casually tell him some guy looked 'pretty', and then abruptly leave. One time Joe came up and started telling him about how important country music was. Scott knew that Joe knew he was in Centauri, so couldn't figure out what that had been about at all. Three or four times last year when Scott was at his locker, Joe would come by, flip his hair up, then give him an obviously fake apology. All of it seemed like harassment but without any particular violent intent. Then there was the generally high-strung way Joe conducted himself. The races in his pickup truck, the arrest that was talked about all over school last year when it was said he had beat up a family member, and the verbal abuse he gave his girlfriend. His two best buddies were known to drink the hardest of almost anyone else in school and Joe was known to keep up. Scott knew Joe had been held back a year but didn't know which one. He didn't think it was a high school year though. The highlight of all Joe's odd nature, of course, was the weird invitation to visit him at the bleachers that one night. Scott had played Dungeons and Dragons several times. Just for fun, one of his characters had been chaotic evil in alignment. But that was just a character. Joe seemed like real live chaotic evil, but Scott wondered when it would be more than just a thought in his head and something a lot more dangerous.

Every time Scott ever saw him, Joe wore tight jeans. And he could tell Joe didn't wear underwear. They always rode up the crack of his ass. He sure packed it in up front, too. There were plenty of other boys and girls in school who were part of the cowboy culture, and dressed the part, too. But Joe acted like he was the Cowboy President since he only wore cowboy attire. He couldn't help himself as he watched that butt once again and checked out the Skoal ring in his back pocket. As much as he hated even being near the guy, he had to find out how he had managed to schedule a band for the Thanksgiving Dance before he did. And maybe he could get him to withdraw his suggestion after all.

"Hey, Joe, wait up!" Scott shouted as he came near.

Joe stopped dead in his tracks. That was Scott Faraday's voice. *Fuck, did he find out who nailed his locker? There's no way.* No one had seen him jam the leather punch from his pocketknife into the keyhole then jimmy it open. He had been very careful and very quiet. Joe turned around.

Scott stopped a couple of feet in front of him and briefly glanced at the side of Joe's face. It was quite the patchwork of zits.

"What is it, Scottie boy?" Joe said it with a lilt in his voice he figured Scott might enjoy.

*What's up with that,* Scott wondered. "I talked with Mr. Turner."

"Huh. I did, too. Last week."

Scott decided not to try to match his tone. "The Jesse Copper Band," was all he needed to say.

"Yeah, they're playing at the Thanksgiving Dance. They have the hottest singers, don't you think Scott, dear?"

"Scott, *dear?*" *What the hell is he doing?* He took a step backward.

One of the things that Scott had always noticed was that he was shorter than almost everyone except most of the freshmen. Joe was formidable as well, with fat heft to him. That made it all the more important to avoid getting in his way.

Joe watched Scott take the step backward, so took one forward. "Pretty girls. You know what those are, *don't* you?" He knew Centauri had a female lead singer, but he was more interested in razzing Scott just now.

Scott ignored him. "Mr. Turner put Centauri on the schedule. It's gonna come to a vote, you know. And we'll win." No venue was unimportant now. He *had* to book the gig.

Some of the other losers that inhabited the shop wing were starting to come into the corridor where they were. Several stood nearby, well within earshot, and were talking among themselves.

"Centauri? No way. Jesse Copper has your band beat by a mile. Besides, country rules in this school."

Scott knew that wasn't true. Perhaps a third of the school's population identified themselves as cowboy or cowgirl. Only slightly more than that listened to or liked country music. What was more important right now was that Joe was taunting him. But there was something more going on here. Joe was acting in a way he usually reserved for when they were alone. Never in the past had he ever been this bold. It suddenly dawned on him that Joe might have been his vandal. But why did he suddenly escalate his previous odd behavior to vandalism if that were so? He tried to determine if there was anything he had done recently that could have precipitated Joe's change of character.

*The kiss? In the parking lot? Did he see it?* But there was no way. He had looked all over and seen no one. Besides, it had lasted, what, one-quarter of a second, if that? How could he have seen that? Scott slowly took a couple of more steps backward now. *What if it's true? What if he* did *see me? What might happen next?*

Joe matched his steps by coming forward again, now looking menacing. "Here's the deal, Fairyday. The Jesse Copper Band is playing and your band is *not.* You can just take your band off the schedule right now if you know what's best for you." Joe didn't take his eyes off him.

Scott wanted to say 'fuck you' and just get it over with. But he knew if he did, he'd never be able to win the fight that would inevitably be next. Joe was simply too big. But there was the whole 'Fairyday' thing he had just produced. He wasn't going to get away with that.

"No way. We're gonna play. And for the record, my name's *Fara*day." He enunciated each letter. "F-A-R-A-D-A-Y."

"Not anymore, *Fairyday*."

Purely out of reaction, Scott made a fist and drew his arm back just as Doug tapped him on the shoulder. Scott swung around. He was completely wound up. Seeing Scott's fist pulled back, Doug threw his arms up into the air, lurched away, and hit another student's backpack with his shoulder as she walked by. "Whoa, dude! What the...?"

Scott relaxed his arm and looked back. There was a smirk on Joe's face. Scott heard him say 'faggot' under his breath before he turned around and headed toward shop class. *Shit. It's true. Joe must have seen me!*

Doug looked at him, then toward Joe. "What was all that about?"

"Dickhead there couldn't say my name right."

"First or last?"

"Last."

"What's so hard about Faraday?"

"He has a malignant brain tumor."

# CHAPTER 9

Scott could have kicked himself for not having checked the schedule weeks before, but the gigs on base and all the practice dates, plus his focus on calculus had had priority over all else. Now it was going to come down to a stupid vote. The way it was done was that Mr. Turner set up a ballot box in the admin office on Monday morning. The senior class president plugged both bands during the morning announcements. It was just a matter of counting votes at the end of the week. It was one person, one vote. Their name had to be on the ballot to be valid.

Scott talked to everyone he knew to get them to vote his way. He figured he'd have Joe beat in a second, but wasn't really sure. And getting anyone beside seniors to vote was going to be difficult. Underclassmen knew that seniors called the shots for the bands. He resisted telling Ryan about the vote because he still felt so stupid for not having done anything earlier.

Instead of bothering himself with votes as the week progressed, Scott concentrated on calculus. All he had to do, he figured, was to pass the class. Seeing Annette was the easiest way to do that, so he visited her twice during the week. He couldn't figure out why Preston declined to go with him. Unfortunately, Annette was just too nerdy for him to relate to her anymore. Either he'd figure out how to do the homework on his own, get another tutor if that were possible, or simply demand that Preston study with him.

The final bell of the day for Scott had rung. He deposited his books in his locker and inspected his handiwork. The permanent marker letters had been completely obliterated by his scribbling last week. Now, Centauri stickers covered most of the scribbling. He even had each band member sign one apiece. He pulled his keys out and when he got to his Jeep, tossed his backpack in. He started it up and turned up the volume. He felt the oddest sensation just as he pulled forward, like he was going over a slight bump, then heard a strange noise he couldn't quite place.

He immediately hit the brake, thinking he had a flat tire or perhaps had run over a bottle. Glass in his tire? That would be bad. He got out and inspected them. No, no flats. There didn't appear to be anything underneath the tires either. He took a closer look at them. It wasn't obvious that anything was wrong at all. He got back in, this time with the door still open, turned down the sound, and eased forward again. He heard a thump and a slightly audible clanging sound as he rolled forward a few inches. Alarmed, he shut off the engine and jumped out again.

He stooped down and looked under the chassis again. He still didn't see anything out of the ordinary. He passed his hand over one of the rear wheels, for no other reason except to make sure it was intact. The one lugnut he touched moved. He zeroed in on it and realized it wasn't even hand tight. He tightened it, then inspected the rest on that wheel. They were all loose. He checked all of them. Each lugnut on all four tires was loose up to the very last thread! If he had been going any faster, it might have been possible that his wheels would have fallen off. Maybe all at once, he realized. He knew exactly who had done it. And he was sure Joe hadn't counted on him hearing that weird noise. He hand tightened the rest of the lugnuts, then pulled out the tire iron to finish the job. His next stop would be the auto supply store to get the locking kind. *Fuck that god damned Joe*, he thought, as he went to each wheel in turn. As he mulled over Joe's little stunt, he figured it had been just a new way to intimidate him. But with a single day left of voting there was no way he was going to pull out of the contest.

Joe glanced down at the tire iron that lay on the floorboard of the passenger side as he pulled up into the parking lot of the machine shop. He checked himself in the rearview mirror then adjusted his two-toned beige cowboy hat. *That was the next taste, Fairyday. And the Jesse Copper Band will play at the Thanksgiving Dance or else.*

Scott had wanted to leave school as quickly as he could today so he could get to the Chamber of Commerce office before they closed. He sped there directly after going to the auto supply store. He arrived with just a few minutes to spare. Even though it was late, the clerk tried to be helpful.

"If you're looking for places to book a stage act you can look through this booklet," she said as she handed it to him. "We have a listing of all annual city and regional events and there are ads for lots of different businesses, festivals, and the like. You might want to look through the paper for Grand Openings. See if you can contact larger commercial business owners as well."

Scott thought it would be easier than this. He figured they would have an open slate of events and all he needed to do was go in and start placing the band's name on some calendars. This wasn't like school at all.

"You don't have an events coordinator or something?"

"A what?"

At first he thought she was hard of hearing, but almost immediately realized she didn't know what he was talking about. "Nothing. How about Grubstake Days next Memorial Day? Is there anyone I can to talk to about that event?"

"Mr. Videlka is the liaison for that particular event since it's so large. He handles everything for it." She pulled his business card from a holder and handed it to him. "He left at three today, but he'll be here all day tomorrow."

Scott took all the materials, thanked the woman, and went back to the Jeep. He sat with the booklet resting against the steering wheel for a few minutes while he thumbed through it. He pulled a pen out of his backpack and started marking some of the pages. Maybe if he acted like a detective he could dig up something unusual for the band to perform at as well. Who knew what he might find? In the meantime, he carefully placed the business card in his wallet. Mr. Videlka would be getting a call from him the next day.

*      *      *

Scott was sure he was getting good at keeping his parents from knowing he was driving Ryan in on Friday nights now. Since Ryan would leave his car at home, it was a simple matter of just coming back after they were asleep or before they had returned from the restaurant.

After getting to sleep late, Ryan woke up an hour after dawn and went for Scott yet again. Scott resisted for show only. Once both his parents left for the restaurant the boys dressed and went for a run. Scott had managed to persuade Ryan to go with him again. He mentioned it last night and had to force Ryan to bring shorts and running shoes with him before he would let him come over.

Scott started them at a very slow pace while they headed toward the foothills. Not used to running, like Scott, Ryan got winded less than a quarter-mile into it. Scott let him catch his breath, and with his second wind established, they took a leisurely pace parallel to the wall of rock formations.

"Oh, I forgot to tell you something about this guy, *huff*, I know in school," Scott said as they ran.

"What guy?"

"His name's Preston. He's, *huff*, in my calc class, *huff*, I think he might be gay."

"Did you, *huff*, figure you were, *huff*, the only gay boy, *huff*, in school?"

"No, *huff*, it's just that, *huff*, I've known him, *huff*, for a while and, *huff*, and just now figured it out."

"So, are you, *huff*, gonna come out to him?"

"Not yet. I'm, *huff*, gonna wait till he says, *huff*, something to me."

"Why bother, *huff*, if you're so sure?"

"I wanna be, *huff*, absolutely sure. I, *huff*, need a few more, *huff*, clues. We're studying, *huff*, together a lot. I'm gonna see, *huff*, what he says first." That wasn't the full truth of the matter. He was afraid he might be too attracted to him. And if he came out to him first, it would be weird for him. He figured it would simply be best to lay low and just wait for Preston to say something. He figured he would any day now. If he didn't, then he'd do it anyway.

"Oh, *huff*, there's this other guy, *huff*, at school."

"Another gay boy?"

"No, he's just a dick." So, Scott told him about the two incidents with Joe.

"If he fucks with you again, *huff*, tell me and, *huff*, I'll kick his ass, *huff*, into next Saturday."

Scott thought he might just do it, too.

They continued talking for another ten minutes before Ryan called for a timeout. They stopped by a huge boulder, rounded it, and rested. Ryan gave Scott a familiar look. He slowly pulled Scott's running shorts down to midthigh. Scott's penis sprang to attention as Ryan went down to his knees. Ten minutes later, he had Scott breathing hard again, but it wasn't from running this time. The outskirts of Yucca Valley seemed to have all kinds of out of the way places to accomplish that endeavor.

After they returned, Scott was on his own today. Howard had asked Ryan to accompany him into Ontario later that morning to help him get a piece of furniture that he wanted to purchase. Ryan had to go with him to help strap it to the roof of the car and then take it into the house.

The band had all assembled for practice and had finished three numbers when Colleen called for a break.

"Hey, I have an announcement everyone," Scott then said. At least one thing had gone well for him in the last week. He had managed to get hold of Mr. Videlka from the Chamber of Commerce yesterday and was able to schedule the band for Grubstake Days as well as a couple of other local events. And he'd booked them for Winterfest at school. He was sure that on Monday they'd be scheduled for the Thanksgiving Dance. There was no way Joe was going to win that vote. He knew he should have said something to the band about his endeavor weeks ago, but wanted to have a whole list of things before he said anything. Hopefully, Barry would understand what he was doing and see that he was trying his best to get him to stay. Everyone's attention was focused on him now. "I've been doing some marketing for us."

Darryl stepped away from his keyboard stand and came up to the soundboard. "Marketing? Since when did you become our promoter?"

"Since before the gigs on the base."

"Footwork by Scott Faraday?" Colleen asked.

"Lots of it. Wanna hear what I dug up?"

"Shoot."

"We have gigs scheduled because of yours truly."

"Really? When, where, and most importantly, how much?" Mitch asked.

"Two for my high school and two publicly. One venue is a long way off, but it's for Grubstake Days! We're one of three bands so far. As for how much, how's nine hundred and six hundred for the school concerts. I don't know what Grubstake Days is gonna pay yet. But I also turned up the Annual Lights Parade next February, which we're on for, and possibly the Miss Joshua Tree Pageant in March, but they haven't decided whether they want a band for that event yet."

"Bitchin'!" Bryce exclaimed. "It's about time we did Grubstake Days. How did you do it?"

"I went to the Chamber of Commerce, talked to the liaison, and he put us on the calendar." Scott was beaming. It was perhaps one of the best events they could do to call attention to their talent.

"And the school events?" Colleen asked.

"In November we have the Thanksgiving Dance. And in December we have our annual Winterfest."

"When in November?"

"Uh, the week before Thanksgiving. Friday, the sixteenth."

"Not the sixteenth."

"But that's when it's scheduled."

"We can't."

"Why not?"

"We're booked for *Stage One Bar* on that day."

"*Stage One*? I went there. No one ever called me back."

"I know. I went there, too. Apparently, after you did. Mr. Henderson, who manages the place, said someone had come by a couple of weeks ago representing us. When I asked him who, he showed me our promo flyer with your name on it. I figured you were up to something, but you never said anything about it."

"How much is *it* gonna pay?"

"Nine-hundred and fifty buckaroos."

"Damn." That was more than the school gig.

"Scott, you should tell us when you're promoting the band."

"I wanted it to be a surprise. I was trying to help everyone out."

Bryce was charmed at what Scott had been up to, all secretly. He patted Scott's back. "Dude, seriously. We appreciate the effort, but how are we gonna do both gigs?"

Scott was crushed and it sounded in his voice. "I guess we won't."

Joe had suddenly won by default. It was going to look bad for him now. Once he withdrew, Joe would certainly take it wrong and think he did it out of fear. He'd taunt Scott even more for giving in like that. "But we can still do the Winterfest, and the other ones, huh?"

"When's Winterfest this year?" Colleen asked.

"December twenty-first. It's a Friday night."

"Winterfest. I love Winterfest," Sparks said. Then he attempted to sound nostalgic. "I was a sophomore and it was the first time I got…" He was going to say 'laid', but didn't the chance to. Colleen knew what he was going to say and playfully whacked him across the shoulder with her calendar book. She opened it to December and marked it down. She then looked at Scott. "How much?"

"Six hundred. It's better than nothing."

She kissed his cheek. "It'll be six hundred more than we have right now. Now let's hear the dates for the other events and how much they're paying."

Scott smiled broadly. At least some of his efforts weren't for nothing. Then he frowned when he realized he'd have to talk to Mr. Turner first thing on Monday.

✳ ✳ ✳

On Sunday afternoon, when Scott arrived at Preston's place, he parked next to Rosa's car. He had his swim trunks on already, along with a tank top and sandals. He didn't want to waste time changing. He knew he was going to enjoy the occasional trips over to here. It was a really nice place and Preston had a pool, cooked food in the fridge, and even a housekeeper. He felt a momentary twinge of jealousy as he thought of the money Preston's father must be making to have all this.

Rosa greeted him at the door and pointed to the patio. Preston was sitting at the glass table. When he reached it, Scott felt some odd kind of energy coming from him right away. He decided to scrutinize every one of Preston's actions now. After having his meter pegged so many times, he was going to log every clue he could get.

"I thought you were able to get rid of the housekeeper," Scott joked.

"She'll be here for a while today. She's here most of the time when I get home from school anyway."

"What about your dad?"

"I hardly ever see him except at night after he comes back from the dealership. He's not gonna be here until after nine tonight. Not to worry, there's fried chicken in the fridge. We can scarf it down. I'm sure it's nothing like the food at Faraday's though."

"Home cooking sounds good to me. I hardly ever get a home cooked meal."

Preston was surprised to hear that one. He figured Scott's parents whipped up gourmet meals all the time.

In the center of the patio table was an 8 x 10 enlargement. Scott put his backpack on one of the chairs and picked it up. "Wow. This is a great shot."

The photo showed him from his knees up to his top of his head. He examined it in detail. He had been leaning back with his elbows on the bleacher behind him. He saw his hand stuck up in a quick wave, his smile, and his hair blowing in the wind. Preston seemed to know exactly how to capture an image.

Preston studied the look on Scott's face. He had almost been reluctant to part with the photo, but had several others in his bedroom safely tucked away in the closet. He was particularly proud of this one, but after all, with a subject as handsome as Scott Faraday, who couldn't get a shot like that?

Scott put the photo down and Preston initiated the dive into the pool. Fifteen minutes later, they were still horsing around. Keep away with the Nerf football was not nearly as fun with just two people as it was with three or more, but it served as a way for Preston to keep tackling him. It seemed innocent enough, but every time Preston touched him it pegged his meter. Especially when Preston grabbed the back of his shorts and kept his fingers around the waistband for longer than he expected. They ended up playing far longer than Scott thought they should. He was ready to do some studying. It seemed liked good timing since Rosa stuck her head out the door and announced she was leaving for the day.

"Time out for study now?" Scott offered.

"Let me take some diving shots of you," Preston responded.

"What are diving shots?"

"I have a Polaroid. I could take some awesome shots of you doing stuff."

"We should really start studying."

Preston looked up at the large-numbered clock behind the bar. "We have loads of time. Just a couple?"

"What'd you have in mind?"

"Oh, you know, just some action photos and other stuff. You can take some with you."

"Sure. Go ahead." *What harm would that be?* The enlargement was so good, he was sure Preston would come up with some excellent shots today, too.

This was the moment Preston had in mind. First, he'd soften Scott up by telling him how great he looked in these photos. Then that'd lead to them feeling each other up, and finally he'd bend Scott over in the shallow end where.... He stopped constructing his fantasy as he dried his legs off, went up the back stairs, and quickly retrieved his camera along with an extra film pack.

He directed Scott to sit on the edge of the pool, stand in the shallow end, flex on the short diving board, dive off it, then pose in other miscellaneous shots. He used up the remainder of the film pack that was already in the camera, the fresh pack, and part of another one that he went back up to his room to retrieve.

When Preston was done, Scott was impressed. He had never had anyone do a photo spread of him before. Now, twenty-three photos were spread out all over the patio table. Granted, all of them were of him, but he was particularly proud of the way he looked in them. He was so busy being impressed that he didn't notice Preston almost drooling over them.

Preston held one of the photos up. "This one is the best." It was one where Scott was sitting on the edge of the pool. He was leaning back on his palms. Preston had come in close. They could see Scott's wet hair, his face with water droplets all over it, his shoulders, and down past his waist. It looked like he was naked since his swim trunks were slightly lower than his tan line and the photo didn't show them. Preston's eyes were practically popping out of his head.

Scott's radar pegged mercilessly. It was exactly what he would do in the same situation. His relationship with Preston, innocuous at first, was rapidly changing. Really, who else would have ever suggested taking this many photos of him? Yet, despite Preston's unusual behavior about the pictures, everything else about him said he wasn't gay. In fact, there was a lot more about how Preston interacted with him that simply said he wasn't. *He's this enigma of being in plain sight and being completely hidden at the same time. How the heck am I supposed to figure him out if he's like that?* "Why aren't you on the yearbook staff? You could take all kinds of pictures for it."

Preston didn't want to say that he thought the yearbook staff students were as lame as they could be. He also didn't mention that he had already stood with one of the photographers at a couple of the track meets Scott had run in last year and already had plenty of photos of him. But these were the icing. The others were crumbly old cake now. Hell, Scott was half naked in his pool in *these* pictures! "Nah. This is my last year of school. I just take pictures for fun. That would be way too much work."

"Okay, study time, huh?"

"Buzz killer."

"We have a test later this week."

"I know. But who really needs to know this anyway?"

"I do. That's why I came over. If you don't want to I'll just go see Annette tomorrow."

"No! I was kidding." He immediately pushed the photos aside and flipped open his book. He didn't want Scott to leave any sooner than he had to.

They started working on the problems right away. Preston couldn't keep his mind on them though. He had to start putting his plan in motion and he had to do it now, now that Rosa was gone. Just as he opened his mouth, the front door opened. His father stepped inside.

*God damn it! What's* he *doing here?* Preston stamped his left foot under the table in anger, banging his knee against the underside of the glass. It rattled their glasses and threatened to knock his over onto his textbook. He got to it just in time.

Scott noticed his sudden odd outburst and wondered what it had been all about. Preston had been acting really distracted ever since they had sat down. He looked up first at Mr. Tyllas, then back to Preston.

Warren tossed his suit coat onto the back of the couch and dropped a folded up newspaper on the end table. He saw the two boys on the patio and came toward them. He then stepped up to the wet bar and started fixing himself a drink. "Preston, who's your friend?"

Preston sighed. "Hi, Dad. Scott, this is my dad. Dad, Scott Faraday." He was terribly disappointed. His father had returned much earlier than expected, ruining his chance right when he was going to say something. But next time Scott was over, he'd do it. And, by God, he was going to have hot monkey sex with him if it was the last thing he ever did.

*               *               *

Early Monday morning Scott started his search for Mr. Turner. His first stop was the admin office. Mrs. Deginski said Mr. Turner had removed the box just a little earlier and had taken it to the teacher's lounge.

Mr. Turner was at a circular table in the far corner of the lounge. The room smelled of cigarette smoke. *Aren't there laws about teachers smoking in school,* he wondered. He didn't see a lit cigarette anywhere. No one else appeared to be there except for he and the teacher.

Scott's sudden appearance caught Mr. Turner's attention. "Uh, Mr. Faraday, students aren't allowed in here."

"I know Mr. Turner, but I have to talk to you."

"If it's about the votes, I'm counting them now. Once I finish, Mrs. Chandler's verifying them."

Scott approached the table anyway. "That's why I'm here. Centauri can't perform then. We have another gig that night."

"Did I hear you correctly?"

"My bad. I jumped the gun." He had never done that even once during a track meet. He suddenly found it odd that while the band seemed far more important than his previous athletic endeavors, he had jumped it this time.

Mr. Turner released his grip of a stack of ballots. "A whole week went by and you're telling me now?"

"I didn't know until the weekend. I'm seriously sorry."

"Can you say The Jesse Copper Band?"

Scott let his shoulders down. *Fuck.*

At lunch, Scott saw Preston sitting down at an empty table in the cafeteria. None of his other friends were around so he decided to eat with him. He had barely gotten out a hello when Joe came up from behind, set his tray down, and took a seat. Joe had never sat at this end of the cafeteria much less right next to him. Scott's heart ramped up a bit.

Joe looked at Preston briefly, then addressed Scott. "Jesse Copper beat your ass, Scottie Fairyday," he simply said. Joe was getting bolder and bolder.

Preston looked at Joe. Cowboys never sat at this table. It was taboo. "What are you doing?"

"I'm talking to Fairyday." He looked at Scott. "If you pull another stunt like that you can suck my dick. And I bet you're pretty good at that."

Scott looked him squarely in the eye. Clearly, he had already talked to Mr. Turner. "Get the fuck lost," he said coldly.

"Gonna wet your diaper?"

Scott had to decide right then what he should do. If he did nothing he was assured of continued torment. If he started anything, especially in the cafeteria, he'd certainly be kicked out of school. He was well aware that the school didn't care why people fought. No matter who started it, both of them would be suspended for three days. He couldn't afford that at all.

Preston was so flabbergasted by Joe's statement he spoke up before Scott could say another word. "How about you leaving." He pointed. "Your table is over there."

Joe hadn't even picked up his fork. He had no intention of staying. He just wanted to come over and give Scott grief. "I can't sit next to a faggot anyway." With that, he picked up his tray and went to the other side of the cafeteria to sit with his cowboy buddies.

At first Preston was sure Joe had been talking about him. Yet, he was sure no one in school knew he was gay. Then he realized Joe must have meant all of it for Scott. But he also knew that calling someone a faggot was just about as common as saying the word 'fuck'. Yet, it was sort of confusing, given what he knew about Scott now.

Preston watched Joe leave. "That was about the vote, huh?" He wasn't so sure. He was actually stabbing in the dark.

"Yeah," Scott replied sheepishly.

"Well, I won't be going to the dance if Jesse Copper's performing."

"My guess is that you wouldn't have a date anyway," Scott replied. He wasn't looking at Preston, but rather watching Joe. And it was a snide comment to be sure. He shouldn't have said it even given his suspicion about Preston, but he was feeling angry and it just came out.

Preston couldn't do it. Not in the cafeteria. He couldn't just come out and say he was gay right here, despite what he knew about Scott. He hinted instead. "You're right. I don't do girls," he said quite casually. Unless Scott was completely dense, he had to have figured it out now.

Preston was grinning. Scott's radar pegged to maximum. It was one weird moment, too. That should have been all he needed to come to the proper conclusion, but Scott didn't want to admit it. Preston was too attractive. Magnetic even. Yes, he'd given Scott as many clues as he needed, so it should have been obvious what was up.

Something told Scott, though, that Preston was treacherous as well as not exactly straight.

# CHAPTER 10

For several weeks now the Iraqi invasion of Kuwait had begun to show itself in the Morongo Basin. That was the disadvantage of living near a military base. No matter how far away a conflict was, the populous was keenly aware of it. The Basin was always crawling with Marines due to the nearby base. Now, though, they were a little more restricted to base. While convoys could be seen along the highway on occasion, Scott noticed a lot more equipment movement in the last several weeks. He didn't like that at all. It was the first time he could remember seeing troop and equipment movements that weren't just war games or the common comings and goings of the nearby military personnel. Whatever was happening in Kuwait couldn't possibly affect them directly. Or could it? Hell, Kuwait was in a desert, and so were they. The C-5 Galaxy aircraft that were taking off and landing from the airstrip on base were probably moving equipment out of the base at Twentynine Palms to halfway around the world. He was so glad he was in school and not in the military.

Two weeks earlier Joe had driven his truck to the Marine Corps recruiting station at the mall. Although he had registered, as required, with the Selective Service at eighteen, he was pissed off now. He went inside and demanded to talk to one of the recruiters. He had watched enough TV news to know what was happening over there and wanted to be involved. After a half-hour talk with two of the recruiters he discovered that if he wanted to join up he'd have to quit school first, but that wasn't recommended. Then he'd have to take the ASVAB test which he'd been putting off, graduate boot camp, get training, and get his first duty station. All that would take up to six months at the earliest and the US involvement over there could very well be over with by then. Once he realized that one didn't just up and join, he took away all the forms and went to Brenda's house to bitch at her about it. She reminded him of his arrest record. He reminded her that the Marines routinely didn't care about that. He'd have to wait until he finished school after all. *God damn it*, he thought.

\*        \*        \*

It was Thursday and Scott hadn't seen Ryan since Monday evening. They'd talked on the phone briefly last night, but it wasn't about anything important. He needed to call him tonight, since he had to know if Ryan wanted to be at the gig they were going to do at *Stage One Bar* tomorrow night. He came in from his run, fed Shakaiyo, then took a shower. His phone rang before he was finished drying off. He sat on the bed, fiddled with his pubes for a second to check if they were dry, then picked up the phone. "This is Scott."

Ryan was upset again, like he sometimes was when he called. "The worst thing happened."

Scott dragged the towel across his hair again with his free hand then tossed it over his shoulder. "Howard kicked your ass out, huh?" he asked playfully.

"Worse. Muh's dead."

He knew Muh as Ryan's sweet grandmother. "That's not even funny."

"Chris came home from school and found her on the couch." Chris was Ryan's sixteen-year old brother who still lived with her.

He was sure Ryan was leading him on. "Why are you saying shit like that?"

"I'm not shitting you. We're leaving tonight. This is awful." His voice faded out at that last word.

"You're serious."

"Oh yeah, I'd just call you up and tell you something like that for fun."

Yes, he was serious, alright. "How old was she?"

"Eighty-two."

"*Eighty-two*? I thought she was like sixty or something."

"She looked a lot younger than she was."

"I am *so* sorry. How long will you be gone?"

"Don't know yet. Howie says it might be next weekend before we get back."

"That's a long time for a funeral. Aw, man, you won't be at the gig tomorrow night! Or here for Thanksgiving. That sucks."

"I wouldn't be in any mood to be with you guys even if I stayed here."

Scott was well aware of Ryan's ability to shift moods abruptly. Usually for the worse. "But why a week?"

"We have to pack stuff up for Chris."

"He's gonna live here, too?"

"He can't live by himself, dumbass."

Scott knew that Chris still wasn't in on their relationship. If he came down to live with Howie and Ryan, the secret would be out sooner rather than later.

Ryan emitted a short moan. "She wasn't supposed to die."

Scott couldn't think of anything profound to say. "She was old."

"But she wasn't supposed to die."

Scott heard the desperation in his voice. *Uh, oh, he's gonna crack.* "I'm coming over."

"We're packing."

"I'm coming over anyway." Silence.

Finally, "Whatever."

Scott took off a few minutes later.

Howard answered the door. "Hi Scott," he said. He didn't look all that happy either. "He's in his bedroom. You know the way." He followed Howard down the hall. As Scott passed Howard's open bedroom door, he saw clothes already laid out on the bed and a suitcase sitting on the floor next to it. It looked like he was wasting no time.

Scott entered Ryan's bedroom. "Hey, I'm here."

Ryan was facing the bed away from him. "I heard the doorbell."

Scott didn't like his response. There was an undertone of anger. He could tell that Ryan was more sad than anything else though.

Scott wasn't exactly sure why Ryan felt so pained by her death. All four of his own grandparents had died before he was born. He never knew any of them. He wasn't aware of the profound influence Muh had had on both Ryan and Chris after their parents had died so many years back.

An unzipped bag was on Ryan's bed. He stuffed a bunched up t-shirt into it. Scott turned and gently closed the door.

Ryan's face was etched with grief. He draped himself over Scott's shoulders and they hugged. He felt terribly vulnerable right now.

*God, he's so moody,* Scott thought. He wasn't sure he'd be able to do or say anything to change it either. He knew Ryan well enough at this point to know that he would have to change it himself.

Ryan continued folding the clothes from the pile next to his bag. Scott stayed for moral support and talked with him until he and Howard got ready to leave. He tried to cheer him up with the occasional joke, a wisecrack, and some silly accents he came up with on the fly, but none of it worked. Several hours later, Ryan and Howard were on their way to the airport in Ontario to start their journey to Crescent City.

⋆　　　　　　⋆　　　　　　⋆

The next night Scott only half expected to see the man he had originally met at the *Stage One Bar.* He never did see him though. The band set up hours before any patrons arrived, ate dinner together, and came back around nine. The manager welcomed them backstage and told them that he'd been advertising them for weeks now. He expected several hundred people to be there despite the relatively small venue. A good local band was hard to come by, he told them. Although Mr. Henderson eyed Scott's under-aged appearance more than once while he talked with them, he never asked how old he was. *Good,* Scott thought, *I'd lie to him anyway.*

The venue was excellent, though, and the crowd was actually larger than the manager said it would be. Scott was, in a way, surprised. His initial foray to the bar was just because he had heard it was a good place to showcase their talent. Now he was sure it was a good one.

Tonight Scott wouldn't be performing. He was strictly sound. It was during their first number when he realized the loss of not having Ryan there for the concert. He was so used to having him there to watch them perform, as well as generally help out, that his absence was noticeable.

Despite his disappointment at Ryan not being there, they were all equally pleasantly surprised later on. The manager came up to Colleen and Barry after the bar closed and told them that he wanted them back one weekend night a month at least through March. Steady income, however short-term? They signed a contract that very evening. Scott was disappointed again that Ryan hadn't been there to see the deal being signed.

*          *          *

Six days now and Scott still hadn't heard from Ryan. It was a strange week. It was the first time since they had met that they hadn't seen each other for more than a couple of days or at least talked on the phone. The feeling was excruciating. Sleeping alone was refreshing since he hadn't been constantly woken up due to Ryan feeling him up at random intervals during the night. Not that he minded that, but the loss of sleep wasn't missed. The separation also held an emptiness he had never experienced. Before June, he had never slept with anyone before. Now it was a familiar feeling that he had grown used to and even craved.

Thinking he'd be able to hold out, he tried to withhold from beating off. That had lasted exactly two days, nine hours and eight minutes from his reckoning. He simply couldn't hold off any longer. It was quite messy, both times, in that half-hour stretch.

Scott arrived at Colleen's before anyone else did that evening. He let Shakaiyo out of the jeep and she took off toward the large boulders at the end of the yard behind the Royal Garage.

Colleen was folding up a lawn chair next to Bryce's drum set. She didn't see or hear Scott come into the garage. When she returned to the mike stand Scott's movement startled her. "Whoa, when did you get here?"

"Sorry. Didn't mean to startle you."

Colleen looked at him. There was something odd about him that she couldn't quite place. "You're early. And you look like your dog just got run over."

"No, she's okay."

"Well, what is it?"

"I haven't seen my boyfriend since last Thursday. I'm going crazy."

"There'll be a time when you can't wait to get away from a boyfriend, you know."

"Mine's not like yours."

"Hey, that's not fair. I've never said anything bad about *yours.*"

"Sorry, I'm just not happy."

"How long could her funeral last anyway?"

"I don't know. I've never been to one. But it was more than just the funeral. They had to pack up his brother's stuff, get him out of school, lock up the house, and all sorts of other stuff, too."

"Oh, he has a brother?"

"Yeah, a younger one. He's a junior." He quickly fell silent.

She studied his face. "You're moping. Scott Faraday doesn't mope."

"I feel like I'm all out of energy. It's the longest we've been apart since we met."

She grinned as she circled him, looking him up and down. Scott followed her with his eyes. She stepped behind him and squeezed his shoulders. "Height, width, depth. If I'm not mistaken, three dimensions means you're all here." She peeked around to look at him and cracked a smile.

He couldn't help himself and laughed. Her sense of humor, similar to his in certain ways, broke his mood. "You win. But it's worse."

"How much worse?" She released her grip and stood in front of him now.

"I'm thinking about him all the time."

"Well, that's it then."

"That's what then?"

"I thought you *were* smart."

"Oh, stop it."

"You're in l-o-v-e."

"Maybe."

Maybe she was just trying to make him feel better. He adjusted some of the line levels on the board as he thought about it. He was feeling something for Ryan. And he was certainly thinking about him a lot. But he didn't know if it was love or not. It flew close, then fluttered off, far away. It resisted his reach. It kept getting blurred when he approached it. He certainly was greatly concerned with how Ryan was feeling right now. And whenever he was alone these last six days he got hard whenever he thought about them being together.

When they had been up in Crescent City together before school started, he had told Ryan he loved him. But it was a spur of the moment statement. Sure, he felt what he thought was love for him, but it wasn't as if he were 'in love' with him. Or was he? Ryan was the last thing he thought about just about every night before he fell asleep. His heart pounded when he thought about him, even now, filling him with feelings that kept getting mixed up. Maybe she was right. But why was it so difficult to tell?

Practice went for just a couple of hours tonight since Colleen only wanted to test some vocals with Darryl. Scott was there to tape then mix the new tracks with previous ones to make sure it was the sound they wanted to achieve. Thanksgiving was tomorrow and nobody else wanted to bother with practice for the long holiday weekend.

When he returned home he let Shakaiyo into this bedroom then dropped down to the floor with her. She rolled over onto her side, front paws groping air, and let him embrace her. He made a sour face and pulled himself away. She smelled awful. Since he had nothing to do right now he started the shower, shed his clothes, and pulled her in with him. He was drying her off when the phone rang.

He wiped his lower legs off again and sat on the bed, still unclothed, and pressed the on button.

"Scott here."

"Hey," Ryan said in a soft voice.

"You're back!" He had left three messages yesterday asking Ryan to call him immediately upon his return. He figured it might be a bit excessive, but he couldn't help himself.

"Can I come over?"

"You have to ask?" Scott realized he was getting hard just listening to Ryan's voice.

"I'll be a few minutes."

Scott was on the driveway when Ryan arrived. Ryan parked his Mustang at the curb and strode up to the gate. Scott noticed right away that a certain spring was missing from his step. "Come into my bedroom," he demanded. He wanted to grab Ryan and kiss him right there, but resisted the urge out in the open.

With her tail wagging, Shakaiyo greeted him with her usual slow meandering walk to his outstretched hand. After a good scratching behind the ears, Scott literally pulled him into his bedroom. He didn't let her in with them.

He pushed the door shut, gently pushed him against it, and immediately planted a kiss on Ryan's lips. As the same time he was rising to the occasion. Scott's head was spinning.

He pulled Ryan toward the bed and they both fell onto it with Ryan on his back. It felt like the first night that they were together so many months back in Parker. Scott hugged and kissed him while slowly sliding himself up and down the front of Ryan's body. Scott's running shorts were shiny nylon and allowed him somewhat frictionless gliding, and before he knew it he was panting and moaning as he quickly lost control. It was like a wet dream, only he was wide awake. It was the first time that had ever happened. He rolled over and was off the bed as quickly as he could get up. A dark wet spot had already started to appear on the front of them.

Ryan was trying to stifle his snickering as he caught a quick glance of the evidence. "I can't believe it. You-you just shot your wad?"

Scott said nothing as he dashed to the bathroom and shut the door behind himself.

Ryan answered himself. "You did!"

Scott cracked open the door. "Shut up!" He couldn't believe how embarrassed he felt.

Ryan heard him step out of his shorts. He saw half of Scott's bubble butt and his right calf, the shorts in a bunch at his foot. Scott wetted a washcloth while Ryan fell backward on the bed and continued to snicker.

Scott pulled the door open a bit more and briefly glared at him. "Stop it!"

Ryan sat up. "I'm gonna tell Chris. He'll laugh so hard he'll be crying."

"It's your fault."

Scott emerged from the bathroom with the washcloth over his crotch. He wasn't exactly sure why he was bothering since they had seen each other naked, what, a hundred times, over the last several months? He pulled on some fresh underwear and slipped into a clean pair of shorts. Finally, he sat on the bed. He was actually a little proud of himself now. After all, hadn't it meant that he missed Ryan? But now he noticed that Ryan didn't seem at all interested in messing around.

"How was the funeral?" Scott thought it might sound odd to ask the question just like that, but what else does one ask? *Oh, well, I couldn't exactly avoid the question.*

Whereas the last several minutes were quite carefree, Ryan's demeanor shifted considerably as he began. "They buried her two days ago." Then Ryan recapped the last week. As he spoke, he started sounding more and more depressed. "When we got there she had already been taken to the morgue. Chris called Adina's parents and he stayed with them that night. He started crying as soon as he saw us and cried the whole next day. We made plans for the funeral and had to notify all her friends and our other relatives. I had to contact the Park Service office and tell them that our lease had expired due to her death and we had to meet with them, then we had to go to the lawyer's office to handle the will and stuff. I still have to go back next month to handle the estate sale, see the lawyer again, sign a bunch of real estate papers, and other things."

"*You* have to go?"

"I'm the only one who can do it. Howie can't take any more time off."

"Did you get, like, anything in the will?"

"Chris and I get everything."

"Is it a lot?"

"My share's gonna be enough to pay for college twice, and a whole lot more. Once everything's finalized with the lawyers Howie told me he's charging me rent. The dick."

"Wow. You are *so* lucky," Scott replied as he thought about the inheritance.

"Yeah, my grandma dies, I have to pay rent now, and you say I'm lucky. Fuck you."

Scott made a face at him. "I'm not saying you're lucky she died."

"Yes, you did."

Scott shoved him. "I did not."

Ryan hesitated for a moment as he studied Scott's face. "I-I'm sorry." He could have sworn Scott had been razzing him.

Scott was shaking his head. Ryan was overreacting again. And what the heck was up with his mood? The funeral was behind him. He just got an inheritance that would make anyone jump up and down. But Ryan was simply down.

"I don't feel so good," Ryan announced.

He pointed to Ryan's crotch. "You will be when I get my mouth on that."

Scott went for the zipper. He was sure Ryan simply needed some cheering up, or at least something to distract him.

At first, Ryan said no. Scott had heard that one before and it had always meant nothing. Scott continued to unzip him. Ryan's pants dropped to the floor and he stepped out of them. Scott was surprised so see that Ryan wasn't even close to being hard. That's when he realized Ryan hadn't been hard at all during his rather frantic release minutes before. And, this was the first time he'd seen him naked and not immediately that way. He decided to fix that and started working on him.

Five minutes later, after using both his mouth and his hand, Ryan had gotten erect but couldn't maintain it very well. Finally, Scott couldn't continue.

"My mouth's getting sore. And are you really empty? You could have waited, you know."

"I'm not in the mood."

"Liar. You're always in the mood."

"Not today."

*What is up with him?*

Ryan was looking down at the bedspread. He wouldn't make eye contact. Something was disturbing him for sure.

*Uh, oh,* Scott thought. He wasn't sure he should ask, but he had to know. "You're not thinking about it again, are you?"

Ryan looked up at him. He pulled on his underwear then stepped into his shorts. There was some sort of forlorn look in his eyes. "No."

"You swore!" Scott stood up now, quickly losing his erection. "You promised you wouldn't try it again. Promise me now!"

Ryan's voice was weak. "I swear." He slipped on his tennis shoes and tied them.

Scott wasn't satisfied. He remembered right then about Kyle Sorenson, his psychologist rock-climbing friend who lived in San Bernardino. He was going to get his phone number this very evening. "Well, don't," he said sternly. He was getting anxious now. *I thought he would snap out of it. But his mood's worse now than when he left. And, this is the first time we've been naked together where he's not had an orgasm. Something's not right here.* He desperately wanted to connect to him so changed the subject. "Did you tell Chris about us?"

"Yeah."

"When?"

"On the plane."

"What'd he say?"

"He just didn't want me to tell any of his friends once he gets into school." Scott tried to be funny. "Why? Does he think you'll go for 'em?"

"His friends? I *have* a boyfriend." He finally looked at Scott. "I have a favor to ask."

"Anything for you." The last minute's scare was rapidly fading away.

"It's not for me. It's for him. He has to get into school and I can't take any more time off work right now. They'll seriously dock my pay if I do. Can you…?"

"Enroll him?"

"Yeah."

"Not to worry. When?"

"Monday morning. He can't wait. He'll be too far behind to catch up if he even waits another week."

"What time should I come by?"

"Before school starts. Like seven-thirty?"

"Make sure he's up." He placed his hands on Ryan's shoulders as they stood face to face and kissed. "How about you and I go out next Friday night, after the holiday's over? On a date."

"Where to?"

"Tower Road Drive-In. Where else?"

"Okay. I'll come pick you up."

"Deal. What're you guys doing tomorrow for Thanksgiving?"

"Our next door neighbor invited us over. They know about the funeral and all and I guess they feel sorry for us."

"Yeah," he said sarcastically. "You know, maybe they're just trying to be *nice*. Faraday's will be open, of course. It'll be a banner day for us, as usual."

Once Ryan left, Scott let Shakaiyo into his bedroom again, shut the door, and called the operator. He didn't have a phone book that covered the San Bernardino area. "San Berdoo. Kyle Sorenson. S-o-r-e-n-s-o-n," he spelled.

"I have a business listing."

"Is there a residential phone number?"

"There's a K. Sorenson on Horseshoe Way."

"I'll take it." While the recording read off the number, he copied it down for future reference. He pressed the 1 key and the system dialed for him.

Kyle's wife answered. "Hello. Lisa speaking."

"Hi, Lisa. This is Scott Faraday."

"To what do I owe this pleasure? Can't find anyone to rappel with you this weekend?"

"No, it's not that. I need some professional advice from Kyle, if he's around."

"Sorry, I just sent him to the store. I give professional advice, too. Is there something I can do?"

"Well, maybe not advice really. I need the name of a good psychologist in Yucca Valley, if you know one."

"Is this for you?"

"No, it's for my boy, uh, my friend," he said obviously correcting himself.

It didn't slip by her. "Boyfriend?"

He sighed. "Yeah, boyfriend." The expected response didn't come.

She didn't mention the short conversation she had had with Ryan several months ago in the Monument when she had last seen them rappelling that weekend. But the conversation combined with what Scott had just said told her everything.

"Oh. I know one but don't have the phone number. Just a minute while I get his address book."

She put the phone down and he heard footsteps as she walked away. He felt embarrassed. He didn't intend to reveal that bit of information, but it had slipped out before he knew it.

She returned a moment later. "His name's Dr. Kevin McGinnis. I happen to know he's very good."

Scott took down the phone number and address. He didn't know when he'd need it so put it in his wallet. "Thanks."

"I hope everything's okay."

"I hope so, too.

"Happy Thanksgiving."

"Happy Thanksgiving," he replied nicely enough, yet feeling awful.

She could tell he wasn't even close to feeling happy.

*          *          *

On Monday, Howard and Ryan had already left for work when Scott pulled up in their driveway. Chris was sitting on the front porch stairs. Scott hadn't seen him in months. He had on a faded green t-shirt with Pennzoil written across the front, jeans, beat up tennis shoes, and had a gray backpack sitting next to him. His hair was considerably shorter now and he didn't look as dopey as Scott remembered. *Maybe he's not smoking as much pot anymore. Heck, I wonder what Howard thought of the pot plants that were in his bedroom?*

Chris waved, issued a brief smile, and stepped off the porch. Scott unlocked the passenger side door and Chris jumped in. "Hey, Chris. Long time."

"Hey, Scott. Thanks for picking me up." He placed the bag on his lap.

"No problem." He put it into reverse and pulled down the driveway.

"This is pretty lame, huh?" Chris said.

"What's lame?"

"You having to take me to school."

"Heck no. After all, you're…" He wanted to say 'my boyfriend's brother' but skipped it. "…gonna need someone to show you around."

"I wanted to be with my friends back home, not in the friggin' desert."

"Hey, there's stuff to do here. Yucca Valley has a bitchin' BMX bike park. It's only a couple of miles from here. The junior class has almost four hundred people in it this year, and I'm sure you'll find someone to replace your old girl-friend."

"The one that dumped me?"

Scott was right after all. He had figured she'd dump him as soon as school started.

"I happen to know that there are plenty of cute junior girls here."

"I hope so."

Scott took a right onto the highway. "So, Ryan told you about us two, huh?"

"Yeah," he said reluctantly.

"You're cool with it?"

"Don't even *try* to 'mo me."

Scott knew that 'mo was high school slang for the made up verb 'to homo'.

Scott wasn't sure whether he was serious or not. He made a gagging sound. "You are *not* my type."

Chris grinned. "Relief."

Scott guessed he was kidding after all.

Chris continued to look at him. "So, you and my brother were, like, you know, doing homo stuff in my house?"

"'Homo stuff'?"

"Kissing and…all that."

"Yeah, there was some kissing but I seem to remember a *lot* of 'all that'."

Chris acted like he was puking. "My brother's weird enough and now this."

Scott wanted to laugh at Chris' antic but held back. "You just have to get to know him."

"I've known him longer than you have."

"Okay, you're right. He's weird. But he sure knows how to kiss and *all that*." Scott looked over at him.

Chris had a horrified look on his face. "My first day of school and I have, like, these images in my head of…. Can you, like, not talk about that anymore?"

Scott was grinning. "Just testing you."

Chris made a diagonal chopping motion with his hand. "Okay, test *over*."

Scott popped in one of his Centauri tape mixes but kept the volume low. The first tune was barely halfway through before Scott spoke up again. "You think you'll be able to catch up?"

"I'm not taking accelerated classes."

"Not even one?"

"Why strain myself?"

He realized that Chris was no brain by any means.

They pulled into the school parking lot and Scott parked toward the end of a row. He had been keeping his vehicle in full view of traffic in case Joe decided to pull another stunt like he did with his lugnuts. He looked down at the front wheel as he got out. The locking lugnuts had cost a lot, but his life was worth it.

Just before they got to the administrative office Preston saw Scott as he came down the hall with Chris, and turned to walk with him.

Casey had been taking up almost all of Preston's free time these last several weeks. It was odd timing, it seemed. Right when he wanted to start executing his plan to get Scott, Casey started pouring on the charm.

Casey had decided that the only way to get Preston to really open up to him was to be with him a lot more. So, he had changed his schedule at work so that it matched Preston's as much as possible. That gave him time to see him more often. He had Preston over to his house a lot and even had him stay for dinner with his family for the first time. Later, they had gone out on a real date for a change during the Thanksgiving weekend. It seemed that things were working out a lot better now even if Preston sometimes talked to him like he were an idiot. And their physical relationship had improved. Preston was totally willing to accommodate his desires. Preston loved it since he was getting more sex than he knew what to do with. In fact, he had been seeing so much of Casey that he almost forgot that the object of most of his desires had been Scott. Still though, he saw Scott every day in class, so he was always within visual range. His infatuation with Scott, while on hold, was still quietly smoldering.

Luckily for Preston, they had both gone to tutoring class twice in the last three weeks. But all conversations about what he had seen in the parking lot were on hold. Heck, he could barely keep up with Casey now, much less try to pursue anyone else. Besides, what use would it be to come out to Scott if he couldn't continue with the next step of his plan, which was to *have* him? Something inside him, this odd feeling he had for Scott, was still calling him to act. Soon. Very soon.

"Hey, Scott. Where're ya goin'?" Preston asked.

Scott pointed to Chris. "The admin office to enroll him."

Preston looked at Chris. "You new?"

"Yeah."

"He's the brother of a friend of mine. He just moved here from way up north," Scott offered.

Chris raised an eyebrow. "Friend?"

Scott elbowed him in the side. Chris attempted to scoot out of the way but was unsuccessful. Preston wondered what that was all about.

"Sophomore?" Preston asked.

"*Junior.*"

"You won't make any friends if you keep up that attitude," Scott said. He was surprised to hear himself sound like that, but Chris was trying to be obnoxious. They reached the administrative office and all three of them entered.

"Just show me who I have to talk to, huh?" Chris told Scott.

Scott took him to the counter and one of the admin staff took his transfer papers. Chris stood at the counter while Scott and Preston sat in the row of chairs that were along the wall and talked. Soon enough the topic came back around to Chris.

"So, why are you enrolling this guy, and so late in the school year?"

"He used to live with his grandma, but she died. Now he lives down here with Ryan and his uncle."

"Ryan has a brother?"

Scott wasn't thinking. *Shit, did I just say his name?* "How do know him?"

"I've known him since eighth grade. So have you."

Scott was totally confused.

Preston looked at him for a moment. "You're talking about Ryan Taylor, right?"

"No, not him. His last name's St. Charles. He's already graduated and he's from Crescent City."

"Way up by Oregon?"

"Yep. Same one."

Preston thought it was a long shot but attempted to put the pieces of the puzzle together anyway. "Does that Ryan drive a Mustang?"

"How did you know?" Maybe he knew his Ryan after all?

"I always remember cars with a Tyllas Nissan sticker on them."

Preston thought he was going to have a heart attack. In just a few seconds he had gone from not knowing who the boy was that Scott had kissed, to knowing the boy's full name and even meeting his brother! This was getting really, really interesting.

Scott's eyes darted back and forth to each of Preston's. How could he have identified Ryan's car out of the blue like that? Okay, so Preston noticed Tyllas Nissan stickers on cars. But when could he have possibly seen it and identified the driver as someone Scott knew? Was it that day Ryan dropped him off at school? If so, then that could make two people who had seen him that day. *Am I completely blind?* Of course, he didn't dare ask if Preston saw the kiss. A few minutes later, they both left Chris to continue his enrollment and went to their respective classes.

*Shit, I wonder how much he does know,* Scott asked himself.

*        *        *

Tower Road Drive-In was a fun spot virtually any night of the week. But on a Friday, it rocked. If he stayed long enough, Scott invariably saw at least a dozen people he knew. Tonight though, he wanted to only be with Ryan. He had been especially scrutinizing Ryan all evening. Something was different about him ever since he had come back from the funeral. He couldn't quite put his finger on it, but it was as if he were no longer happy about anything. He could tell the three times they talked on the phone this last week and the one time he saw him briefly at Faraday's on Wednesday. It seemed to have gotten worse as the week progressed.

Ryan only finished half of his burger then set the rest down. "I'm not going to UCLA." He regretted having said it like that, but he couldn't help himself.

Several thoughts ran through Scott's head just then. The first was that he had already sent his own application to UCLA last Tuesday. His school counselor had had one after all, had seen him in the hall, and had invited him back to her office so he could get it. Scott had forgotten all about the aborted conversation he had had with Ryan when they were coming home from the first gig on the Marine base. Ryan had been trying to tell Scott that UCLA might not be the best place for them to go together. Scott hadn't really been listening then anyway. And while Ryan had been gone, he had filled out the application and had sent all the requisite paperwork to their admissions office, along with a check. The second thought Scott had was that it suddenly meant that it was no longer predictable where he would be going either. He had figured he would automatically go wherever Ryan was going.

"You-you what? Why didn't you tell me?"

"I just did."

"What the hell am I supposed to do now?"

"You don't do anything."

"I mean about us. I'm supposed to go with you."

"You shouldn't. I tried to tell you before."

Scott felt he had been deliberately dealt a losing hand in a card game. "*What the fuck?*" he exclaimed.

The miscommunication was twofold. Nothing mattered anymore in Ryan's mind. Everything seemed to have taken on a meaningless tone ever since he exited the plane when they got back. He had even noticed his own mood swiftly degenerating as the week went by. What's more was that he didn't bother to tell Scott right now that he had already tried to tell him that UCLA wasn't the right place for both of them to attend together. He still hadn't gotten any of the information he had sent for from the other three schools, but UCLA was definitely out. There was a whole lot more going on inside him, too. He doubted having told Howard he was gay. He doubted it was a good idea to have Chris live in the same house with them. He doubted what he wanted to do with his life. His lower back had been hurting on and off for the last several days for no apparent reason. But it was worse. He doubted his relationship with Scott.

Muh's death was affecting him in ways he never could have predicted. All of his confusion doubled the feelings of insecurity and self-doubt he usually kept just at arm's length. And now, here he was in a public place with Scott wailing on him.

"I'll talk to you in the car. Just don't bitch at me here." He wanted to get home anyway since his back was starting to hurt again.

Scott could barely contain himself. First Ryan didn't want to have sex with him after his return. He was still uninterested in even making out, much less making up for lost time. Now, he was essentially saying that he wouldn't be going to college. What was next?

They got in the car and Ryan cranked the engine.

"What the hell is going on? Will you just tell me?" Scott asked.

Ryan refused to look at him. "I don't think it's gonna work out," he simply said. He didn't elaborate. He didn't want to. He felt completely worthless. And a new feeling was coming up when he finally looked at Scott. A feeling of dread. Intense, overwhelming fear and dread. He didn't know what that was all about, but knew he had to make it go away. The only way he could do that was to not see Scott just now. A sinking feeling overwhelmed Ryan at that moment, making his breath lurch. *Despair...spiral downward...love...no, death.*

Scott was instantly panicked. In fact, his mouth dropped open. "It will, I swear it will!" His normal calm demeanor had completely disappeared. Despite Ryan's mostly unpredictable moods, they hadn't indicated this at all.

"I'm not sure about anything anymore."

Scott was incredulous. "You can't do this to us!" He had no clue about the torment Ryan was feeling.

"Just let me take you home." Ryan winced as his back spasmed. Scott noticed and wondered what that was all about.

Scott wanted to tell him he would walk home. He hesitated though, as Ryan put the car into reverse. He thought he might say it, but decided he didn't need to help the situation deteriorate any more than it had so far. He figured that if he stayed cool and didn't say anything else that he might open up a bit. Maybe he was kidding? Was he just faking him out? If so, he was doing a pretty good job of it. He tried to keep his thoughts still, just trying to be with him without anything in the way, no words, none of his own frazzled emotions, nothing. It wasn't working.

A few minutes later, they arrived at Scott's house. Scott had carefully not said a word. When he pulled up in the driveway Scott hesitated before he got out. He looked at Ryan. Ryan didn't speak at first, waiting for Scott to say something. But Scott was waiting for him.

"I'm sorry. I just don't feel anything is right anymore," Ryan finally said. It was as cryptic as it could be.

Scott was almost too numb to understand any of it. Things seemed to be in slow motion as he got out of the car. Everything was going badly all around right now, what with Barry still not telling the band what his decision might be; Joe's harassment was going to be worse at any moment, and now this.

He stood there, unbelieving, while Ryan backed down the driveway and took off. Shakaiyo was in the house and he saw her at the sliding glass door. Seeing her usually made him feel good no matter what his mood, but the numbness was getting worse and she wasn't the antidote he needed just now.

He didn't bother to get her as he simply went in and sat on his bed. He sat there in the dark and in the silence. It was the first time in a very long time he hadn't immediately turned on some music when he entered his bedroom. It was disturbing listening to the quiet. He sat there, not thinking for almost two minutes. Things had gotten way too serious way too fast about everything. His tranquil world and relatively simple responsibilities were evaporating. Everything was different and he didn't like it at all.

Then it started. He picked up his small pillow and pressed it against his face. The first tears dropped to his lap before it even got that far. He angrily tossed it across the room. It smacked into his chair, which caused it to crash into his desk quite loudly, startling him with the sudden noise. Before he knew it, he was laying face down on his other pillow so it would muffle the sound. His throat constricted and his entire body shook as he let it out. It had been a very, very long time since he had cried like this or felt this way.

Saturday morning Scott barely heard the phone ring due to having cranked up his stereo quite loudly. The louder the music was the better, since it was the only way he could study successfully when he was by himself. He pressed the amplifier remote's mute button, then pressed the phone's on button. He was sure it would be Ryan calling to apologize for last night. It wasn't.

"Hey, Scott?"

"Mr. St. Charles?"

"Yeah, it's me. I was hoping you could tell me something."

"Something."

"Good try, but this is serious. Have you noticed that Ryan is acting a little, how should I say, odd lately?"

"You noticed?"

"So, it's true."

"Yeah, he's a complete asshole." He didn't care if Howard didn't like his choice of words. He expected Ryan to get on the phone any minute now to apologize.

"More than the normal asshole that he is?"

"More. Why, did he do something to you?"

"No. He's been lethargic ever since he came back from the funeral. He's barely eaten all week. Chris said he came in last night and went straight to his bedroom without saying a word to him. That, in itself, is unusual. And he wouldn't get out of bed this morning. He said his back was hurting him."

"He said he doesn't want me to go to UCLA with him. He even said *he's* not going. What the hell is going on with him?"

"I was hoping you might tell me."

Scott tapped his pencil while he bit his lip. He had to tell him. "There's more. I doubt he's said anything about it either."

"Let's have it."

"He's tried to commit suicide before. Several times. You know his so-called 'car accident'?"

"Oh, boy. Yeah?"

"That was the most recent attempt."

Scott heard Howard exhale loudly. "The signs are all there then."

"What signs?"

"Depression. I figure that's it, but I'm not a doctor. And if he's tried to kill himself then I have to take this seriously and get him some professional help. I'll make some inquiries and see if I can find someone."

"Wait! I've got a name already. I can give you his number."

"Why do you just happen to have the name of a therapist?"

Scott told him why. Howard took down the name and phone number and thanked him.

"Mr. St. Charles." He hesitated before he found the right words. "I-I don't want him to be all screwed up."

"Not to worry. I'll call their office tomorrow." He heard Scott's unsteady breathing. "Scott?"

"Yeah?"

"I figure that was supposed to be secret. But, I'm glad you told me. You're a good guy, you know that?"

"Thanks."

"I'm not just saying that. I know you guys mean a lot to each other."

Scott's chin trembled. "Yeah, he does to me."

Howard said goodbye.

Studying was out of the question now. Scott was far too agitated to keep his mind on calculus. He'd have to see Annette this week despite making relatively decent grades now in class. At first, he had been worried about his ability to keep up but now was somewhat happy with his C average. Nonetheless, he'd call Preston and see if he wouldn't mind him coming over. The weather hadn't turned all that cool just yet, he could use a dip in the pool, and Preston was a friendly face he would love to see soon, especially since Ryan was being so bizarre recently.

# CHAPTER 11

Scott was still pissed off about Ryan as he drove over to Preston's house. Ryan had refused to return his calls all weekend and Howard wasn't being all that helpful. Last night, he said that Ryan was going to have his first session with Dr. McGinnis today and would most likely call him either tonight or later this week. That was an ambiguous as it could be as far as he was concerned, so he didn't bother to be home tonight in case he 'might' call.

Luckily, Preston was the light-hearted one in the midst of all this seriousness. He had talked with him three times in the hallway today. And Preston was much more friendly than normal in class. He had been especially animated, and there was a lot of eye contact. Because of that, Scott was going to find out once and for all whether he was gay. Maybe he was unconsciously being drawn to gay boys and just didn't know it. After all, he only started figuring out who might be several months back with Ryan.

Preston greeted him at the door, which indicated they were by themselves. That was good, Scott thought. With Rosa out of the picture, he would have plenty of time to find out as much as he could and ask 'the question'. Preston was barefoot, wearing a tank top and swim trunks. He was looking especially delicious.

"I have to get my stuff. Come on up," Preston said as he led the way. Scott tried to avoid staring at the back of his smooth tanned legs but couldn't help himself. He noticed how distinct his calves looked. *I worked hard for my calves, and he's not even a runner,* he mused.

Preston led him through the back hallway where Scott briefly checked out some of the pictures along each wall. They went up the stairs to the second floor. This was the first time he'd seen Preston's bedroom. He observed a queen-sized bed with the ornate metal headboard, a big walk-in closet, a private bath, a desk with a computer and printer on it, and a tall bookcase with a couple of rows of books in it. Two of the walls had been painted yellow and the other two were a more muted mustard color. He thought that painting two adjacent walls one color and the other two another was a brilliant idea, and thought to do it himself in his bedroom. There was nothing in the room to indicate that Preston might be gay, he thought, as he looked around. There wasn't even a poster on any of the walls to indicate which famous personalities or bands he liked. There was just the usual school memorabilia scattered throughout. Preston grabbed his backpack from the foot of the bookcase and they started down the back stairs to the patio.

Scott had noticed on his second trip over that the fence surrounding the yard was quite high. High enough so that none of the neighbors could possibly see anyone in the pool. The patio was completely isolated from either of the neighbor's views because of the L-shape that the house made to the left. That made for perfect privacy and Scott was sure that Preston had done his share of swimming in the nude.

Scott had his swim trunks on under his shorts this time. They stopped by the patio table and Preston placed his backpack on it. He pulled off his tank top and glasses. Scott pulled his shorts off after kicking off his sandals. Preston was watching his every move. Scott noted that. *Strike three, Preston.* He wondered how he would ask the question now. He wanted to make it dramatic when he did.

They splashed around in the water for a while when Preston made his announcement. "Hey, wanna skinny-dip? No one's around."

That was the moment Scott figured might happen. Asking the question would be totally easy now. He untied the string on his swim trunks, slipped them off, and slung them up on the edge of the pool. Preston stopped dead in the water. He didn't think Scott would just up and do that, and certainly not immediately.

"What're you waiting for?" Scott asked with a wide grin. He could play this game, too.

"Uh, nothing." Preston slid his trunks down and off. He wadded them up and slung them to the edge, too. *Scott is more of a god than I imagined. Now it's just a matter of seeing him up close.* Without his glasses, his vision was just bad enough to not be able to see Scott all that well right now. It disappointed him that he never wore contacts. But that issue was going to be moot in a few moments, he figured.

"Race ya!" Preston exclaimed.

"From where?"

Preston pointed and they waded to the shallow end. "Three laps, back and forth."

"All underwater?"

"No, you can breathe."

"Say when."

"On three."

They stood with the water up to their waists. The water's constant movement along with his own slightly bad vision made Scott's crotch a total blur as
they stood there. *Damn it*, Preston thought.

Scott, on the other hand, could see the top of Preston's firm, but not very
meaty, butt. *Nice*, he thought, *very nice*. Somehow, though, he managed to contain himself enough to not stare too much.

Preston counted to three and they took off. At the completion of the third
lap, Scott was wiping his hair back from his forehead while Preston was still
catching his breath. In the shallow end the water only went up to his navel.

Preston boldly waded over to Scott and stood right in front of him. Scott's
meter pegged to maximum and stayed there. It was dizzying. Preston was good
looking, they were naked, and no one was home. The inevitable was next.

He was right. Preston simply reached his hand down to Scott's crotch and
touched him right there in the water. No waiting, no pretense about it. Scott
didn't even jump since he expected it. Preston reached out, grabbed Scott by
the waist, and pressed their bodies together. Scott was hard in seconds. Preston,
on the other hand was feeling nervous even as he was doing it. He had
dreamed of this moment for months. It had been a part of so many of his fantasies that it seemed almost unreal that it was now actually happening. He was
so surprised that he had been this bold that it kept him from getting hard right
away. But as soon as he felt Scott's hard penis pressing up against his crotch, he
finally swelled to full hardness. Preston now had Scott's butt cheeks in each
hand. His boldness had always worked for him and it was paying dividends
right this second.

Scott figured Preston would at least have tried to kiss him on the lips but he
seemed to be avoiding that. He leaned in to Preston, but for some reason
couldn't quite bring himself to do it either. While they placed gentle kisses all
over each other's pecs, shoulders, and necks, he realized he was cheating on
Ryan. His next thought wiped that one out a split second later. Ryan had totally
withdrawn and Scott was not only angry with him, he was feeling lonely as well
as horny. And Preston's flirting had indeed been exactly what he thought it
was. In a way, though, he was surprised since Preston was so unassuming at all
other times.

No words needed to be exchanged. Preston pulled back only enough to
massage Scott's penis. Scott did the same. It was a completely different shape
and feel from Ryan's. It had less of a curve, was shorter than either Ryan's or his
own, and was dangerously thick. As he massaged it, Preston leaned in and

started sucking on Scott's left nipple. It was as if an electric current went through Scott's body. The waves of pleasure that shot through him were relentless. Despite having relieved himself several times this week, that was exactly what did it for him. He gritted his teeth to help stifle his moans. He didn't want to make any noise that the neighbors might hear. It happened far more quickly than Scott anticipated: the point of no return. Scott's soft moaning reverberated against Preston's body.

*Holy shit! Scott came in my pool!* Preston was in heaven. Scott not only totally got into it, he had figured out exactly what turned him on in mere seconds.

Scott was finally able to open his eyes. He felt incredibly embarrassed. It had happened so fast he felt he had been under some sort of spell. Granted, he was usually a hair trigger anyway, but Preston had hardly begun.

Preston released his grip and pulled his hand up out of the water. Thin white strands clung to his fingers. He figured it was all over their legs, too. He knew what it was like since this wasn't the first time someone had come in the pool. Finally, someone else besides him had, too.

Scott quickly got over his embarrassment as he started working on Preston. He was so hard, it was as if he were handling a piece of fleshy steel. With his other hand, he gently kneaded Preston's scrotum. In another moment, Preston leaned back slightly as he shut his eyes and let out a series of quiet guttural sounds. Scott watched him grit his teeth. He then held his breath, stuck his face just under the surface, and opened his eyes. It was his first good look at his penis. Preston had both hands on Scott's shoulders, clutching his traps. Each squirt shot out fast, then quickly lost velocity as it hit the water. Scott's ears weren't under the surface so he could hear what sounded like gurgling from the back of Preston's throat. He had missed the first two squirts, but was able to count three forceful, then four weaker ones. White globs floated all around his hand, clinging to his knuckles, some sticking to Preston's belly, some to his pubes. It was a marvelous sight and one which Scott couldn't believe he was observing. But now it was over. He pulled his head up and took a deep breath.

"Come up to my bedroom," Preston whispered once he was able to catch his breath.

"Why?"

"Duh. Guess." Scott instantly understood him.

Preston waded to the steps at the shallow end. He hadn't lost much of his erection. Once the water had drained off them both they observed the white amorphous globs that clung to them here and there. Still mostly hard from excitement, they pulled the sticky residue from their groin and legs, then wiped themselves dry with towels. Scott grabbed his shorts, while Preston retrieved his, then his glasses from the patio table. Leaving two sets of slightly damp footprints up the back steps, they went into the bedroom.

Preston shut and locked his bedroom door using his quick one-motion technique. By the time they had gotten up there, they had lost most of their erections. But now, with their warm naked bodies pressed against each other again they both were pointing toward the ceiling.

Preston slowly eased Scott backward onto the bed. Scott sat down, then lay back. Preston knelt down and placed his legs onto his shoulders at the knees. He stood up, but not to full height, and pushed Scott's legs down against his chest. Scott held onto the backs of his thighs. He wasn't sure what Preston was up to at first, but another second later he found out. Preston found his belly on fire as he knelt in front of him and made Scott spread his legs apart a little bit more. He slowly but deliberately used his tongue where he knew Scott was most sensitive. *Red hair here, too. A ring of fire,* Preston thought. *Burn him up.*

Scott felt intoxicated at the sensation. The next thing he knew Preston had reached up to work on his penis at the same time. He was enveloped in the pleasurable feeling of Preston's tongue pressing against him, lapping, stopping, then starting again, the occasion poke inside, and the steady slow rhythm on his dick.

The pressure built up almost as quickly as before. Three minutes later, with hardly a moment of rest, he unloaded again. He was so scrunched up from holding his legs up that a blob smacked against his right cheek. Another one hit his neck and another his right pectoral just below his nipple.

Preston stayed still as he listened to Scott moan. He could feel the contractions against his tongue. He pressed it harder, trying to get as far as he could inside him. Scott moaned even louder. He counted seven long moans before Scott's body started to relax. Scott was finally able to catch his breath as he released his legs.

Preston leaned over between Scott's legs and started rapidly beating off. Scott alternately watched Preston's face and his penis as three spurts shot out in rapid succession. Then half a dozen little droplets landed all over his abdomen. Preston's penis finally went somewhat limp, sticking out straight ahead of his body. He dropped to his back on the bed beside Scott as they both rested.

Scott realized right then that their friendship would never be the same. His classmate had chosen an odd, but certainly exciting way, to come out to him. It was at that moment that he realized exactly how to interpret the constant signals he'd been picking up. All the subtle clues were carefully logged and categorized in his mind. *The next time my radar goes off, even slightly, I'm going to know exactly what's going on.*

*          *          *

It had taken a little effort on Howard's part last night: twenty minutes of escalated haranguing and a threat to kick Ryan out this morning after he said he wasn't going. But he finally gave in. Now they were in Howard's car on their way to see the psychologist. Howard wasn't about to let Ryan go by himself or even drive his own car. "You're lucky I'm in good with the boss," he said. "He's being very accommodating allowing you to be late for work this morning. And me, too."

Ryan tried to deflect the real reason why he was being taken to see Dr. McGinnis, but only half-heartedly cared what it meant about his current mental state. "I told you, my back is killing me."

"Did you take more ibuprofen?"

"Yes, but it hasn't done any good."

They drove in silence for another minute before Howard decided to tell him. "I know about the suicide attempts." He figured he shouldn't say anything else until they got to the doctor's office.

Ryan glanced at his uncle. He was embarrassed about that, but felt so worthless right now that he didn't want to talk about it. Scott had called a number of times over the weekend. He wondered if that's when he divulged it to Howard. As far as he knew, Howie had never known anything about that. Ryan hadn't called Scott back and had been alternately angry with himself about it, or feeling just numb to everything that was going on around him. He didn't know what he was feeling right now. Nonetheless, a little anger again peeked through. *Fucking Scott.*

The office building was located in the town of Joshua Tree in an unassuming one-story building several blocks off Highway 62. Once through the front door, they saw the names of three doctors listed in the lobby's entryway. The woman sitting behind the window at the far end of the quiet waiting room smiled warmly as she pushed the little glass door aside. Howard signed in. Five minutes later, after he had Ryan fill out all the forms, and sign where required, they were called down the hallway.

Dr. McGinnis's office was cozy and inviting. Ryan was motioned to the plush comfortable couch. Two overstuffed leather chairs were opposite it. A low glass coffee table sat in the center of the arrangement. Howard sat next to him and Dr. McGinnis took a seat in one of the chairs. Ryan surveyed the room. A small desk was in one corner and another wall had two bookcases filled with books. Three walls were paneled with dark wood. The room reminded Ryan of a well-appointed study. The fourth wall framed three tall picture windows that looked out over a private courtyard. It enclosed a small slice of highly landscaped desert flora. It was more than a continuation of what surrounded Yucca Valley since it contained a miniature waterfall and a curious selection of bonsai trees. Ryan could hear the water running over rocks from somewhere and wondered briefly if it were real or if there were speakers piping the sound in. He took one of the little pillows off the couch and placed it on his lap.

Dr. McGinnis was thirty-three years old, had wavy dark brown hair parted on one side, and well defined facial features. He was a very pleasant man to look at, or so Ryan thought. He was dressed in khaki dress pants, a black pullover shirt, and wore highly polished black loafers.

From San Luis Obispo originally, Dr. McGinnis had received his Ph.D. years previous, and had opened his practice four years ago. He didn't exactly consider himself a beginner, despite the short amount of time he had had his practice, but he nonetheless didn't consider himself an expert just yet either.

Despite his dour mood, Ryan felt attracted to him. That in itself seemed good and bad. He thought he'd end up seeing someone who was old and gray. But instead of being turned completely off, his interest was there now as he checked out Dr. McGinnis' nicely proportioned body and trim outline in his casual clothing.

They went through the usual introductions and the doctor took the short silence that followed to get started. He directed his statement to Ryan.

"Thank you for coming today and for being on time. Being punctual is important. For this session, I'd just like to get to know you and find out the nature of the issues you feel you have. Don't feel as though you have to say anything more than you're comfortable with today." Dr. McGinnis then looked at Howard. "Any questions before we begin?"

Both Ryan and Howard shook their heads.

"Okay," Dr. McGinnis said. "First off, I rarely go by Dr. McGinnis. Dr. Kevin will do just fine. I don't like to be too formal despite what my office looks like. The paneling was already here when we moved in," he said, then pointed to one of the walls.

Ryan chalked one up for the guy. He was professional, but was certainly not a dickwad. He wasn't expecting that at all.

"Ryan, you want to begin?"

Howard leaned back a bit, trying to get a little more comfortable. Ryan was tied up in knots despite his initial liking of Dr. Kevin.

"I don't have much to say." He winced as his lower back went into a spasm.

Dr. Kevin noted that, but wasn't quite sure what it indicated just yet. "You can start with why you're here."

Ryan tilted his head toward Howard. "He hauled me over here."

Howard took a deep breath then started. "His grandmother died recently. Now he's moping around the house, won't get up to go to work on time and his, uh, his friend told me that he's attempted suicide a number of times."

Ryan was alarmed that he just out and said it. *Damn it. Did he have to tell him that?*

Kevin responded. "Sounds like it's been a difficult period for you."

Ryan looked first at his uncle then back to his lap. There was a long silence. "That was a long time ago."

Dr. Kevin spoke. "What was?"

He still wouldn't look up at Kevin. "I haven't tried to kill myself for a long time."

Howard spoke up again. "Last May he wrecked his car on purpose. Totaled it."

"On purpose," Kevin stated.

Ryan thought about how to respond. He took a while again to say anything. "I don't know," he said now looking up at him. He decided he didn't like Dr. Kevin after all.

Despite wanting to know them better before he began, Kevin had some initial impressions about this case. Ryan was displaying classic symptoms he had dealt with before. Of course, there was a lot more to delve into, but he was already aware of some things he needed to focus on.

"Is there anything else you want to tell me before I ask you to the waiting room, Mr. St. Charles?"

"I think he's depressed. But that's why he's here. To get a proper diagnosis. That's all I want to add."

"Thanks." He noted that Howard was indeed correct in his assessment.

Howard rose up, briefly touched Ryan's shoulder, and closed the door behind him as he left. Ryan felt a lot more comfortable now that he had left the room. He squeezed the little pillow in his lap.

"So, Ryan, do you feel depressed?" That much was obvious from Ryan's demeanor. His slow replies had already told him that, too. He would get to the real serious issues later. Right now though, he wanted to see how much Ryan was willing to talk.

"I-I don't care about anything anymore."

"Overwhelmed?"

"Yeah, I guess."

"When did your grandmother die?"

"Two weeks ago."

"What happened to her?"

"I killed her."

*That's unlikely*, Kevin thought. "You want to tell me about that?"

"I was here when it happened. My brother found her."

Kevin had to coax it out, but Ryan explained everything to him. Once he finished relating his perspective of her death to him Kevin had a much better understanding of where Ryan was coming from. It seemed simple enough so far. Ryan blamed himself for her death and felt guilty about it. He would get to the bottom of that one shortly.

"How long did your grandmother take care of you?"

"Almost eight years. My little brother and I lived with her after my parents died." He winced as his lower back spasmed again.

"What was that?"

"My back. It hurts like hell."

Kevin was well aware of the many and varied somatic responses people had when they felt depressed.

"Our work together may provide you with relief for your back."

Ryan wondered if Dr. Kevin had some drugs he could get for it. He shifted positions on the couch a little.

"So, how did your parents die?"

Ryan gave him the details, which took a while. Kevin made notes as Ryan talked, noting that his patient's eyes were showing emotion he seemed to be trying to keep at bay.

"And you had to be strong about it, huh?"

"I had to. For Chris." Ryan's eyes went from red to teary. A couple of them slowly rolled down his cheeks. He made no move to wipe them away.

Kevin watched a tear drop from his cheek. "Are you trying not to cry?"

Ryan didn't look up. He rubbed his forehead in a failed attempt to hide his obvious emotion. Kevin handed him a tissue from the box at his left. Ryan took it, sniffled, and wiped his cheek. He continued to clutch the semi-wet tissue.

"You want to talk about it?"

"There's nothing to say."

"Sure there is. For starters, how did your parents treat you?"

"They hated us."

"Hate is a pretty strong word."

"Well they did. They fought all the time and sent me to my room for no reason."

"Tell me about that."

"My dad traveled a lot for his work. He did some kind of insurance adjusting. I don't remember exactly. Whenever he was home, he would get angry about something with my mother. They would argue and when we would ask them to stop, my dad would tell us to shut up and go to our room. I spent a lot of time there."

"How did that make you feel?"

"He didn't love me." Ryan hadn't said that before.

"Hmm. He didn't love you."

"He made me go away when they were angry with each other." Ryan tried to swallow the lump in his throat. "I just wanted to be near him when he was home, but he wouldn't let me most of the time. So, what would you think?"

"What do you think?" Dr. Kevin was surprised this was proceeding so rapidly. He didn't expect Ryan to start out with this kind of dialog at all.

"I think he hated me and I think that my mother just went along with it. That's what I think."

"And your grandmother? Did she hate you, too?"

Ryan's chin was quivering now. "No...she...loved me." Tears filled his eyes again. Two fell to his lap.

"You loved her, too?"

"Of course I loved her." Ryan was angry again.

That was a good sign, Kevin realized. Depressed patients usually didn't experience anger, especially during an initial session. "Why are you angry about that?"

"Because I didn't-I didn't tell her before she died."

From what little Kevin had gathered so far, he was already beginning to form some conclusions. Ryan was the older of two boys, his parents had both died when he was young, and they had essentially emotionally abandoned him before that. But their deaths were a physical reminder of the initial emotional abandonment. Now Ryan was transferring those feelings associated with that abandonment to his grandmother who had been his surrogate caregiver. In addition, he appeared to feel tremendously guilty about her death and felt traumatized about being abandoned by her now.

Dr. Kevin was beginning to see that due to the chaotic and apparently unstable home life Ryan seemed to have endured, one of the issues facing him was not having been connected to a source of emotional strength during his formative years. He knew that for a boy to achieve a healthy dose of self-worth, an early connection to a consistent empathic parental figure was essential. That appeared to be have been interrupted. His grandmother most likely took over that role, but she wasn't male. And Ryan seemed to have needed that most of all. There was most likely a whole lot more going on.

"She was there for you, wasn't she?"

"Yeah. But Mom and Dad never were," he spat. "I *hated* sitting in my room waiting for them to let me out. I *hated* them fighting so much. I *hated* that when they let me out that they wouldn't talk to me."

"Wouldn't talk to you?"

"I would ask them if they were okay and neither would ever tell me anything. So, I never knew when they were or weren't okay. I always had to figure it out, and I was mostly wrong. And then they would either lie to me, tell me to shut up, or send me back to my room. They hated me!"

Kevin was seeing a pattern. Ryan's parents had obviously been disturbed. Clearly, they took a great deal of it out on him. Perhaps he had been lucky they died when they did. He may have been spared a lot more emotional damage because of it.

"It's possible they didn't like themselves. And they clearly didn't take care of each other. Sounds like they took it out on you."

Ryan clutched the pillow tightly as anger spread throughout his body. He started to feel extremely hot and began to sweat. Maybe they hated each other? He was totally confused now. "Why didn't they just get a divorce?"

"Maybe they were on their way."

Now he was seething with anger. He had never heard it put this way before and was surprised. "So, I got *punished* for *their* problems? Fucking assholes!"

Any form of punishment, however light, unconsciously reminded him of being sent to his room as a child. It had been that way as long as he could remember. It wasn't about the punishment as such, but rather how he felt about it. Being alone, with no one to talk to was what had started it. And now, in this setting, he remembered the first time he had been sent to his room for merely asking how his father was. The feeling of confusion was the worst. All he had done was ask if they were still fighting. The feeling of being thrust aside and ignored, had compounded his feeling of isolation. The continual feeling of being worthless, like he didn't matter, seemed to come up a lot for him back then. He fought desperately for his father's attention, but when he got it, he got punished.

Kevin kept the rest of the session much lighter. He had already gotten his diagnostic impression based on Ryan's speech patterns, his body language, and the way he had responded to his questions. He wanted to know about Ryan's background so asked about Crescent City, going to school up there, and how he liked it down here in the high desert. "For the record I have to ask you a few other questions."

"Like what?"

"Are you doing any drugs?"

"No."

"What's kept you from them?" He was well aware that some depressed patients used alcohol or other drugs in an attempt to relieve their symptoms.

"I've done some, but they're for burnouts."

"What about marijuana?"

"I've smoked pot."

"How about now?"

"Not recently. My b…I have a friend who doesn't like it." He almost said it but caught himself.

"Alcohol?"

"I drink. My uncle doesn't need to know about that."

"How much?"

"Just a little. Like everyone else."

Kevin leveled his eyes at him, testing his honesty, but could tell that Ryan didn't seem to have the signs of addiction.

"I swear. Just every once in a while."

The fifty minutes were up much faster than Ryan had anticipated and he decided that he liked Dr. Kevin again by the end of the session.

Kevin wrote down more notes. "I'm going to the office next door to talk with my colleague. Her name's Dr. Maine. She's our psychiatrist and can authorize the prescriptions I think you'll need for a while. I'll see if she'll script a muscle relaxer for your back, and I think you would benefit from an anti-depressant. I would also recommend warm baths with Epsom salt for at least a week, and a couple of massages so you can get some relief. Ever heard of Prozac?"

"No."

"It's the anti-depressant. Most people find it quite helpful. It has minimal side effects. It takes a few weeks to get established in your system so I'll want you to take it regularly. My job is to make sure you get properly taken care of, okay?"

Ryan nodded his head.

Howard knew not to ask any questions when Ryan came out to the waiting room. Dr. Kevin consulted with Dr. Maine and a few minutes later both Ryan and Howard were called into her office. Dr. Kevin shook their hands and went back into his office.

While Ryan was next door, Kevin made his first post-session notes in his new patient folder. His first thoughts were that it's too bad this good looking kid had had such a horrendously dysfunctional family. Nonetheless, he hoped Ryan would provide all the information he needed to help nudge him back to being a happy smiling young adult. It usually worked, except that one time, which he still felt somewhat guilty about. It was the regret at not having been able to properly treat Ted that had made him stick with it. Ryan wouldn't be his second disaster.

Dr. Maine, an older woman, with nicely coiffed white hair, and wearing a two-piece gray dress, ushered them in where they took a seat in front of her desk. She smiled a lot, and seemed genuine, which put Ryan completely at ease. He inspected the wall behind her. It was filled with diplomas, certificates, and other awards.

She wrote out the prescriptions and explained the effects and side effects of the anti-depressant. He and Howard left a few minutes later. Their next stop was to have the prescriptions filled.

When they got to work, Howard made sure he watched Ryan take the anti-depressant. Not that he didn't think he would. He just wanted to make sure that his effort hadn't been wasted.

Later that night, as Ryan lay in bed, he listened to two crickets outside his window. One was close by and the other was some distance away. They seemed to be chirruping in some sort of bizarre syncopated rhythm that didn't quite work.

He thought about what he should be trying to accomplish in therapy. In a way, Frank back home reminded him a little of Dr. Kevin. But, he didn't allow himself to open up to Frank and wondered if it had been a big mistake after all. Slowly, but surely, he realized that he knew he would have to allow himself to trust his therapist. No more getting pissed off at people who were trustworthy. No more clamming up when he knew he should be open. Sad smiles, hurt feelings, confusing thoughts, and angry remarks needed to be a part of the past. Maybe it was time to trust those that were trying to help him. He could do it, despite his failures at doing so in the past. He just knew it.

But now he hated himself at how he was treating Scott. Scott was the most trustworthy person he had ever known and he couldn't bring himself to even talk to him.

There it was again. That feeling of intense dread every time he thought about him. It didn't make any sense. He couldn't fathom why he felt this way.

*Despair…spiral downward…love…no, death.*

With that, he pulled the sheet up to his face and pressed it against his eyes which had started to brim with tears. *Please don't die, Scott. Please don't die*, he thought. He had no idea why he thought Scott was next.

# CHAPTER 12

Casey sat at Preston's desk while he showered. Preston was particular about his privacy in the shower, so he had no intention of joining him. He was odd like that, Casey thought. *Just like he's odd about so many things.*

Preston's computer had been running when Casey had arrived about a half hour previous. The word processing program was up on the screen. Casey absentmindedly inspected the last several lines on the monitor. Preston had been writing a paper for English and was typing the last page when Casey came over. After they had had sex on Preston's floor he had upped and jumped into the shower. Casey hadn't even attempted to put his clothes on yet. If Preston wanted him to leave in a hurry and Casey wanted to linger and be with him instead, it would invariably make him angry. He wanted to see if this would piss him off, too.

He looked down at his dark blonde pubes. The head of his penis was touching the seat. A drop of semen was oozing out. It would be his little 'gift' for Preston to sit on later. The translucent drop was making its way out. There. As it liquefied, it spread out slowly like a drop of honey.

The desk drawer was opened slightly, inviting him to look. He pulled it open slowly and looked at all the items. A couple of pens and pencils. A protractor laying next to a metal ruler. A large eraser with both ends used. Several other miscellaneous items were scattered throughout. But what was that toward the back corner? It looked like a stack of Polaroids wrapped in a rubber band. The stack was upside down. His interest was piqued.

The shower was still running.

He pulled the stack out. It looked like there were a dozen and half pictures wrapped up. He turned it over and was immediately captivated by the image in the first one. He pulled the rubber band off and started looking through them.

He had no idea who the boy with the dark red hair was, but was nonetheless enamored. He was cute as hell with those thick thighs, the killer smile, those

135

rosy cheeks, and the cute swim trunks. Wet as they were, they clung to him very nicely. *What a butt,* he thought as he continued to sort through them. But the setting of the pictures disturbed him. They were all taken in or around Preston's pool. The last one had a date written on it in pen. *Hmm, weekend before last. This year? And who is this boy?*

He sorted through them one more time. One had the redhead sitting in one of the chairs at the patio table. There were two schoolbooks laying in the background on the table. One was closed. He tilted the photo slightly so he could read it better. Introduction to Calculus. There was a backpack and a couple of glasses of soda in the background on top of the patio table as well. *He must be one of Preston's classmates.* He looked over at the bookshelf. There it was, the same book from the photo. *So, it was last weekend.* He reached over to pick up the book and opened it to a page where a folded piece of notebook paper was. It was a sheet of problems worked out in pencil in Preston's handwriting. In small cursive letters between two problems in the textbook he saw a single sentence. It was distinct enough to determine that it was in Preston's handwriting, too. It said 'Scott Faraday is a god'. *Scott Faraday?* He had never heard that name before. But what was worse though was the intense feeling of jealousy he felt upon reading it.

On the top shelf of the bookcase were three yearbooks. It was only a hunch, but he just had to know. He quickly pulled off the most recent one, thumbed through the index, and found the name almost immediately. He turned to the first of three pages that indicated where Scott's picture could be found. It was his junior class picture. He compared one of the Polaroids to the yearbook picture, and sure enough, they matched. The hair and cute-as-hell smile were the key indicators to his identity. At least he knew who the boy was.

He put both books back on their respective shelves, took the top photo off the stack, and wrapped the rest back up in the rubber band. He stuffed the photo into a pocket of his pants, which still lay in a heap on the floor.

The shower stopped running just as he put the photos back in the drawer, in the exact spot he had found them, upside down. He pretended now he had been doing nothing but reading the computer screen when Preston came out of the bathroom. He had the towel across his back, drying it off. There was a touch of anger in his voice. "Will you get dressed?"

*Poor Preston,* Casey thought. *Not even a hint of a hug or a kiss from him?* Casey desperately wanted to roll around on the bed with him. What he would give to feel Preston's body so close, so warm. He wanted to whisper in his ear. He wanted to kiss Preston until they were both hard again. He wanted to sleep with him. Just once. They'd done virtually everything except sleep together. He wanted Preston to tell him he loved him. But it was never like any of that.

Being the nice guy that he was, he sighed and merely responded, "Sure. No problem, P."

✶        ✶        ✶

Scott was faced with an odd dilemma. Day before yesterday he had had sex with his friend completely unexpectedly, twice. It was so hot and so fast he couldn't believe it. And now Preston had carefully been avoiding him in class yesterday and today. The same went for the couple of times he saw him in the hall. He knew why. He didn't want to talk to him either.

How strange, too. It was embarrassing and a relief at the same time. Embarrassing because he hadn't expected what had happened, and with someone he had known for all this time and only recently suspected. A relief since he had been fed up with having no sex.

Despite the awkwardness of what had changed for them both, Scott knew he had to have a talk with him, even if it was at school.

Scott spotted Preston in the lunchroom eating way off in the corner. *What an idiot. Does he think I won't find him?* He had a sack lunch with him and came up from behind. No one else had taken a place at the table yet. He figured that if he snuck up on him and immediately engaged him in a conversation he wouldn't leave in too big of a hurry. He sat opposite Preston in one quick motion, while setting his sack down.

"You could have just said something earlier," he immediately began.

Preston had just sunk his teeth into an apple. He almost choked on it. He had just looked back, hadn't seen Scott anywhere, and suddenly he had appeared, seemingly out of nowhere. He had been avoiding Scott for a very good reason. He was in his own quandary. If Scott were a new potential sexual partner, even occasionally, he wanted to make sure he was going to make the right decision if he told Casey to get lost. And what was to be his red-letter day forever was that the object of most of his fantasies had actually done it with him in his own house even! It had all been so totally unlike anything he had ever conjured up before.

"About what?" Preston replied.

Scott whispered. "About *what*? That you're gay. You didn't have to do it that way, you know."

Preston finished chewing, swallowed, then countered. "You didn't seem to mind." He put his apple down.

It was true. Preston's come-on was not something he could say no to. Starved for sexual attention, he couldn't help himself and simply gave in to whatever Preston had in mind. Besides, he had been suspicious for weeks. And he had seemed quite experienced in Scott's estimation. Plus, Ryan still hadn't bothered to return his phone messages, something which he was even more angry about now.

"You *still* could have said something first."

"I had to be sure," Preston lied.

"What a way to do that. But how did you know I would, you know, do it? I've never advertised to anyone that I'm gay."

Preston wasn't sure yet whether he should say anything about seeing The Kiss. So far, Scott hadn't said a word about having a boyfriend, so he wanted to avoid that topic at all costs. *If neither of us told the other, then what could be wrong with that?* Who could possibly get hurt if no one knew about the other's boyfriend? Especially if what they were going to be doing in the future was purely for fun.

"I can tell about other people. I don't know what it is, but I can tell," Preston offered.

*So, Preston has the same sort of radar. Maybe it's only gay people that have it,* Scott thought. Still, he had no idea it would lead to them having sex just like that. He figured there would have been an excited conversation, a revelation of some kind that would lead them to being closer friends. But Preston's initiation had shifted them from being just friends to sexual partners. "I knew about you, too.

"I knew the second time I came over to your house."

"How?" Preston wondered.

"I can tell, just like you. Besides, who took all those pictures? That tipped me off."

Preston had looked through the pictures just last night after Casey had left. Somehow, his favorite one was missing. He knew he shouldn't have put them in his desk, but rather in his locked box in the closet where the rest of his 'chestposé' was. He had dumped the entire drawer out looking for it, had looked in every book he had touched in the last couple of days, moved his computer, looked under the bed with a flashlight, and had pulled the duvet, the pillows, and every sheet off his bed in his search. He still couldn't find it. The stack was secure in the box now where they should have been in the first place.

"I'd like them if you don't mind," Scott said.

"I don't think so. They're mine. Besides, you got some."

Preston's heart was beating rapidly. He felt terribly possessive about the photos, especially for the lost one. Regardless of whether they were innocuous pictures of Scott, they were pictures of his one and only god and he was going to keep them.

"Fuck it. But you're not taking any more of me."

Preston didn't mind. He now had in his possession the best photos he had ever had of him. He also had the mental image of his tongue in the very place he had always wanted it, his hand on the exact place he had dreamed about for months, and a spot on his duvet that, despite his annoyance of it being there, was from Scott. He wished he could touch it even now and felt himself starting to get hard just thinking about it.

Later that afternoon, after calculus class was over, Scott waited by Chris' locker. The freshman lockers were several wings over from his and he had to make a special trip to get there. Less than a minute later Chris and a new friend of his came up. Chris acknowledged Scott's presence, then looked embarrassed as his friend stood there with him.

"Chris," Scott said.

Chris opened the locker. "What?" He gave a furtive glance back to his friend. He was sure Alex would be able to tell that Scott was gay and the association would instantly rub off onto him.

"What's up with Ryan? Why isn't he calling me?"

"I told you he's weird," he whispered.

"Yeah, yeah, so he's weird. But he can use a phone can't he? And why are you whispering?"

Chris used a normal tone of voice now. "He knows you called. I gave him the message last night."

"Tell him I can't wait all freakin' week, huh?"

"I'll tell him again." He pulled out the book for his next class, then shut the locker. "I gotta go, okay?"

Scott knew he couldn't keep using Chris as a courier. Nonetheless, he hoped he would at least relay this one last message for him. "Yeah. I do, too," Scott said as they left in separate directions.

*　　　　　*　　　　　*

Ryan lay on top of the sheet in his bed in the dark that night. It was just past eleven-thirty and the house was quiet. His back was beginning to feel a lot better now that he had been taking the muscle relaxers. The hot bath tonight helped as well. The psychiatrist had said the anti-depressant wouldn't kick in for a couple of weeks, and he wondered why he was even taking it if that were the case.

His sleep patterns were completely off. He had been waking up at all hours of the night for the last week, falling asleep in the first place was turning into a random event, and he had slept for over ten hours at a time last weekend. At least his back had nearly quit hurting. That had been the second worst part.

The worst part was that his experience of being horny all the time had just about disappeared. He noticed it shortly after they had gotten to Crescent City. It was most obvious when he saw Scott the day they had returned. It got continually worse as the week progressed. Now he had next to no interest in sex. He wasn't used to that and it disturbed him. He had tried masturbating earlier and had gotten hard, but after a good twenty minutes of stimulating himself every way he could think of it just didn't feel good and he quit. He had no idea it was even possible to give up on beating off.

He felt terrible about how he'd been treating Scott. He hadn't bothered to call him back yet. Scott had been talking to Howard instead. He had heard them on the phone several times now. Chris had even slipped notes under his door yesterday and today. They simply said, 'Call Scott!' He hadn't. That was about to change.

He pulled on some underwear and went to the kitchen. The cord was long enough to reach the back deck. Even though it was late, he felt that he should at least tell Scott he was alive. He was very quiet now as he dialed Scott's number, then went out on the deck and slid the door shut behind him. The cord wiggled as he slid down on his haunches, his back against the warm outside wall.

*It was a labyrinth of wet and slime. Every time Scott turned right someone laughed. Every time he turned left someone screamed. It was getting louder and louder. Should he stand still? What if he backtracked? If he went to the beginning and started over again he would be able to follow the route perfectly. The jeering started when he took a wrong turn a little way back. Maybe if he asked for a guide? He was allowed a guide, wasn't he? Another left turn. The screaming was even louder now. Maybe he wasn't allowed a guide after all. Another scream. That was weird. Simply thinking about that caused the screaming this time. Maybe if he quite thinking and felt his way through with his eyes closed and his ears plugged up…*

The ringing woke Scott up. This late at night, it had to be a wrong number and he was ready to give the caller a piece of his mind. He put the phone to his ear. "What!"

"It's me," Ryan said quietly after he returned the phone to his ear. He knew Scott wouldn't be happy about being woken up like that.

"Ryan!" Scott sat up.

"I'm sorry I'm calling you so late, but I haven't been feeling so good lately."

Scott wasn't thinking clearly. The strong feelings the dream had stirred up were still with him. "I'm not feeling so good myself. You killed my chance to be with you. You killed *us!*" He hadn't meant it to come out with such anger but it did.

Ryan shut his eyes tightly. The way Scott said it stung. "You don't understand."

Scott hadn't been listening when he had told him weeks previous. Ryan had tried to explain it but Scott hadn't been in the mood to hear him. Perhaps he shouldn't have said anything then, but it was on his mind. Nonetheless, Scott didn't understand, and here he was complaining about it again.

Scott was faced with quite the predicament. Should he say anything about having been with Preston? *No way.* "You said you didn't want me with you."

"I didn't mean it that way."

"Then why did you say it? Was it another joke like when you lied to me about Little Trout?"

*Fuck,* Ryan thought. That lie was in the past, like all the other lies he'd told. And now, Scott dragged it up to haunt him. No, to taunt him. "Please Scott. I swear it's not that way." To be sure, he wasn't being forceful enough about the point he wanted to make. He simply didn't have the energy to explain himself better. And he was beginning to feel extremely fearful again. Just talking with Scott was doing it.

Scott wasn't convinced and wondered whether he should just hang up. But hadn't Ryan reached out, even a little? Nonetheless, he was feeling even more angry now. He calmed himself down anyway. "Can I go to sleep now? I'll call you tomorrow."

Ryan was awash in grief. It seemed Scott still didn't want to hear him. "Please don't go away," he said even while feeling the fear of making the request. Both feelings were confusing him to no end. He needed Scott like never before, but at the same time he felt fearful about it, terrified even.

Scott heard the plea in his voice. It was genuine enough. Maybe there was something else going on here that he didn't understand. "I'll call you. I promise." He swallowed the lump in his throat and hung up.

Ryan heard the click and the phone went dead. He continued to sit there and hugged the handset as warm desert night breezes blew over him. He hoped they would evaporate the tear that slowly rolled down his cheek and hung there on his chin.

It took another hour and a half before Scott was able to return to a fitful sleep.

# CHAPTER 13

Scott called his aunt the moment he returned from school the next day. She always seemed to have helpful insight. Perhaps she could help him sort through his feelings.

Scott explained to her how it seemed that his relationship was faltering, about how Ryan was in therapy, and that he had called last night. He didn't dare say anything about Preston though. He just couldn't.

She waited until he was through with his long monolog. "I'm so sorry to hear about all that, honey."

"He's trying to ruin our relationship."

"If that's true, why would he call to apologize?"

"He doesn't want me around him. I think he wants to stop going out with me."

"Did he say that, or are you just thinking that's what's so?"

"When someone tells you you're not going to school together, that's pretty clear."

"I don't think you heard him right."

"It sure seemed clear enough."

"You should be *absolutely* sure about this." She was sure he was either not getting the point or there was something else he hadn't said.

"I thought relationships were supposed to be fun. It's not fun anymore."

"I wish relationships were supposed to be fun all the time, honey. But they're not. People sometimes get married even though they're not ever having any fun."

"Then why bother?"

"Sometimes people get together for the wrong reasons. There's an initial attraction, but when that wears off sometimes there's nothing left."

"But I'm still attracted to him. I can't let him go. I still feel that there's something left. And…I think about him all the time."

"Well, that's good and bad. But don't beat yourself up about it. Sometimes things just don't work out and you have to move on."

"Please don't say that."

"Scott, honey, I'm just being realistic. Besides, rarely do relationships work out over the long haul at your age anyway."

"Please, please don't say that." *But...what if she's right?* His eyes started to smart.

"I have to be honest. I'm not going to lie to you, even now. I know you're having problems. Unless you two talk it out you're not going to get past this. Look, you and your father are talking now, huh? I know you can do it."

"Yeah, but he's still not connecting with me. I don't think he really knows me."

"I'm sure he knows you quite well. You just don't have the perspective of—and I'm sorry to have to say this—his age."

"Like, I'm not old enough to have a brain?"

"No, honey, of course not. It's just that age allows you see things differently. Time has this great way of making us wiser. Well, it works on some people."

"You think it's working on him?"

"I'm sure it is."

"I can't wait all my life."

"You won't. Trust me. You won't."

They talked for another ten minutes about school and how the most recent concerts had gone. Finally, he said goodbye. He looked at the phone for a moment while he debated calling Ryan. He had a paper to write. If Ryan turned out to be in a bad mood, it would rub off on him and make it difficult to concentrate on it. But he decided he had to find out what he meant last night. He dialed the number and paced in his bedroom as he waited for some-one to pick up. Ryan answered on the fourth ring. He stopped pacing and sat on the bed.

"Hey," Scott said tentatively.

"Hey," Ryan answered softly.

"I'm sorry I yelled at you last night. I was in the middle of an awful dream, that I can't remember at all now. It was weirding me out."

"I didn't mean it like that," Ryan began.

"Mean what?"

"I was confusing you. I'm sorry. What I meant was that I'm not going to UCLA because it's not the right place go to *together*."

"Then were are we going?"

"I don't know yet."

"Then how could you know I shouldn't go with you?"

"Because I looked into it. I said I would. If I go there you won't be at the right place for music school. I was looking out for you. But you're being a bastard about it. Why?"

"I'm not the bastard, you are!"

"Why are you twisting my words?"

Why? Because he was feeling terribly guilty now. That's why. His liaison with Preston was staring him in the face. It shouldn't have happened, but it did. He had deliberately not told anyone and it was gnawing at him now. But, at the time, he was pissed off. Ryan had been distant and didn't want to talk. Yet, as far as he could tell, they were still going out. Just barely, it seemed, but still, no one had called it off just yet. "I'm-I'm sorry," Scott offered.

"Please Scott. Don't mess with my head. I can't deal with it. I'm confused about everything right now."

"Confused? You're confused? You don't call me. You don't want to have sex with me. You don't even want me around you. You're not going to school anymore. And *you're* confused?"

Ryan was taken aback at Scott's outburst. He didn't dare answer him. They could hear each other breathing while neither said anything else. It took tremendous effort on his part, but Ryan said it despite his feeling of dread. "Nobody's home. They went out to get some food for dinner. Maybe you can come over and we can talk before they get back. Okay?"

Scott thought about it for a moment. Despite the guilt he felt about his indiscretion with Preston, he ached to be with Ryan. He wanted to hug him more than anything, but he was getting the oddest vibe from his voice, his intonations. And Ryan was admitting to being messed up. Did he want that in his life right now? Yes, he did. His paper could wait. It couldn't wait long, but it could wait for now.

A few minutes later Scott was knocking at the door.

Ryan tried but he couldn't quite muster a smile. He was trying his best to keep the feeling of fear from coming up now that Scott was there in front of him. Ryan led him to his bedroom then pushed the door with his foot. It didn't close all the way, because the air conditioner was cycled on. They sat down on his bed. Scott heard a car pull up, muffled voices, then car doors shutting.

"I'm going to the bathroom," Krysta told Howard as they came in. Chris pulled the patio door shut as she started down the hall. She noticed the light on in Ryan's bedroom and the door slightly ajar as she entered the bathroom. She'd seen Scott's Jeep in the driveway and realized that she hadn't seen him since they all went to get Ryan's car down in Palm Springs. The bathroom was down the hall from Ryan's bedroom. After she was finished, she opened the door then checked her hair.

She could hear Ryan and Scott talking. Distinctly.

Ryan: "I'll make it up to you, I swear."

Scott: "My dick can't wait forever."

*My dick,* she wondered. That's an odd thing for a boy to say to a male friend. She stopped primping and stood in the bathroom doorway to hear more.

Ryan: "I'm sorry. I-I just can't keep it up."

Scott: "Fuck."

Ryan: "I can kiss, you know."

Then she heard it. The obvious sound of kissing.

*What is going on in there?* Then she remembered the sketchpad she had looked through on the dining room table months ago. In it had been drawings of all sorts of things. The ones toward the back had especially gotten her attention. They were of Scott. He had been naked, in different poses, and in various states of arousal, including one where he was fully aroused. Now it was clear what that was about after all. Howard's nonchalance at that time now seemed to be a clear indication that he was in on it, too.

She knew she shouldn't do it, but had to find out for herself. She walked down the hall, pushed Ryan's bedroom door open a bit, and stuck her head in. The boys were lying on the bed on their sides. They were obviously French kissing and their arms were wrapped around each other. Startled at what she was witnessing, she put her hand to her mouth and inhaled noisily.

The boys sat up at once. Scott was immediately embarrassed. Ryan was instantly angry at her intrusion. "What the fuck? How *dare* you barge in my bedroom!"

She stood there, dumbfounded and from the anger with which Ryan had reacted.

Ryan looked over at Scott who had jumped up and was now standing. Scott was sure kissing was completely benign. And he was glad his partial erection wasn't noticeable due to his untucked t-shirt.

"You were *spying* on us!" Ryan charged.

"The door was open," she shot back.

"Yeah, right. Get *out* of my fucking bedroom!"

Howard heard the loud exchange and made a fist. Chris was pulling food out of the bags and the noise was masking what was going on down the hallway. Startled, he jumped when Howard pounded on the countertop.

"What was that all about?"

He didn't answer as he started down the hall.

She heard Howard coming and pushed opened Ryan's bedroom door even more. She looked back at him. "They-they were tongue kissing each other!"

Howard looked at them both. Ryan had just stood up. He pointed at her. "You was *spying* on us! *I* live here. *You* don't! I can kiss *anyone* I want to."

She turned to Howard. "Are you going to do something about it?"

Howard let his shoulders down. It wasn't going to do any good to lie to her since she had apparently seen something. He briefly surveyed the boys. They had all their clothes on and everything appeared to be buttoned or zipped up. The embarrassment he thought he might have to endure wasn't there. "Like what?"

She gestured toward them with both hands. "This is horrible."

Scott had never heard a tirade like this and was alternately amused and taken aback. She was upset because they were kissing? *Fuck, how dare she!*

Howard didn't really know what to tell her. "I think they…do that sometimes." He realized he'd never even seen them hold hands.

Chris was at the door now. He rolled his eyes after listening to part of the verbal exchange. It seemed that chaos was returning to his life and he didn't want to be involved with any of this.

Ryan saw him do that. "Don't *you* start!"

Chris ducked purely out of reaction, and without saying a word, went straight back to the kitchen. He still hadn't completely assimilated the revelation of having a gay brother. And it was going to be difficult now having Howard and Krysta mad at each other.

Krysta kept her attention on Howard and continued. "You condone it?"

"I can't stop them."

"You certainly *can*. And you *should*."

"It wouldn't be fair to them even if I could." Howard was trying to be diplomatic, but Krysta was becoming noticeably more agitated as she pressed the issue.

*So*, she thought, *he* is *in on it*.

He continued. "Besides, it's his bedroom. He can do just anything he wants to in here, short of drugs or murder." He looked back at Ryan as he said that.

Exasperated, Krysta turned around and headed for the kitchen. Chris had just turned on the oven to warm up the food. He stood with his back to it as she picked up her purse from the counter. He pointed his thumb back to the oven.

"Where 're you going? I'm heating everything up."

"I'm leaving. If that's what's going on in this house I don't want to have anything to do with it." She dug into her purse for her keys. By that time, Howard had made his way back to the kitchen. Ryan and Scott stayed put for the moment.

Howard spoke up. "Look, I can explain this."

"Explain what? That you condone boys kissing each other? What's next? You telling me that they're...they're..." She couldn't bring herself to say it. She slid open the door and virtually launched herself out onto the deck.

"Krysta! Don't be ridiculous," he exclaimed as he followed her down to her car.

Chris, his pulse racing and not budging an inch, had watched the brief interaction. But now he moved. He went back down the hallway. Scott had a slat raised up on the window to see if he could see them on the driveway. Ryan was trying to look around him through the window.

Chris stood at the doorway. "Do you have to fuck up everybody's life?" he yelled.

Ryan whirled around. "*Fuck* you!"

Scott dropped the slat in reaction. The energy with which Ryan had said it was almost tangible.

Chris fired back. "Fuck *you*! You fucked up *my* life and now you're fucking up Uncle Howard's. You dumbass!" With that, he turned around, went into his bedroom, and slammed the door. They heard him yell 'fuck' and something fell to the floor.

"Come here, you *butthole*," Ryan shouted. He started for the doorway.

Scott reached out and grabbed him by the wrist. Ryan tried to pull free but Scott used that moment to grab him around the chest where he pinned his arms to his sides. "*Don't!* You'll just gonna make it worse."

Ryan wrenched himself free, angry as hell, but stopped short of leaving the room.

Scott looked at Ryan's face. It was beet red. Ryan was really, really angry. Scott moved to the doorway to make sure Ryan wouldn't leave the room, and watched as Ryan's hard breathing settled down. Finally, the angry red color left his face.

A moment later Howard came back into the kitchen. Scott let Ryan leave the bedroom now and followed him to the kitchen. Ryan kicked Chris's door as he passed it, but not nearly as hard as he wanted to.

"Where's Chris?" Howard asked Ryan.

"I sent him to his room."

"You what?"

"He's pissed off."

"Well, *I'm* pissed off, too. And *Krysta's* pissed off. Scott, are *you* pissed off?"

Scott didn't know what to say. Howard didn't appear to be directing any anger at him specifically, but he didn't want to exacerbate the situation at all. "I think I'll just leave. I'm sorry I came over. I had no idea this would happen." He pulled the sliding glass door open and went the same way Krysta did.

Ryan followed him. "Please don't leave," he pleaded.

Scott stopped once he got to the driveway. "Don't leave? Are you serious? You think your uncle wants me in his house after what just happened?"

"She's a bitch. He shouldn't be dating her anyway."

"I think he should decide that, not you."

Scott yanked the Jeep door open and jumped in. Ryan grabbed his bicep through the open window. "But it's her fault. She was spying on us."

"I gotta go," was all Scott could say. He shook off Ryan's grip. Ryan stood on the driveway looking terribly upset.

Scott couldn't exactly say to himself why he felt he had to leave. Sure, part of it was the sheer embarrassment at the whole scene she'd made over a simple kiss. Maybe it was partly because he was still feeling awfully guilty about Preston. Mostly though, he was just plain feeling odd about Ryan now. He didn't know Ryan could get so angry. What if Ryan took something out on *him*?

Ryan stood on the driveway watching Scott back out as quickly as he could. *Despair…spiral downward…love…no, death.*

*          *          *

On Friday, Scott sat in class, looking forward to the end of the day. This week had been way too hectic and way too long. He was ready for the weekend and being around the familiarity of the band. The bell rang and he went into the boy's bathroom at the end of the corridor. It appeared to be empty. There was a row of eight tall recessed urinals along the wall. Scott chose the second one from the sink. That's when he noticed the tennis shoe under the last door of the stalls. That stall door was the only one closed. He was almost done when he heard the bathroom door open. Joe strode in and chose the first urinal right next to him. Scott almost peed on himself when he saw Joe staring at him. Joe slowly unzipped and pulled his penis out. Scott couldn't help himself and glanced at it.

"I knew you'd like it, Fairyday. Why don't you suck it?"

"Fuck you."

"You can deny it all you want, but I know you're a faggot. I saw you kiss that guy out in the parking lot. Come on. Deny it."

*He saw me kiss Ryan? How in the fuck did he see that?* "So what? You don't tell me who I can or can't kiss." *This is way too bizarre. First Krysta freaked out last night over a simple kiss and now Joe. Why is kissing so horrible that people have to become unstable because of it?*

Scott had fast zipped up and stepped back now, ready to bolt. Joe apparently never intended to pee yet he still had his dick hanging out. A lengthy portion of it. Scott couldn't believe he could be so casual about it. And whoever was in the stall had just heard their conversation. They could easily report what they heard to whoever his friends were and make life totally unbearable for him. He just hoped whoever it was didn't know him.

"Suck it. I know you can do it," Joe said. He turned slightly and wiggled it just enough so Scott could clearly see him doing it. It was the first time Scott ever thought of a penis being menacing. Joe was facing away from the stalls. Clearly, he didn't know anyone was in there, or he certainly wouldn't have carried on like this.

Scott hefted his backpack and started for the door. "Suck your own dick, fuckwad."

Joe squinted. He quickly pulled his dick back into his pants and zipped up. He grabbed Scott's shoulder before he could get even a foot away. Pushing him up against one of the sinks, he pressed his body against him. Scott could feel Joe's crotch against his waist. For a brief instant, he wondered if this was what rape victims felt like.

Scott didn't dare throw a punch. The entire bathroom was tiled and he figured he'd end up with his head busted in for sure if he did. Nonetheless, both arms were tensed as he pushed back. If Joe punched him, he would certainly defend himself.

Joe leaned forward, his pimply face just inches from Scott's. "I'm gonna get you, Fairyday. I'm gonna get you and fuck the shit outta you," he whispered. It was loud enough. Whoever was in the stall hadn't so much as moved a muscle and heard every word of it.

Scott didn't know whether to just take it or attempt to get out of the bathroom. Joe had the most bizarre tone in his voice. He had a disturbing look in his eyes and his breath smelled foul, like Skoal. None of it made any sense. *Why would he dare say anything as disgusting as that? All over a kiss? And in the school bathroom? He's not just bold anymore, he's freakin' psychotic!*

The bathroom door swung open. Three longhaired burnouts from the junior Hacky Sack crowd came in. They stopped dead in their tracks. They knew a fight when they saw one. Joe stepped back, released his grip, and pushed Scott for good measure before he left. Scott took a deep breath, then pressed past the burnouts, who reeked of cigarette smoke. They gave him a wide berth. Joe was already nowhere to be seen, due to the crowd of students streaming through the corridor.

Scott reached his locker, searching the hall in both directions. He still didn't see Joe anywhere. He swiftly worked his combination. When he looked up again, he saw Doug standing beside him.

Doug had a concerned look on his face. "Scott," he said.

"What?"

"Come with me."

"Where?"

"The stadium."

"Why?"

"Because we have to talk. *Now.*"

"I have a class."

"You don't anymore."

"What the fuck, dude?"

"Just come with me." He was serious.

Scott took his books with him anyway. They went around the back of the school grounds to the football stadium. Scott was confused at first that Doug wouldn't say a word to him, but now he was outright incensed. They climbed the bleachers and stopped sixteen rows up near the twenty-yard line on the east side. Doug sat down, placed his books between them, and Scott did the same. No one else was around.

"Okay, so why are we here? There's no football game going on."

Doug ignored the question. "How come you *never* told me?"

"Never told you what?"

"Duh. That you're *gay.*"

At first, Scott didn't know what to say. He hadn't figured Doug had seen the kiss in the parking lot, too. *Does the whole fucking school know?* "You saw me kissing Ryan, too?"

"Ryan?" Doug asked. He only knew one Ryan.

Scott was freaking. He reached for his books, then started to stand up. Doug placed his hand on them. "Sit down!" he ordered.

"So you can punch me? No fucking way!" Scott replied. He tried to wrench the books up.

Doug rose up a little so he could hold them down with more weight. "Why do you think I brought you here?"

"You saw me kiss him," Scott assumed.

"No I didn't."

"Then how…?"

"I heard you in the bathroom with that redneck punk."

"That was *you*?"

"You knew I was in there?"

"I saw a tennis shoe under the stall door." He looked at Doug's tennis shoes now. They were the same.

"You're lucky it was me. Now what the *fuck's* going on here? And how come you never told me?"

Scott was speechless.

Doug released his weight from the books and looked directly into Scott's eyes. "I've thought for over two years that you were my *friend*, and I find this out right when you're about to be punched out by some stupid dickweed cowboy?"

"What?" Scott heard him. Doug wasn't trying to be nasty at all.

Doug was shaking his head. "I thought you were the coolest dude. But maybe it's not like that after all. I must have figured you out completely wrong. No, I *did* have you figured out wrong. If you're *not* my friend just tell me right fucking now."

Scott sat down. He was still breathing hard. He could also see that Doug was genuinely hurt. *Oh, fuck, I just ruined our friendship.*

Doug studied his face. "I've known for months. And I don't care."

"You *have*? You *don't*?"

"God, Scott. How many times have we partied together? How many times have the Wolves won because of each other? Huh? Dude, you're like the brother I never had. You're the most decent guy I know. I'd defend you to the *death*. When I heard that fuckwad saying that shit to you I nearly flipped out."

Scott could list a dozen reasons why he liked Doug. His heartfelt admission of defending him to the death now topped everything he knew about him.

Scott knew Doug was an only child. There was some sort of rapport they had that Scott never really understood. After all, he had a brother and was used to that kind of relationship. Apparently, Doug couldn't get enough of it.

"If you knew…why didn't you ever say anything?" Scott asked.

Doug looked away for a moment. "I kept telling myself it couldn't be true, despite all the clues. You and I went on dates together. You taught me how to rappel. You don't, like, you know, act gay. Fuck, we've seen each other naked in the locker room! I just didn't wanna believe you were actually, you know, that way."

Scott let out a long sigh. He gave up all pretenses. His withhold was no more. He was completely himself with Doug for the first time ever. And God, did it feel like a burden was lifted off him.

"I'm that way. And I'm going out, I think, with Ryan."

"You think?"

"We're having…some problems."

"I think your bigger problem is Skoal Man."

"*He's* been after me since last year."

"Ugh."

Scott snorted. "Not that way. At least I don't think so. Jeez, now I don't know after what he just did. He's a twisted motherfucker, that's for sure."

Doug had a funny look on his face. "Ryan Taylor is gay, too. I had no idea," he stated.

*Jeez. First Preston, now him.* "No, not *that* Ryan. He's straight as far as I know, too. His name's Ryan St. Charles. He's a year ahead of us. And he never went to our school."

"Oh. Why did you, you know, kiss him in the *parking* lot?"

"It just happened. He dropped me off one day. I looked around. No one was watching, or so I thought, and I kissed him. It was nothing. But Joe must have seen us. Now he's spazzing out about it."

"How come you never said anything about Joe?"

"The full scale attacks only started a couple of weeks ago. He just harassed me last year every once in a while. I thought he was just weird or something. But now it's completely different. It wasn't until I...kissed Ryan that it got like this, or this bad. I think he wants to kill me now."

"It won't happen on my watch."

"On your what?"

Doug sat up a little more straight as he looked out to the fifty-yard line. He then looked back to Scott. "Not while I'm friends with you." He saw Scott's eyes redden. "And why didn't you tell me?"

Scott rubbed his, eyes then tried to gather his thoughts. *Because you're my best friend, and you're one of The Nine, and I was sure you'd hate me, and...*"I just couldn't do it. I-I didn't want to lose you as my friend. My-my best friend."

In a way, Doug was disappointed that Scott didn't think he deserved his trust. But he knew enough about him to know that once he knew someone supported him, they were friends for life. "Not everyone's an asshole," he offered.

They stood up at the same time. Without hesitation, Scott wrapped his arms around Doug in a tight hug. Both their books fell off the bleacher seat as their shins brushed up against them. He tried to release his arms to pick them up, but Doug held on. Scott tightened his arms around him as a single tear fell onto Doug's shoulder. He really had no idea Doug would react like this. Like the friend that he really was. He also realized he needed to reevaluate how he handled his friendships. Nonetheless, he knew right there that no matter how old he got, he would always know Doug first and foremost as his best friend.

∗          ∗          ∗

Kevin welcomed Ryan into his office. This was only his second session and they chatted for a few minutes after he took a seat.

"How do you feel about being here on a Friday evening? Don't you want to be with your friends?" Kevin asked.

"I don't have any friends, except one, and I don't think he wants me around right now."

Ryan had debated whether he should say anything about being gay yet, but had decided against it. Besides, it didn't seem relevant to anything so far. Yet, he was still quite disturbed at what Krysta had done the other night and couldn't figure out why Howard wanted to forgive her. *She must be some piece of ass. And she sure is one hell of a fucked up person to let Howie fuck her and then go off and be so freaked out about a kiss between Scott and me.* He figured that Krysta was history anyway despite Howard saying just the opposite after she and Scott had left last night.

When Chris had finally come out of his bedroom—once his stomach had gotten control of his emotions—Ryan apologized for yelling at him. That only made Chris more sullen. He hadn't been expecting an apology. Besides, he was still angry at what he thought was Ryan provoking Krysta anyway.

And at three in the morning, when Ryan had woken up and couldn't quite get back to sleep again, he felt that she had not only intruded in on his privacy, but had done exactly what his mother, his father, his grandmother, and what Scott had done to him. She had abandoned Howard. Why did people have to continuously do that?

Kevin noted that Ryan was in a better mood today, yet seemed a bit agitated about something. "How's the back?"

"It doesn't hurt as much. I still can't sleep through the night, though."

"That's likely to happen for a while until you're feeling a little better. Are you taking the anti-depressant?"

"Yeah."

Kevin lowered his chin.

"I swear."

Kevin felt satisfied he was.

Ryan looked out to the miniature waterfall in the courtyard, then to the books in the far bookcase along the opposite wall. He finally looked at Dr. Kevin.

"You can talk about it if you want to," Kevin said.

Ryan didn't know what to think just then. Everything seemed to be painted in shades of gray or black. The early darkness, due to the time change at the end of October, and the shorter days, weren't helping any either.

"You can play hide and seek with your feelings, or you can decide to change things."

"Change things? Change what? That everyone leaves me?"

"Everyone?"

"Mom, Dad, Muh, Scott…"

"Scott?"

"He's…my friend."

*Present tense*, Kevin thought. "So, Scott's not dead?"

"He's next."

"You're sure of that?"

"He's gonna die, too. I just know it. Why do people I love have to keep dying?" His eyes got red and he tilted his head downward so Dr. Kevin couldn't see.

*That was too easy*, Kevin thought. *He must really like his friend.* "Do you think your grandmother died on purpose?"

"No!" he replied angrily, completely inappropriate for the question. He almost said he was terrified that Scott would abandon him. That was the real issue he didn't dare broach yet. Deep inside, almost hiding, he felt the most intense joy whenever he even thought about Scott. It was his beautiful red hair, his smile, his fuzzy little ears, the curve of his biceps, those thick thighs. It was the little squiggly red birthmark on his waist over his left buttock, the soft touch of his hands. It was the odd and interesting accents he pulled out of nowhere, those awesome lyrics he wrote for the band. It was the beautiful way he played that flute and, of course, his intense passion when they were naked together. It was *everything* about him. But he was more scared right now than anything. The more he thought about Scott, the more terrified he became. Scott was going to leave him like everyone else had. He was sure that if he completely acknowledged that he loved him, it would happen. *Despair…spiral downward…love…no, death.*

"It makes you angry to think about that?"

He picked the little pillow up and plopped it onto his lap. He fidgeted with it for a few moments. "Huh. You'd be angry if your parents wouldn't talk to you, and then just left, permanently, without even saying goodbye. Then you'd-you'd…" Ryan couldn't continue as tears filled his eyes. Kevin was at the ready with a tissue, which he slid across the coffee table. He then placed the box in front of him.

Ryan didn't all out cry though. And the tears weren't for his parents. They were about Scott. Several of them followed the contour of his left cheek and stopped at the bottom of his chin as he thought about what Scott would do. If he said goodbye it would be the end of the line for him, too.

"Does your fear that people will abandon you cause you to think you need to end everything?"

Ryan took the tissue, blotted the tears, then sniffled. Odd. He felt like he was fourteen again and couldn't figure out why. "No."

Kevin realized that wasn't it either, and hadn't keyed into what it was just yet, but would eventually find out the source of it. He just had to keep probing.

"So tell me then. Why the suicide attempts?"

Ryan was feeling terribly exposed. They were an attempt to gain control over his completely chaotic life. It hadn't been until Scott appeared and totally stabilized him by the simple fact that he existed that he had cast off that idea. "Everything was too confusing."

"So when did you decide to not end it all?"

"When I met Scott. If it weren't for him I-I wouldn't...be here now."

"In my office? Or alive?"

"Alive. Both. I don't know."

"You must really trust him."

"I do. But he hates me now."

"There we are again with the hate thing."

"He hates me. I just know it."

"Why would that be?"

"Because I-I...can't do it with him anymore." He shut his eyes tightly. There. He hadn't meant to tell him but it was out now. He opened his eyes and looked up.

Kevin was busy interpreting 'do it', but figured he had zeroed in on it already. He shifted in his chair. "Are you gay?" He didn't have any idea until just now.

"Yeah, and don't try to change me."

"That's not why we're here, is it?"

This revelation changed everything. *Reality is trying it's best to teach me that lesson, isn't it?* The memory of the patient he'd been unable to help came to mind. It dealt with the only openly gay boy he had had in the four years of his practice. It was right in his face once again.

Ted was fifteen and almost militantly out to his family. It had caused enormous pressure on his parents, who at first, had tried to suppress his announcement. Ted's paternal grandfather was a fundamentalist Protestant preacher in nearby Landers. Ted's parents didn't want the 'secret' out to him or his congregation. Ted's father wasn't as much of a fundamentalist, but was ardent enough with his religious beliefs. When their attempts to suppress his continual statements about being gay failed, they tried punishing him. When that failed, they tried family counseling. They could have used pastoral counseling, but felt the moral issue was too great to let it be known to them. When family counseling didn't work, they scheduled private sessions for Ted. But both of Ted's parents kept retarding the incremental progress they had been making. Ted kept fighting back with them. None of his real issues were being resolved due to their continual confrontations. The misery Ted felt about his family's denial of his basic feelings and needs became too difficult for Kevin to treat. He had consulted with his practice partner, Dr. Jerome, who had a few years more experience, and had had several gay patients in the past. Unfortunately, that didn't work either. The last they heard about the kid was that he had run away and was living somewhere on the streets of Hollywood. The family seemed only too happy to have rid themselves of their youngest son. How awful they must all be, Kevin had thought. They kicked their own flesh and blood out of the house over something as basic as real life.

"So, the issue between you two is sex?"

"I'm just not interested in doing it. But he's my boyfriend. I-I don't want to lose him."

Kevin bit down on his pen. Already this was different from the Ted case. Ted had never been in a relationship. And Ryan wasn't about to run away. All cases were different, but he couldn't help but recall what had happened before. Nonetheless, depression could seriously affect one's libido. If Ryan had been engaged in a sexual relationship, and it were being affected by his loss of or diminished sex drive, he could see the problem for sure. He was aware that Prozac wouldn't be helping things either. "How long have you been in this…relationship?"

"Since July."

"Does your uncle know about it?"

"Yeah."

"And?" He didn't want Ryan's current home environment to be any worse than anything he'd already come from.

"He's okay with it."

"So, he hasn't tried to stop you, or force you out of the house or anything?"

"No. He likes Scott." Ryan then told him about what Krysta had said to them and how Howard defended them.

Kevin was very relieved that Ryan's case was nothing like Ted's. And now that this issue was on the table, it lent a whole new dimension to what might be going on with him. He already knew that being gay wasn't an issue in itself. It was evident that the problems that existed between he and his boyfriend were due to Ryan's fear of abandonment and his concern about the state of their relationship. The situation would probably just get worse due to common side effects of the anti-depressant. He would consult with Dr. Maine about that later.

This was beginning to fit together quite nicely. Nonetheless, he had to ask the hard questions, just to be sure. "Were you ever sexually abused?"

Ryan hesitated before answering. "I don't think so. Why?"

Kevin noted the hesitation. It suggested that he felt some sort of abuse somewhere. He didn't try to pursue it just now though. "Sometimes it can cause males to be confused about their sexuality."

"I've known I was gay since I was eight."

*Huh?* "You knew you were gay when you were *eight?*" Kevin asked, incredulous.

"No. It's just when I look back I knew. I didn't have the right word for it until-until I met Scott." He then told Kevin about his friends back in Crescent City.

The word up until last summer had always been faggot or something worse. Crawford's word for it was fag or queerboy, but Ryan didn't mention him. He felt too weird about that just now. Nonetheless, the word had never simply been 'gay' until he met Scott.

There it was again. Another reason Scott seemed, well, perfect. Something he wasn't even close to being.

Kevin made a few more notes and they talked about innocuous subjects until the session was over. He knew he had some research to do later that day before he got more into the real issues he had uncovered.

Later that evening, at the public library, Kevin closed the magazine he had in front of him. There were several psychological journals scattered on the table. In addition, he had looked through microfiche on the topic. He had pages of notes on his notepad. What he had uncovered was some interesting information he never realized before. One significant item was that gay teens were several times more likely than non-gay teens to not only attempt, but to complete, suicide. Not surprisingly, that particular bit of data seemed to have been carefully suppressed in the popular media. Actually, he found it odd that the Surgeon General didn't want it published but then blamed it on politics.

Of course, in high school peer pressure to conform was enormous. He was well aware of that fact. What he hadn't been aware of was the high rate of death among gay teens about Ryan's age, at their own hands, due to this particular phobia. Although Kevin still felt somewhat badly about how things had turned out with Ted, he hoped he'd be more help to Ryan.

\*           \*           \*

Ryan felt a lot better since seeing Dr. Kevin last night. He was amazed at the change in his ability to see things more clearly already. Unfortunately, his sex drive was still on hold, which was greatly disturbing him. After Dr. Kevin had gone into more depth about its sexual side effects, he had dumped the remainder of the anti-depressant pills in the toilet. The concept of a drug that killed one's sex drive mortified him.

Nonetheless, it wasn't right that he couldn't get off very easily. Last night, even after using plenty of lube, it had taken him almost half an hour to have an orgasm. He was determined to finish himself off this time. It was a gusher if he ever had one since it had been almost two weeks. And it was painful. That just wasn't right. Nobody who was eighteen should have that kind of experience, or take that long, he had decided. Kevin assured him that the new anti-depressant he had Dr. Maine prescribe wouldn't contribute to any sexual dysfunction once it kicked in. But it was depression that was still causing the problem.

The last two of the three college packages that he had sent off for had finally arrived in the mail this afternoon. He laid all the forms out on his bedroom floor. His biggest concern was how late in the year he was doing all of this. He was well aware of the fact that classes may all be filled by this time. Quotas may already have been made. Dorms were hard to get this late, too. He mentally crossed his fingers. Hopefully, starting during the summer semester would be a plus.

After an hour and a half of careful reading, he finally settled on one. Cal-Poly Pomona. It was clearly the best place for them. It had a good engineering school and a perfect music business college. Both were highly rated and it seemed that the choices in classes was nearly perfect. Cal-Poly had on-campus dorms, the university was relatively close to the Morongo Basin (affording easy returns home when they wanted), and best of all was that it wasn't all the way into L.A.

He dug into his back pocket for his wallet and pulled out the piece of paper that had Scott's social security number on it. He started filling out the forms. It took him an hour before he was done. He even managed to forge a decent signature for Scott. He then got out his checkbook and wrote out two checks for the admissions cost. One for himself, the other for Scott.

He would make it up to Scott if it were the last thing he did. How to get him to understand what he had uncovered and done for him was going to be the hard part. He was sure Scott didn't ever want to speak to him again. Somehow, though, he had to get Scott to talk. Somehow, he had to get Scott to understand that he couldn't stop thinking about him either.

*                    *                    *

Preston caught up with Scott in the school parking lot after school. He had deliberately not talked to him during class and Scott was acutely aware of it.

"Need a refresher?" he asked once he got close enough. He said it in that certain way that Scott was all too familiar with now.

Scott didn't want to think about his baffling relationship with either Preston or Ryan right now. On the other hand, he was horny as usual and wondered how long Preston would drag him along like this.

"Refresher?"

"My dad's not home till late. We could, you know, study a little."

"Study, my ass."

Preston lit right up at the remark. "That, too."

"I didn't mean it like that."

Preston knew what he meant. He licked his lips seductively. Scott watched his tongue as he did it. "So, you wanna?"

"I have to work tonight."

"You could stop by and we could just go over one problem...area." He stuck his left hand in his pocket.

He looked down at Preston's hand groping around. There were people all over the place going to their cars and Scott was feeling really uncomfortable with Preston's boldness right out in the open like this. "Quit it," he said.

Preston continued to grin as he started to feign beating off in his pocket. His careful, deliberate movements, which a bystander wouldn't even glance at twice, was making Scott terribly horny. "Just one," Preston offered again.

*God, if he isn't the hottest,* Scott thought. He sighed, then looked at his watch. If he got home fast enough, he could make it to his house fifteen minutes later. That would leave another forty-five minutes before he had to be at work. He could do it. He took his backpack off his shoulder and held it in front of himself. He was getting hard just thinking about it and didn't want it to be noticeable. "Okay, just one."

"See ya in...?"

"Fifteen, twenty minutes."

Scott pulled up at the driveway at Preston's house eighteen minutes later. It was all he could do to contain his excitement. This time there was no pretense. They weren't going to study. They weren't going to study, then have sex. They were simply going to have sex. It was so easy and no one would know except the two of them.

Preston was alone in the house. He hurried Scott into his bedroom, where he immediately shut and locked the door. Preston's nice school dress shirt had been unbuttoned. By the time they were upstairs, the collar was across his shoulder blades and the ends of the sleeves were down over his hands. Scott pulled each of Preston's sleeves down and the shirt dropped to the floor. He had decided he was going to waste no time either. He only had on a t-shirt, his shorts, and sandals. He hadn't even bothered with underwear. A fresh pair was in his bag back in the Jeep, along with the rest of his work clothes.

Preston pulled Scott's t-shirt up and off, then immediately went for his left nipple. He wanted to get right down to business. Scott, at first, tried to slow him down, but as Preston started flicking his tongue across it, quickly bringing Scott under his control, the idea evaporated.

He groped around for Scott's waistband, and when he got to it, pulled his running shorts down in a slow continuous motion. He was pleasantly surprised. It was evident that Scott had nothing on under the shorts since by the time he had made it into his room the front of them were already pressed firmly outward from his fully erect state.

Now, with Preston half-naked and Scott's arousal at DEFCON 1, Preston dropped to his knees to give Scott what he figured he needed the most. A slow deliberate blowjob. Scott eased himself to a sitting position on the bed, taking care to not let Preston's mouth come off his penis. Preston was relentless.

Even as he was receiving perhaps the most intense blowjob he'd gotten in weeks Scott noted one important thing. Preston only wanted him for sex. Well, it was mutual. But it was completely different from being with Ryan. There was always something more in the background with them. Sure, they had gotten off like any boys. But he knew that what had been going on between them, even that first time back at his aunt's place in Parker, had been far greater than just lust.

Preston sucked while he fumbling around with Scott's sandal. He finally found the release catch. Snap, thump. One off. Snap, thump. The other. Scott's shorts silently fell to the floor. Scott spread his legs wider to accommodate Preston, who had moved in a little closer.

Preston's penis was hurting since he hadn't pulled his shorts off yet. He was harder than he ever felt before. Nonetheless, he made sure he didn't touch himself. He was right on the edge. He had deliberately not beat off for a day and a half, and had told Casey he was too tired last night, having anticipated this moment. If Scott had said no to him back in the school parking lot he would have gotten off, it just wouldn't have been with Scott.

Scott's back started to arch as Preston continued to work on him. He could hear Scott's laborious breathing. When Scott placed his hands on Preston's head, he knew it was only a matter of seconds.

He pulled his mouth away, gripped Scott's dick, and started stroking. Scott dropped onto his back. His slick wet penis was incredibly beautiful as it squirted out all over his torso. Preston continued to slowly stroke as the last of it oozed out over his knuckles. He was surprised at how rigid Scott stayed even a minute later.

He scooped up all the semen into his palm, spit several times into it and slicked up Scott's penis. Scott rose up on his elbows and watched.

"You are my god," Preston whispered.

Scott pulled himself up onto the bed a little more. With his free hand, Preston shed his shorts. His penis sprang out, hard, pulsating. Scott reached out to touch it, grasp it, stroke it. Preston straddled him. He slowly slid his butt across Scott's hard wet penis and let it slick his backside up. He spit into his palm a couple more times, reached around behind himself, and rewet Scott's penis and himself. He stopped only long enough to get a tube of hand cream from his nightstand. He squirted some into his fingertip and poked himself a couple of times. He was well lubed up now.

He slid back enough to let Scott penetrate him just a little. Preston was a top. At least he considered himself that. But with Scott, he didn't care what he was just as long as he could feel every inch of him.

"Whoa, no way," Scott said as he felt himself going in.

"Just let me feel you inside me." With that, he lowered himself down harder. It was about halfway in when Scott half-heartedly attempted to stop him again. He pressed his hand against Preston's chest, but he weighed a lot more than him and had control in this position. Plus, with him already inside, it was difficult to pull out or otherwise maneuver away. Besides, it felt great, so why stop him?

Preston was in heaven. He couldn't believe how good it felt. He started working on his penis while he flexed his thighs and bounced up and down. Not more than twenty seconds later, he released himself onto Scott's cheek, the duvet (*not again!*) and Scott's abdomen. Finally, letting his full weight down, he sank completely onto Scott's still-rigid penis as the rest oozed down his fingers.

Preston's head was thrown back. He could barely breathe. He wondered if his eyeballs hadn't gotten lost somewhere inside his brain. He thought it was the longest and perhaps the most intense orgasm he had ever had. He still felt contractions long after the oozing stopped.

Scott had to pull him off since it was beginning to hurt staying this hard and with so much attention focused on his dick. Preston slid off the bed and stood with the mess all over his left h nd, his penis still pointing toward the ceiling. He staggered backward a step c h egs quivering a little.

Preston's sticky handprints w er Scott's chest. "That was incredible," he said.

It was impossible to get Casey that. He just didn't like being the active partner. And Scott had just fucke , or more accurately, he had forced Scott to fuck him. Without a condom e Casey always insisted on them and Scott hardly protested when he started ing down on his uncovered dick. Just for an instant, he regretted never having written John back from last summer. It was with John when he first had that experience and he realized how much he missed it.

They spent the next several minutes at Preston's sink. After they were cleaned up, Scott went back to the Jeep to get his clothes bag. Preston didn't mind at all. It was an opportunity to see Scott get naked in his bedroom all over again, which Scott had to do to change.

Finally, about halfway to work, Scott realized some important things. The sex was incredible and Preston was an animal. But he was cold, too. It seemed to have something to do with there being no feeling attached to what they did. And he completely changed when they were naked. Mild-mannered Preston was really a sex fiend. Sure, Scott loved sex. He'd proven it over and over again with Ryan. But they were careful. Preston was careless. He didn't even bother to get a condom before sitting down on his dick. And that thing about him being his god was disturbing. Why did he say that? He was certainly no god. He did-n't even have a classic build, not like Tim on the wrestling team. Now *he* was a god. At least Scott thought so. Something was wrong with Preston, but he couldn't put his finger on it.

He let go of his thoughts because of the expanding emotion he was feeling. Anger. Anger at himself for having seen Preston yet again, and this time only for sex. He fumed all during work and Clark noticed it. He was used to seeing Scott and Beth, one of the swing shift waitresses, trade good-natured jokes, or throw innocuous insults at each other. Tonight he was more serious than he'd ever seen him. He went to the host station and waited for him to seat the next couple. Scott returned a moment later.

"You and I need to talk."

"You, too?"

"Someone else noticed your mood?"

"Everyone's noticing. Even my mom."

"Wanna talk about it?

"I don't know…"

It was obvious he did. "I'm going to *Stanton's Nursery* to pick up some mums tomorrow. Go with me."

"Sure. I-I need a shoulder to cry on anyway."

"Hmm. Sounds serious."

"Maybe it is." They made the plans since neither would be working that next evening.

*           *           *

Scott parked his Jeep at the apartment complex where Clark lived. He went up to the second floor, found the right door, and knocked. As he waited, he glanced out over the railing to the parking lot. His vehicle was almost directly below. He saw an odd looking mark on the top and wondered if it was bird poop. As he squinted, trying to figure it out, Clark answered the door.

"Hey. Come on in."

Scott stepped into the living room. He saw an upright piano along one wall, a long sectional couch along the other, and a stereo and small TV in a sparse entertainment center along the third. He couldn't believe the carpet was white. A white carpet in his bedroom would be filthy in a day. Clark's was spotless, as was the rest of the apartment. He didn't get to inspect much else as Clark grabbed his keys off the kitchen counter and they took off in his car.

Once they got going, Clark started with the questioning. "So, why the mood, buddy?"

"It's my boyfriend. We're not doing so well lately." He didn't dare say he had cheated on him. That was just a little too much information. God, it was weird. He knew he should tell someone, but how? And what would happen if he did? Would everything fall completely apart?

"So, what's up with that?"

"We were doing it, like, all the time, and now it's gone to exactly zero."

Clark chewed on his thumb. He hadn't had sex with anyone except his VCR for quite a while. He knew exactly what it was like. "Sorry to hear that. If I were your age, I'd probably explode. Oh, wait. I did, in my hand, on a regular basis," he said with a funny look on his face.

That got a reluctant grunt of laughter from Scott, which made Clark laugh as well. He reached out and briefly touched Scott's arm. "So what happened?"

"He's depressed."

"We all get depressed sometimes. Like you now."

"I'm not seeing a shrink like he is."

"Oh. I've seen a shrink."

"You have? Why?"

"Long story, but when the love of my life died in my arms, I thought it was the end."

"Fuck. What happened?"

"What do you think?"

"AIDS?"

"You win the prize."

"Sounds like you didn't.

"I won nothing but a black hole of emotional turmoil."

"It was that difficult?"

"It was the hardest thing I ever had to live through."

Scott thought for a moment. "It's not that bad for me."

Clark noticed the downcast eyes, the tone of his voice, and now the way he was biting his cuticle. "I think it's worse than you're admitting."

Scott dropped his hand from his mouth. "He's supposed to be my boyfriend, but he's all fucked up now. I don't think it's gonna work…" He couldn't finish the sentence and stifled the intense sadness he was feeling all the sudden. He, of all people, wasn't one to just up and break down like that, especially in front of people he didn't know all that well. But here he was doing it in front of Clark.

Clark noticed and was troubled by the unexpected shift of emotion. No, he didn't know Scott all that well either, but he liked him and didn't want him to feel bad. "Well, then our little trip won't be in vain. Ever been to *Stanton's Nursery*?"

"No."

"Do you know Tony Stanton or Dan Pate?"

"Never heard of them."

"Well, they're an inspiration to me."

"How?"

"For starters, they've run the most successful nursery in the Morongo Basin and have done so for almost nine years. Second, they give money to AIDS charities every year since they're so successful. But the most inspiring is how and when they met."

"Go on."

"They met right here in Yucca Valley, nineteen years ago, and 've been together since then."

"No way."

"Serious."

"Nineteen years ago? Jeez. That's longer than I've been *alive*."

"Wanna know where they met?"

"Uh, in jail?"

Clark grinned. "Sorry, but no."

"Okay, where?"

"On your high school swim team."

"Yeah, right."

"I'm not kidding. You can ask them yourself."

"I don't even know them."

"After tonight you will."

They arrived at the nursery a few minutes later. Since it was December, all the usual spring and summer flora was well behind them now. The nursery

sustained itself like most other nurseries past prime season by selling pump-
kins, gourds, and hay bales for Halloween; Indian corn and other
Thanksgiving items in November; and now a wide variety of different colored
mums, Christmas trees, and ornaments. The parking lot had about a dozen
cars in it when they arrived, and shoppers were scattered all over the place
inside the enclosed greenhouse. Some, though, were inspecting the trees,
which took up a good portion of the parking lot.

"Why didn't you just get a mum at the grocery store?" Scott asked as they
exited the car.

"Huh! Are you insane? These guys not only have the best selection, I *support*
them."

Scott had no idea what he was talking about. He still didn't know why they
drove past two grocery stores just to get flowers.

They strode up and down rows of multi-colored mums while Clark stopped
ever so often to pull pots forward for inspection.

A man with thick dark hair that was just graying at the temples, nice jeans,
Timberland boots, and the whitest smile, came up the aisle and greeted Clark.
The two men shook hands, then briefly hugged. Scott felt a little uncomfortable with their open display of affection. It was something he had never seen
before between men in public.

Clark introduced Scott. "Dan, I believe you've heard me mention this guy
before."

"Hi. Dan Pate. Clark told us about you, but he never said you were cute." He
looked at Clark. "In fact, you never mentioned anything about it."

Scott looked around. He was sure someone had heard him. But none of the
other shoppers seemed to be within earshot. In a way, Scott liked the unexpected attention, but also felt embarrassed.

Dan saw him hesitate and realized he probably shouldn't have said that.
"Sorry. I'm happily married, so not to worry." He stuck his hand out.

As they shook, Scott noticed how strong and firm his hand was. He immediately recalled an image of Frank Gaviota, Ryan's friend from Crescent City.
He couldn't help but smile at the memory. He had just dropped his hand when
another man walked up and briefly placed his hand on Dan's shoulder.

Tony Stanton looked to be about the same age as Dan. His light brown hair
was extremely short, and thinning considerably on top. Scott noted the contrast with Dan's hair. His was longer and thicker. Tony was at least three inches
shorter than Dan's six-foot two, and leaner. He wore a thick blue button-down
shirt with the name 'Stanton Nursery' embroidered over the left pocket.
Invoices were held by a clipboard in his right hand. He placed a pen behind his
ear then shook Clark's hand.

"Haven't seen you since, what, last weekend?" he asked then grinned.

Scott instantly liked him. From that one sentence he seemed to exude high energy.

Dan turned to Tony as he pointed to Scott. "This is who Clark was telling us about."

"Yikes. I bet you drive the boys *insane*," he said as he shook his hand. "Love the hair," he added.

Scott looked all around. "Will you guys stop it? You're embarrassing me."

Clark shook his head. "Scott, Scott, Scott. Eat it up, kid. When they stop complimenting you on your looks you'll wonder what happened to the years."

The three adults laughed heartily. That's when Scott saw Dan and Tony's matching rings. They were on their ring finger, but on their right hands. That was the first time he had ever seen anything like that and realized they were married, in a fashion. And, he was sure this was the first time he had been in a group, however small, of grown gay man and instantly loved it. He felt so comfortable with them now he just had to ask.

"Clark was telling me that you guys have been together for nineteen years. Was he lying?"

"It's been *eighty*-nine years, hasn't it?" Tony asked Dan.

Dan answered pensively. "No, it's been a *hundred* and nine years. That's not counting the amount of time I was passed out due to that awful cologne you wore on our first date."

"When did you really meet?" Scott asked.

Dan made a face. "Ouch, do we have to say?"

"Oh, don't worry. He probably can't count. He's too pretty to know how," Tony replied.

"Uh! Come on." Scott was somewhat confused at the odd rapid banter.

"See, I told you. He's way too pretty," Tony said, now smiling.

Clark was grinning from ear to ear at the repartee. He knew them quite well and loved their ability to do what amounted to improv. He was sure that was one of the reasons why they had lasted so long together.

"All right. We met back at Morongo Basin High, now called Yucca Valley Regional High," Tony began.

Dan then spoke. "We'd known each other since junior year. It was the first week on the swim team during our senior year and we were changing into our swimsuits. I was checking you out again in the locker room."

"And that was the first time I noticed you checking me out...that way. I still don't know why I never figured you out before then."

Scott looked around again, hoping no one could hear them. There was still no one in earshot.

"Leaving out the long, involved, and very boring story, it's been a love made in heaven ever since," Dan added.

"You were really on the swim team at *my* high school?" Scott was sure Clark had also been making that up.

Dan nodded his head. "No lie. I was MBH Backstroke Champion, Class of '71. They still have the trophy. It's probably collecting dust in some storage room."

"And because of him, I became master of a completely different kind of stroke," Tony whispered.

Dan gave him a dirty look. "You wouldn't know anything about that," he told Scott.

Scott couldn't help but laugh. "Are you kidding? My boyfriend and I..."

He stopped in mid-sentence. He was so caught up in the moment he had completely forgotten that he and Ryan were barely speaking to each other. Then he remembered his liaisons with Preston and the light-hearted last few minutes completely disappeared.

"Uh, something I said?" Dan asked.

"I forgot for a minute that we're having problems."

"Problems? What are those?" Tony asked as he batted his eyelashes.

"Tony," Dan warned. "Problems?" he then asked Scott in a serious tone.

"It's complicated, but I don't think he wants me in his life anymore."

"It's just illusions," Tony offered.

At this point, several people were nearby looking at flowers. Tony pointed the group toward his office. They left the floor of the greenhouse and retreated to a small room that just barely fit them all comfortably.

Dan shut the door. "So, what's this about problems?"

Scott briefly described his confusion concerning the state of their relationship, the appearance of Ryan's mental distress after his grandmother had died, the fact that he was seeing a therapist now, and his reluctance to talk about anything. He almost told them about Preston. *Say it, say it! No. Shit.*

"That's what shrinks are for, Scott," Tony said.

"Raise your hand if you've been to one," Dan said somewhat comically.

Scott watched three hands go up.

"See, it's not so bad. I'm sure he'll be okay. Besides, when you're depressed you can't think right. You say and do stupid things. Everything is a blur. Life has no meaning, you're confused..." Dan paused.

"You realize you used too much awful cologne on dates," Tony interjected.

Dan grinned and squeezed Tony's forearm.

Scott loved that they felt so easy and casual about touching each other. He missed that so much, even if it had always been in private with Ryan. He hated himself now for having done anything with Preston. It was beginning to weigh very heavily on him now.

"So, what did you mean about 'illusions'?" Scott asked Tony.

"If you really like someone, or hell, if you love them, they end up pushing all your buttons either on purpose or unconsciously. I do it to Dan on purpose. It doesn't mean anything."

"You do it all the time, I might add," Dan put forth. Then to Scott, "But you get used to it, or you ignore it, or you work through it. I haven't heard anything about how you've been working through this rough spot."

"Rough spot?"

"Yeah, it's just a bump in the road. Who says you're through?"

Scott hesitated before he answered. "Well, nobody really."

"Hmm. I think you're caught in the illusion," Tony said.

They saw a person's shadow at the frosted glass window of the office door, then a knock. Tony opened it. An employee needed his assistance with something for a customer.

"We can talk about this some other time. But remember. *It can work.* You have to give it a chance," Dan said. He gently squeezed Scott's shoulder. It sent chills through his body.

*Wow, he's actually concerned and he doesn't even know me,* Scott thought.

Clark took the employee's interruption as his cue to get the mums he came for, pay for them, and get home. Scott needed to get back anyway to do at least some of his homework.

Close to eleven, while Scott was laying in bed, he went over some of what had transpired this evening. Those guys had met on the swim team? He had been in the swim team locker room only twice. He wondered which bench they had sat at, where their lockers had been, and where they first kissed. That led him to wonder when they first had sex and he started getting hard as he thought about it. But he never made it to a full hard-on as he thought about the tangled mess he felt he was in with Ryan. And now with Preston.

*          *          *

It was midweek now. Ryan was at his next session with Dr. Kevin.

"You feel Scott hates you?" Kevin asked.

"He thinks I don't want to have sex with him anymore, but it's not true. I want to but I just don't feel up to it. I can't, you know, keep it up. And he thinks I don't want to go to school with him. He thinks I'm a total head case."

"Can you be more specific about the school issue?"

So, Ryan explained how Scott wanted to go to school with him. How he had investigated and had discovered that UCLA wasn't the best place for both of them to go together. He told Kevin about secretly getting Scott's social security number, about having called his high school, successfully getting his grade information by faking his way through being a university employee, and having sent off for other university packages. He also explained how he had even gone so far as to send signed applications to Cal-Poly Pomona.

Kevin took all of it in and realized that sex didn't seem to have much to do with it really. Ryan clearly not only cared deeply for Scott, he was trying his hardest to keep him close. Scott seemed to be pulling away for some unknown reason. He didn't know what that was all about, but Ryan would have to dig into it with him to figure it out.

Kevin grinned. "Did you tell him you were depressed and that's why you couldn't, uh, keep it up?"

"No, I didn't know what the problem was."

"It's one of the unfortunate effects of feeling the way you do."

Ryan covered his eyes with one of his hands. "He means everything to me. I don't want to lose him."

"Perhaps you won't." Actually, Kevin wasn't so sure about it.

"He hates me. I just know it. I don't want him to. And I don't want him to go away."

Dr. McGinnis put his pad down and leaned forward. He pulled a couple of tissues from the box as a couple of tears slowly ran down Ryan's cheek. Kevin was genuinely concerned for their relationship anyway.

Although Ryan hadn't said it yet, Kevin was sure that Ryan was in love. Despite the depression and the dysfunctional background he had endured, he seemed to have a healthy ability to love Scott, however hidden the deeper emotions were to himself just now. Ryan dried his eyes with the proffered tissues.

"Tell me about him."

Ryan told him as much as he felt he needed to: about how they met, about Scott's background, that he felt Scott was a dynamic ball of energy that he was going to seriously screw up if he wasn't careful, and that his whole world right now seemed to revolve around whether Scott still liked him or not.

As Ryan talked, Kevin became more and more intrigued. Both boys seemed thoroughly into each other, and from Ryan's perspective, he seemed to be more into the relationship than Scott. There was no way he could be sure that Scott wouldn't leave him. But another thing was becoming evident. Ryan simply wasn't asserting himself. Why, he wasn't sure just yet. "Why don't you tell him how you really feel?"

"I've tried. But I'm afraid to."

"Seems to me that you guys talk."

"Not about this. And I'm afraid of what'll happen to him."

"Tell me more about that."

"I'm afraid he'll...die." Ryan's chin quivered a little as he clamped his mouth shut.

"Die?"

"Like her. Like Muh."

"Aren't Scott and your grandmother two completely different issues?"

"No. If I tell him how much I...want to be with him...he'll be dead, too." *Despair...spiral downward...love...no, death.* "Why do all the people I love have to keep dying?"

Kevin was glad that Ryan had finally used the word 'love'. "Feels like you're taking a big risk to love others?"

Ryan looked up at him. "What?"

"If we love other people, we run the risk of losing them. Everyone dies. Everyone. I will. You will. Scott will. But Scott certainly won't die just because you *love* him."

Ryan leaned back and pinched his lower lip. He was trying to absorb what Kevin said about death and accepting the risk of loving someone.

Kevin continued. "Anyone who's left after someone dies gets to look at how sacred life really is. When it's their time, well, hopefully someone else will get that fact, too."

Ryan lit up. Kevin noticed that he'd latched onto something. "Sacred?" Ryan asked.

Kevin shrugged his shoulders. "Perhaps more than we can really know." He actually wanted to stop this train of thought. They really needed to get back to their original intention of the session. "So, that reminds me of another very important issue. Your suicide attempts. You want to talk about them yet?"

Ryan looked at the floor, then sighed loudly. "I guess."

"What you were trying to do?"

"Crawford. It had everything to do with him."

"Crawford?"

Ryan told Kevin about how he met Crawford and about their relationship that lasted his entire senior year. He told him about his girlfriend Little Trout, and more about his so-called buddies. It took a while to do. A lot of that time was spent working through his embarrassment of even telling him any of it.

*So, that's where the sexual abuse Ryan had alluded to had come from,* Kevin thought as Ryan told him about the handcuffs and the whipping. *And that's why he seemed to have hesitated in saying anything about it earlier.* It couldn't be categorized exactly as sexual abuse in a clinical sense, but rather more like masochism. After all, he stepped right into it. On purpose.

"You were brave," Kevin said.

"Huh! I was a coward the whole time."

"You're much braver than you can imagine. It takes guts to endure what you did, and then get out of it. Granted, the choices you made weren't the best, but you endured. You survived not only your emotions, but you also endured the tests you concocted for yourself. And you're still alive. You didn't do it after all. It takes a bravery to not go through with a scheme to end it."

"I don't see how."

"You endured the confusion and chaos. You endured the fantasy you created with Crawford about how your life would work with him. You kept your buddies—the predators—at bay despite everything. That takes bravery, regardless of how bad some of it turned out."

Ryan wasn't quite sure he was being completely truthful with him, but he liked the sound of it. Nonetheless, he couldn't recall a time when anyone had ever told him he was brave.

They continued to discuss Ryan's flirtation with suicide. Ryan told him about every one of them. He finished with what Scott had thought was a suicide attempt but wasn't really, that night under the bridge. Their fifty minutes was rapidly ending. But Kevin had extracted information about them and how Ryan had felt afterward. That gave him a greater understanding of what Ryan was really trying to do, since he clearly wasn't successful.

Dr. Kevin ended the session shortly thereafter. Ryan drove home feeling a hell of a lot better than just this morning.

# CHAPTER 14

After Scott came into his bedroom after school he saw that his answering machine light was illuminated. He listened to the message. "Hey. I'm going up north for Muh's estate sale. I won't be back until Sunday evening. I also wanted you to know that I-that I *love* you."

He rewound the message and listened to it again. Something started to form in his mind. It was only a kernel at first, but it fast loomed larger until it overwhelmed all other thoughts in his head. It was as if everything just shifted all the sudden.

What if…what if *he* were the sole source of everything that had gone wrong between them. What if he took responsibility for Ryan's feelings? Did he know how to? Could he sort through them? Hell, he had no idea how to do that. Or, what if he took the blame for everything? He certainly was to blame for at least part of it. He had had sex with Preston and he couldn't take that back. That had permanently altered everything he and Ryan had together. What if he simply changed his mind about it? What if it could work between them no matter what? It was getting really complicated as he thought about it.

He had thought about Dan and Tony continuously for the last two days. He had no idea what ups and downs they must have gone through in all their years together. *They've managed to keep their relationship going for nineteen years, damn it. Hell, they met in high school! And they're what now?* He counted the years. *Jeez, they're like thirty-six. And they're still together. It can work. I just know it can. Please let it work for us, too.*

*        *        *

Ryan had his chin on his fist and had been looking out the little window the last half hour of the decent into Crescent City. He saw nothing except the rain wetting the outside of the window. That was okay, though. The gray background was the perfect canvas for him to think without being distracted.

Finally, the clouds parted and he saw a carpet of green below. He was finally back to a familiar landscape of rainy cold, but home was no more. In fact, once he was done three days from now, he would be a lot richer, but everything about his past would be erased—scattered to his relatives, to complete strangers, and to Goodwill. The sale would be both Saturday and Sunday. With the amount of things they had to sell, he figured the pace might be pretty intense.

The estate sale would take place directly on the property. Howard had done most of the preliminary work over the phone. He had placed several ads in all the Crescent City periodicals. He had notified most of their relatives in the area. And he had instructed the Goodwill people to bring their van by on Sunday evening to haul away all the remaining items that wouldn't sell.

Ryan was to be the moneychanger and the coordinator. After all, he was going to be the recipient of most of the money this weekend, so he had most of the responsibility. It seemed so final. But when it was done, he knew his life would be transformed.

In a way, Muh's death was soon going to be the impetus for a whole new life. All of his studies would be paid for. Chris', too. He'd even have enough for living expenses, a graduate degree, and a whole lot more, even after all the taxes had been paid. He'd return to Yucca Valley to a small fortune. *How ironic that something good could come out of this,* he thought.

He went to the rental car booth and, after signing for a vehicle, zipped up his rain slicker. After finding it in the lot, he threw his bags in the trunk and flipped on the windshield wipers before heading out. He looked up at the familiar gray skies and tall evergreens. The lush surroundings seemed to cradle him, to welcome him back, despite the bleakness he felt about the whole situation. He shivered at knowing he was back home, at least for a short while.

He glanced at his checklist in the passenger seat. He had to go to the lawyer's office first to sign the remaining papers regarding Muh's will, then visit the bank to handle the transfer of all the funds left to he and Chris, and lastly be at the real estate closing office where he would officially sign away the land in the property transaction to the park service. Afterward, he would see his cousin where he was staying for the weekend.

The parents of Adina Stephens, who was his second cousin, had lightened up considerably about him after Muh had died. Perhaps it was because he no longer lived there. Perhaps it was out of simply being nice to family. At the funeral, they had been quite consoling to them all.

It was just about dark when he completed his tasks. Lunch had been late since the bank took an hour longer than he expected. The closing officer he needed to talk to at the title company wasn't in until the second time he went back. He had finally tracked everyone down, though, and now had a neat pile of papers on the passenger seat, along with several receipts totaling over $215,000 from her various funds and accounts. All the monies had been electronically transferred to his bank account in Yucca Valley. For about fifteen minutes, he felt like he was walking on air. His personal checking account had over two hundred grand in it and he couldn't believe it. Yet, his mood shifted back down once he got over the initial elation.

Adina ran to him when he pulled up in the driveway. She hugged him tightly when he stepped out of the car. "Gosh, it's good to see you again." She pulled back and looked at his face. Maybe he was just tired? "You feel okay?"

"My entire life is being sold off tomorrow. Including my prized Packard. How do you think I'd feel?" He was referring to the fact that the Packard Super 8 that had been willed to him by his grandfather was also being sold. Howard had also placed ads in two car trade papers. He figured there might be a bidding war due to its value.

"Well, not to worry. I'm gonna be there to help and so are Mom and Dad. We'll make sandwiches, change money, help move stuff for the buyers. It's gonna be fun."

He smiled for the first time today. She was always bubbly, and he noticed she was getting even better looking now. More so than when he left.

"I have to ask you something later. But first let me get you inside," she told him. She pointed upward. "The weather forecast is sunny tomorrow with possible scattered showers on Sunday. So it might just be perfect for the sale."

Adina's parents insisted that he not help clear the table after dinner. She went upstairs with him and sat on the bed as he pulled a few things out of his bag. They could just barely hear the stereo going downstairs and the dishes being scraped into the sink behind the closed door.

"I have to hear this from your mouth," she began.

"About what?"

"Dolf told me you're gay."

He stopped what he was doing, astonished at her revelation. He didn't think Dolf would actually tell anyone. "He *told* you?"

"It's true?"

"Yeah. It's true. Surprised?"

"Hmm, not really. As you know, people talk here. Little Trout said something a long time ago. That made me mad at her for a while. But then I remembered something from when we were freshmen and everything came together."

Little Trout, his old girlfriend, had talked more than he realized. "What thing?"

"About you nearly passing out every time David O'Bright talked to you."

He sat on the bed as his head started to swim. *Oh my God, David O'Bright.* Memories came flooding back like a half-forgotten horror movie. The one movie he hoped he'd never have to see again.

She continued even as she noticed that he seemed to be in some sort of a fog now. "He was only the cutest boy in our class, after *you* that is, and before he— you know." She had always thought Ryan was good looking. Being his second cousin, she never thought anything bad about it. "And, who didn't fall for David? Only it was all girls and *one* guy, now that I think about it. I even wondered whether you guys had a little extra going on."

"There was never 'a little extra' going on."

"What about that guy you brought up back in August? Scott."

"What about him?" He was still feeling lightheaded.

"He's way cute." She was hinting. He could tell.

"Yeah, he *is* way cute. And yes." He looked at her, hesitating. "He's…my boyfriend." He hoped it was still true, he hoped to God.

"I figured," she said. "You both had that look."

He knew exactly what she was talking about. He tried to organize his thoughts. He had no idea it had been obvious to her. His head finally stopped spinning. Now he felt crushed as he recalled that awful event. The movie was starting to run in his head. The movie he had done such a good job of trying to forget. He dropped his eyes away from her gaze, afraid he would completely lose it. He couldn't believe the feelings that were coming up now. "When David died I-I felt like I-like I died, too." He barely got the sentence out.

David had died in an accident. He had been climbing to the roof of their house to help his father fix their chimney. The roof was slick since it had been raining all day. But it was the ladder that had fallen over, with him still on it. He landed on his side on a sharp branch in the leafless bushes two stories below. It went deep enough between two ribs to puncture his lung and the pulmonary artery. The coroner said he died almost instantly. Ryan heard about it the next day. He cried then and at the oddest moments for months afterward. Actually, a lot of the kids in his class cried. It was the first time they had had a classmate die.

Ryan cried for an entirely different reason: David was the object of his first adolescent crush. His emotions had been completely unchecked, although he couldn't remember them being of an overt sexual nature. By that time, he had known David for months. They played street hockey in the school parking lot with the guys at least twice a week. They ate lunch together every day. They often got into trouble in homeroom. They called each other at home. They spent virtually all their free time together. The weird part was that he had deliberately forgotten about him until just this minute. But it had always been there, hovering close by. Until the day he acknowledged it again. Like now. He was so glad he had been talking with Dr. Kevin. He wondered if he'd be able to handle what he was feeling if he hadn't been doing so.

Adina stood up and held her arms out. He stood with her and let her give him a tight hug. He hugged back as tightly as he could, holding tears at bay. He could smell the pleasant scent of her shampoo, a hint of perfume at her neck. "You don't have to go around and tell everyone, okay?" he told her.

"I haven't, if that's what you're thinking. No one would believe me anyway."

She pulled back and kissed him gently on the cheek. He kissed hers in return. She saw a glint in his eyes and was nice enough not to say anything else as she quietly left the room.

After the door shut, sad tears soaked the bunched up t-shirt he had pressed against his eyes.

*               *               *

When Ryan woke up it didn't appear as if it was going to be, but by seven o'clock, it was perfectly clear and sunny. Last night when he woke up at two-thirty, and couldn't get back to sleep right away, he found himself with tears in his eyes when he thought about David again. He softly cried himself back to sleep and now was thankful he hadn't just tossed and turned until morning. He felt like a total head case as he showered. Crying about Scott. Now crying about David after so long. Crying about everything. *Stop it, you fucking wimp!*

Ryan, Adina, and her parents Nolan and Pamela, got to the house shortly after seven to unlock the gate to the property and the doors of the house. Inside, the place looked the same as when he left. A musty odor greeted them due to it having been closed up for several weeks. The chickens and goats Muh had kept out back had long since been given away to their neighbor a quarter mile away. The fenced in areas that once housed them now held nothing but tall brown weeds and patches of grass. The orchard-tree he enjoyed for so many years was leafless. It was so tall and old he couldn't see any of the grafts, even without its foliage. This weekend would be the last time he would see it. The smokehouse was just about kaput, and his mouth watered just a little as he thought about the rich feasts of salmon he'd had over the years from it.

Just as he set up the cash box on the card table on the front porch a couple of pickup trucks pulled up. One of them had several people riding in back.

Right behind the two pickup trucks was a much larger one with a crew cab pulling an empty car trailer. Ryan's eyes grew wide immediately. He figured someone would want the Packard but didn't expect anyone there before they barely got through their donuts.

A tall thin man in his early thirties, with dark sunglasses and a very expensive-looking brown leather coat, got out of the passenger side after it came to a stop. The driver was a barrel-chested Hispanic man. He wore an expensive-looking light jacket. He and the passenger got out. Two shorter Hispanic men sitting in the crew cab didn't get out. He was down the stairs before the men got out of the car.

"You look like you're in charge here. That right?" the tall man asked. The Hispanic-looking man stood next to the tall man with his hands clasped in front of him. He seemed to be taking up a classic 'bodyguard' position.

"Ryan St. Charles." He stuck out his hand.

The man shook it. "Thornton Winquest. I'm here to look at the Packard." He held up the trade newspaper, which showed the car circled in black ink.

Ryan held his right hand with the other one. Thornton had quite the grip. "You're not wasting any time, are you?"

"Am I the first to see it?"

"We just got here. I haven't even unlocked the barn yet."

"Let's take a look. I don't want Monty to even see it." Ryan didn't know who he was referring to as Thornton smiled at the Hispanic man. The man grinned back, looked down, and shook his head.

Ryan ran upstairs to tell Nolan what he was doing and he came out to handle the cashbox. Ryan and the two men went to the barn to inspect the car.

After the tarp came off, Thornton inspected the engine briefly, looked under the chassis, and checked out the interior. He issued a toothy grin and went for his wallet. "I have a cashier's check for $41,000. Take it or leave it."

Ryan thought he would pass out. They had set a value which was printed in the paper, by consulting a price guide, but he had no idea anyone would offer him cash just like that, and the check was for two thousand dollars more than he had asked.

"Take a look. It's drawn off a bank here in town." Thornton gave the check to Ryan to inspect.

Yes, Ryan noted, there was a proper watermark on the back. The ink was properly printed. He knew the bank name. It was serialized. It looked legitimate. "Sold," Ryan said not more than two seconds later.

Thornton took his hand and pumped it several times. Ryan stifled a grimace as he did so. "You got a good deal, son. I'm sure you know that." He whistled. "Hot damn, Monty's gonna shit bricks," he said with glee. "My men will have to bring the truck around and load it on the trailer. You have the title?"

"Do whatever you have to do." Ryan was still reeling with the amount he had just been given. "I'll go get it."

He dashed back to the rental car, pulled out a gym bag from the back seat, and yanked out a manila folder. He found the title and dashed back with it. He realized he still had the cashier's check in his hand and thrust it into his front pocket. He was out of breath by the time he got back to the barn. He gave the title to Thornton who inspected it, then had Ryan sign it over to him. They all went back to Thornton's truck. There was a short discussion in Spanish by the barrel-chested man. The men in the crew cab laughed briefly after they heard the name Monty. *They must really hate that guy*, Ryan thought.

They pulled the truck around and disconnected the trailer. While Ryan watched, the two shorter Hispanic men slowly but surely removed the car from its blocks and got it onto the trailer using chains and hydraulics. Half an hour later, with Thornton lighting a cigar, they pulled away. Ryan was over $40,000 richer than yesterday.

As the day progressed, three other men came specifically asking about the car. The first one pulled up with almost the same type of trailer rig pulled by a van. He had introduced himself as Monty Alberts. He seemed angry with himself when Ryan told him the name of the man who had beaten him to the purchase. Ryan didn't want to have anything to do with their apparent feud and was happy to see him leave. It was too bad that Muh's station wagon and Chris' step-side truck had been sold by Adina's parents weeks ago. Maybe he could have at least offered those vehicles.

The elation Ryan felt from the huge initial sale made everything else seem trivial in comparison, despite the brisk business the rest of the items generated. The Stephens were going to get ten percent of the proceeds, minus the profit from the car which was strictly his, so everyone was happy about the number of interested people who were leaving with paid-for items.

By late afternoon, all the larger pieces of furniture had been carted off into trucks, station wagons, and vans. Several items in the cellar still had yet to be purchased and Ryan figured they might be gone by the end of the day or tomorrow latest. People were still milling around all over the place. At any one given time, there were at least fifteen people in and around the house. *The whole freakin' county must know about this*, he thought.

Ryan was in his bedroom where he had just sold his old nightstand. There were two people in the hallway coming toward him and he opened the door a little more so they could come in if they wanted to. But the man in the lead turned and exited out the side entrance. Behind him was a very familiar face.

Ryan saw him stop cold as they locked gazes. "How the hell did you get here?" Ryan asked.

Crawford came into the bedroom. He was wearing a red flannel shirt, a baseball cap, which he had on backwards, a two-day growth of beard, crisp clean jeans, and high-top hiking boots. He looked like a lumberjack if Ryan ever did see one. "I wanted to see if you were here."

"How did you know where I lived?"

"Did you really think I didn't know?"

"This is a coincidence, isn't it? You just read about the sale in the paper."

"You're half right. I saw the sale in the paper. That's why I came by. Come on Ryan, I knew where you lived the third weekend after we met."

"What the fuck?"

"I can read a driver's license, you know. After all, your pants were on the floor along with the rest of your clothes at the time." He grinned as he surveyed the bedroom, wondering if it had been Ryan's. "Your little brother looks a lot like you," he said off-handedly.

"You met Chris?" He hadn't meant to reveal his brother's name like that, but hell, Crawford seemed to know a lot more than he ever had divulged before.

"He was in a step-side pickup truck, I think, just coming down the driveway when I drove up here one day. I asked him if you lived here. He said you weren't home. So, I pulled up to the house, turned around, and left. Nice place." He patted the doorframe. "They don't bother to build them like this nowadays. Too bad you don't live here anymore."

"Yeah, too bad." He pointed toward the side entrance door. "And you can leave now."

"Look, we need to talk."

"Just leave. I don't have anything to say to you. This is hard enough selling off everything I've ever owned without you being here."

He stepped a little closer to Ryan and lowered his voice. "That's not fair." He gave Ryan that familiar look. Ryan couldn't help himself. He looked directly into his eyes. "I love you. I've *always* loved you. You know that. Don't write me off. Please."

Ryan was totally confused. He had no idea Crawford would say that. He had never said it before. He had no idea that Crawford could possibly love anyone, much less him.

Ryan reluctantly let Crawford shut the bedroom door. The room was empty of everything except some miscellaneous items scattered on a shelf and in the closet. The curtains were shut. No one in the yard could possibly see in.

Crawford took off his cap and smoothed his hair back. He was exactly as Ryan remembered: handsome face, solidly built, and seductive. He came forward and touched Ryan's cheek. Ryan took his wrist, but before he knew it, Crawford had his chin in his hand. Ryan desperately didn't want it to happen, but it did.

They kissed.

In an instant, every emotion he had held in check about him flooded to the surface. He was with Crawford again. He hands were warm, his breath smelled like peppermint, his eyes were as beautiful as he remembered. How could this be? The last time he was here, he hated him. He didn't ever want to see him again. Now this.

They kissed for a good thirty seconds. All the while Crawford rubbed Ryan's shoulders. The baseball cap dropped to the floor. Ryan found it more and more difficult to catch his breath as his blood pounded in his head, as his dick swelled in his pants. He pulled away and turned his head. It couldn't be like this. He couldn't possibly feel this way.

Crawford rested a palm on Ryan's ear. His fingers stroked the back of his head. He didn't want to leave. Ryan no longer wanted him to either but there was a knock at the door. It startled them both.

Almost at the same time as the knock, Ryan heard a woman's voice. "Hello," she said in a warbling voice. A short, very old woman entered. She looked at them, at the items in the room, then looked back briefly to another equally old woman. "There's not much in here, but we should look anyway." They came in.

Ryan thrust his hands into his pockets. Luckily, his shirt was untucked since his dick was sticking straight up now. Crawford stooped to pick up his cap. They smiled at the old ladies, quickly left the room, and went out the side entrance.

Ryan briefly saw Adina and Nolan at the front of the house as they helped someone load up the back of their station wagon.

"Please come over tonight," Crawford said huskily.

"I-I can't. I'm staying with someone and they expect me there."

"Just this one night. We need to talk. Really talk."

"This isn't right." *He's gonna make me give in.*

"Just come over. Please." Crawford gave him those eyes again.

Ryan's heart was beating rapidly. His palms were sweaty and he felt weird standing with Crawford essentially in plain sight of his relatives. It was a first. And it was difficult to say no. He sighed. "What time?"

"What time are you ending the sale tonight?"

"Once it gets dark we're outta here."

"I'll be there." With that, he put the cap back on and went to his pickup truck. Ryan stood there and watched him go. Crawford looked back, smiled, and took off down the driveway behind the well-laden station wagon. Ryan felt distracted for the rest of the day, but tried his best to hide his agitation from his relatives.

Ryan knocked on Crawford's door later that evening and waited. Shortly after dark, it got foggy and had started to drizzle. Now it was coming down a little more steadily. A wispy cocoon enveloped Crawford's house there on the side of the hill. Ryan had his hands in his coat pockets and saw his breath as he stood on the front porch. Light shined through every window. He knew he shouldn't be here, but he was feeling so mixed up now that he couldn't help himself. He debated it the whole way up. He should have turned back miles ago, but couldn't. He had to find out what Crawford really wanted. Besides, hadn't he used the 'L' word? Scott had only said it once and that was months ago. But he knew Scott hated him now. And he hated himself, now that nothing was going the way he wanted it to.

Crawford opened the door. Ryan shed his coat on the porch, shook it off, then stepped in. Crawford took it and hung it up on the peg next to the door. The house smelled like cinnamon. Potpourri was simmering on the stove in a small pan. Ryan was surprised. Crawford never cared for feminine things like that. Perhaps he had changed a little in the past few months.

Crawford didn't say anything. He just took Ryan in his arms and hugged him. Ryan hugged him back then looked up at him. Crawford looked into his eyes and kissed him. Ryan was flush with emotion.

After long minutes, Crawford finally led him to the couch opposite the fireplace. A fire was snapping rapidly from some dry logs he had apparently just put in. The bearskin rug was still in front of the hearth. It was on that very same rug where he had lost his innocence.

*David O'Bright*. He couldn't figure out why, of all times, David popped into his head. The memory was growing, swelling in his mind, presenting itself in a way he didn't fully understand just yet.

"I was wrong not to tell you how much I love you," Crawford began. He placed his hand on Ryan's thigh. "When you left last summer I thought I was gonna go crazy. I didn't know where you were. But then I found out you're living way down south. Some town in the Mojave."

Ryan wasn't exactly listening. Curious about the memories of David spinning around in his head, he watched the flames leap higher and higher in the fireplace. He searched for the first time they met and found it. It was their first day as freshmen. David sat across from him in homeroom. He had come from a different junior high school so no one knew him. There was the eye contact, the furtive smiles, then the introduction. Ryan had been the first person to become friends with him. And it didn't take long before they were best buddies. Looking back on everything, Ryan was sure David would have become the most popular boy in school if it hadn't been for...hadn't been for...the accident several months later. The terrible accident that took the first boy he ever loved away from him forever.

Crawford scooted a little closer and slid his arm around the back of Ryan's waist. "Mmm. Same lean boy I grew to know and love." With his other hand he started to unbutton Ryan's untucked shirt. Ryan let him while he continued to meander through the images in his mind. Underneath the shirt he was wearing a thick black t-shirt. It wasn't tucked in either and once Crawford got all the buttons undone, he moved his hand slowly underneath. He placed his hand at first on Ryan's stomach, slowly rubbed back and forth, then edged his hand up to his chest. He caressed the soft skin of Ryan's pec. "Mmm, still as hot as the night we met."

The images were transforming. Crawford could have been a million miles away right now. Everything Ryan had felt about David was now flooding his emotions. Everything. The love he had felt, the pain he had endured. The memory of that day came flooding back in his mind. Brightly.

*Ryan and David were walking along the side of the road going to David's house from school. It had been an unusually nice late fall afternoon. Sunny, clear. About this same week, years ago. It was magical. They were alone together. They both had their hockey sticks and skates over their shoulders. Occasionally, they would smack the blades against each other, dueling it out behind themselves. Ryan could hear David's regular breathing as they trudged along. The breathing of his best friend. The breath of love right next to him. The side of David's face glistened with a trickle of sweat. As it ran downward it matted the soft hair in front of his ear. The trickle descended lower and lower with every other step as they talked. Ryan reached out. David was smiling. Ryan's field of vision narrowed to that one tiny trail. He touched it with his finger. The droplet was a river, engulfing him, sweeping him up in its current, spinning him around, making him dizzy. His finger to his tongue. It wasn't sweat. It was David. Salty life. His soul in liquid form. The taste of love.*

That very same day he was no more.

It struck Ryan like a hammer. This was terribly, terribly wrong. Crawford was *lying*. He hadn't changed a bit. He only wanted him for one thing. Sure, it was hot. Crawford was perhaps the most intensely sexual person he'd ever met. But Crawford only wanted to stick his dick inside him, get off, then do it again, preferably as soon as possible. There was really nothing more than that between them. But Ryan knew what it was like to have more. He had been in a real relationship for a change. He found himself feeling so angry with himself that he jumped up, nearly ripping his t-shirt due to Crawford's reach.

"W-what's wrong?" Crawford asked. There was a noticeable tent in Crawford's pants.

"What's *wrong*? I'm an *idiot*. *That's* what's wrong. I'm a fucking *idiot!*" He started to button his shirt. As he did so, he started for the entryway and spoke. "What did you tell Dolf after I left? That you loved him, too?"

Crawford stood and adjusted himself. "Who's Dolf?"

"Oh, you remember. My buddy at the lumberyard? When you came on to him, did you tell him you only wanted to kiss him, or did you tell him you were fucking me, too? How much did you tell him anyway?"

Crawford was in a panic. "What are you talking about? Where are you going?" He finally remembered who Dolf was though. He had just forgotten about that incident.

"Where? *Where?* Back to my life. That's where. And you wanna know something? You're not in it. *Nowhere.*" Ryan unbuttoned his jeans, lowered his zipper, and started shoving his shirttail in.

"You're making a big mistake. I love you!"

"You love that I was a hole for your dick."

Crawford looked away briefly, then back at him. "Okay, I admit I have it bad for your hot body. But I *love* you. I…"

Ryan held up his hand, then continued to stuff in his shirttail. Crawford abruptly shut his mouth. Ryan hoped Dr. Kevin had been right. Was he brave? He hoped he'd be able to make it to the car before he gave in again to Crawford's almost perfect job of sucking him back into his life. No, God damn it, he'd *make* Kevin right. He'd be braver than Kevin ever imagined.

Crawford stood in front of the door, his arms crossed.

"No. See," Ryan said. "You just want me for one thing. Well, here it is." He rebuttoned his jeans, then zipped up. He grabbed his crotch, thrust his pelvis out at him, then pulled his coat off the peg. He quickly donned it.

"Look, it's not like that. I just wanted you to feel comfortable."

"Funny thing. I felt more comfortable when you weren't around." With that, he pushed Crawford aside, not too forcefully, but certainly not gently, and opened the door. Crawford stood on the cold slab of his front porch in his socks. His arms were still crossed in the foggy night air. Ryan opened the car door. He looked back at Crawford.

"When you come back, call first. I might have some other boy over," Crawford said acidly.

Ryan shook his head. "There won't *be* a next time. Ever."

"We'll see."

Ryan scowled and gave him his middle finger.

On his way back he didn't tear up even once. He felt like he should be crying at this point, but he wasn't. He stayed angry. Angry at how he had shut down years ago. Angry at how he had lied to himself about what he felt after David had died, stuffing his feelings in until they were almost calcified.

He had attended the funeral with his other friends, the ones who had gotten to know David. It had been so painful wanting to touch him again even in death, if only to kiss his cheek as he lay in that casket. He was sure no one had ever known that he had been the one who cried the most at the viewing, at the funeral, at the cemetery, the next weekend, two months later that one night, that time three months later in the car while he was waiting for his grandmother in the drugstore parking lot, and that day he broke down while fishing by himself a full six months after the funeral. That one was, oddly enough, the worst bout. It kept coming back to haunt him. It was that last time when he had told himself that he never again wanted to feel the agony of loving a boy who couldn't love him back the way he wanted. The way he needed. He had told himself that love was what caused so much pain. He squashed his feelings. Hid the reason for his lingering grief. The ache had been so unbearable that he had to push it away. His whole life had changed that day. He had no idea that something like this had the power it had: his parents dying, Muh dying, but especially David.

But now he knew the truth. And he willingly acknowledged it for the first time. *I loved you David. I loved you so much.* His anger softened as he felt warmth at remembering David's easy smile, his cherubic face, and his awesome boyhood friendship.

*Scott's like David in so many ways.* Fear slammed into him. *Why do I feel so scared when I think about him?*

＊                    ＊                    ＊

The weekend was almost over now. Preston and Casey had just gotten to the merry-go-round at the club when they heard two car doors shut in the parking lot above them next to the dining area. It was just past eight in the evening and dark in their rendezvous spot. They heard a woman giggle and a male voice telling her to be quiet. Preston put a finger to Casey's lips.

They heard footsteps coming down the sidewalk near them. A bush moved like someone had hit it, then they heard an *awk!* as the man fell over and tumbled down the hill next to the sidewalk. He came to a stop not more than ten feet from them. The two boys froze where they were sitting, hardly breathing even. Preston was thankful they had all their clothes on. There had been many times in the past when that wouldn't have been the case. But the couple didn't even see them; they were both clearly drunk. The boys would have easily been identified as employees due to their attire if the couple had had their wits about them. The girl helped the man up; they both laughed, then took off further down the hill from them past the entire play area. Finally, they were completely out of earshot.

"I-I don't want to be your boyfriend anymore," Preston announced right out of the blue.

Casey was so taken aback that he had to ask himself if he had heard it correctly. After all, he was just about to turn his head to kiss him. "You *what?*" He stood up.

"I don't wanna go out with you anymore."

Preston had deliberated all weekend about what to say. He had decided that he'd first tell Casey to get lost, then tomorrow, Monday, he would tell Scott that he wanted him. He knew it was the wrong thing to do but he had had enough of Casey. He was way too romantic. He continuously referred to him as 'boyfriend', which was becoming annoying, and Preston just didn't like that Casey was so nice to him. It made him feel claustrophobic.

"*You bitch!*"

Preston shushed him and quickly looked around.

"Don't shush me. Why are you doing this? Why do you *hate* me so much?" All the time they had been together and Preston kept pushing him away, like just about every time after they had sex, or when they were with other people they knew, came to Casey's mind now. All the time he had spent these last several weeks trying his best to get Preston to see how much he liked him. It had done no good.

"I don't *hate* you. I just don't want us to be together anymore. It makes me feel all fucked up." He knew he wasn't doing a decent job of explaining it.

The Polaroids came to Casey's mind. "It's Scott, isn't it?"

Preston's mouth dropped open. "How do you know about him?" He instantly regretted saying that.

"So, it's true. Are you going fuck him over like your fucking me over right now? You *bitch!*" This time he pushed Preston hard against the merry-go-round.

"Ow!" he exclaimed, then rubbed the back of his head. *How could he possibly know about Scott? Had they talked?* "W-what did he tell you?"

Casey ignored his question. "I thought you liked me. I thought you *loved* me." He had only hoped that part was true. But the opposite was indeed true. He was in love with Preston.

*Shit. That's exactly what I thought he'd say,* Preston thought.

Despite the difficult time Casey always had with him, he was used to Preston being there. Where else could he find such a cute boy to be with? Despite Preston's quirky personality, he was a familiar source of intimacy, however unevenly it was meted out. As their relationship had progressed, he had found himself falling deeper and deeper in love with him, something he simply couldn't help. He hadn't dared tell him, knowing what might be in store if he divulged it. But now this.

"I'm sorry. I-I just don't want to go out with you anymore."

Casey's mind went on overdrive. He didn't know whether to try to salvage what little they had together, or just simply walk away. He decided that next instant.

"You're a fuckwad, Preston Tyllas." With that, he went up the hill, got into his car, and drove off.

Casey's world had crashed down hard on top of him.

Preston didn't even try to go after him. He felt bad about it, but wanted to end it as quickly as possible. For several minutes, he felt guilt and regret at what he'd done. He finally managed to stifle all the feelings except for the pain from the bump on his head. Otherwise, it would ruin the plans he was already formulating about how to tell Scott tomorrow at school that he wanted him to be his boyfriend.

He still couldn't figure out how Casey even knew Scott existed.

*    *    *

The clock silently changed from 7:29 to 7:30 and buzzed. Scott jerked awake and smacked it with his open palm. He was really hard. It was as much from having to pee as from some particularly erotic imagery from a dream that was still lingering in his mind.

After he exited the bathroom, he looked over at his answering machine. He had deliberately kept the message Ryan had left on it from Thursday and had listened to it repeatedly. He rewound and re-listened to the last three words again: 'I *love* you'.

A reminder of what was most important.

It was as if he had been slapped in the face. He couldn't hide the one most important thing about his relationship with Ryan. He had been so busy feeling hurt, nursing his miscommunications with and from him, and being angry with himself about Preston, that he hadn't allowed himself to be fully cognizant of how much…he…loved…Ryan.

It went way beyond kissing, way beyond sex. It was the subtle measure of his intelligence. How about his ability to draw just about anything? What about his incredibly sensitive core? And there was his butch attitude which he secretly admired. There was something between them that transcended their conversations, when they touched, even when they were merely silent together. It was the way he did everything. Scott had few words to adequately describe it. But it was real, almost solid in its intensity.

Colleen had been right. He had been in colossal denial. *This is what it's like to be in love,* he thought. The answering machine message filled his thoughts, echoed. 'I *love* you. I *love* you.'

Scott's legs ceased being able to hold him up. He slowly dropped to the floor next to his bed and grasped the sheet in his fists as he rested his forehead on the mattress. He felt angry at his foolishness. The anger slowly faded and was replaced by the same feeling he had that day when they were coming back from Parker months ago. When Ryan said he would be Scott's boyfriend. A feeling greatly magnified now. His heart pounded in his chest. He let the feeling rise until it almost overwhelmed him.

He...was...totally...in...love.

No. No!

*Yes!*

That explained why he couldn't stop thinking about him. That explained why he could barely concentrate on his homework recently. That explained why he wasn't as attentive at band practice as he normally was. That explained why he kept the message on the machine instead of erasing it right away; why he listened to it over and over. That explained why, despite their thoughtlessness at what was going on between them, they still hadn't called it off. Even though he figured it should be over, it wasn't.

It wasn't even close to being over.

Scott glanced at the clock. He badly needed to talk to Ryan, but he had to get to school. Besides, he knew Ryan was on his way to work just about now. It was going to be a weird day. He had to be at work early tonight. Somehow, he'd have to contain himself all day about this. But tonight he'd see him. *Tonight!*

Scott reeled with the feeling the entire first half of the day. He really expected it to fade away, but it didn't. It stayed the exact same way, a steady simmer. At his locker, his heart pounded when he even thought Ryan's name. In his first three classes, he couldn't concentrate, nor could he keep the silly grin off his face as he wrote Ryan's name repeatedly on a piece of notebook paper. He filled three columns. At lunch, he just stared at his food, wondering why he even bothered to enter the cafeteria. In a way, he wasn't sure why he had denied his deepest feelings recently, or even how he had managed to do so. But he figured that maybe it was because of how volatile Ryan was and he didn't want to admit he loved someone like that. He thought he would be the first one to make that giant leap to full-blown acknowledgement of being in love. It seemed so out of character for him not to.

No.

Yes...*yes!*

After lunch, other things slowly crowded his thoughts. Important things. The calculus midterm was coming up on Thursday. He had been avoiding Preston in the hall, ignoring him in class, and making sure he wasn't in the cafeteria when he saw him there. He had had to find another way to study for the exam. Annette had been his only alternative. Today would be the last time he'd really need to see her this week. Reviews were scheduled in all his classes until the exams on Thursday. His other midterms were a piece of cake. He was only worried about this one.

His study session with Annette later that day was quite involved. Luckily, there was no one else that needed her attention today. He was alone with her, one-on-one. She asked twice why he was grinning. He said 'Ryan' the second time and left it at that.

Preston saw Scott through the narrow vertical window of the classroom door. He waited outside in the hallway until just before the bell rang then went down to the end of the hall, through the double doors, and out onto the sidewalk.

It was getting worse. He couldn't stop the feelings he was having for Scott. Before, it had been pure lust. Now, though, it was heart palpitations, romantic feelings, thoughts about them being together. It was completely different from being with Casey. *I don't get it. I never felt this way about anyone.*

A few moments later, Scott emerged through the same doors and went toward the parking lot. Preston had been waiting where Scott couldn't see him. Scott heard someone approaching from behind and turned his head to see who it was. He turned around and dropped his shoulders when he saw him.

Preston stopped not more than three feet from him. "Scott, I need to talk to you," he said as he caught his breath. His adrenaline was pumping now.

"Make it quick. I gotta go," he said, obviously annoyed.

"Don't go. I-I wanted to tell you that I really, *really* like you. And I wanted to know if you and I could see each other more often. Like, as boyfriends. Besides, I like studying with you."

Scott couldn't believe what he was hearing. "Studying? With *me*? You mean studying my *dick*. And did I even hear that come out of your mouth? You wanna be boyfriends? We haven't even been on a date."

*Why is he acting like this?* "Why not? Why couldn't we go out?"

At this point, despite the acknowledgement of his feelings, Scott wasn't sure whether Ryan was his boyfriend or not. But he was certain of one important thing: Preston was definitely not anyone he could ever bring himself to even think about dating. "You must be delusional. We're not gonna date. We're not gonna be boyfriends. And we're not gonna have sex ever again either."

Preston grabbed his arm. *"What?"* He was panicking, reacting instead of taking the lead. He had just gotten rid of Casey once and for all, was ready to take Scott as his, and his heart was talking to him for a change. But Scott was acting completely off the wall.

"Here, I'll say it again. We're…"

Preston cut him off. "No! I just dumped…" He realized he had just divulged the big secret and clamped his mouth shut.

Scott heard him. "Huh? You just *dumped* someone?"

Preston had already misspoken, so it couldn't hurt to say so. Besides, Casey was history now. He released Scott's arm. "Yes."

"You were going out with someone? While we were…?" Scott's voice trailed off. He was greatly alarmed at the news.

"Well, *he* thought he was my boyfriend."

Although Scott couldn't do calculus all that well, he certainly could do the math. This was too weird. He never had any intention of messing up another relationship, much less his own. "Fuck you," he said. But he had been one of the guilty parties and knew it even as he said it.

Preston was furious. Now was no time to keep any more secrets. He pointed a finger at him. "I saw you kiss him. Right here in the parking lot. You're going out with someone, too. Aren't you?"

Scott was speechless. Preston had seen the kiss, too? *Fuck!* "And I still am," he shot back. God, he hoped it were still true. *Tonight!*

"Well, let's see. After I tell him, he'll dump *you.*"

*Fuck, fuck!* "Huh! You don't even know who he is."

"Let me guess. Ryan St. Charles."

Scott grabbed the front of Preston's shirt and twisted it until it was tight in his fist. "If you say *anything* I'll kick your fucking ass. And you *know* I can do it." He released his grip, surprised at his outburst. He had totally overreacted.

Preston hadn't been prepared for Scott's aggressive reaction. He straightened his shirt while Scott went to his Jeep. This time he couldn't stop himself from feeling terrible.

Other students were walking by him on the sidewalk to their cars, too. Preston stood there watching Scott get in his Jeep. *Damn,* he thought. He had no idea how to contact Ryan anyway. His brother was certainly out of the question. And now he wondered how he had messed things up so quickly and so badly. He had been a master at all of this and now it had bitten him in the ass. *There's no way Scott would beat me up.* He watched as the Jeep pulled out of the parking lot. *Jeez, maybe he would.*

Adrenaline coursed through Scott's veins. *Why did I react like that? Because he threatened to ruin what little is salvageable between Ryan and me?* But it brought up the one thing he knew he had to handle. He had to tell Ryan every-thing. He'd have to divulge everything about his liaisons with Preston if he were to get through the rest of the week with his emotions intact.

*Love. Pounding mercilessly in my heart. Guilt. Hovering over me like a guillotine.*

Preston was pissed off at not only Scott, but with himself. He should have used another approach. Yet, he hadn't expected Scott's odd reaction. *Something must have happened. Something I don't know anything about.* But he had some-thing else to attend to now as he carefully, methodically, squelched his feelings for Scott. It was refreshing feeling this way about him, but also annoying at the same time. *It just isn't right to fall for someone like that.*

He had been studying for midterms, but knew full well he'd get a very poor grade on the calculus one. Although they were going to be reviewing in class tomorrow and Wednesday, it wasn't going to be enough for him. Now, with Scott being a dick he wouldn't be able to concentrate in class either. It was going to be really awkward again this week. Jeez, this would be so much easier if he didn't sit in the very next row. But he'd figure out what was going on with Scott. And if Scott didn't come around, like he expected, Ryan would find out all about it, regardless of Scott's threat.

Luckily, he had been planning his next move since the end of last week. He knew exactly where Ms. Dunn's mailbox was in the admin office. He had been in the office often enough to know that they were usually unguarded in a sep-arate smaller room off to the left. He also knew that Ms. Dunn had a freshman class assistant copy her tests, with the questions and answers, and he would put them into her box in advance of exam days. Starting on last Thursday, Preston had been clandestinely checking her mailbox, glancing ever so briefly into it after making his quick trips to the little mailroom when no one was looking. He also knew that the old ladies that worked in the office weren't as sharp as they used to be. No one had seen him come by the last several times. Today was going to be no exception. He went back into the building, wondering how he was going to get Scott to come around, yet at the same time, wondering again if that damn exam was in the box yet.

Once again, he'd timed it right. No one was around. He peeked at the stack of wooden boxes, pulled hers out, and quickly leafed through the contents. There were several items in it, but the most conspicuous one was the large sealed white envelope. He quickly pulled it out and pressed the cover against the contents. He could just barely make out the words 'Calculus Exam, 5th period.' Ah, ha! As quickly as he could, he stuffed it into his backpack and, with considerable trepidation, exited the office. His next stop would be to the copy shop down the street. He'd be able to have the envelope back in the mailbox in less than half an hour.

Ms. Dunn was at her desk in her classroom. On the lesson plan in front of her for fifth period for the next two days was a review of a series of sixteen questions for the midterm on Thursday. She had already randomly selected four questions of the sixteen for them to answer on the exam. If her students worked out the questions properly during the review, then most of the class would not only pass the exam, but her grade curve would look picture perfect as well.

Andy, her freshman classroom assistant, said the exams would be in her admin office box by 3 p.m. She headed out of the classroom and went down the wing to the office. The only other person she saw was Preston just coming out of the office and briskly going down the corridor in the opposite direction. He didn't see her.

No one was in the office when she came in. And the exam envelope wasn't in her mailbox yet. She took the rest of her mail anyway. As she went back down the wing to her classroom, she saw Andy through the library window sitting at one of the tables with some other students. She didn't want to go in and bother the kids, so motioned to get his attention. He saw her and came out to the hallway.

"Hi, Ms. Dunn. Something wrong?"

"I thought you would have those exams copied already."

"I did it two hours ago. The envelope's in your mailbox."

She looked through her mail again. "I don't see it."

"Everything was there: the answer sheet, the worksheet you made, and twenty-eight copies of the exam. In a big white envelope. I sealed it myself in the office."

"Was anyone there when you did it?"

"Mrs. Griffith. She was back there sorting mail. I told her what I was doing."

"Maybe she moved it for some reason. I'm sorry I interrupted you."

She took a quick look through the library window. The two freshmen girls at his table were trying to hide giggles while looking at Andy with furtive glances. They were clearly talking about him. Andy hadn't noticed since he was facing away from them. She briefly smiled at him and went down the hall. She wasn't concerned now so she went to the teacher's lounge to get a soda, turned on the little TV to catch up on some news while she drank it, and read the mail. Twenty minutes later, she went back to the admin office. Mrs. Griffith was at her desk.

"Hi, Marge. I came looking for my midterm exam package that Andy left in my mailbox this afternoon. Have you seen it?"

"Why yes. I was back there when he put it in the box. Have you looked?"

"I got my other mail earlier, but it wasn't there."

"I'm sure I saw him put it in there." She stood and went to the mailboxes with her. When Marge pulled her box out, the white envelope was the only thing in it.

Ms. Dunn looked flustered. "I don't understand it. I was here not more than thirty minutes ago. It wasn't here."

Marge touched her glasses frames. "I guess we're *all* getting old, Nancy."

She didn't know what to say, but nonetheless took the envelope and headed back to her classroom to get her things.

*          *          *

Howard commented on the incredibly good mood Ryan was in several times since he had returned late Sunday evening and twice today at work. And Ryan looked forward to his session with Dr. Kevin tonight. He had all sorts of interesting things to tell him. He pulled up in the parking lot at dusk and looked at magazines in the waiting room for a few minutes. At his scheduled time, Dr. Kevin greeted him as Ryan entered his office. They made small talk for a few minutes.

"You seem to be in exceptionally good spirits today. I know you just came back from your grandmother's estate sale. Turned out well?"

Ryan had indeed walked away with a boatload of money. He had already transferred the requisite amount of monies to Chris' account and had handled the trust account issues earlier over the phone. He told Dr. Kevin about what he had done up at the house. How they had sold virtually everything off. How the Goodwill truck had hauled off the rest. How he had walked the property and then locked up the house for the very last time. How he and Adina, along with her parents, had stood on the driveway and hugged each other that Sunday night under the light pole next to the house after it got dark out. About the delayed flight coming back from up north due to some weather they had to skirt around near San Francisco. That chapter of his life was now over. His adult life was somewhere other than in Crescent City now.

"My entire college education is paid for now. Undergraduate, graduate, and more. That's a burden off my shoulders."

"But there's more than that, isn't there?" Kevin could see the sparkle in his eyes, the completely different tone of his voice, the confidence in his speaking.

"I understand some really important things now. I remembered something while I was up there that I tried to make myself forget, but couldn't.

"There was this boy named David when I was a freshman back home. He died in an accident when we were kids. I-I was, like, in love with him. But I just shut down. Completely. I even tried to make myself forget he was ever alive.

His death made me so afraid that if I ever loved anyone again they would die. Just like my parents had. When Muh died, that feeling was there, but I had shut off why I was feeling that way."

Then Ryan told him about seeing Crawford and the swirl of emotion that seeing him had caused. How he couldn't help himself and let Crawford kiss him. About exactly how he felt when he finally realized who Crawford had been for him. *Really* understood this time. He had been hardly more than a security blanket. At he discussed it with Kevin he came to realize that Crawford was his father who had abandoned him years earlier. Crawford was a substitute David who Ryan hoped might love him back. Crawford was a convenient teenage sexual outlet. He fulfilled multiple roles in his life, but he wasn't who Ryan thought he was and now he knew it. Completely knew it.

And why was he so afraid when he thought of Scott? He knew what it was all about now. He had slowly figured it out while coming back on the plane. Scott wouldn't die if he loved him, just like Dr. Kevin had said. It was David who had died. But the emotional torment he had felt had been rearing its head at him all that time. His unrelenting love for Scott had simply restimulated that long forgotten memory. Whenever he consciously acknowledged it, even a little, he felt terror. He had been constantly feeling the same as on the day he heard about David's death. As his love for Scott kept overflowing, it kept restimulating the same feeling.

"So, while I was at Crawford's place there was this moment of, I don't know what, maybe like clarity or something, when I realized how much I loved David. But my love for Scott is a hundred times more…intense." He almost didn't get that last word out. He stopped and fought for composure. It certainly wasn't from sadness. It was from the feelings that were coming up. Finally, he poised himself and continued. "Everything changed because of Scott.

"You used the word 'sacred' once. I'd been thinking about that ever since you said it. He made me realize how sacred life is. He made me see how sacred *he* is, how sacred *I* am. He's the only person in the world right now that I-that I…*love.*" It wasn't red eyes and simple tears down his cheeks this time. It was all out crying. It was so wonderful understanding it, feeling it, and now saying it, that he couldn't contain himself anymore.

Kevin's was quite moved. He thought Ryan would find this inside him, but he didn't anticipate it would be so cathartic or this soon.

He pulled three, four, then five tissues from the box in quick succession. He rose up, took one of Ryan's hands, and forced them into it. Ryan pressed the mass of tissues against his eyes. Kevin could only see his mouth in a crying-frown, his nose as it started to drain, and his cheeks completely wet even though the most of his face was obscured.

*He's certainly accomplished a lot of difficult therapeutic work and all in a very short period,* Kevin thought.

Although it was bad protocol, Kevin sat down next to Ryan. He reached out and touched his shoulder. Ryan responded and wrapped arms around Kevin. Kevin smiled as they rocked back and forth a little, then stopped. Kevin continued to hold him, feeling Ryan shake as he sobbed, amazed at the intensity of Ryan's feelings.

At intervals Ryan cried so hard he couldn't breathe. He loved Scott so much it seemed to hurt. No, the hurt was from the time he had spent hiding it. His bout lasted a good four minutes while he purged. Finally, it was over, swept away.

*Pain gone forever.*

*Death?*

*No death.*

*Indescribable joy.*

*Love?*

*Love.*

Kevin was still sitting next to him, smiling brightly. Ryan smiled back at him. Even with his puffy eyes he looked like a little boy who had just gotten the biggest stuffed animal prize at a carnival.

Everything was different now.

Everything.

*     *     *

It was shortly after nine when Scott left work. Ryan had called him earlier and insisted that he come over as soon as he could. There was a tone in Ryan's voice he couldn't quite place. Peace, calm.

He wanted to see Ryan so badly he could taste it. He had to tell Ryan everything. He had to apologize and do it fast. He had to do it so he could feel free to tell him how much he loved him. The waiting had been killing him all evening. The more he thought about Dan and Tony together, the angrier he had gotten with himself. If they had been able to stay together for that long, then by God, he could do it, too. *But what if I damaged us beyond recognition,* he thought. *What if Ryan simply says no? Please don't, please don't. I love you too much for that to happen.*

Ryan was sitting on the driveway in the dark when Scott pulled up. His legs were stretched out in front of him and he was leaning back on his palms. Scott shut off the engine and looked down at him. Ryan wiggled his feet a little upon seeing him but continued to sit there with an amusing smile on his face.

Scott stepped out and sat down on the driveway with him. His heart was beating rapidly. He felt giddy. "This is a pretty strange place to hang out."

"I was watching satellites. You can just barely see them even if you stare for a long time. Sometimes they look like they're blinking, but it's really because they're spinning. You can hardly ever see them up north since the sky's not so clear up there."

Scott looked up, didn't see any, but marveled at the wide expanse of the starry sky anyway. "Let's go up the street." Scott helped him up and they held hands as they started down the driveway in silence.

They just passed the last streetlight when Ryan stopped and looked over at him. "I love you. I love you like nobody else in the world." He squeezed Scott's hand.

Scott was mustering up the courage to tell him. He was feeling incredibly guilty. Stupid. Heart pounding, he didn't know how to say it so he just blurted it out. "I have to tell you something that's really bad. I-I had sex with someone. Someone else."

"When? With who?"

"That guy from school I was telling you about. Preston. We did it-we did it…a couple of times. He even dumped his boyfriend. I'm so sorry, you just don't know." There. It was said.

Ryan winced at the revelation. Here he was, totally in love with Scott and now this. He was filled with anguish at the news. "Why?"

"It's all *my* fault. I didn't know you wanted me anymore. He was giving me these signals, flirting with me. We were studying for fucking calculus and he just came on to me. I'm so sorry it happened. I didn't mean to. I really didn't."

"But you did. You had sex with him."

"I was mad at you, and I was horny and-and you weren't there."

"That's convenient. What else is going on between you two?" It was as if the fire in his heart had suddenly been extinguished by very cold water.

"Nothing. I swear it. I had to tell you because…" Scott stopped talking because Ryan yanked his hand away.

Ryan's face changed, contorted, took on the look of pain. He looked away. "Maybe it won't work out after all. I should have known better. This was a big mistake. I've been such a *mess* all this time. Fuck. *Fuck!*"

There was silence. Intense, deep silence. Scott could feel the blood rushing in his neck, could hear it in his ears. His tether came loose. He was pulling away the ship, pulling away rapidly, faster than he could imagine, plummeting out of orbit, into the atmosphere. He grabbed Ryan's arm, held tightly, hoping that re-entry wouldn't burn him to a cinder. "*No! I* made the mistake. I'm sorry, I swear I'm *sorry!*"

Ryan's eyes were teary. "Well, he dumped his boyfriend. Did you just kiss him or did you let him *fuck* you for that?"

*Stabbed, deeply.* "I didn't do *anything* for him. I didn't even know he *had* a boyfriend."

"I bet he didn't know *you* had one either, right?"

"*Please.* I wasn't sure what was going on between us. But, it's not what you think! I *love* you. I swear." He slowly let go of Ryan's arm.

*I won't hear this. I can't!* Ryan started breathing in an odd staccato manner, as if he were trying to hold something in. Emotion. *Spiral downward, again.* "You love me? And this is how you show it? How could you do this? Right when everything was so perfect."

Scott bit his lip as he heard the intense grief in Ryan's voice. His throat was tightening up and he could barely speak. *Swallow.* "Everything was 'so perfect?'" His throat tightened even more. *Swallow again before you completely lose it.* "It wasn't perfect at all."

Ryan hadn't had a chance to explain everything just yet, and neither had Scott. But the 'perfect' he meant was that he had discovered the source of his most deeply held fear. The forgotten issue about David. It had colored everything about his relationship with Scott. Hell, it had colored his relationship with everyone until this last weekend. And when that had been uncovered, when it was all out in the open, he had discovered how much he had loved Scott and for how long, too. But Scott's sudden disclosure on top of his wonderful new revelation led him to doubt right now just how important that was. He didn't exactly know how to explain it either. He had never been any good at explaining his feelings. Dr. Kevin was the only one he had ever divulged so much to, or so fast. He hadn't even opened up that much to Scott before, despite what had happened between them while they were up north all those months back. And now Scott seemed like an enemy. How that was possible he couldn't begin to say. He was still in love with him! It was unbelievably confusing. *Spiral, ever downward. Cushion the fall. Stop.* He looked down at the asphalt.

"I need to sort this all out. Just give me some time to decide what to do," Ryan told him.

"Sort what out? Decide to do what?"

"Us. I love you and now you're telling me that you have to just…hurt me."

"I swear I love you." Scott's vision blurred from a veil of tears. "I swear."

It didn't help. Scott went from feeling awful to outright despondent. He was sure that if he started with the apology it would clear the way for him to tell

Ryan that he loved him. Really, really loved him. It wasn't supposed to be this way when you loved someone. But both of them were too stirred up, angry, crazy with confusion to listen to each other clearly. Nonetheless, he took Ryan in his arms and hugged him. Hugged him hard. His nose ran, getting Ryan's shoulder wet.

The wind picked up. As they held on to each other it picked up even more, swirling around them like the sad emotion each was feeling inside.

# CHAPTER 15

M rs. Dunn handed out the exams to the head of each row and watched as
they were passed back. She had announced just five minutes previous
that the exam would consist of four of the sixteen questions they had already
reviewed in the last two days. That got a look of surprise from some of the students. Others groaned. They were to show their work on a separate sheet of
paper and hand that in with their exam. Any student who handed in a worksheet without a name on it would automatically fail. Everyone signed their
blank sheet right away. Their incentive to be in class tomorrow? She would be
grading them this evening and have their results tomorrow before Winterfest.

Scott was nervous as hell, but he felt totally prepared. He had worked with
Annette enough, understood every one of the exam questions they had
reviewed, and was sure that if the test was merely four of the ones they had just
reviewed that he would pass for sure. He couldn't believe the luck.

They had been told they could leave as soon as they were done. Forty minutes later when he was done, there were only five other students left. It was
harder than he thought. He couldn't imagine how Preston was the third student to leave, but was so busy working on the second problem by then that it
didn't cross his mind again.

Once he was outside the classroom Doug caught up with him. "Some test.
Just memorize everything we went over and spit out the answer."

"That is, if your memory is perfect. My worksheet was filled up," Scott
answered.

"Well, I think I aced it."

"Funny thing. I think I did, too."

"Hey, Jill, Evan, and I, and a bunch of the other guys, are gonna go to the
Powerlines tonight to celebrate the end of midterms. Wanna go?"

"Have I ever said no to the Powerlines?"

The Powerlines was the place to party. Underneath the high-tension line towers fifteen miles from the edge of town, people would bring their vans, pick-ups, and other vehicles, pile out of them, and party on the nearby rock formations. The road leading to the area was one and a half miles of undulating, rugged terrain off the two-lane highway. More or less isolated from authorities, the cops had made an appearance exactly once that Scott was aware of. So, it was a great place for under-aged beer drinking; and for the stoners, to smoke pot and do the occasional harder drugs.

They started for the parking lot. Doug turned to Scott. "Are you guys ready for tomorrow night?" He was referring to the fact that Centauri would be playing at the school for Winterfest.

"Are you kidding? It's gonna be the bitchin'est' party this school's ever had."

Doug smiled brightly. "Awesome. Centauri *rocks!*" He held up his fist. Scott made one and they smacked their knuckles together.

Ms. Dunn sat at the kitchen table that evening, where she always graded papers. The stack of exams was to her left, the big white envelope to her right, and the worksheet was on top of the envelope. She had manually worked out all the steps on the worksheet in longhand days before. Then it caught her eye. She noticed that she had made an error on her worksheet. She had that ability to see a math error at a glance, and it worked this time, too. Mr. Zemchenko, the senior English teacher, had the same uncanny ability to spot a spelling mistake in virtually any document. She had even taken two papers to him in the past for him to check for her, for a continuing education course she had been in. His eagle eye had caught three errors.

This was odd, too. She had transposed one of the variables, while working out the solution to the second question, which had made the result completely wrong. She looked at the solution to the third question and was even more flabbergasted. She had written down an incorrect log value. That made the result completely wrong, too. *Now how in the heck did I do that twice?* She recalled that she had been working out the problems while watching TV. She remembered her attention being diverted when the weatherman said that it would be warmer toward the middle of the week, but with record cold coming in tonight. The Dunn's had a three-season porch in the back of the house and she had stopped what she was doing to make sure the two rows of windows had been firmly shut back there. Her young kids never shut them properly. When she had returned to the kitchen, and was working on the third problem, the pot of rice on the stove had boiled over, and that had diverted her attention yet again. The dog was scratching at the door at the same time. She must have been so flustered that when she had returned to the worksheet both times she made the mistakes.

*Maybe Marge* was *right. I must be getting old…no,* senile*!* Luckily, though, it didn't affect the exam in any way. She'd simply work out the solutions again and use the addendum worksheet as a reference, if needed.

Doug came by Scott's house to pick him up shortly after eight. Jill was in the passenger seat.

"You better bring a jacket. It's supposed to get cold," she said through the window as Scott approached.

He was wearing an untucked flannel shirt, a tucked in t-shirt, jeans, and hiking boots. He looked at her, unconvinced. "Are you sure?"

"Yeah, record cold. It may even get below freezing."

Scott went back to his room to get his letter jacket. *Record cold? Below freezing? That hardly ever happens, even this late in December.* He looked at the thermometer screwed to the outside window frame next to his bedroom door. *Besides, it's sixty-five now.* He returned just moments later and they took off.

Tonight was a perfectly clear night, with a waxing quarter moon hanging just between the low notches of the far mountains in the southwest. There were two sets of low-piled boulders near the parking area. Students from the various schools, all of which knew this party spot, rarely mixed, sticking mostly near their own boulder pile. It kept fights to a minimum. Regardless, they parked their cars near each other in the long ago well-established area.

Once Scott, Doug, and Jill piled out, they found some of the track team and other students milling about already. There were already a dozen people on the west side of the near boulders.

When the place got crowded, groups of students would invariably end up at various compass points of both mounds. Tonight there was a small group they knew standing between the two mounds. Someone had brought some bottle rockets and they were clustered together while one of them fired them off. When their lighter would no longer function, Jill announced she had one in her purse and gave it to one of the boys. They watched while a half dozen more were launched, one at a time.

Evan came along with a couple of their track buddies in his car. Directly after him was what everyone was waiting for. From the back of a pickup were produced two small washtubs with iced beer in them. Everyone had to pony up three dollars and there was a free for all to get their bottles and cans. Scott twisted the cap off his beer and clinked Doug's bottle. They talked for a few moments about midterms while they continued to watch the remainder of the bottle rockets being fired off. None of them noticed Joe arrive and park his truck. His two buddies, Carl and Stu, were together in another truck behind him. They pulled up and parked next him.

Ryan sat in Kevin's office looking through a magazine that had been left on the coffee table. Kevin came in and shut the door. Ryan tossed the magazine aside.

"Sorry, I got paged. It's good to see you again. How are things going now?" Kevin asked with a big smile.

So, with a downhearted look on his face Ryan told Dr. Kevin all about Monday evening. The roller coaster ride still hadn't stopped. He thought it had ended. But, oddly enough, although he felt saddened by what had transpired between Scott and himself, he had no intrinsic grief left. It was gone. What had replaced all of it was a little bit of anxiety, but mostly he felt peace and calm. It was the oddest sensation. He thought he should be feeling so despondent he should be shrouded in tears. It just wasn't happening.

Kevin noticed that too. "No more grief. I think you truly found the source of your most un-welcomed feelings. What do you think you're going to do with this issue? Do you think Scott really loves you after all?"

"I'm sure he does. I just know it. He said it so many times that night. I just kept ignoring him. I'm such a shit. I called him tonight but he wasn't home. He wasn't at work either. His mother said one of his friends was going to come by and they were going out someplace. I left a message for him anyway."

"What was in it?"

"I told him that I was upset. That I just spun out again. I had just gotten used to feeling really good and then he told me he, like, cheated on me. And, well, it made me think he was trying to leave me and…you know." Ryan looked away.

"Your feeling of being abandoned got all stirred up."

Ryan nodded, feeling more stupid than anything else. "He was *apologizing* and I didn't even hear it until this afternoon. God, I hope he doesn't hate me." *Kick myself. Hard.*

"Perhaps you should ask him. No, better yet tell him you don't hate *him*."

Ryan heard him, but he was looking out toward the courtyard at the water-fall. *Emotion gliding over the rocks. Gathering peacefully into a pool of calm water.* "I *love* him. I love Scott even right *now*. My heart's beating so fast just *thinking* about him. About *us*. About us being *together*." *Our sacred love.*

Even though he felt stupid for not hearing Scott's apology, he hoped that when he got home tonight he would hear from him no matter how late it was.

Ms. Dunn had graded seventeen of the twenty-eight tests so far. She had been plotting the grades onto a piece of graph paper. The letters A through F were along the X-axis and she was building columns as she marked the exams. She wanted a rough estimate of the grade point spread. So far, her bar chart was looking exactly as she expected. She wouldn't have to apply a curve after all. She marked another grade on the graph paper, then turned the exam over onto the finished pile. Next was Preston's. He had maintained a C minus average and she hoped he would pull this one off to raise it a bit. She started going over his worksheet. By this time, she had seen so many of them she knew what to expect. She didn't expect what she saw now.

"This can't be," she said out loud. "This is not possible."

Casey knew he shouldn't be pissed off anymore but, after all, he had never been dumped before, so he was still quite angry. René Geiger, his friend from down the street, was driving them to the Powerlines. They had gone there several times over the years. She had heard from some of the other Yucca Valley students that there was going to be a little get together to celebrate the end of midterms. Since Casey was her friend, and he had told her about what had happened between he and Preston, she decided he needed some cheering up. She didn't know any of the details, but knew enough to realize that Casey needed a diversion from his hurt feelings. Casey knew from conversations at school that there would be at least half a dozen fellow students there tonight from Teller.

He had just finished telling her about that night at the merry-go-round.

"He's just awful," she said. She knew Preston from school, but had never talked with him. He didn't seem the least bit gay and as far as she knew no one from school suspected he was either. Casey wouldn't make it a week before people knew he was gay, though. Funny how gay guys could be so different from one another, she thought.

"Thanks for listening. You're the best, René. I'm still pissed off though."

"Well, a night partying with your friends will be just what you need. And when we get there, don't go running off like you do all the time. I hate when you do that."

Whenever he didn't drive, he had a tendency to leave with anyone who offered him a ride. Never mind that René drove him those last two times. When she had been ready to go he was nowhere to be seen. He was like that because he was way more social than she could ever hope to be, and he just got caught up in whatever crowd he was with at the moment. At least that's what he told her. She decided he was either absentminded, flaky, or a combination of the two. Regardless, she loved him.

"You never know who's gonna show up. I can't help it. I just get involved in conversations. You know me," he told her.

"Yeah, I do. That's why I said it."

"I'm sorry," he said genuinely. "I love you, René." They blew each other an air kiss.

Once they arrived and parked, they immediately saw two Teller students that they knew from their neighborhood. They went to the group and started talking with them.

Scott noticed as the evening was wearing on that Doug and Jill were getting a lot more amorous. She kept leaning into him, giving him those eyes, and generally making him horny by sticking her hands in his back pockets. Doug was doing his share of touching, too. He knew what Doug was like when he got horny. Not personally, of course. More like when he was with Jill.

Scott snapped the buttons of his jacket together. The evening was turning considerably colder, just as Jill said it would. He was glad she told him to bring his jacket.

Soon enough Doug came up to him. "Hey, Scott, uh, Jill and I are gonna go back early. You might wanna find someone to take you back."

Scott snickered. "Have fun. I'll ask Evan for a ride later."

"You don't mind?"

"Just go and do it before I have to see the whole thing happen here." Actually, he wouldn't have minded it at all. He would have loved to see Doug humping away even if he were having sex with a girl.

Doug grinned as he realized that Scott knew what was up. He went back to Jill, and they took off a few minutes later.

Ryan came back into the TV room. It was several hours after his therapy session. Chris had also noticed the considerable change in Ryan's mood recently and had been having decent conversations with him this last week. Ryan was greatly aware now he had been the source of most of their non-communicating and was relieved when Chris was being nice to him. It felt odd, but good to have a whole different way of interacting with his brother.

Ryan set the bowl of popcorn down between them on the couch and they shared it while watching a re-run. He suddenly realized it had been over a year since they had sat so close to each other, shared anything, or watched the same program together.

"Thanks," Ryan said.

Chris tilted his head back to get the handful of popcorn into his mouth. His voice was muffled. "For what?"

Ryan took the remote from the coffee table and raised the volume a little higher. "Just for being my brother."

Chris stopped munching as he knitted his brow. He slowly turned his head to look at him when he realized he did indeed hear him correctly.

Howard had somehow managed to get Krysta to talk to him and he was over at her house. She didn't want to come over to Howard's place right now but he was welcome to come over to her place anytime. Ryan felt a little jealous. Howard was willing to salvage his relationship with her despite her pitiful attempt at shoving her silly morals into their faces. *He's probably over there boinking her right now. Boink. Boink.*

That reminded him of Scott. He had called Scott several times after he got home. He had hung up twice due to just getting his answering machine. He called a third time and left a message. It was getting close to ten and, since it was a school night, he figured Scott couldn't be all that late coming back.

*Endless emotion. In my head. In my heart. In my pants.*

*I love you Scott.*

He kept munching popcorn as he grinned to himself.

Ms. Dunn's suspicion aroused now, she pulled her original worksheet out of the stack to her right and placed it in front of her. She laid Preston's worksheet next to it. She compared the second and third problems on her worksheet with his.

They were virtually identical, line for line, including her errors. She leaned back as she tried to figure out how it could have happened. She noted several clues as she thought. First, when she went to get her mail last week she had seen exactly one person in the hall. It had been Preston. He had just come out of the admin office. Then when she went back to get her mail the second time, the envelope was there, looked like it had been ripped open, although carefully, then taped at the top. She would ask Andy tomorrow if he had taped it. But the third clue was the fact that Preston had been one of the first people to turn his exam in. That particular clue was the most telling. She knew Preston was in a tutoring class. She also knew Scott Faraday was in it. Scott's class performance had improved because of it. Preston's hadn't. Yet, despite the tutoring class, Scott was still working on the last problem right up to the end of class. Preston had been long gone by that time. Was Scott involved, too? Something wasn't right.

She still hadn't gotten to Scott's exam, so she sorted through the remaining tests. His worksheet was a mess. He had used virtually all the space on both sides of the paper. As she carefully scrutinized it, then graded the exam, she noted with considerable delight that his didn't contain her errors, and that he had scored a 93. An A! That was his best score to date. She placed his score in the A column. There were only five A's so far, and now one was his.

Now she went back to Preston's and graded it. With her errors in the mix, he made a 61, which was an F. That was odd. If Preston was able to memorize an entire worksheet, errors, and all, why wasn't he a better student? Was he that lazy or was it something else?

She reluctantly marked her graph paper. His score was the only one in the F column.

Unfortunately, all of the clues were there. She knew exactly what had happened. She shook her head at what she had to do tomorrow. It wasn't going to be pleasant. This hadn't happened in six years.

*God damn that Preston Tyllas. He just ruined my class record.*

Casey eventually moved from the crowd he had been with to mix with some other Teller students. He didn't see René anywhere now and figured she had also moved on to talk to some other people, too. He was wearing only a light sweater, jeans, and tennis shoes, and noted that it was becoming a bit chilly. *Damn it, I should have brought a coat,* he thought.

One of the students in the crowd he had joined said he brought a Roman candle and some other assorted explosives. The student was going to outdo the lame bottle rocket launches he had seen earlier from the Regional students. Casey hadn't seen the earlier fireworks. He followed them as they set up their stuff where the earlier fireworks had been lit.

One of the students Scott was with pointed and noted that the Teller students had fireworks. They all slowly migrated in that direction when they saw the Roman candle going off. They wanted to be as close as possible to see and hear what else they might have. Hey, it was cheap entertainment.

Casey saw the knot of Regional students coming up to their group now that the Roman candle had been lit. The flares it was spitting out illuminated the area quite a bit. Now that they had come to stand near them, he saw that several had on letter jackets. He surveyed them to see if there were any cute faces worth looking at.

Scott and his entourage consisted of five other guys. He, along with two others, had on their letter jackets. Evan wasn't among them right now as he had gone to talk to a girl who had arrived a few minutes before. They all stopped a short distance away to watch the spectacle.

The Teller students, including Casey, added up to four kids in a semicircle. One had the bag of assorted fireworks in his hand. He was setting up the louder explosives in front of a large rock to the right of the Roman candle.

Scott had almost finished his second beer. He thrust his free hand into a pocket. The wind had picked up and it was getting even colder. He saw a group of people heading to their cars to leave. He figured would have to mention something to Evan soon about getting a ride back. Evan lived the closest to him, so was the most obvious prospect.

Casey's eyes went from one student's face the next as the Roman candle continued to spit balls of light. Then he stopped on what seemed to be a familiar one. Where had he seen that boy before? The one to the left wearing the letter jacket. He was short, and in this light, he appeared to have dark red hair and a smile to die for. He had a stocky build and nice thick legs. His mouth dropped open.

*No fucking way!*

He yanked his wallet out of his back pocket and pulled out the folded up Polaroid he had stolen from Preston. He should have thrown it already since it was a nasty reminder of that dickhead ex-boyfriend of his, but he had forgotten about it until just this second. Another Roman candle flare shot out and he looked at the picture. The faces matched exactly. *That's Scott Faraday, the very boy who stole Preston away from me.* He dropped the picture to the ground and dug the heel of his tennis shoe into it. Even more angry now, he decided right there he'd make Scott pay for his transgression.

It was ten-thirty now. Chris had gone to bed fifteen minutes ago. Even though it was relatively early, Ryan found his eyelids getting heavy. He figured he might hear from Scott, but felt particularly saddened now that he hadn't called yet.

He had just gotten to his doorway when he heard the unmistakable muffled moaning of a boy having an orgasm. The interior walls in Howard's house were way thinner than the home he grew up in. That made three times this week he'd heard Chris from the hallway or from the bathroom. Tomorrow he'd say something to him about being more quiet, which would no doubt embarrass him. He grinned at the thought of deliberately doing that.

Finally, the Teller students had exploded all their fireworks and the Roman candle had gone out. Some of the students around the far sides of the rock formations had peered around to watch, but not many others appeared to be all that interested in coming any closer.

"Hey, Scott, we're gonna go back. Wanna ride?" his old teammate, Jeremy, asked.

"No thanks, I'll ask Evan." Jeremy would have to go way out of his way to get him home.

"Whatever." Scott started in the opposite direction from him. "Where are you going?"

"To take a leak."

"See ya tomorrow in school." Jeremy, and the two students he was with, turned to leave.

As Scott started for the rocks, he thought about tomorrow night. The band was ready for Winterfest and so was he. He couldn't wait to help Centauri make a permanent impression on the school.

Casey was still with his Teller friends, but with one ear on the conversation between Scott and his buddies. When Scott turned toward the rocks, Casey followed.

Joe buttoned his jean jacket to the top button. He had five bottles lined up on Stu's open tailgate and a sixth in his hand. Stu and Carl had just raced to pound down their sixth apiece and finished when the last explosion from the fireworks went off. They slammed their empty bottles down on the tailgate at nearly the same time. The vibration knocked three of Joe's down.

"Joe, we're leaving," Carl said. He noted that people were slowly migrating to the remaining cars and trucks now. There were only five vehicles left, excluding their two trucks. "It's getting cold. Everyone else is leaving too," he added. He picked up the empty beer box and started stuffing their empties into it.

"Pussies," Joe responded.

"Freeze your fuckin' ass, then." He knew Joe was just trying to sound ornery.

Stu pulled out his keys, then exhaled through his mouth. He could see his breath now. "Come on, Carl. Joe, can you drive?"

With bleary eyes, Joe looked over at Stu. He had driven drunk before. A trek back to his house under his current six-pack conditions would be easy.

"I can drive better than either of you with one eye shut," Joe boasted. He started away from them both.

"Where the hell are you going now?"

Joe held his hands in front of his crotch, with the mostly finished bottle in one of them, to indicate he was going to take a leak.

"Yeah, yeah. See you in shop tomorrow." Stu shut the tailgate. He and Carl then took off while Joe walked toward the pile of rocks.

Casey was following Scott. *Where the hell is he going?*

Scott had walked further into the rock pile than he expected. Casey was somewhat concerned now because he noticed that lots of people were leaving and he still hadn't asked anyone for a ride back yet. But he had to have it out with Scott now. This was a perfect opportunity and it would only take a minute to get it off his chest.

Scott unzipped and started peeing against the curved rock surface. He wanted to hurry so he could find Evan to bum a ride off him. Just as he zipped up, he heard footsteps crunching behind him.

Casey stopped when Scott turned around. The smell of urine was pretty strong here. After all, it was the favored boys toilet out here. "You're Scott Faraday, aren't you?"

Scott sized Casey up. He noticed his tight curly blonde hair, the evenly tanned face, but that was just about all he could see of him in the dim light of the crescent moon. He also noticed his unusual accent but didn't recognize him at all. *Maybe he's from Teller. But, whoever it is, he's gotta be gay.*

"That's me. Who are you?"

Casey was the one asking the questions. "And you know Preston Tyllas, right?"

"Yeah, you know him?"

"He *was* my boyfriend until *you* stole him."

*Oh fuck, this is the guy Preston dumped!* "Whoa, wait a minute. That's not true."

"Then why did he take all those pictures of you?"

"Pictures?"

"The ones in his pool? I'm sure you remember."

Scott wondered for a second if he was Russian; then realized what he was saying. "I don't even know who you are."

"Casey Sekalic. I *loved* Preston and you stole him, you bastard."

Joe had thought just about everyone had left. In fact, he was sure what he just heard was caused by a drunk-induced stupor. But the voices were as clear as they could be. He was sure he heard Scott Faraday and some other faggot talking about stealing boyfriends. He quickly zipped up and looked around to determine where the voices had come from. The rocks here carried sound oddly, and in his current state of mind he wasn't sure where to look. No, he *was* sure. Most of the guys used the semi-circular area over to his right to pee.

"It's not what you think. He never told me about you."

"That's no surprise. He's an asshole like that. But you took him away from me. Why?"

"That's just not true."

"Liar!" He came forward and pushed Scott just as Joe found them both.

Joe laughed and Casey wheeled around. Scott moved to the side a bit to peer past Casey. Joe was breathing heavily and looking quite drunk.

All the way back to his truck he had been whispering under his breath, "Don't leave yet. Don't leave yet." Once he had gotten to the cab, he removed the two-foot long length of steel pipe he kept on the floor just inside the driver's side door and had come back with it to the rocks. Now he stood there with it, wondering who he should take a swing at first.

Scott was mortified. *How the hell did he know I was here?* Scott hadn't seen him all evening and now he showed up with a pipe in his hand and a menacing look on his face right when he was getting ready to leave.

"I got me *two* queers in the piss trough. That's where you should be in the first place. You, I know," he sort of pointed the pipe at Scott. "You I don't, but you're gonna love sucking my dick, too."

Scott spoke up. "H-how did you know I was here?"

"I know where to find queers, Fairyday."

Casey spoke up. "You're wrong. We're not queer."

"Shut up," Scott warned. This was no time for cowardice. Not anymore. All the times he had avoided fighting Joe came to mind. He had wanted to take a swing so badly and couldn't. So what if Joe had a weapon now. He wasn't going to avoid him this time. "It's true Joe. We're gay. But no one's sucking your dick."

Casey's mouth dropped open as he looked back at him. *What the hell? Why the fuck did he tell him that?*

Joe couldn't believe what he heard. He shook the pipe again. "Come here and suck my dick, you God damned faggot trash!"

Casey was totally freaked out now. Whoever this guy was he was sure he was going to kill one of them! And was Scott trying to invite murder? There were no small or even medium-sized rocks anywhere around, just boulders and hard gravel. He had no weapons, not even a pocketknife, and he didn't know how to fight at all.

Scott was almost equally frightened now. Joe was slurring his words, so he was certainly wasted, and he had a formidable weapon, which they were defenseless against. What was worse, though, was that they were completely blocked in, with Joe standing at the only way out. The rocks were too high to scale over them so that escape route was out. He went over wrestling moves in his head but they were for open spaces with room to move around. That wasn't going to help in this situation. Maybe they could rush him at the same time. He tried to prepare himself for the worst.

Joe pointed the pipe at Casey. "*Come here, right God damned now!*" His voice was filled with rage.

Casey winced, then started forward. Scott realized that it was because he was going to comply. He grabbed the back of Casey's sweater and forcefully pulled him back. Joe advanced a couple of steps. He swung the pipe and it hit the boulder to his left. Rock particles went flying, pelting both Casey and Scott's pant legs.

The force of the blow reverberated back into Joe's hand. That made him even angrier since it hurt. "*Fuck!*" he yelped. He pointed to Casey. "Get over here right fucking now!"

Scott heard Casey suck in a ragged breath. He could tell he was terrified. Scott yelled as loud as he could. "Back the fuck off, you closet case mother-fucker!" Someone had to have heard that. If they did, perhaps they'd come running and hopefully help them.

Joe took another step forward. He had to hit Scott to get him to shut up. No one was going to call him a closet case to his face, or any other way for that matter. He raised the pipe up. Casey yelled as loudly as he could. "Help! Help!"

So far, no one had come to investigate. But that was the moment Scott was waiting for. The cry for help. This would most likely be the moment that Joe was off-guard. It was going to be close and totally daring and Scott was really scared, but their lives appeared to be on the line. He had a split-second to decide whether to tell Casey to move or not. If he did, Joe would have the advantage. If he didn't, then Casey would just have to figure out what he was doing.

He thought it instead, trying to will him to step aside. *Casey move!* Scott launched himself forward while raising both hands in the air. If Casey moved right now, it might work. He rushed toward Joe, moving past Casey just as the pipe came almost straight down. He figured he would be able to take advantage of the possibility that Joe wasn't fully in charge of his motor functions. He was executing his plan even as he was formulating it. He was going to take Joe's downward momentum by grabbing his wrists. Then, at just the right moment, he'd move to the side and direct the pipe downward toward Joe's knee, all while continuing to guide Joe's wrists with his clenched hands. Hopefully, he'd make Joe hit himself, then they'd be able to make a run for it.

Casey didn't know what was going on. He was so startled by Scott's rush past him and the fact that he was just plain frightened, that he froze. His legs wouldn't budge.

Scott timed it just right though. Almost as if it were in slow motion, Casey watched Scott grab Joe's wrists and turn. Joe was moving forward. Four hands came down with the pipe. Casey raised his arms up in front of him and turned his head. He still couldn't move his legs. The pipe struck the center of his right forearm. Scott heard a sharp *crack* and a scream. Casey's scream. He went straight to the ground like a rag doll being dropped. Joe staggered from Scott's launch at him. Dust went flying from their feet scuffling the ground.

Scott still had a little momentum and was able to push Joe against the boulder to his right. The back of Joe's hand scraped along the jagged, weathered granite, tearing a couple of layers of skin off his knuckles. He howled in pain but still held on to the pipe. Scott lost his footing on the loose gravel, which made him twist more than he intended. He landed on the ground in a heap on his back.

It had all happened in the time it took to take a deep breath.

Joe wasn't expecting any of what just transpired. He took that moment to try to do as much damage as he could. After all, Scott was flat on his back directly beneath him.

His intention was to stomp Scott's throat. He had to make him shut up! But he was disoriented from the alcohol, and now from the pain to the back of his hand, and he miscalculated. He completely missed his throat. The heel of his cowboy boot came down squarely onto the middle of Scott's chest instead. Blood was dripping from his raw knuckles and a couple of drops landed on the side of Scott's face. Joe turned and ran as fast as he could in his current inebriated state back to his truck. He threw the pipe into the truck bed where it landed with a loud clatter. A moment later gravel and dirt went flying like sideways hail as he sped away from the Powerlines. The parking area became a quiet eerie moonscape devoid of all sound. Joe's had been the only vehicle left.

Scott heard Casey screaming in pain, but he was having trouble himself now since the blow had caused him to start hyperventilating. He tried to get up but he couldn't catch his breath. It was as if a huge weight had been placed on his chest. He fell smack down onto his back again. Adrenaline coursed through his bloodstream causing him to start panicking. He was scared he wouldn't be able to catch his breath at all. Finally, he stopped struggling and was finally able to sit up. He listened for Joe while he tried to fight off his fright. *Where the fuck is he?* Finally, by holding his breath for a few seconds at every other inhale, he was able to kill his hyperventilation and get his breathing under control.

No longer limp, Casey was writhing in agony. He knew his arm was broken. The pain was so bad he could barely open his eyes. He had heard Joe run away and knew that Scott hadn't been killed in the attack, but was sure he had been hurt. He was finally able to stop screaming long enough to hear that Scott seemed to be moving nearby, but his own fright had started him crying now. All of this because of that God damned Scott!

Scott tried to stand but stopped himself as a sharp pain stabbed him in the chest. He knelt instead. He unsnapped the buttons of his jacket and quickly unbuttoned his shirt. Even though it was quite cold now he pulled his t-shirt up to briefly look at the damage Joe had done to him. A squarish-looking spot was lacerated and extremely painful.

Scott crawled over to Casey. He coughed hoarsely several times. "Casey, I'm going for help," he said through his pain.

"Don't go," Casey squeaked out. He saw blood all over the side of Scott's face. It was gruesome looking and frightened him even more.

"I can't yell out. I have to go for help."

Scott could barely speak. For some reason his voice just wouldn't work right. He stood, stumbled. Then, while leaning against the rock walls, he exited the rocky formation. He emerged to the bleak, still landscape. He stood stark still as he looked. Not a single car was anywhere.

*Oh my God, we're stranded!*

Scott dropped to his knees and started to whimper, which almost immediately turned into full-blown crying. He didn't know why, but it did. It lasted perhaps five seconds.

He pulled himself together and went back to Casey. He had to get him out of the piss trough. It smelled awful here. He was starting to cough now, more from having cried than from anything else, and it hurt like hell every time he did. He helped Casey up while he held his broken arm with his good hand. Scott looked at his arm.

"Are you bleeding?" He hoped Casey didn't have a compound fracture.

Casey sucked in a painful breath. "I don't think so. But you are."

"Where?"

"Your face. *Agh!*" he exclaimed as he moved his fingers.

Scott touched the side of his face. Blood came away on his fingers. He realized it couldn't have been his. He wasn't cut anywhere. "It's Joe's, not mine. Is your arm broken?"

"No fucking shit, you dick! Why didn't you get help?"

Scott felt awful. He didn't even know Casey and now he had a broken arm, partly because of him, but mostly because of his own enemy. "No one's here."

"*What?*"

"Where's your car?"

"I, *agh!*, rode here with one of my friends."

"Why aren't they still here?"

"It's a long story. How did you," he winced in pain again, "get here?"

"I rode with someone who left early. I was going to catch a ride with another one of my buddies. I didn't get to ask him." The irony of their situation eluded him just now.

When they emerged from the rocks they both stopped and stared at the deserted parking area, the tall steel towers, and the electrical lines trailing across the sky far above them going from the southwest to the northeast. It was perfectly quiet except for the cold wind singing overhead

It was getting even more chilly now. When he started to shiver Scott realized that Casey only had a light sweater and a t-shirt on underneath it. Casey's eyes were starting to get droopy.

"Are you alright?"

"I feel like...I'm gonna...pass out." He sounded like he was in a daze.

*Fuck, he's probably going into shock.* Scott knew enough first aid to know that. "We gotta get out of the wind. Then we'll, I don't know, we'll go out to the highway and flag someone down." He wondered how they were going to reach the highway with Casey in such pain. Besides, it was quite a ways away and Casey wasn't dressed for the cold.

By the time Doug pulled up into Jill's driveway she had unzipped his jeans and was working on him over his underwear. He hated when she teased him like that. He should have just pulled over and let her give him a blowjob, but wanted to get to her bedroom and do it right. He wanted penetration.

They finally made it to her bedroom and Doug pulled off his shoes. Her parents were asleep at the other end of the house so he knew if they were quiet, no one would discover them. Besides, they had done it several times in her bedroom and had never been caught.

Doug had his shirt and jeans off now. He had just gotten her top off and was going for her pants when she stopped him. "Not until I see the condom."

"Get one then."

"They're in my purse. Damn it, I left it in the car."

"I'd go out and get it for you, but it's cold out," he whispered as he looked down. His erection pressed against the white fabric.

"I'll go get it," she told him.

He scrounged for his keys from his pants pocket while she quickly donned a thick pullover sweater. He stopped her and kissed her for almost a minute before she pulled him off and went out the door with a quiet giggle. She returned a moment later and turned on the little light next to her bed.

He squinted. "What's up with that?"

"We have to go back."

"Back where?"

"The Powerlines. I left my purse there."

"We can get it later."

"No we can't. Everything I own is in it, including the condoms. You're not doing anything with me unless we have one."

He dragged his hand across his hair. "Shit. I knew I should have kept some in my car. You're going on birth control starting tomorrow."

"No way. It'll make me fat."

"Well, this just screwed up my night."

He was angry, but knew that he had to go back so she could get her purse. Whispering angry remarks to himself he started getting dressed.

Jill pulled off the sweater and put her bra back on. Then she put the sweater back on. "I'm sorry. When I got outside, I remembered I gave Todd my lighter for the fireworks when his ran out. I left the purse out on the rocks. I know exactly where it is," she said sheepishly.

"It's gonna be midnight before we get back."

"I said I'm sorry. I'll make it up to you. I promise," she said in a seductive voice. With that, she gently pushed him down on the bed and started kissing him. He didn't bother to resist as she raised his arms over his head and caressed his armpits. Unfortunately, it got him totally hard again.

Joe passed out twice on the drive back to his house. He came to both times within a couple of seconds. He somehow managed to stay out of the ditch, but ended up in the oncoming lane both times. After he pulled up to the house, he shut off the engine but, in his stupor, forgot to turn off the headlights. He stumbled out of the cab and made a somewhat noisy entrance into the house.

Bob, his step-uncle, was in the kitchen and saw him as he passed by. He sneered. *Drunk again.* It was too dark in the hall for him to see the dried blood all over the back of Joe's hand.

Joe went straight to his bedroom. *Fairyday admitted to liking boys. Hell, he probably even likes having sex with them.* Sitting now on his bed, he wondered if he should have left so fast. He should have hurt them both even more. Like he had been hurt by his father. So, tomorrow in school, everyone would know exactly what Scott liked. That would be hurtful enough, at least for starters.

Scott pulled his jacket off and draped it around Casey. Casey was shivering uncontrollable, which was making Scott scared. He led them to a place amongst some boulders well away from the urine smell, but it wasn't going to shelter them from the cold. He figured it probably wasn't quite down to freezing just yet, but the wind chill was the real problem. The sky was clear and the moon was still visible despite the incoming clouds from the south, so at least they could see.

Scott spied a dead branch wedged in a crack and pulled it out. "Do you have a lighter?" he asked Casey.

Casey's teeth were chattering so much he couldn't speak. He shook his head a couple of times. His arm was throbbing mercilessly and he was trying his best to keep from yelling out in pain.

Scott didn't have one either. "I'm going over to where they were doing the fireworks to see if I can find one there." He dropped the branch.

Casey nodded his head a few times and sat down. His fingers were beginning to grow numb from the cold and he couldn't move them or his hand now.

Scott walked, rather than ran, to the fireworks area. Whenever he took a deep breath, it hurt his chest. He figured he didn't have any broken ribs but knew he'd probably have one hell of a bruise. He looked all over the place, but didn't find anything except cans, bottles, trash, and burnt fireworks. He found one lighter that was crushed, then another with a missing striker, but it was empty anyway. This was bad. If he didn't find a way to make a fire soon, they might freeze to death. He picked up his pace and went in a spiral pattern while searching on the ground for anything that could make a flame. Dizzy from his quick maneuvering, he stopped walking, coughed some more, then stopped moving altogether so he could catch his breath. His adrenaline was still surging at full speed.

He leaned on a rock. He was really cold now since he wasn't wearing his jacket anymore. Due to the pain it caused, it was hard to hold his arms across his chest, too. As he pondered what to do next he saw an amorphous black shape wedged between two stones to his right about ten feet away. He noticed it because of the glint in the moonlight of something metallic. At once, he recognized it as a purse and dashed to it. He knelt to the ground and, without ceremony, grabbed it and unsnapped the buckle. He dumped the contents out. He quickly sorted through the mess in the silvery moonlight. A wallet, three tampons in wrappers, five condoms in packages, tissues, cosmetics, two hair scrunchies, a brush, and the one item he was looking for. A lighter. He quickly snatched it from the pile and flicked it once, twice, then adjusted the flame level. On the next try it lit with a steady flame.

Scott didn't care about the pain in his chest as he gathered the tissues, then some nearby paper. Gripping the lighter tightly, he made a beeline back to Casey, picking up small sticks as he went. By the time he returned, he had a small armload of things to burn.

He dumped everything, found a flat stone, and dug out a shallow bowl-shaped area in the gravelly dirt. He wadded the tissues and a few pieces of paper with them.

All his Boy Scout fire-building skills came into play as he layered small pieces of kindling against the pile, then larger sticks. He flicked the lighter and attempted to catch the tissues and paper on fire. The wind blew through their little confined area which immediately blew out the flame and knocked over his hastily built pile. He adjusted the sticks upright and flicked the lighter again, this time shielding it with his cupped hand. The tissues lit. He blew on them.

In a few moments, acrid smoke filled the area, making him cough, which made his chest hurt even more. He blew on the tissues again and heard some of the kindling crackle. That was a good sign. The flame was large enough now to ignite them. He puffed on the flames a few times until all the kindling lit. He took that moment to check on Casey.

"Casey, I fucked up. I let him come on to me and I shouldn't have. But I didn't steal him from you. I swear it. We're not going out. We never will either. And he never told me he was going out with anyone."

Casey was fighting the haze of pain that was still threatening to make him pass out. He managed to speak, if only a little. "I loved him and he dumped me for you!"

"Fuck! I didn't know that. But it's not my fault. It was him that started it. Please believe me. I *swear* it." He looked at Casey's arm. "Shit. I-I can't believe Joe did this to you."

Casey's teeth chattered loudly as he spoke. "Y-you kn-now h-him?"

"He goes to my school. He's got some bug up his dickwad ass. He was after *me.*"

More teeth chattering. "L-like P-Preston?"

*Will you listen to me?* "No. Not like him. He was just in my calc class. I didn't even know he was gay until just a few weeks ago." *Fuck.* "How did *you* know him?"

He winced, then panted a little before he spoke. "We work together."

"If you were his boyfriend, then why the hell did he want to do anything with me?"

He managed to talk through clenched teeth. "'Cause he's a royal pain in the ass! Uhh!"

"And because of me you got hurt. I am *so* sorry this happened. I swear I'm sorry. Joe was after me, not you. Look, I'm gonna go for help. I'll have to leave you here so I can flag down a car....*God damn you, Joe!*" he hissed between clenched teeth.

Scott scooted over to the fire and blew on the flame again.

Casey had been sitting up, but now slumped over onto the ground. Scott scooted back over to him. He felt his pulse along his neck. He could still feel something. *Thank God.* "Hey, can you hear me?" Casey just groaned and moved his head but he didn't say anything coherent. "*Fuck!* Casey please don't die." Scott was terrified now. Here he was attempting to save his life and he might be slipping into a coma for all he knew. *God damn that Preston! If it hadn't been for him.*

*If it hadn't been for me.* After all, he'd been the reason Preston dumped Casey in the first place. All because he had let Preston come on to him. And if he hadn't been at the Powerlines, Joe would never have tried to kill them. Again, his fault. He still couldn't figure out how Joe even knew he was here.

He heard Casey say something but wasn't sure what it was. *He must be in shock.* He moved over to blow on the flames again. After that, he went back to make sure Casey was covered a little more with his jacket.

Scott was shaking as much from the cold as from fright. But he had to get more wood. He stood and left their little confined area. He held his hands up to his mouth and blew on them. He could barely feel his fingertips now.

All he found in his search were some dead Joshua Tree branches and crushed Cholla cactus wood. He gathered as much as he could and brought it back. His little flame was still lit and he slowly but surely added more of the wood.

The wind died down to almost nothing and the smoke finally rose straight up. *At least we won't suffocate.* The fire was finally starting to take on considerable height and warming him up a bit. He took that moment to move Casey a little closer, making sure he wasn't so close that he'd get burned.

Scott drew his legs up and attempted to wrap his arms around his shins, but that hurt his chest too much. He leaned back with the fire to his side. Random thoughts went through his mind. *Joe tried to kill us both. We might freeze to death. No one is going to rescue us.*

He started rocking back and forth, thinking he should be terrified. But oddly enough, his fear and anxiety receded, replaced by hot anger which held steadfast in his mind as he held his hands up to the flames.

Joe. A line from a lyric came to Scott's mind by Bruce Cockburn, one of his favorite Canadian recording artists. *"If I had a rocket launcher, some son of a bitch will die."*

Jill had Doug's jeans unbuttoned, his zipper all the way down, and his underwear pulled down just enough while he drove. This wasn't the first time he'd gotten a blowjob while driving. But out on the completely dark and desolate highway, it was the best sensation. He eased the seat back a little more as her head bobbed up and down. Just as he came, he released the gas pedal. Since his eyes were barely open it was much easier to steer if he didn't press the gas. They were down to twenty miles an hour by the time he regained complete control of his senses. After she sat up, she grinned. That was something Doug really liked about her. She was no stranger to a penis.

"Told you I'd make it up to you."

*She really needs to quit doing that. No, what the hell am I thinking? She needs to perfect it!* He was busy trying to zip back up when the turn came to the dirt road leading to the Powerlines.

The adrenaline that had saturated Scott's bloodstream was rapidly ebbing. The pain in his chest was throbbing with every breath, even shallow ones, and it was becoming quite annoying. The fire had warmed him up, but every time the wind found them he got chilled again. But it wasn't just the wind Scott was worried about. He wasn't too sure he'd be able to find many more sizeable pieces of wood nearby. His pile was growing smaller much more quickly than he had anticipated. Cholla and Joshua Tree wood burned hot but very quickly. The moon was just about to disappear behind the thickening clouds, which would make it impossible to find more without getting hurt or stumbling on a live cactus. He knew exactly how painful Cholla spines were.

He stood and looked over the rock barrier that separated them from the deserted parking area. He decided he'd make one last foray before there was no more light left. Then he'd just have to hope that whatever he found would last long enough while he trekked out to the highway to try to flag down a car. He had waited because he knew no one would be out this late. He knew he'd probably become hypothermic long before he managed to get someone to help them, but he couldn't just let Casey stay in pain or possibly even freeze. That's when he saw the headlights. He first thought they were far away, but when he saw a dust trail and then the vehicle, he realized they were coming directly toward them. Before he knew it, he was shouting. "Hey, over here! Over here!" That sent him into a spasm of coughs. He dashed out from their shelter and trotted as best as he could, despite the pain, toward the oncoming car.

Jill saw him first. She grabbed Doug's arm. "Look out!"

Doug saw someone running into his headlight beams and slammed on the brakes. The car skidded several feet on the gravelly desert floor and came to a full stop not ten feet in front of him.

She clutched his arm even tighter. "Oh my God, that's *Scott!*"

Doug shoved the transmission into park and left the engine running. Both of them quickly opened the car doors as he came running up to Doug.

"Doug! Jill! How did you know to come back?" *Cough. Cough.*

Doug was completely confused. "What the fuck are you *doing* out here?"

"I got stranded, but it's worse. Some kid from Teller got his arm broken. *Cough.* Joe did it. Joe Engle tried to kill us! The kid's back there." Scott was pointing and moving sideways, gesturing with his other hand as he tried to get him to come. "He's freezing to death. We have to get him to a hospital!"

Doug didn't even try to calm Scott down. He simply ran with him, wondering why he wasn't wearing a jacket, and clutching his chest. "How did this happen?"

"Joe snuck up on us just as everyone was leaving. He said some awful things to us. *Cough.* He had a pipe and hit Casey with it."

Scott stopped and tried to hug Doug. Doug hugged him back but that only made the pain in Scott's chest worse. He was quite chilled, and his teeth were starting to chatter, but getting Casey was a priority. "He's over there in the rocks," he said as he pointed.

Doug stopped and turned around. "Jill, pull the car up here!"

She was standing in front of the headlights and he saw her nod her head yes. She went to the driver's side, pulled the car closer, and put it in park. She quickly pulled a flashlight out of the glove box and dashed to where she had left the purse. It wasn't there. She figured someone had probably stolen it, but then she stepped on its contents. At least her wallet was there, and it appeared to be unopened. That was a surprise. She quickly shoved everything into the purse which was nearby after all, then snapped the buckle shut. She dashed back to the car and threw it into the passenger seat.

The boys reached Casey seconds later. Doug stopped short and tried to swallow the lump in his throat. He'd never been confronted with something like this before, but Scott's resolve and determination were keeping him going just now.

"Be careful of his right arm. It's broken," Scott said.

"Fuck, he looks dead."

Totally wound up, Scott shoved him. "He's not *dead!* He's breathing, isn't he?"

Doug shoved him back. "I don't know! I just got here!"

"Here, you get his legs. I'll take his shoulders. *Be careful.*" Cough. Cough.

"Okay, okay. I'll be careful." Then he shouted. "Jill, open the back door!"

She complied and stood there waiting for them. When she saw them pulling what appeared to be a dead body out from the rocks she emitted a brief scream, then covered her mouth with both hands.

Doug responded immediately. "No screaming! Put the heater on high. He's freezing!"

She reached in and twisted the knob to high. Heat started blasting out.

Casey weighed as much as Preston. It was difficult to move him with Scott in pain and Casey being limp. They set him down, managed to get him partially conscious, and he was able to help them get him into the back seat. Doug popped the trunk and pulled out an old blanket. It wasn't exactly the cleanest thing in the world, but it would do the job. Finally, they were all back in the car with Doug in the back seat spreading the blanket over Casey; Scott trying to warm up on the passenger side in front, now with his jacket back on; and Jill driving. She didn't scream again, but rather mustered stupendous courage and determination while she carefully traversed the rutted dirt road back to the highway, then drove them to the hospital as fast as she could.

The phone only rang twice. Nonetheless, it woke Ryan up. He looked over at the clock briefly. It was just after one in the morning. Moments later, just as he was almost asleep again, there was a knock on his bedroom door. It was Howard.

Ryan was fully awake as he sped to the hospital. Scott's father had called to let Ryan know that there had been an accident and that Scott had been involved. There were no details. He realized that despite the late hour his dad had bothered to call. Ralph thought enough of him to call them in the middle of the night? The implication choked him up.

He was surprised at how cold it had become. He had been wearing a t-shirt when he went to Dr. Kevin's office earlier, but was forced to don a heavy sweatshirt before he took off. He thought the worse things as he sped down the highway. Ralph said he could find them in the emergency waiting room. As soon as he was able to park, he ran to that entrance.

He found Elaine, Ralph, and Scott almost immediately, along with two other kids he figured were students, sitting in a cluster of chairs off to the right. There was another family nearby, looking far more agitated than the Faraday party.

It was the moment from hell for Ryan. He didn't know what had happened or how to feel. But Scott felt it for him. He stood up and dashed toward Ryan. They stopped in the middle of the room. No words were exchanged as they simply held on to each other. Scott's heart pounded as he fought back tears. Ryan shut his eyes tightly, sure that at any moment he'd break down right there in front of everyone.

Doug and Jill, along with Ralph and Elaine looked on, knowing they were observing a hug that was derived from more than mere friendship. Scott yelped when Ryan squeezed him. He instantly released his grip. "I'm sorry, what did I do?"

"It's the bruise on my chest." Scott stepped back. He raised his t-shirt to show him. Ryan saw a bandage taped between his pecs. Scott told him everything, then introduced him to Doug and Jill. By this time Scott had not only calmed down, he had also given Jill a big kiss when he had discovered why they had returned and that it was her purse he had pillaged. He was sure her forgetfulness had saved his and Casey's life.

Scott pulled him aside and apologized over and over again for not explaining himself quickly enough earlier in the week. Ryan continuously apologized for not having listened to Scott that night. Scott pulled him into an empty corridor. Through some minor tears, he begged Ryan's forgiveness about his indiscretions with Preston. Ryan showed him he was forgiven by gently leaning him against the corridor wall where he kissed and hugged him, this time much more cautiously. They vowed to make sure they heard each other in the future.

When they came up for air, they realized they had been in full view of two of the night cleaning crew who were buffing the far end of the corridor. Scott didn't care. *Kiss. Embrace...careful. Warm. Love.*

Embarrassment be damned. Nothing else mattered.

On the way over to the hospital, the worst thoughts of Ryan's life had been going through his mind. But Scott was safe, in his arms, touching his lips, pressed against his body. It almost happened again...*almost*. But Scott was not a repeat of David. He was just shaken up. Best of all, though, was the fact that he was absolutely sure Scott was still his boyfriend. *Unequivocally. Undeniably. Most definitely. His boyfriend.*

Casey's parents had been with him in the ER. Shortly after the boys returned to sit with the others, they came out with their son walking slowly along with him and told everyone that he was okay. Casey had been filled with painkillers, his arm had been x-rayed and set, and a cast had been put on it. Although he was very sleepy, floating even, at least he wasn't cold anymore, the pain had been eliminated, and he was happy to be alive. The situation had brought him out to his parents and to all these complete strangers. It would have happened sooner or later anyway.

Scott was relieved that Casey was okay. "I'm so sorry this happened. God, I'm so sorry," Scott told him.

Casey looked down at first, then gave him a tight smile. "I'm-I'm just thankful you saved my life. I might have died if it hadn't been for you."

Casey looked at Ryan, realizing who he must be, since Scott was holding his hand. Ryan looked at Scott. He didn't know what to say and squeezed Scott's hand even more tightly. Casey noticed all of it even while he floated. Jealous and happy. Enjoying the buzz, but wanting to sleep. At least someone had come out of this with their relationship intact. *Damn.*

Ralph stood with the rest of the group now and turned to Casey's father. The police had been at the hospital earlier to take statements. Ralph looked at his watch, then spoke to Dr. Sekalic. "They should be there by now."

Scott raised his shirt up briefly to press the bandage into place. It kept coming loose on one corner. Hidden beneath it was an ugly black and purple bruise, outlining a heel print. Luckily, he had only minor lacerations due to having had several layers of clothing on during the attack. It could have been much worse if Joe's foot had had come down any harder or he had stomped him where he had intended.

Elaine's eyes filled with tears again as she clasped her son's free hand. The other one was still firmly in Ryan's grip. *How could anyone want to murder my child?*

Ryan was seething with anger. Although he knew the police were on their way to take care of Joe, he wished he could go over there instead. Images of stabbing Joe with a rusty knife, or stuffing a concussion grenade into his mouth, or throwing him from a tall cliff onto some jagged talus came to his mind. Huh, maybe he'd just strangle him very, very slowly with his bare hands.

# CHAPTER 16

Officers Whalen and Travis were quite familiar with the chaotic Pitley household. Whalen was particularly familiar with Joe. He had been the officer who took him in for the domestic battery charge last spring. Now though, the situation was completely different. This time the charge involved a weapon against two unrelated victims.

When they arrived, the house had some lights on and the place seemed quiet. Several cars were in the driveway. Whalen called in all the license plates and positively identified Joe's truck. It was the one with the headlights left on. They left the squad car to check it out. Travis noted a steel pipe in the bed along with some empty beer bottles and other debris. His flashlight showed blood in the cab and on the driver's side window. By that time, the second squad car arrived.

Whalen was at the door. Travis stood behind him in the correct cover position while the two other officers went around to the back of the house. This was a serious call and no one was going to make a run for it. Whalen knocked. Someone pulled a curtain back then dropped it at the other end of the house.

Liddy Engle was dressed in her robe. Her face expressed a mixture of shock and concern when she opened the door, but she didn't look scared. Whalen let his guard down a little. Whatever was going on hadn't seemed to have affected the rest of the family so far.

"Ms. Pitley?" Whalen asked.

"What's going on here?"

"Where's your son?"

"Why? What did he do?"

"Is he here or not?"

"He came home a little while ago. He should be in his bedroom. What did he do?"

"He attacked two students."

*Gasp.*

"Two students were attacked with a pipe. One has a broken arm. They said your son did it."

She clutched the front of her robe just as her husband came down the hallway. He was dressed in nothing but dirty jeans. Officer Travis's hand went to his holster at his sudden appearance, but when Liddy went to hug him, Travis dropped his hand. They conferred for a moment, then Roger's face tightened.

Roger's brother appeared. Liddy told him what happened. "He came home drunk," Bob told the officers.

"Which way to the bedroom?"

They led the two officers down the hallway.

Roger knocked on the door. There was no answer. He knocked again. "Joe, open this door right now!"

There was no sound behind the door. He tried the doorknob but it was locked. The policemen drew their weapons. Roger waved them off while Bob kept his distance down the hallway. It was a cheap doorknob. A slender object inserted into the hole in the center would easily open it. Roger went into the bathroom to his left and pulled out a cotton swab from a box that was on the messy countertop. He returned to the door and pushed it into the hole. They heard the lock pop on the other side and he moved aside. The officers rushed into the bedroom.

Joe was laying on his bed face down and fully clothed. His left hand was bloody despite it having been wrapped in a bandanna. Blood had soaked through it and had contacted the sheet where he lay. The small room reeked of alcohol. It was no surprise about the alcohol. Teens drank all the time and got into trouble. This one, though, had deliberately harmed two students. That made it all the more important to get him on a Breathalyzer as soon as possible. He tried to roust Joe.

Joe regained partial consciousness and, with considerable trouble, turned over and sat upright on the bed. Joe knew he was no longer dreaming when he saw his mother, his stepfather, and two policemen standing in his bedroom. He also didn't know why they were all there.

Then, even in his current state, he realized something else. He looked down briefly. Due to the thickness of the denim, only a small wet spot had developed alongside the zipper. No one but him knew that there was a much larger sticky mess all over the inside of his jeans. From the looks of things, he wouldn't get the opportunity to go out to the garage to punch another hole in the drywall.

"Joe Engle? You're under arrest," Whalen said. He told Joe the charge and read him his rights. One of the other officers who had been covering the back entrance came down the hallway with the pipe from Joe's truck bed in an evidence bag. He briefly held it up for the officers to see and returned to his vehicle.

Joe thought about taking a swing at the policeman, but his head was spinning. So instead, he stood on wobbly legs and held his arms up to allow the policeman to put the handcuffs on. Whalen held one wrist, turned him around, applied the cuff, then snapped the other on. Joe passed out again and fell face first back onto the bed.

Crawford had been sleeping soundly when he heard the crackling. That woke him up. Then he smelled smoke. But it was much stronger than he had ever smelled before. He sat bolt upright in the bed. Beyond his bedroom door, he saw the flames. His couch was on fire!

"*What the fuck!*" he exclaimed.

He jumped out of bed and pulled his jeans on. Already the smoke had been building up along the ceiling in the bedroom. He coughed, then quickly dropped to the floor, crawled down the hallway, and exited out the back door. It was the usual chilly drizzly night and he was shirtless and barefoot. He quickly went to the shed, flipped on the light switch, and pulled out the twenty-pound fire extinguisher. He raced around to the other side of the house, kicked open the front door and attempted to douse the flames with the extinguisher. It did no good. He ducked into the kitchen, pulled the cordless phone off its cradle, and dashed back outside to call the fire department. Smoke poured out the front door. He knew he shouldn't have left the fire screen off after he put that fresh log in. Now he was paying dearly for it. And he should have just purchased those God-damned smoke detectors like he was going to do all year.

He was sitting inside his truck when the fire truck arrived. He had a jacket in the cab, which he was wearing now, and the heater on.

The front door was still open and he could see the entire room in flames. The fire had already broken the window nearest the fireplace and flames were dancing against the wooden siding. He had been motionless, just staring at the scene. It was awful, right out of a horrible movie. He sat there realizing that his life would never be the same again. Everything he owned was in there. And all of it was slowly becoming smoke damaged or turning to embers. Now that the volunteers were dousing his house with water in the foggy drizzly night, he realized that Christmas, less than a week away, was going to be ruined as well.

\*　　　　　\*　　　　　\*

Word had spread all over Regional the next day about what ended up sounding like attempted murder. Rumors were flying everywhere. One said that Scott was gay, had tried to get into Joe Engle's pants at the Powerlines, and that Joe had beat him up. Some heard that Scott was gay and that some boy from Teller Academy had beat him up. Others heard that Scott had beat up Joe, but that Joe had been arrested. Some heard about the second victim, some didn't. None of it made any sense to anyone since there were so many different, even conflicting stories, going around.

Doug didn't get to school until third period due to having slept late from last night's events, heard all the rumors by fourth period, and started to straighten things out. He told everyone he could that he and Jill had been there, had rescued Scott, that a student from Teller had had his arm broken by Joe, and that they had taken Scott and the other student to the hospital. He also emphasized that it was Joe who had been arrested on a charge of battery. Finally, all the rumors died down and the correct version of the story was being broadcast faster than water could run downhill. Both Jill and Doug were being hailed as heroes for saving Scott. Scott was already being spoken of as a hero for saving a Teller student's life.

Turns out that Chris had started the rumor. He had divulged a little too much information in his attempt to relate the tale to his freshmen friends and it had quickly transmuted into a completely different story than what he had originally told.

People from the track team and some of Scott and Doug's mutual friends had been coming up to him all day in support of Scott. Without exception, not a single person had said anything bad about the fact that they knew Scott was gay. Not one. Some were surprised, others didn't believe it, but all were supportive. Doug felt proud of them and himself. *See Scott, everyone is not an asshole.*

Preston had only heard one of the varied and assorted rumors before he was called into the principal's office during first period. He couldn't believe what he had heard. Why would Scott have tried to kill Joe?

Ms. Dunn was there, along with Andy. Mr. Harris, who was the principal, had Preston in the chair in front of him. Ms. Dunn was sitting to one side and Andy was in a third chair. Preston was totally freaking out.

"Mr. Tyllas, do you know why you're here?" Mr. Harris asked. He looked deeply disappointed. On his desk were her original calculus worksheet along with Preston's.

Preston didn't see either since he was too nervous to focus his attention. He had never been called to the principal's office before either. He had a terrible suspicion since both Ms. Dunn and Andy were there, but he certainly wasn't going to admit to anything. "No."

"Ms. Dunn, would you like to tell him what you told me?"

"Of course. But first, Andy, sorry for alarming you. And thank you for confirming everything for me." That was his cue to go.

"Sh-sure, Ms. Dunn." He picked his backpack up from the floor. He glanced one last time at Preston. *He's dead meat,* he thought, as he left the office.

Ms. Dunn turned to Preston. "I graded all the exams last night for the midterm. The grades were just as I expected except for one. Yours. You want to explain it?"

"Explain what?" There's no way she could know what he did. There wasn't a sole in the admin office. There were no security cameras in the office. How could Andy have known anything about his scheme? There was no way! And so what if he aced the test?

"How you got an F on your calculus midterm."

*"An F? That's impossible!"*

"I rest my case, Mr. Harris." A clear admission of guilt. She knew he expected a perfect score or very close to that.

Fifteen minutes later Preston was headed for his car. He had been suspended for ten days, as well as summarily failed out of calculus. Since he couldn't graduate without this class, his only recourse was to go to summer school and accept a late graduation. This was not only bad for him, but also the school. A senior hadn't been failed for any reason for a number of years.

Preston felt not only humiliated for being caught, but had to go to summer school with total losers. *God damn it. That just ruined my chance to leave Yucca Valley next summer.*

As he drove home, he thought about several things. He had wanted to see Centauri tonight, and especially Scott, but his suspension had made that impossible. He was barred from campus until after New Years. He had been planning on talking to Scott again about being his boyfriend. He had tried, but still couldn't shake his feelings for him. Now, even talking to him wasn't going to happen either.

What was worse was that his father was going to be so pissed off at him he would lose the car. He knew it.

By fifth period calculus, word had gotten out that Preston had been failed out of the class. That would be at least one empty chair in class. By that time, Ms. Dunn had also heard the correct story concerning Scott. She didn't expect him to be in class either and figured she'd have a second empty chair, too. She was shocked that two of her students had been involved in disturbing situations at the same time. She would call the Faraday house tonight to give Scott his exam score and offer her support. *Oops, maybe not. The band he's in is play-ing at Winterfest tonight. Maybe on Saturday instead.*

The mood was somber in class when she handed out their graded midterm exams. Everyone kept looking at Scott's empty desk and wondering if he was okay. No one would look at Preston's desk. Somehow, it seemed bad luck to even glance at it.

Ryan got to work on time despite the fact that he had stayed up all night with Scott. But he had no intention of missing Centauri's performance tonight even though he was sleepy as hell. He decided he would be there no matter what.

Chris always got home from school earlier than either his brother or his uncle and usually sorted the mail. It was on the dining room table as usual. When Ryan got back home, he spotted the conspicuously large envelopes from Cal-Poly Pomona right away, quickly ripped the first one open, and read the cover letter.

"Fuck, yeah!" he exclaimed.

He quickly ripped the next envelope open and read a nearly identical cover letter. "All right!" This changed everything. And Scott had better not say no.

As the band members loaded up equipment into Barry's van and the other vehicles, Scott told the whole story several times, each time in more detail.

Even though his chest still hurt, he was perfectly willing to not only lift things, but also to perform tonight. Colleen had insisted. She said that no mat-ter what, he was going to play his flute. It was important to show everyone that he was not only okay, but also in excellent spirits. Scott was reluctant at first, not sure he would have the breath control for it. He also didn't want to deal with the embarrassment of surely having been outed to the entire school. He gave in when the band threatened to punch his bruise—which he had shown everyone—if he didn't. He practiced breathing deeply and realized that although he still felt the bruise he seemed to have full use of his lungs.

The auditorium was quiet when they first arrived. The security guards had the doors chained shut, as was protocol, so they could set up without interrup-tion. Scott realized that although they were under cover of darkness that a good portion of the student body probably wondered if he were going to be there.

Doug and Jill came in the back entrance and found them. Jill made sure she didn't hug Scott too hard. Scott couldn't believe the amount of hugs he had been getting recently. "Everyone's talking about you," she told him.

"I figured. What're they saying?"

"They know everything. We had to set them straight though, as it were." She grinned at her remark, then continued. "Weird rumors were flying all over the place."

Scott's face showed his concern.

"Not to worry. The team was totally cool after they found out you're gay," Doug offered. "The stupid football jocks were another story."

"Surprise," Scott replied.

"When Devin and Thad started talking shit I told them that we would have a 'team talk' with them, if you know what I mean, if they didn't shut up or if they did anything to you." Devin, one of the Wolves tackles, and Thad, one of the running backs, were well known for their anti-gay rhetoric. "Evan's with me. And Aubrey, Spence, Cody, and Drew." They were the other track team members who were ready to defend him as well. "And there 're others. *Lots* of others."

A wide smile crossed Scott face.

Sparks pointed to his wrist as the security guards started unchaining the doors. He motioned to stage right where the soundboard was. It certainly wasn't the best place for the board, in fact, one of the worst, but they didn't want to take up any seats in the auditorium, as was usually the case. Scott would have to do his best from there.

Students poured down the two aisles and started taking their seats. Some of them saw Scott offstage and insisted he come over to see them. Some of them patted him on the back. Four girls gave him hugs. Two students congratulated him for getting rid of Joe. Some just stood there, listening to as much of the story as they could. A junior boy who Scott recognized, and a senior girl from his history class, clandestinely passed him folded up notes. When he later went backstage, he opened them. They were unsigned but said that he was their hero. They simply wanted to come out to him. He thrust the notes into his pocket and wondered how this was happening. He had become a catalyst for classmates to come out to him? He'd talk to them later for sure. This wasn't anything like he expected. He figured he'd be lynched by everyone, not by just the dickheads on the football team. *The last vestiges of my stupidity are being erased, whether I like it or not.*

As he took his position behind the soundboard, he wondered where Ryan was. He was supposed to have been here by now. But that could wait since the MC was announcing the band.

When Scott had come out on stage to adjust a microphone stand during their intermission, he finally saw Ryan. He had been there the whole time, watching the band from the audience, and now approached the foot of the stage. Other students were milling around nearby, talking and visiting with each other while the lights were still on. Ryan's smiling face was the most radiant in the crowd of kids. Scott came forward to one of the monitor speakers while a cassette of his favorite tunes by Loverboy played at a reasonable volume. Ryan hoisted himself up onstage and stopped next to it in front of him. He went down on both knees. No one else was onstage except them two.

Doug and Jill were talking to Evan and several others near the first row. Doug tapped on Jill's shoulder, then pointed to the boys. The group watched what unfolded.

Scott wasn't sure why Ryan was on his knees as he began. "Scott, like I said last night, I love you more than you can know. And I have a surprise."

"What?"

"We've both been accepted at Cal-Poly Pomona. You for music, and me for engineering. I even got us a dorm room. You're accepted pending your final grades. For now on you're studying calculus, and all *other* math classes, with *me*." He pulled the acceptance letters from his back pocket and handed the one marked for Scott to him.

Scott briefly looked at it. His mouth dropped open as he read the letterhead out loud. "College of Music Technology?"

"They have the exact classes for you. The perfect combination of music technology and music theory, all with a business minor. And it's a great place for me to get started on my engineering degree. Here's the best part. I'm paying for everything. *Everything*. And I want you with me. As my roommate." He listened to the music for a second, then grinned. "As my own lover boy." He clasped his hands together in front of his chest. "Do you accept?"

Scott didn't care who was watching. He dropped down to his knees in front of Ryan and hugged him as hard as he dared due to his injury. When he opened his eyes, he happened to be looking directly at the row of his friends and teammates bunched up at the foot of the stage. There was Doug next to Jill, along with Evan, Aubrey, and Spence. Other guys from the team were there, too, behind them. Some were giving Scott a thumbs up and grinning. Jill smiled radiantly. Scott raised his fist and gave them a thumbs up as he smiled back at them all. Doug pounded the wooden stage floor with his fist a couple of times. The rest of the guys did the same as they howled the Wolves cry.

Ryan let go of Scott and turned his head to see what the racket was all about. He chuckled as they pointed at him and howled again. He turned back to Scott. "Well?"

"*Hell, yeah!*"

Before intermission was over Scott donned one of his shiny metallic-threaded shirts. He wanted to be as noticeable as possible for what was coming next.

Elaine, Ralph, and Howard had shown up a few minutes before and were in the audience toward the back. Scott didn't see them since he could barely see any of the seats from where he was offstage. Chris was there, too, but was with some of his new friends in a completely different part of the auditorium. When Colleen announced that Scott would be coming out to play a special tune, the place went wild.

Scott took his flute out of its case and twisted it together. Ryan, standing next to him, slapped him on the back, then took off to find the family in the audience. Scott went to center stage and bowed gracefully next to the microphone stand. He inserted the mike pickup, then stepped over to Colleen's mike where he asked the audience to quiet down a little.

By the time he was halfway through the tune the kids were wild with enthusiasm. He saw his mother, father, Howard and Ryan as they pressed down one of the aisles. When he saw them, he pointed ever so briefly in their direction. In fact, seeing them all there emboldened his step, quickened his heart, and livened his playing even more.

Ryan was in ecstasy. Scott seemed so much more confident and seemed to have honed his sound even more so than just a couple of weeks ago. He was amazed as he watched Scott dance around, dip, even twirl once, while he played like a madman.

He held his lower lip between his teeth as shivers went up his back. This whole experience made him recall when Scott played his flute for him the first time way back in the summer at the VFW. This time it was ten times more exciting, ten times more thrilling, and he felt ten times more love for Scott than he had ever felt before.

Ryan shook his head. *Wow. And he's mine!*

# CHAPTER 17

The clerk handed Elaine the receipt and she took her bag of non-perishables through the checkout lane at Safeway. It was the usual sunny day this last week of August. As she headed toward the exit, she could see heat waves in the parking lot through the big picture windows by the customer service booth. Earlier, the newscaster on the car radio said it was one hundred seven outside. It was the end of the workweek and she was looking forward to a busy night tonight at the restaurant.

She had already driven out of the parking lot when she remembered the one last errand she had been putting off. The picture frame. The photograph had been sitting in that drawer now for several months, ever since the first week of June. *I can't believe I keep forgetting to buy it.* She looked at her watch. *I still have a couple of hours before I need to be at the restaurant.* She turned off the highway to the nearby mall. She had no excuse this time. She locked the car, and walked up the sidewalk to the main mall entrance.

The film store was on the second floor just off the escalator to the right. She knew they had the largest selection of frames of any store in the mall. When she entered the shop, she was immediately confronted with several display aisles of them. The 8 x 10 photograph needed just the right one. Wooden or pewter? A red frame or a black one? It was difficult to choose as she examined them all. Finally, though, she found it. It was about one and a half inches wide on all four sides and was made of thin wedges of alternating light and dark wood. It was put together in a pattern that was somewhat reminiscent of slender rays of light radiating from the center. It also happened to be one of the most expensive frames on the shelf.

Once she got home, she set her purse and the bags down on the kitchen counter. She pulled out the glass cleaner from under the sink, and pulled the frame out of its box. She cleaned the glass until it squeaked. After placing the glass back into the frame, she went to the chest in the living room. Inside the top drawer was the stiff paperboard holder that protected the photo. She brought it back to the kitchen, then carefully pulled it out of its plastic sleeve. She put it upside down on the glass, placed the backing down against the photo, and closed the tabs. She turned it over and examined it.

Scott was in his green satin high school graduation gown, still wearing his mortarboard. The green and white tassel was positioned to the left with the shiny gold '91 plainly visible. He had the biggest smile she'd ever seen on his face. Ryan was dressed in a dark suit coat, red tie with a pure white shirt, and khaki trousers. He had visited the barbershop that day and had a perfect haircut. His smile, equally as radiant as Scott's, crossed his face with a glow unlike she had ever seen on a young man. Ryan had his arm around Scott's waist, holding him tight. Scott had an arm around Ryan's waist holding him close as well. His other hand held a rolled up scroll with a green and white ribbon tied around it close to this chest. Scott was looking directly at the camera and Ryan was looking at Scott. She could see Ryan's love for her son even in a photo.

It was a scene she hoped would never leave her memory as she kissed the glass twice. Once for Scott, then for Ryan. *Now I have three handsome sons,* she thought, as she brought it to the living room and put it next to the picture of her elder son Steve, his wife and their new baby daughter.

*         *         *

It was almost eight on Saturday morning. Ryan was on his back holding his breath. Scott was on top of him probing his mouth with his tongue as he rested his upper body on his elbows. Both of his hands were busy thoroughly messing up Ryan's hair, which Ryan hated. Finally, he couldn't stand it any longer and pushed Scott away. He exhaled loudly, with his head turned to one side, and drew in a deep breath. The sheet slid off Scott's shirtless back and stopped at his waist. Ryan pawed at his hair to smooth it back down.

"We have to get up. And your breath! Ugh," Ryan told him.

"I'm not done yet," Scott countered.

"Yes you are. They're supposed to be here by nine."

Scott glanced at the clock as he rolled over to Ryan's side. "Yeah, nine."

During their first semester—the summer one—they had roomed in a dorm on-campus. They both hated the room since it was small and only had two twin beds. So, despite the fact they were in the same room, sleeping together had been a pain. That changed halfway through the summer when they moved out of the dorm. Now they had a big room in a two-story four-bedroom house three blocks off-campus. They had their own large adjoining bathroom, too. Their awkward sleeping arrangement was solved as well. The room was spacious since Ryan had insisted on the largest one they could find. He had the money and wasn't about to let them have something cramped again. So, they had a king-sized bed now. At first, it had been difficult to stay off each other when they studied, but they had figured out when to keep their clothes on and they had been studying a lot more productively now.

While Ryan hit the shower Scott brushed his teeth. Still undressed, he started picking up the room. His mind on idle, his thoughts went back to April, four months ago. Barry had announced that he was going to join Pacific Moon in San Diego after all. He simply couldn't refuse the offer. It had been a huge disappointment to Scott. Well before that, though, he had told the band that his relationship meant more than anything else did. He would be leaving Yucca Valley after he graduated. He had to be with Ryan no matter what. Centauri was on a major break. They still hadn't found a decent lead guitarist or a soundman.

Last month Barry sent Scott a copy of their pre-release tape. In less than two weeks, it had become his favorite one, which was a surprise, since he was sure he didn't like jazz. Maybe it was because Barry was such a good guitar player. Maybe it was because his taste in music was expanding. He didn't know for sure, but he was already humming two of the tunes on occasion, one of which was right now.

Ryan's pocket-sized schedule book was open on his desk. As he draped Ryan's t-shirt and shorts over his desk chair, he glanced at it. Ryan had stopped seeing Dr. Kevin for his weekly sessions just before they moved away from Yucca Valley. He had regularly been seeing a school counselor since their first term started back in June. His next session was Tuesday, directly after his last class.

Scott was so thankful for how things had completely changed for them. Shortly after New Years, Ryan started becoming a different person. And not in any bad ways either. His mood swings had gradually tapered off and now he was the most stable person Scott knew. He had completely dropped what had been, at times, his somewhat hostile nature. He had even embraced being gay in ways Scott couldn't believe were possible for him. Heck, they both went shirtless to their first Gay Pride Parade back in late June. Ryan had insisted on wearing all six necklaces which had been given to them by that group of older guys who kept whistling at them. Because of the many changes, Ryan's libido had completely returned, their embraces had become more passionate, and kissing was almost a spiritual experience. And what they had now wasn't sex. It was lovemaking. Sure, sometimes it was just pure animal lust. But the love that moved between them was different now; it was more than just sticky. It was glue. Holding them together. Solidly. Two into one. Scott had a difficult time believing it could be better than it had been before they started college, but it was. Last night had been that way, too. A grin slowly widened across his face.

Ryan was drying off when Scott led him to the still unmade bed, not saying a word. He gently pushed Ryan onto his back, hovered over him on his hands and knees with a fierce erection, and gave him a long tender kiss. Ryan merely gave in and passionately kissed him back. Scott lowered his hips just enough so that their stiff penises touched. He rubbed back and forth a little, teasing him as he kissed.

Still fully erect, Scott finally hopped into the shower, while Ryan started making the bed. Scott was drying off when he heard a knock on the bedroom door from behind the mostly closed bathroom door. Ryan was already dressed and opened it.

Justin, one of their three other housemates, came in. He had been anticipating their houseguests as well. He couldn't wait to meet them after hearing all about them for weeks. A freshman like themselves, Justin was Ryan's height, of medium build, and had thick wavy dark blonde hair. He had tiny stud earrings in both ears, a patch of dark blonde hair on his chin, and was a decent acoustic guitar player. When Justin realized he had two gay boys living in the house with him, and that they were a couple, he immediately came out to them. The fact that he was a musician and gay made he and Scott instant friends. Scott couldn't bring Shakaiyo to school with him, so lost her as a constant companion. But the boys had both gained a new one.

Justin was generally high-spirited, but lamented the fact that he didn't have a boyfriend. Lately, he carried on like he was desperate. They would exacerbate his whining by French kissing in front of him when he complained about it in their room. They'd lay on the floor or flop onto the bed and start up. Justin would complain about that, too, but it only made them mock him more. They had done that to him three times in the last two weeks. It was good-natured fun, but they knew Justin needed a boyfriend of his own.

Once Scott got dressed, the three of them went downstairs to the kitchen to toast some bagels. Their other housemates weren't up yet. A few minutes later, there was a knock at the front door. Scott went to it and flung it open.

Jill's smiling face greeted him. "Happy belated birthdays *and* anniversary!"

The boys had decided that their anniversary was to be celebrated one year after Ryan had agreed to be Scott's boyfriend that day last summer. They had already celebrated it weeks previous, along with their eighteen and nineteenth birthdays.

Her large shopping bag, filled with birthday and anniversary gifts, smacked against his back as she stepped in to embrace him. Doug was right behind her. He shook Scott's hand, then pulled him forward to hug him briefly.

Casey was right behind Doug. Scott got misty-eyed as they hugged long and hard and slapped each other's backs several times. Scott kissed his cheek, then ushered him in. The group came into the den. With a wide smile, Ryan hugged everyone, too.

It had been months since high school graduation and he hadn't seen any of them since then. Now his three best friends from back home were here for a joyful reunion, a barbeque in the backyard this afternoon, and belated celebrating for both he and Ryan tonight. The boys had gotten them a room at a hotel down the street, and tomorrow they were all going to take a drive to the north rim of the L.A. basin to hike in the mountains. *What a great way to end our summer break*, Scott thought.

Scott noticed that Casey and Justin were checking each other out right away. He introduced them and could tell they took an instant liking for one another. Their coy smiles told him everything.

Scott shook his head ever so slightly as he grinned. *I bet Casey's not even gonna see that hotel room tonight!*

# About the Author

Mark Ian Kendrick is the author of five novels.

*Desert Sons* is the first of two stories that trace the relationship between Scott and Ryan.

Scott Faraday, sixteen, has no idea that his world is about to radically change. Scott is in a small-town rock band, is fun loving, and out—but only to a select few. When Ryan St. Charles comes to live with his uncle in Scott's hometown of Yucca Valley, CA, they meet and form a tentative friendship. Ryan is a brash seventeen-year old who has just severed a long relationship with a man, but still considers himself straight. As Scott and Ryan's friendship develops, Scott begins to suspect that Ryan might be covering up that he's gay. Scott is sure Ryan has no idea that Scott is gay, so he comes out to him. The result is that Scott transforms their friendship into his first real relationship. Then, Ryan's hidden past comes into view. Scott is not at all prepared for what he discovers. Despite their vast differences, Scott sticks with him, and learns more about himself and relationships than he ever thought possible. This novel spans the summer that forever changed them both.

*Into This World We're Thrown* is the sequel to *Desert Sons.*

In this dramatic conclusion to *Desert Sons,* Scott and Ryan's relationship takes on new twists and turns. They both come out to those they love and have to confront their responses. Ryan's grandmother, his long-time care-giver, dies, which causes Ryan to re-evaluate his entire life. The band Scott is in might break up. Scott discovers he has secret allies, a schoolmate who's bent on having Scott be his no matter what, and a twisted foe. Will his secret admirer permanently ruin his now tenuous relationship with Ryan? Will Scott's foe turn his life into a living hell? Will Ryan pull himself from the depths of his emotional turmoil? Can the boys remove the bitterness that develops as a rift opens and widens between them? Can they uncover and express their love for one another before it's too late? All of this and much more is revealed, explored, and concluded in this exciting sequel.

*Stealing Some Time* is a gay science fiction adventure story. Told as a trilogy, this series follows Kallen and Aaric and the two time periods they come from.

### Book I: World Without You

It is 2477 CE. Much of the world has long since become desert due to the unchecked use of fossil fuels in centuries past. But the world of the 25th century is an advanced one, where technology rules, where ruthless leaders have the upper hand, and where water is the limiting factor for all of civilization. Eighteen-year old Kallen Deshara is entering his obligatory 5-year stint in the North American Alliance's Air Defense Force. While in boot camp, Kallen comes to terms with the fact that he's gay. He even finds his first gay relationship with a fellow graduate recruit, but is dumped shortly after it starts. While nursing his wounds, he finds his second relationship in a fellow student while in the ADF's Schools Division. After being dumped again, Kallen is shipped off to his first duty station in the mountains at the edge of North America's Great Central Desert. There, Kallen becomes a force to be reckoned with as his natural talent in photronics, the 25th century form of software, comes to the fore. Another relationship follows. This time with an officer. But it falls short again. When called to Central Security, he's sure he's walking into a court-martial due to being found out since gay activity in the ADF is a serious breach of military law. Instead, he finds that he's been called for a secret mission to 1820. *Time travel!* He and a hastily assembled team have been called to rectify a problem caused by the very device that opened the portal to the past. Not expecting more than to do his duty, Kallen isn't prepared for what awaits him.

## Book II: Chance Encounter

Sergeant Technician Kallen Deshara's mission to 1820 Kentucky hasn't prepared him to meet young handsome Aaric Utzman, whom he literally and figuratively falls head over heels for. And, while on the mission, one of the scientists who invented the device that opened the time portal, uploads to him the real history of how the world became burning hot. Kallen couldn't be any more ill-prepared for that long-suppressed truth. In addition, before he left, he hacked into the base commander's personal files. Once he goes through them it brings him face-to-face with the awful truth about the commander, his country's President, and a long abided-by water treaty. Everything he thought he knew about the past, his present, and his allegiance is put to the test. In fact, he's forced to challenge the limit of his sanity as he tries to absorb the truth of the world and of his heart.

## Book III: Journey's End

Kallen Deshara now knows his world's origin, nature, and destiny; and has fallen madly in love with young Aaric Utzman. His decision to stay with Aaric, knowing full well that his presence might change all of history, brings him to the very edge of reality. But his colleagues who have returned to the 25th century have other plans. They intend to bring him back before he changes anything, even if it means killing him. But first they have to find him. Traveling along the Wilderness Trail with his new companion, Kallen is totally unaware he's being stalked. In the meantime, he realizes what had been missing his whole life, deepens his love with Aaric, and sees more water than he thought possible. Slowly but surely, he recognizes that he has more to offer than he ever knew. In fact, he may even be able to shape the future that should have been! But he learns an even more important lesson. He discovers that love knows no boundaries—not even of time itself.

More information is available on Mark's website at www.mark-kendrick.com. You can contact him from there as well.

## If you enjoyed this book,
## check out these iUniverse authors:

**Mark Roeder**
### *A Better Place*
**A Better Place** is the story of two boys from two completely different worlds struggling to find themselves amongst a
whirlwind of confusion. The unlikely pair struggle through
friendship and heartbreaks, betrayal and hardships, to find
the deepest desire of their hearts.

**Ronald Donaghe**
### *The Blind Season*
*Book Two of the Common Threads in Life Series*
In **The Blind Season**, the sequel to the best-selling novel
*Common Sons*, Joel and his husband Tom decide to start a
family. Knowing that two gay men will never be able to
adopt, Joel and Tom decide to find a surrogate mother to
carry their child. What they find is a lot more than they bar-
gained for.

**Josh Thomas**
### *Murder at Willow Slough*
A gay reporter, a straight cop and thirteen dead men: will
the good guys get the killers, or will the killers get them?
**Murder at Willow Slough** is simultaneously terrifying, tough
and tender, as two very different men stare down danger
and discover the truth: the only defense against evil is people who care for each other.

**Buy these books through your local bookstore**
**or at www.iuniverse.com.**

0-595-21468-1

Printed in the United States
15930LVS00003B/150